More praise for *The Birthdays* and Heidi Pitlor

"Heidi Pitlor rolls family life on its back, exposing the soft underbelly of generational shift and conflict: the grievances, the need for love and approval, the rank and file of birth order, the parental need to know and protect. . . . Pitlor's eye for the good in this emotionally arrested crew is straight and honest. Just when you want to throw up your hands and hope you never meet any of these people at a party, some shining light pierces the Millers' flood, and you smile, because after all, this is life. In Pitlor's competent hands, *The Birthdays* is a character-driven narrative with an impeccable plot. The Millers ponder and struggle and cry out on the page in refreshingly direct prose. . . . This is what Pitlor's special vision illuminates: resolution and a stab at redemption."

—Catherine Parnell, *Milwaukee Journal-Sentinel*

"The kaleidoscopic effect of the roving third-person intimate point of view creates a crystalline portrait of each pivotal personality, while at the same time illuminating how each is seen by the others. The result is undeniably gratifying. . . . Pitlor isn't afraid to contemplate and explore such great and grave questions, while at the same time evoking memorable moments and a subtly riveting plot. This isn't just a terrific family novel; it's a terrific novel through and through. 'You're surviving the family reunion so far?' Joe at one point asks his distinctly wayward daughter Hilary. Of course they all do, but through Pitlor's gifts they do more than that: they endure."

—Fred Leebron, *Ploughshares*

"Rich in symbolism and a strong sense of place, Pitlor's debut novel, with its overlapping narrative perspectives, creates a multilayered portrait of a family in all its fragility and its strength." —*Publishers Weekly*

"[Pitlor] has ably homed in on trenchant modern issues revolving around fertility, marriage, and aging." —Joanne Wilkinson, *Booklist*

"Beautifully rounded, wonderfully balanced, *The Birthdays* offers a rare portrait of a family caught exactly at the moment when generations shift roles. Heidi Pitlor is a wonderful writer, and her characters come alive on the page." —Andrea Barrett, author of *Ship Fever*

"In *The Birthdays* Heidi Pitlor demonstrates a wonderful sense of setting, plot, and occasion, but what makes this novel so absorbing, and so masterful, is her sense of character. In some magical way Pitlor manages to make us feel what it is like to be both a parent and a child, both old and young, both bitter and hopeful. An exhilarating debut." —Margot Livesey, author of *Banishing Verona*

"Heidi Pitlor has fashioned an elegant and enormously satisfying family drama that takes a refreshingly unsentimental look at the vagaries of long-term marriage and even longer-term parenting. She writes with compassion for even the most flawed members of the Miller clan and, in doing so, shows us that family love can be messy and garrulous, that the responsibilities of that love only increase with the years, and that it requires the kind of super-human strength of which we are all, in our own flawed ways, entirely capable." —Marisa Silver, author of *No Direction Home*

"Just when you think there's nothing more to say about the madness and mystery of family life, along comes a book like Heidi Pitlor's first novel, *The Birthdays*. Boldly, lovingly, she takes the archetype of the weekend reunion and uses it to reveal the never-ending growth pains of one ordinary yet fascinating family. Anyone who knows firsthand the modern-day struggles of veering into middle age alongside siblings, in-laws, and elderly parents (and isn't that most of us nowadays?) will find this book captivating, moving, painfully funny, and so very, very true."　　　—Julie Glass, author of *Three Junes*

"I loved spending a weekend on Great Salt Island with the Miller family. Pitlor deftly introduces each member, drawing a reader into their knot of confusion and love. I didn't want the story to end, and dreaded the last ferry home."
　　　　　—Amanda Eyre Ward, author of *How to Be Lost*

"Heidi Pitlor's first novel—about family, pregnancy, sex, and loss—is always acute and elegant, at moments terribly sad, at other moments (and this surprises) extremely funny. She has an amazing ear for the heartbeat of family life, and I have no doubt but that in the future we'll be hearing more of what she hears. An auspicious debut."　　　　—David Leavitt

The Birthdays

a novel

Heidi Pitlor

W. W. Norton & Company
New York London

For information about permission to reproduce selections from this book, write
to Permissions, W. W. Norton & Company, Inc.,
500 Fifth Avenue, New York, NY 10110

Manufacturing by Courier Westford
Book design by Anna Oler

Library of Congress Cataloging-in-Publication Data

Pitlor, Heidi.
The birthdays : a novel / Heidi Pitlor.— 1st ed.
p. cm.
ISBN-13: 978-0-393-06127-7
ISBN-10: 0-393-06127-2
1. Pregnancy—Psychological aspects—Fiction.   2. Maine—Fiction.
3. Domestic fiction.   I. Title.
PS3616.I875B57 2006
813'.6—dc22
2006000421

ISBN 978-0-393-32993-3 pbk.

W. W. Norton & Company, Inc., 500 Fifth Avenue, New York, N.Y. 10110
www.wwnorton.com

W. W. Norton & Company Ltd., Castle House, 75/76 Wells Street, London
W1T 3QT

3 4 5 6 7 8 9 0

1
Genetics

Daniel no longer liked the color he and his wife had painted their dining room walls. Faded, marbled ochre, it was an almost physiological shade. More the color of indigestion than peaceful meals and a happy home—what had they been thinking? He didn't like the walls and he didn't like the pea green place mats Brenda had just bought, or the matching cloth napkins with pea green flecks. She'd found them at a British housewares shop in Boston, a store she visited when she felt homesick for London.

"More pancakes?" she asked, already on her third serving. Her stomach rested on her legs like a small pumpkin beneath her T-shirt.

"No more for me, thanks."

She helped herself to the last two pancakes and drizzled threads of maple syrup in large circles over her plate. It was the first morning of her twenty-fourth week of pregnancy, and she'd been up since before sunrise. Through his dreams, Daniel had heard her in the kitchen moving pots and pans, dropping them on the floor. Most likely trying to wake him. Granted, her new body—and their new house just outside Boston with its narrow hallways and doors—made her clumsy. Small yellow bruises lined her hips and thighs, for she still hadn't gotten used to cutting corners so tightly. He'd lain in bed "like a dead person," as she sometimes proclaimed from her very high horse, and he'd listened to her clang about. Daniel had wondered if she'd want a second child, and then they'd need to move yet again to a bigger house with more rooms. She seemed to truly enjoy being pregnant. She forgave herself her new clumsiness and mood swings, her lapses of memory and constant trips to the bathroom.

"Oops," she said now, dropping a square of pancake on her lap. Just six months ago, she was reed thin with narrow, almost boyish hips, and her size made her look even younger than she was. Thirty-one years old, and fourteen years younger than Daniel, Brenda was short, a mere five-three, and had tiny bones, impossibly small wrists and ankles. Even now, six months in.

"You never used to like pancakes," he said.

"I know. Isn't it weird? I could eat ten more."

"Who are you? Where is my wife?"

She grinned through her stuffed mouth. Daniel noticed a spot of syrup gleaming on her chin, and he reached over to wipe it off. Food used to be an inconvenience for her, something that only disrupted the flow of her days and evenings, and though at times her small appetite grated on him, he secretly loved being so much bigger than her. He'd loved wrapping his arms around her waist in bed and being able to touch his own elbows. He'd loved the faint trail of her verte-brae down her back, the shadow of her breasts on her flat stomach in the mornings—but these things had disappeared over the past months. He felt his whole body frown.

Daniel and Brenda had recently moved from a loft in a mostly empty building in Brooklyn. He didn't miss the musty smell of vacancy, or the cracked windows and occasional rat he saw sniffing around the dumpster out back. But he often missed the galleries and plays they used to go to, the weekly dinners they had with their neighbors, Evan and John. He missed the buzz of life in New York. Most of their new neigh-bors were older and bore an air of sadness, a sense that they'd sacrificed great things in their lives and had made a fragile peace with this fact.

After she'd finished washing the breakfast dishes, Brenda stood in the shower, her mouth open to the water raining down her face. Daniel could see her—she'd left the door ajar and the shower curtain halfway open. She clearly hadn't heard him come in. She rubbed her hands over the arc of her belly and breathed a contented sigh.

"You look happy," Daniel said. More and more he found himself examining her and reporting what he saw.

"God, Dan, you scared me." She covered her nipples.

"I've seen those before. You don't need to hide them."

She reached for the shampoo and squeezed the bottle directly over her head, allowing the liquid to stream down the sides of her cheeks.

"You look free. Liberated."

She glanced out at him. "I do?" She leaned her face toward the water again. "From what?" Her accent seemed to be returning lately, and she pronounced this last word through tight lips.

"I can't tell." He lifted his glasses from his face and wiped the fog from the lenses with the bottom of his T-shirt. "Liz is already saying that she wants her old body back." Daniel's sister-in-law was just over seven weeks pregnant. And his sister Hilary was pregnant too—maybe that would be enough for Brenda, their child not having any siblings but at least a couple of cousins. He made a mental note to broach the topic later that morning, maybe on the drive north to Maine. His family would gather at his brother Jake's summer house for the weekend to celebrate their father's seventy-fifth birthday.

The last time all of the Millers had been in one place was four years ago, for his grandmother's funeral. Afterward, they drove to a steakhouse near the cemetery and squeezed into a plush burgundy booth. In the artificial darkness, amid the smell of charred onions, his family discussed the funeral service, which his mother thought had been a little cursory, the eulogy a little rushed. They discussed Hilary's travel plans the next day, and soon enough those who usually drifted to the forefront of the family conversations did so, and those who did not—Daniel's father, Daniel himself more and more—focused on their plates. He remembered he'd grown a little sleepy, as he often did in their presence. A comforting sort of sleepiness. No matter how infrequently the seven gathered, they talked about the same topics—their jobs, politics, their travel plans—in the same lulling rhythm as if they had never parted. Once the babies came, there would be ten Millers and conversations would inevitably change. They would certainly no longer fit in the booth of a steakhouse. They would turn into a completely different family. Most likely, this weekend would be the last time they would be just seven. Daniel often grew apprehensive about it all. But then again, he thought too fondly of the past—he knew he did.

"Liz says she's already outgrown some of her clothes," he said to Brenda.

"She's probably just being vain," she said. "Anyway, it can't be all that bad. She's only seven weeks. Maybe she's just eating too much."

"I don't think it was vanity." Daniel slid his glasses back on. "And she wasn't really complaining, more just filling me in. I can understand her being a little anxious." He turned himself around, and his left wheel caught on Brenda's old pink towel that lay across the floor. He reached down and walked his hands forward.

"I suppose."

The towel stretched and tore beneath the wheel, and he began to lose his balance.

"We've got to leave in ten minutes," she said behind him. "Will you be ready?"

"Goddammit," he muttered, and jerked his chair backward.

The sperm donor was from Milwaukee—twenty-nine years old, five-eleven, 175 pounds, brown, blue. A self-described "freelance landscaper," he had strong visual and verbal skills, weaker math. Their counselor had described him as gentle but confident. She wouldn't tell them why he'd sold his sperm, as he'd opted not to disclose this, and Daniel couldn't help thinking that the man probably was desperate for money, that he was unemployable in some fundamental way that might get passed along genetically. Still, the counselor said he came closest to what Brenda had said she wanted: someone healthy, intelligent, creative and happy. This thing, this sperm donation, had been her idea.

Daniel was forty-five, five-eleven when standing, 170 pounds, brown, brown, with a square jaw and the close-set eyes characteristic of the Millers. He was a commercial illustrator, but he wasn't afraid of numbers like the other illustrators and artists he knew. He took care of his and Brenda's budget and bills, their taxes. He would have described himself as detail-oriented, but maybe this was just a function of the wheelchair, since before the accident he'd been markedly less organized. Though the accident was only a year and a half ago, he remembered life as absolutely different before it. More driven by amorphous ideas and concerns: When would he be able to do his real drawing and painting full-time? Where should they travel to next? Where would they ideally like to settle down, in what sort of place? His old life often came back to him in what seemed like passing memories of a dream: the sensation of running toward a soccer ball, of sprinting to catch a bus into the city, wet grass beneath his toes in the summer, a heavy cloth napkin blanketing his lap in a restaurant. Now his legs hung from him like a doll's, useless. And his days were composed of floods of details: how much time to leave for getting to the physical therapist, where to meet Brenda for her ultrasound. The goal now was to prevent flukes and mistakes, to control the surface layer of life. Even his conversations with Brenda had seemed different and easier, at least more playful before the accident. Sometimes when they'd lie in bed on Sunday mornings, she'd ask him to imagine that he was painting a part of her body, and to talk her

through each stroke. She'd never picked the obvious parts—
never her breasts or legs, never her face. She'd say that she
wanted to keep him guessing, so she'd ask him to draw her
thumb, or her left knee, her chin. As he spoke in as much
detail as he could, she'd sometimes interject with random
thoughts about fantasies she had—living near the Mediterranean, starting an artists' cooperative. Their words took on a
lazy air of reverie, and they'd stay in bed through the afternoon and into the early evening, dozing on and off, making
love, rising only to get something to eat or to change the
music on the stereo. Lounging in bed, describing Brenda's
perfect body parts and dreaming about living in France
seemed almost silly now, indulgent and irrelevant. And sex
was no longer the spontaneous, transporting experience it
used to be. On a good day, Daniel could manage to get it up
for five seconds or so—actually, on a good day, he could manage anything at all. It was obvious that Brenda missed their
old talks, as well as their former sex life. Sometimes she still
asked him lofty questions about art and travel and love
(always, it seemed, as they were falling asleep, when he had
little energy for abstract thoughts), but overall, she seemed
more and more preoccupied with her pregnancy and getting
ready for the baby. Daniel supposed this satisfied her need for
something hopeful and positive, given his moods lately. He
often felt he'd aged threefold in the past year and a half.

After their first appointment at the sperm bank, Daniel
said, "Isn't it strange, thinking about the donor, this very significant person that we'll never know?" Andrea, their genetic
counselor, had explained the many varieties of sperm that
were available, the endless varieties of men that had offered
up their genetics (straight, gay, black, white, Hispanic, tall,

short, broad, lanky—the list was truly infinite). She began to seem like a god, so many possible lives at her fingertips. Daniel noticed that she spoke primarily to Brenda, and that she included him in the conversation once or twice merely as an afterthought. Daniel and Brenda sat in the car, stopped at a traffic light.

"Maybe a little," she said. "Just try not to think about him as a person. That's what I'm doing. It's just sperm. It's just science, really, and in the end it'll be our baby. You'll be its father."

"Sort of," Daniel said, though he was relieved to hear that Brenda had in her mind reduced this man to a faceless shot of liquid. Unbelievably, they hadn't more fully discussed this before now, but then the whole process had moved so quickly. Initially he'd looked into various new types of surgery and processes with sinister names like "electrical ejaculation" and "testicular sperm extraction" and immediately rejected them—he'd had enough of surgeons and hospitals and machines and drugs in the past year and a half. He and Brenda had briefly considered adoption, but she'd been opposed to it. She'd heard horror stories about adopted children growing up to be schizophrenic, psychotic, and when Daniel argued that even their own child could turn out this way, she put her foot down and said no. No adoption. Period. And then she came up with the idea of using a donor. Half of their genetics was better than none, she said. The logic made sense at the time, and seeking a donor the best option. They barreled ahead with her plan, and he didn't stop to think twice about it.

"This guy will have nothing to do with our lives in the end," she said.

"Except for providing the genetics."

"Half of the genetics."

"True, but still. I'm starting to hate how tangential I am in this whole process. Andrea talked to you like you were the only one in the room."

"Come on. You'll be right there when I'm inseminated. You'll come with me to all these appointments. You'll take Lamaze with me. Pretty soon you'll forget about the donor." She sounded tired.

"I guess," he said, but as the insemination drew nearer, he found he couldn't forget at all. And afterward, as the weeks and months passed after that day, he thought about the donor more and more. Daniel tried to imagine what the man looked like, his face, his clothes, what his house looked like, his car. Daniel wanted him to be perfect and imperfect at once, flawless and profoundly flawed. When he mentioned his thoughts to Brenda, she humored him at first—"I'm seeing a tan guy who wears flannel shirts and jeans. He drives a non-dad car, something sporty, something red"—but soon chafed at this game and grew more and more exasperated with Daniel wanting to talk so frequently about the donor. One day she finally grumbled, "To be honest, I think it's getting unhealthy, this obsession of yours," to which Daniel responded, "I guess I just need to make myself think about other things."

Daniel sat beside the living room window now, waiting for Brenda to finish packing. He saw their neighbor, Morris Arnold, step out his back door. A paunchy, elderly hermit, the man regularly hung his stained underwear on a line that faced their back yard. His terrier, Rex, peed on their rosebushes and ravaged their trash, leaving chunks of cardboard and coffee grounds and plastic and pens strewn across their lawn. For some reason, Brenda had taken a liking to Morris. Right in the middle of dinner, just as Daniel began telling her about his day, she would jump up, fill a plate with food and head for the back door. Daniel would hear her next door talking to Morris, cooing at his new rhododendrons, making sure he remembered to reheat the dinner if he wasn't going eat it right away. People she hardly knew were endlessly interesting to her.

He heard her in the bathroom, doing whatever she did in there and singing loudly. She had a mediocre voice, and she chose to sing octaves higher than her natural range. It was unlike her, at least unlike her old self, to so openly revel in her bad voice.

He looked out at five pairs of Morris's underwear flapping in the breeze. A glass of something in one hand, Morris raised his other hand to Daniel. He wheeled behind a curtain and peered out at the old man cushioned in so much flesh, sitting on his rocker, gazing at his underwear and the clouds that gathered like a family of whales above. A woman Daniel didn't recognize stepped out from behind Morris. Brenda had told Daniel that he was widowed and had been for years. This woman was short and scrawny with a high, beaklike nose and a pile of pinkish hair stacked on her head—the sort of woman who could be drawn easily in caricature. She placed her hands on his shoulders and rested her chin on the top of his head. Rex pushed the door open and ran onto the back lawn, jumping and picking a fight with a light blue pair of underwear. Morris just sat there and watched.

"Who's she?"

Daniel hadn't heard Brenda come up behind him. "I don't know. His sister?"

"No, he doesn't have any living siblings. And his kids live in Oregon."

"You think she's his girlfriend?"

"I doubt it. He just doesn't seem the type."

"The type of what?"

Brenda moved beside him. "I guess the type who dates. Maybe she's an old flame or something, a widow whose husband just died and she's been in love with Morris her whole life."

"And now here they sit, so romantic, watching his underwear billow with the breeze."

"I don't know why that bugs you so much, love. It's just clothing."

"It's an old man's underpants. It's clothing that's been somewhere I don't want to think about." He leaned back and made a pinched expression.

"Oh, lighten up. It's too early for the gloom show."

—

Brenda helped him into the car—she'd gotten good at this. Her arms had grown tight and muscular, and despite her size, she was able to use enough force to prop him up and over so he could grab the handle above the window. Even at six months, she still had the strength to help him into his seat. He'd become a little lazy; initially he'd trained himself to do such things entirely on his own. He'd lifted weights daily, and worked his arms into good shape at the gym. But lately he liked Brenda's help. He could build himself back up another time, another year. And anyway, doctors were taking big steps toward understanding and even reversing some spinal cord injuries. Every once in a while Daniel allowed himself to hope.

When they got going, Brenda dipped back into her song. She exaggerated her accent, and what was this awful song anyway? He didn't recognize the words.

"Bren," he said, "could we have some quiet?"

"I feel like singing."

She sounded so young, but then again, she was. "Fine."

"Oh, just forget it." She reached forward and turned on the radio—anything was better than listening to him complain. Or listening to silence.

"Go ahead, sing. The windshield might shatter, though." He looked out the window at the squat, toylike houses on their street—teal, white, seashell gray.

"That was unnecessary."

She was right, and he began to feel small sitting beside her in their car, a small-minded man withering beside his wife flourishing. It was perplexing, really, that he couldn't embrace her happiness lately.

"What do you think his name is?" Daniel asked. "Why do you think he wanted to be anonymous?"

"Who?"

"The donor."

She sighed heavily. "Does it really matter?"

"I'm thinking his name is Peter. Or Jonathan. A good WASP name. Jonathan White. Something completely bland and boring."

"You mean something anonymous?"

He smiled. "I guess."

"I don't know why you dwell on this. It only makes you feel like shit. Mum said she knew this would be a problem, that the whole donor thing would bring up issues."

"What the hell does she know about sperm donors? I wish you wouldn't tell her so much about every little thing we do."

"I wouldn't exactly call this little," she said. "At any rate, I thought you agreed to make yourself think about other things."

He rested his palms on his lap. "I guess I did," he said. He could feel the rough, crisp denim of his shorts, but he could not feel the weight of his hands on his legs.

Ten years ago he never thought much about having children. They seemed something that would remain a part of his future, never his present. He met Brenda when he was teaching a figure drawing class at her college. She was endearingly awful, so stuck on getting every detail just right ("Exaggerate, make things up, make the model yours," he'd told them, and later he thought it made sense when she chose photography as her major), but she hovered near him at the end of each class and in her thick accent asked him question after question about his work. She listened to his answers with reverence. She was deferential in talk, but the way she carried herself—her firm posture, her emphatic gestures, even her black hair cut close to her head and her pale blue eyes—lent her a different dimension. A sense that she knew more than she let on, that she was wiser and more adult than her years. She had an endearing habit of licking her lips twice before she began speaking, and though he'd told himself not to pay such close attention to a student, he found that he couldn't help it.

Two years later, they married and bought an apartment in Brooklyn, and once their friends began having children, they discussed doing the same but decided to wait. Things were busy for them—Daniel's work would soon be featured in magazines and books, and Brenda, now a commercial photographer, had been contracted for several assignments in Africa. Their careers were thriving, and they didn't want this to change. Then Brenda was returning from a trip to the Serengeti, where she'd been photographing running shoes. A storm had moved much quicker than predicted, and the airplane rose and dipped through the lightning in the sky. *The turbulence was like a wave, like we were inside a tidal wave*, she said. *I felt this sinking so intense my stomach went from my throat to my toes in less than one second, and then my head smashed into the seat in front of me.* After the plane landed in Memphis, she was transported to the nearest hospital, and—miraculously—her injuries turned out to be only a mild case of whiplash and a bruised head. Others on the plane had not been so lucky. An elderly woman had suffered a heart attack and died; one man had been hit on the head by a falling suitcase and had slipped into a coma.

As Daniel drove her the twenty-one hours home from the hospital so she wouldn't have to endure another flight, Brenda sat rigid and still beside him, drumming her fingers against her knees. "I want to have a child," she said after a while, and he nodded. "Then we'll have a child."

Now Daniel liked to think back on this time and savor the drama of this decision made so soon after that flight. He couldn't remember actively engaging in any thought process, only yielding to something bigger than them. That night, and every night for the next two weeks, they climbed into bed and tried to make a baby, and Daniel brimmed with a sense of purpose and a renewed adoration of his wife. Weeks passed and she got her period, so the next month they tried again, as well as the next.

Neither of them could have expected what came two

months later, which was eventually followed by their move to Massachusetts. Here they could more easily own a car. Here Daniel's parents could come over and help when needed, and in a smaller city, everything seemed more wheelchair-accessible. It was like a poorly written movie, he often thought, Brenda's near miss followed so closely by his own tragedy—tragedy? Was the word too extreme? Well, no, he thought now, and he shouldn't have to apologize for hyperbole, and especially not to himself. Brenda survived a near plane crash virtually unscathed, and he couldn't bike to the store to pick up sugar and milk without getting crushed by a hatchback.

She fiddled with the radio dial. He had behaved like one of those men in the supermarket who shouted at their children when they spoke too loudly and snapped at their wives for no good reason. Surly, tired, predictable men who did nothing to prove that they weren't the more volatile gender. He would think before he spoke from now on. He would lighten his tone.

They drove in silence and Daniel looked out the window at the passing houses, their shingled roofs sloping toward the road. He rolled down the window, leaned out his arm and cupped his hand into the wind. The air lifted and dropped his curled hand and pushed between his fingers. It seemed he could feel every cell in his palms. They tingled and cooled with the breeze.

—

Ellen Miller stood at the stove, waiting for the kettle to whistle. She imagined her fingers losing sensation, then her arms, her shoulders, her neck. She pictured each part of herself shutting down, then the memories, the knowledge, the sound of her own breath each night, the look of the melon-colored sun setting over the abandoned playground at the end of the street, all of it fading to black. Or would there even be black? Perhaps there wouldn't be color or anything she could possibly imagine given the equipment she or anyone else on this earth had. Her husband Joe would call her ghoulish for thinking such things, but MacNeil would understand. MacNeil, whom she'd known only as her good friend Vera's husband for years.

Joe sat behind her at the kitchen table waiting for his tea. His flesh hung on his bones, sagging and folding with age.

"Seventy-five years. You're an old man."

"And you're an old lady," he said in his quiet baritone, and what could she say to this? *Of course I am. Give me something better than that.*

"I'm younger than you."

"Not by much." He was reading some library book about a war. He read only books about war and danger and suspense and murder, books she found boring given the amount of action they provided. She supposed he must have gotten something necessary from them, as he himself had once served in a war—she often had to remind herself of this fact.

The kettle sang and she filled two cups and brought them to the small table. They'd been talking about buying a bigger one for years, but there were always more urgent things to buy—a new clutch for the car, a new boiler. It was only seven A.M., and they had hours to pass before they would drive to Maine and board the ferry that would take them to Great Salt Island and Jake's undoubtedly large summer home. At least someone in the family had made a lot of money. At least someone had realized a dream.

MacNeil was in San Francisco visiting his daughter. He'd be

back in a couple of days and that following Wednesday they would go to Boston, to the Gardner Museum for a concert of Bach and Schumann in the Tapestry Room. She'd never been disloyal to Joe in her life and she knew he'd not been either. But she wondered where her newfound friendship with Mac-Neil would lead—and how funny, she thought, how perfectly strange to wonder such a thing this late in life. The last few times she'd seen him, she'd noticed a distinct charge in the air between them, a quickening in her chest. She'd become more self-conscious with him, more aware of everything he said and the way he said it. And it seemed as if he'd been responding to something too. He'd started standing closer to her, and touching her more—gently on her arm or her hand as they walked together, on the small of her back as he opened a door for her, and she couldn't help it, she liked it. Objectively, their relationship was just a friendship. Platonic. She knew MacNeil would have agreed, but she couldn't keep herself from speculating about the possibilities. And when she did, she questioned what it was that she truly wanted from him—to feel the beginnings of desire again? To feel desirable and interesting, or at least interested? To act on these feelings? Or something more permanent, more life-changing? This thought seemed too cumbersome, its ramifications too enormous to even entertain. *What do you really want?* was the question that kept people up at night, and she'd gotten through the years mostly by not asking it of herself, just continuing on, and contemplating only that which was directly before her, that which was easily answerable: the logistics of life, of work and home and family. Her children, especially Jake, were plagued by questions of fate and human will and it did them no good. Since Jake was a child, he'd been hunting for something that was just out of his

reach—more friends, different girlfriends, athletic achieve-
ment, academic success. It seemed that he finally got what he
wanted when he met his wife Liz, and later, when he found his
astonishingly high-paying job in finance. But even now he
wasn't entirely content. He complained constantly to Ellen
about his brother and sister never calling him, about how he
wished the family were closer and saw each other more and
how he worried that his child would barely know its cousin.
Jake didn't seem to see his own role in the matter—that he
tended to complain too much. He tried too hard to impress or
at least to please people. He was too forceful with his love, and
he inadvertently made people recoil, which made him try even
harder. It seemed that he might never be truly happy. His wife
Liz was a minor saint. Or perhaps, Ellen thought with a
twinge, perhaps she had a MacNeil in her life.

"Do you think Liz is happy?" Ellen asked Joe.

"She's finally pregnant. It's what they've been working on
for years, a family." He didn't look up from his book. The air
conditioner next door whirred and the neighbor, Dorothy
Wenders, coughed. There was no quiet in this neighborhood.
No privacy at all.

"Happy as in deeply happy, satisfied with her life and their
marriage, not just relieved that she's going to become a
mother."

He slid a finger between the pages of his book and looked
above his glasses at her. "I do think she's happy," he said.
"Sugar?"

She rose to find the sugar bowl and nearly tripped over
Babe, Joe's box turtle, who had planted himself a foot from
her chair. "Must you let him out so often?"

"He needs to stretch."

"He's a turtle, he doesn't have muscles that need stretching. He has a shell. He has turtle flesh."

"Come here, Babe," Joe murmured, snapping his fingers near the floor.

"It's just not sanitary, letting him have the run of the kitchen."

"He's the cleanest turtle you'll ever find."

"Because it's almost your birthday, I'll give you this," she said as she handed him the sugar bowl and sat. She wished she didn't have the desire to fling the turtle out the window. As a boy, Joe hadn't been allowed pets or toys or anything, really. The only child of a poor Russian couple, he had grown up in a small, bleak apartment in Buffalo. Constantly afraid some tragedy would befall him in this new country, his parents rarely let him play outside with the neighborhood children. It wasn't a surprise that Joe now treasured the things that filled their small house with life.

Babe stared up at her, and she sighed. MacNeil did not have pets or a house filled with the clutter of old newspapers or piles of clothes heaped on chairs. He did not have leaking ceilings and a prehistoric boiler and stained, threadbare carpets. His house was clean and spare and spacious, the house of a man who lived alone and kept only that which fed his soul—soul! A word MacNeil used with regularity, a word that previously Ellen had never thought to use in daily conversation. In his living room were original paintings, photographs, rare books—he could afford the finest. Ellen lifted the tea bag from her cup and wrung it against the spoon. She supposed Babe filled a small hole in Joe's spirit, one made in his childhood, but in the end it just seemed so ignoble, his obsession with his pet, his rock with four legs.

"Happy almost-birthday to me," Joe said suddenly, and stood. He moved behind her and lightly kissed the top of her head. "Come here."

"What is it?"

"Let's dance," he said, and clumsily pulled her from her seat.

"Joe." He was acting like someone else. Her husband Joe wasn't the sort of man who just up and danced with his wife. He was a car salesman, a bargain shopper, a man who organized his receipts. Everything about him was practical (everything except Babe, of course).

"Come on," he said, and led her into the living room, where the morning light cut across the furniture in hard triangles. He gently slid his arm behind her back and guided her around the coffee table, and she practically tripped. It'd been years since she'd danced. He swept her back and forth as if in time to a waltz, and she noticed a flurry of dust winking like snowflakes in the sunlight.

"Joe, what music are you hearing?" she asked, but he only grinned in reply.

Pleasant. Silly. Pointless. Inane—words filled her mind.

Ellen met Vera and MacNeil at an exhibit of young photographers at the DeCordova Museum thirty years ago. Ellen had dragged Joe and the kids out to Lincoln on a sunny Saturday afternoon, though they'd had other ideas of how they wanted to spend the day. The five drove the hacking station wagon fifteen miles westward on the skinny highway through larger and larger towns. They turned onto the road that led them up and down hills and through maples, elderberries, pines, oaks, past big old wooden houses with large porches and long driveways. Ellen had once dreamed of living in Lincoln in a sprawling antique farmhouse on acres of land, but she and Joe never could have afforded it, and in the end she'd accepted their small but sufficient Cape.

At DeCordova, two outgoing and seemingly parentless children tagged along with their bored three, and eventually an attractive couple appeared and apologized vacantly for their kids' rambunctiousness. Dressed in a loose black tunic and slacks, Vera was petite, with a long ballerina's neck, curtains of silky brown hair, and MacNeil was twice Vera's height but thin, broad in the forehead and square in the chin. Attractive. "Have you seen the Gartsons?" Vera asked Ellen after introducing herself and her husband. "We met the man a few years back at an opening downtown. A real genius, though he was out of his mind drunk at the time. Come on, come look at them. They're unbelievably gorgeous," and tugged her into the next room to show her the wall-sized color photographs of entwined nudes. The children followed and Ellen felt a blush fill her face as she watched her children giggle at the enormous breasts and legs and even the hulking shadow of a penis. Joe followed far behind, stopping to glance at each photograph, his hands held in a knot behind his back.

Later, he said he'd thought the couple was pretentious about art and completely careless with their children, but Ellen told him that she'd found them refreshingly exuberant, so obviously smitten with the world and each other. "You can just tell they squeeze every ounce they can out of this life." Joe looked at her straight on and said, "Just make sure her pretense doesn't rub off on you." She pivoted, rushed out of the room and secretly vowed to befriend Vera.

The next week, on her day off, Ellen found herself sitting

on Vera's large front porch in Lincoln, listening to the history of the two massive apple trees in her front yard—they'd been planted as symbols of hope by MacNeil's Scottish ancestors— and sipping fresh-squeezed limeade that tasted like candy. And every Wednesday that followed, Ellen traveled to Lincoln and experienced a different life. Vera took her on long, hilly walks and identified the many different birds in the trees above. The two cooked risotto with truffles or prosciutto or goat cheese for lunch, and on rainy days they sat beneath Vera's eiderdown comforter on her sofa and watched French and Italian films about young lovers, films that seemed to Ellen at once frivolous and profound. Occasionally Vera asked if they should meet at Ellen's house, but Ellen always found an excuse for them not to. *After all*, she almost said once, *we don't have a VCR or leather furniture or a view of the trees or anything, really, that you'd want to see.* The months and years passed, and Vera and MacNeil came to dinner a couple of times, but not once did Vera come alone, and not once did Ellen invite her.

At Vera's funeral decades later, MacNeil looked like a stripped leaf—blanched, tired, finished. When they arrived, Ellen said to him, "It doesn't get worse than this"—as if she knew, she now thought—and he said, "I hope not." He'd had no time to prepare for Vera's death, a massive heart attack that struck her one morning when she was yanking up weeds in her flower garden. He'd only just retired as dean of the university.

Two weeks later, Ellen bumped into him at a gourmet grocery store where she liked to shop once in a while for produce. He stood perplexed before a wall of milk. "I've never noticed what sort of milk I've been drinking all these years," he said to her. It was their first time alone. "Vera took care of all these things and I let her. I am a terrible person."

"You are no such thing." Ellen knew Vera preferred whole but pulled out a carton of skim. "You want something low in fat," she said in her wife-and-mother voice. She remembered Vera mentioning his high cholesterol a few months back, and that she'd been plying him with red wine every night, but Ellen couldn't imagine all that alcohol would do him any good. She led him through the store, filling his cart with oats and organic vegetables and eggs, deli meat and freshly baked bread—there was no need to bargain-shop for him—and in the health aisle, she picked out several bottles of vitamins and aspirin. One should never go, she always said, without aspirin.

"Let me thank you with tea," MacNeil said in the parking lot as they filled the trunk of his car. She stood beside him, carrying a large plastic bag with a couple of Vidalias inside.

"I should probably be getting home."

MacNeil nodded.

But Joe wasn't at home. He was out with his friend Bill Dooley pricing new air conditioners, not that either would ever buy one. Joe loved to price things. New houses for them and the kids, kitchen sinks, new cages for Babe. "You know, why not? I'll come for one cup of tea. I'll follow you."

He drove badly—slowly, drifting toward the lines on the road—and Ellen thought it was sweet. She drove at a distance behind him, careful not to crowd him. A few of his bags in her hands, she followed him inside his house at a distance too. The place was eerily quiet and immaculate, the floors shiny and smelling of ammonia. He must have hired a cleaning person. Vera'd always been a mess. She'd been far more concerned with her gardens outside than cleanliness within her house, and her kitchen had always surprised Ellen, the dishes piled in the sink like old books, the empty food boxes strewn across the counter. "Life's too short to worry about dishes," Vera once said.

Ellen began to set the groceries on the counter as MacNeil filled the kettle and set out cups and saucers. Before long, the kettle shrieked and he served them. "You're the first guest I've had in days," he said. "Except a Moonie trying to sell me books."

"Maybe it's good for you to have people here," Ellen said.

"Good, bad, I'm sure there's some way you're supposed to go about this, some way the doctors prescribe."

Ellen tried to smile and took a seat at the table. She wondered if it had been where Vera used to sit.

MacNeil began talking about the approaching presidential election and the two men running for office, one a child, the other a ghost. As she lifted the tea bag from her cup, Ellen thought she and Joe never had conversations about such weighty subjects as politics. They planned, they talked about their days and their children and neighbors, but rarely, anymore, did they discuss anything else.

Joe had left the room now and Ellen looked down at the sofa, its green fabric worn but its cushions still firm. The sofa had lasted thirty years—a minor miracle. She went to the bedroom for the yellow Samsonite, which she'd packed last night, and lifted it, careful to use her knees. Soft blankets of clouds kept the heat away today, and she felt a chill as she carried the suitcase outside to the car and hefted it into the trunk. For one of

Joe's birthdays, before Hilary was born, they brought the boys to Maine—was it Great Salt Island? Her memories were so specific, too specific. She could never recall the basics—the wheres (was it this island?), the whens (which birthday was it?), and it made her want to pull off her head right now. How could she not remember where they went? At any rate, she did remember that they found their way to the motel with the huge clam-shaped sign, and she did remember feeling somehow significant with two sons and a husband, a house outside the city. *I am very much an adult now*, she thought as she unpacked their bags and unfolded the cots for the boys. She and Jake played their game—*What would you do with a million dollars?*—and later that afternoon, when the boys were kicking a ball around outside the room, she and Joe made love quickly and feverishly, careful not to let them hear. Afterward, she curled up beside him and he said, "I'm happy. I really think this is happiness." She nodded drowsily, gratefully, knowing Joe's one dream in life had been to start a family.

Now she wondered what her one dream in life had been. To start a family? She'd certainly wanted one, and she was certainly grateful for hers, but she supposed she'd just always assumed she'd have one. To win a million dollars, as she and Jake used to fantasize? This seemed to approximate a small part of the dream, but it had been more than just this. Perhaps she'd wanted the side effects of money, the deep comfort and pride and sense of fulfillment of a person endowed in some way. With money, yes, or perhaps talent or brilliance or luck. Not just money. Maybe not even money. She looked up at the bleached sky. She couldn't remember really having one unified dream, just the sensation of moving forward and following Joe's lead. Trying in some aimless manner, when she thought of it, to achieve the buzz of happiness.

In some respects, she was more adult then than now, she thought as she pushed the suitcase to the side of the trunk. She had gotten the responsibility of raising children out of the way, and now she was preoccupied with indulgences like Mac-Neil and museums, especially the Gardner, where Vera had taken her just before she died, and MacNeil a few times since then. It was one of his favorite places. Just a couple of weeks ago, the two stood under one of the stone archways that framed the courtyard and admired the new orchids. The sunlight filtered in from the skylights above and gave the place an almost holy glow. It was breathtaking, the beauty there. The flowers in the courtyard were changed seasonally: in the spring were nasturtium, freesia, jasmine and azaleas; lilies and cineraria at Easter; chrysanthemums in the autumn; and of course poinsettias at Christmas. MacNeil said this courtyard could have been what Eden looked like, and though at first the sentiment struck Ellen as too much, she chided herself for her reaction. She was not used to a man expressing such feeling, and so poetically. She was used to men keeping such things to themselves, experiencing happiness (with books, gadgets, cars, all the predictable tangibles) in the privacy of their own minds. The light above softened, then strengthened, and she let her own emotions take hold and form words in her mind. *It would be all right to pass away here.* She pictured her whole body falling in a sigh onto this stone floor. Perhaps in a moment of profound empathy MacNeil would fold too, and one of the guards would find them, two spent bodies lying flat, their eyes open to the heavens. *But what about Joe? He would die alone.* She pushed the thought from her mind. The guard would page another guard, and the two would carry her and MacNeil into the Blue Room, the closest room, where paintings of Henry James and Madame Auguste Manet and friendly letters from Henry Adams and T. S. Eliot and Oliver Wendell Holmes would welcome them into their own long-sleeping world.

How noble Isabella Gardner was to have left so much to the public—her house, her art, her most personal letters. MacNeil had read all about the woman, and had given Ellen a biography. At the elementary school where Ellen was a librarian, she often tried to interest the children in the anecdotes she'd been reading. Her favorite was the one about Isabella bringing home a lion from a nearby zoo. Passersby gaped as this regal woman, pearls in triple strands around her neck, strode toward them down Beacon Street—*one of the richest streets in all of Boston*, Ellen explained—her hand resting on the plush yellow mane of the ferocious beast. *Some said she even tried to ride him.* The children sat cross-legged on the floor in front of her, their eyes bright. *She was not a particularly friendly woman*, she said, *but rarely are the most influential people. And anyway, she had something more valuable than a sunny disposition. She had character and good taste.*

Ellen left the trunk open for Joe and went back inside. She hadn't returned to Maine in years, since that visit with the boys. She thought a moment—was that in fact the last time? No, they went again with the boys a couple of years later. And she went to an art show on Great Salt, a benefit three years ago for her friend Emma's cousin's organization that raised money for Alzheimer's. She'd stayed at an inn, one she could barely afford. Jake kept saying he'd have them up once they'd redone the house, but they'd only just finished. Ellen still remembered the two-lane road from the ferry landing that wound through the small town and out to a steep rise where the ocean ahead looked like what she pictured it to look like in Ireland—tossing, endless and alive like a storm. The road then traced the circle of the island, leading through the hippie commune on the north end where a few run-down houses huddled close to each other, on past the clusters of artists' bungalows to the east, the tall, grassy dunes and narrow beaches to the south and finally back to the ferry slip and the few stores, the health clinic, the post office. Just after the ferry slip stood an inconspicuous little diner where the fishermen went. Here, Ellen, Emma and Vera had eaten fried cod sandwiches and whispered giddily like teenagers about all the handsome men around them. These fishermen were throwbacks from history, Ellen thought now, these men who worked out at sea. They exuded physicality and bravery and masculinity. And their wives beside them were weathered and pretty, deeply tanned and ragged, and seemed to her to possess some sort of ancient wisdom. The weekend was like a happy dream in hindsight.

She'd have liked to bring MacNeil there, as she imagined the brisk sea air and slow pace would do a mourning man good. And was he still mourning? It had been seven months: of course he was. One never stopped. This thought weighed on her. She had an urge to call him and make sure he was feeling all right, but she saw Joe heading toward her, struggling to carry their suitcases. She would call later, once she had a moment to herself, if she could get one.

"Be careful there," she said.

"I'm trying to impress you." He dumped the bags at her feet. He smiled up at her and turned to go inside again. When he came back, he held the large cage in his hands and a plastic bag of carrots in his mouth for Babe.

"Tell me you're not bringing him," she said.

"It's my birthday."

"Is your family not enough for you? You absolutely need that thing too?"

"You've got Jake's phone number?" Joe set the cage in the back seat of the car and stood, his legs apart.

"Jake will faint when he sees this."

"Here are the keys, right in my pocket. I've been looking all over the place for them."

Too often they talked at each other. Each heard at most fragments of what the other said, and she wondered if it had always been this way, this selective hearing.

He took his seat at the wheel and she went back inside to make sure they hadn't forgotten anything. Standing alone in their living room, even Babe out of the house now, she felt a swell of nostalgia for something she couldn't quite pinpoint. She made her way through the rooms, checking under the beds—so many things like wallets and socks and shoes were forgotten under beds—and turning off the lights, then headed to the front hallway and pulled the door shut. From behind the steering wheel, Joe gazed at her. She started, for it had been some time since they'd looked each other directly in the eyes.

—

Jake Miller followed his wife into their kitchen, where she'd arranged the food for the weekend by meals. Next to a carton of eggs on the counter sat a brick of cheddar, a red onion, a bag of mushrooms, a package of sausages. The canister of coffee sat beside the bag of sugar; the baguette beside the raspberry jam; the cantaloupe beside the blueberries. He loved when she arranged items this way, by theme or function—he supposed it gave him a sense of peace and of being tended to. Other men might not have appreciated this, he often thought. She even took the time to arrange their shampoo and conditioner alternately on the shelf in the shower: his, hers, his, hers. She kept the whole house orderly and clean (and he helped, but he didn't need to do that much when it came down to it). They certainly could have afforded a maid or a housekeeper, but Liz wouldn't have been comfortable with that. When Jake was promoted to CFO, vice president and partner of his investment firm and paid a much larger salary, Liz had made him promise that their lifestyle wouldn't change all that much. She continued to teach art at a public high school in the city. She continued to volunteer at a nursing home once a month, and hadn't bought any new clothing or art supplies or anything, really, since the promotion. She even still drove her beat-up Volkswagen. Jake didn't know anyone quite as virtuous, deeply virtuous, as his wife, and when he told her so once, she blanched. "I'm not doing this stuff to be honorable. It's just that I like my job and my car. I like my clothes." "That's one of the great things about you. It comes so naturally, virtue," and she'd said, "Sometimes you give me too much credit." She was a difficult person to compliment—she was uncomfortable with overt praise. And the more she squirmed about it, the more she insisted that he was putting her on a pedestal she didn't deserve, the harder Jake tried to convince her that she was wrong. She deserved every syllable of what he said, he insisted, and the only thing wrong with the pedestal was that it wasn't high enough. "You can't love your wife too much," he told her, and she responded, "I'm not a hundred percent sure about that." His face sank, and she added, "Oh, sweetie. Maybe ninety-nine percent," and reached over to touch his cheek.

Her ultrasound had shown two embryos the other day. They'd gone to her doctor before their first scheduled exam because she'd bled on her way home from work—quite a bit at first, which was beyond alarming to both her and Jake. When they reached the doctor's office early that evening, both shaky, as she was still bleeding, he led them into a small examining room and turned down the lights. A man—the ultrasound technician—stood by a desk typing on a laptop. Liz unbuttoned her skirt and lay on the table as instructed while the ultrasound technician closed his laptop, turned and slipped something that looked like a condom over a plastic vaginal probe. Jake stood close beside Liz and watched the man, tall and stooped with curly red hair, squirt lubricant over the probe. The doctor briefly introduced him as Claude, and Claude murmured, "Careful, cold," and inserted the probe. "You're going to be fine," said the doctor. "No cramping, and you're not passing any tissue. These are good signs." This immediatly made Jake breathe easier. The screen next to Liz's head lit up and swam with blurry gray images. Claude turned his wrist, shifted the probe and pushed it farther inside. Jake looked at him and was sure he saw the man glance down at her breasts. Did he find her sexy? Liz squeezed her eyes shut for a moment. But Claude couldn't have been thinking about sex—it was all business to him. Vaginas were his clients. Ovaries his spreadsheets. Claude moved the probe left and right and finally stopped, and an image of what had to be Liz's uterus appeared on the screen beside her. Jake noted a couple of tiny black swirls inside a patchy gray cloud. Maybe Claude had incredible sex with women since he knew where and what every little thing was. Jake looked down to see whether he wore a wedding ring on the hand that was not between Liz's legs. He did not. The man wasn't exactly attractive. His eyes bulged beneath heavy lids, his red hair was frizzy and thinning on top. Still, he touched women like this every day. Slid his hand right inside.

"Hold on, we're getting there," Claude said.

Jake hadn't gotten his wife pregnant. Well, technically his sperm had. Locked in a closet-sized room with only a TV, an old VCR and two videotapes hand-labeled "The Firm" and "Mean Girls" (whether these were the actual movies or porn knockoffs he didn't know, since he couldn't get the damned VCR to work), Jake had encouraged his sperm out of his body and into a blue plastic cup, which he handed to an obese young male nurse standing behind a desk. The next stop for the tiny fish was a petri dish, where Liz's drug-stimulated eggs were waiting. Once the sperm swam into the eggs, the mixture sat inside an incubator while it fertilized, and two days later got injected into Liz's womb. Jake's body hadn't gotten her pregnant, or more specifically, more accurately he supposed, sex hadn't. Love hadn't. He hadn't even been present for the embryo transfer—he'd been at a meeting in Minneapolis. He and Liz had unsuccessfully tried IVF several times before, so Liz had told him just to go to his meeting and not to worry about it. He hadn't wanted to leave her—he'd told her he could skip the meeting, or at least try to postpone it, but she insisted that they'd given up enough of their lives to infertility. This IVF might be no different from their earlier ones, and she would be fine, absolutely, positively fine doing it on her own. "You don't want me there?" he asked.

"Jake."

"It wouldn't be such a big deal for me not to go to the meeting."

"Jake. End of discussion. Go to Minneapolis."

It seemed to him as if she didn't, for whatever reason, really want him there, but he wouldn't press the point. He was aware of his tendency to misread her signals, and he often had to keep himself in check.

Now, in the exam room, he refocused on the task at hand and searched for something that might be a heartbeat. Suddenly Dr. Mancowicz said, "I think we've got ourselves twins!" Claude shifted the probe again and Dr. M. pressed his thick finger to the screen. "There's one heartbeat. And," he said as he moved his finger to the second black blob and the tiny flickering mass inside it, "there's the second."

Jake swallowed a pocket of air.

Liz laughed nervously. "Can we see them again?" she asked.

Claude pointed more slowly to each pulsing dot. He then removed the probe and its condom, casually tossed it in the trash and dropped the probe on a side table with a small thud.

"Congratulations, you two! Let's go to my office and talk about this good news," Dr. M. said. "Meet me there when you're ready."

Claude pulled the door shut behind him and Jake worried for a second that he'd said all his thoughts about him aloud.

"Hurray!" Liz sang. "We'll have our two children all at once! No more treatments! Hurray!"

Jake took her hand and pulled her off the table, only then fully realizing the enormity of what they'd just seen. Two babies. At once.

"Come on," she said. "It's so great. It's good, at least, isn't it?"

He nodded, reached for her purse on the chair and watched her turn and rush out of the room. *Two babies at once.* He clutched her purse to his side.

In his narrow, bright office that smelled of rubber, Dr. M. explained the risks they faced: early birth, infection, birth defects, death in utero. He spoke plainly, as if he were selling them windows. And for Liz, he continued, there were more risks. High blood pressure, gestational diabetes, hemorrhage, infection. She would need six more weeks of shots and would probably spend at least some of her third trimester on bed rest. After a brief silence and a long sigh, Liz asked him about traveling to Great Salt ("Fine, just don't push yourself") and vitamins, caffeine and exercise. "What about sex?" Jake blurted. They hadn't had any since before she'd gotten pregnant. She'd been too tired, too nauseous, too preoccupied, too something virtually every night. "Is it okay?"

"By all means, just not for three days."

Jake glanced at Liz, but her eyes were on her lap.

He had told his family that she was pregnant, but he hadn't told any of them about the twins yet—they would all be together soon enough, and he wanted to tell them in person. Jake and Liz had hoped for children since before he could remember, and he thought having them should feel more singular, more monumental than it did in the context of Brenda's pregnancy. But now there was the matter of two, he thought as they drove home from the doctor's office that day.

Not that he was competitive, not that he wanted to outdo Daniel in any way, but as the middle child, he was aware that he was always—consciously or subconsciously—vying for the spotlight in his family. He'd read several books about birth order, and middle children finding themselves less special, less visible to their parents than the eldest and youngest. *Middle children grow up feeling squeezed, without the rights of the eldest or the privileges of the youngest children, and often seek to establish an identity separate from the family. While doing so helps them assert their individuality, it can also lead to feelings of exclusion and loneliness within the family.* He'd read a few passages aloud to Liz, perhaps to explain a few things about himself. She'd seemed interested at first but after a while had begun to fidget, perhaps because she was an only child and couldn't relate to any of this. Or perhaps because she'd grown tired of listening to Jake constantly try to understand himself, something he couldn't seem to stop doing despite his best efforts. At any rate, he had read somewhere that psychologists were giving birth order more credence in personality studies and that it could be used in certain cases as a predictor. He wondered now what it would mean to have two children born at the same time. Would there even be a real birth order? Who knew what would happen to such children, and how would this determine their identities? Would they be more competitive with each other?

Jake and Liz had started trying in earnest to have children five years ago. The first night they'd tried was on the island. Liz had lined the windowsills of the bedroom with candles, and the smell of them—lavender, vanilla, lilac—made his nose itch and run. He must have told her thirty times before that he couldn't stand scented candles. The waves crashed predictably outside the walls. As she brushed her teeth, he lay in bed and, smoothing the sheets around him, was struck by the force of expectation. The moon was full, crickets chirped outside the windows, a warm breeze blew across his face. The world seemed to be aligning itself in expectation, and he told himself to relax, it was just another night. He'd made love to his wife before—he certainly knew what he was doing. The curtains billowed with the breeze and sank. Liz stepped out of the bathroom wearing her green flannel pajamas. She looked like a big child, a wing of hair poking out from the left side of her head. When they did make love it was no different than it ever was, though perhaps quicker, and afterward, they lay side by side on their backs and stared up at the shadows of moonlight in stripes across the waves, reflecting off the beams of their ceiling. Light twice removed from its source.

The island was like another planet for Jake as a boy. His parents had taken them a couple of times before Hilary was born. He'd first swum in the ocean here, first seen a girl's breasts (a big wave had tackled her and yanked off her bikini, leaving her tangled in strings of seaweed on the rocky beach, the poor thing); he'd first gotten poison ivy here; first eaten clams. Everything about the place was rugged and natural and raw. And quiet. A quiet so thick his thoughts and words seemed to hold much more significance here. Jake's parents joked with each other in their bed, and deep under his blankets against the night cold, he heard them across the room of the bed and breakfast, whispering and laughing, then shushing each other lest they wake the boys. They were lighter and more affectionate here with each other, as well as with him and Daniel.

After he and Liz married, they visited the island frequently

and even discussed moving here. But eventually they decided
against it. Their friends and jobs were in Portland, and he
could certainly never work from home—the other partners
wouldn't agree to that. Plus life on the island would be too iso-
lated, the frequent winter nor'easters oppressive. Normal
people just didn't live here year-round, not that he'd ever
admit this thought to Liz. She idealized the islanders, those
earthy men who fished for a living, the innkeepers and reclu-
sive artists and aging hippies. But five years ago, when Jake
and Liz were walking along the beach to their bed and breakfast, they spotted a FOR SALE sign in front of a run-down bun-
galow, its clapboards weathered gray. The house was empty
and the walls rotted through in the back. Termites spilled
from the side of the kitchen wall. One window was broken,
the others etched in jagged cracks, but Jake had not been promoted yet and they couldn't have afforded much more. The
two sneaked around back, looking in at the bowed wood
floors and stained walls, the fireplace filled with trash. The
sun had just begun to set, and the light blinked at them from
a small, dusty mirror on the wall. "Think what we could do
with this place," Liz said, and Jake admitted liking it too. Well,
liking its location, really. The house was a complete dump, but
Liz had always wanted to live by the water—it'd been her one
big dream in life, she'd said. "We could fix it up slowly, just do
it in little increments that we can afford. Think of what this
land is probably worth. I mean, it's right on the beach." And
though he had deep reservations about the condition of the
place, about the dangers of storms and the possibilities of ero-
sion, about the financial and logistical burdens of maintaining
a second home, Jake sold off some stock, drained his retirement account and called it a birthday present to her. She

melted with gratitude and excitement and the most palpable love when he first told her about it, and he knew then that he'd done the right thing. He'd never acted this spontaneously before, he often mused, and fortunately they soon had the resources to fully renovate it.

Jake imagined that when they had children, they'd bring them here and spend days on the water, canoeing or kayaking, and nights shucking clams and husking corn and telling ghost stories. He'd give them the clichéd happy childhood he never had. Most of his family vacations had involved accompanying his father on business trips to auto conventions in Detroit or Chicago, and most of what Jake could remember about such places was fighting with Daniel or Hilary in the lukewarm hotel pool. When Jake was small, he was a little afraid of the water, but Daniel loved to swim. As Jake dog-paddled around the shallow end, he'd watch his brother sprint to the end of the diving board, fly into the air in wriggling motions and land with as much weight as possible. Then Daniel would tear across the water toward Jake, pounce on top of him and hold him under the surface for what seemed like minutes. When Daniel finally let go, Jake would pop back above the water, gasping for breath, choking, streams of snot pouring from his nose, his eyes stinging. Hilary, also fearless in the water, would laugh at him and yell, "Sick! You have green snot all over your face!" and all the other kids in the pool would turn to look. He'd lunge for Daniel, who'd duck underwater and swim off, and then the whole thing would start again. His mother never stepped in and told Daniel to stop or Hilary to be quiet. His father always off at conventions, Jake remembered his mother calmly holding court on a chaise lounge beside the pool, drinking cans of Tab and chatting with the other parents, whose kids splashed around beside them, her bobbed brown hair held back from her face by a navy blue and white scarf, her chest and stomach bulky in her navy swimsuit with its polka-dotted skirt. Completely oblivious to the torment going on right in front of her.

Jake's father returned to the hotel room each night, flopped across the bed and switched on the television as their mother helped them into their pajamas. He would, however, read to them before they drifted off to sleep, and sometimes tell them stories of his day, of a strange new car he'd seen that was shaped like an egg, of a salesman he'd met who had ten children, and another who'd visited every baseball park in the country. Because they didn't see him as much, he came to seem more mysterious than Jake's mother, more intriguing and thus important. With an unremarkable sentence or two, Joe had the power to put Jake utterly at ease. When he once pulled his father aside and told him about what had happened in the pool earlier, Joe said solemnly, "I'll have a talk with your brother and sister, all right? Try to put it out of your mind now." Jake nodded and, amazingly, his frustration toward his siblings completely dissolved.

Liz sat in the car as Jake carried out their bags and slid them into the trunk. Jake had forbade her from helping him pack or load the bags in the car. He doted on her these days, though she continually reassured him that she felt fine, that she wouldn't break in half, nor would the babies. "I'm pregnant, not dying," she said as he'd walked her to the car just now, and he replied that he was well aware of this fact, and he was. He simply enjoyed taking care of her. "I got it," she said as he opened the door for her and guided her forward. "I feel just fine, I promise." A thought popped into his head: *Then perhaps you'll be in the mood for a little something once we get to the island.* After all, it had been four days since the bleeding, longer than the doctor recommended, and eight weeks or so since the last time they'd made love, and they had to enjoy themselves now because once the pregnancy progressed and especially once the babies were born, he suspected that they wouldn't have the opportunity or simultaneous desire or energy level for sex, at least for a very long time.

She drummed her fingers against the window and gazed out at their house. Once he'd filled the back seat with the plywood he'd bought to make a ramp over the front step and the new bathtub bench for Daniel, he walked to the passenger's side and pressed his lips against the outside of her window. She made a disgusted face, and when he took his seat behind the wheel, she said, "That window's dirty."

"I don't care," he said, and leaned toward her again.

"Get those filthy lips away from me," she barked, and he pushed his face against hers. "Yuck! Stop!" she howled, and shoved him a little too hard. His arm smacked the steering wheel and then the horn, and he felt a quick ache in his wrist, as well as a flash of irritation that she wouldn't just kiss him. She was now laughing at a squirrel that had been next to the car and leapt into another squirrel after it heard the loud honk of the horn.

They headed out and Liz reached for the radio dial.

"You feeling up for a little something this weekend? Maybe before everyone gets there?" he asked.

"What?" She settled on classical music. Chopin, he guessed. "I don't know, maybe."

"Dr. M. said it was fine. It's been four days. And, what, eight weeks before that?" He immediately regretted saying it this way, as if he'd been keeping track.

"Frankly I am happy to take a prolonged break from doing it so much." She looked at him. "Come on, you got tired of it too. I distinctly remember you saying you were worried that your pecker would fall off from overuse. Remember, before that last IVF?"

"I guess you're right." He gazed at the traffic light ahead of them. "But my pecker's still here. It managed to hang on."

"All right, all right, we'll give it some attention later," she groaned.

It was as if he were demanding the moon from her right now. But she was just tired because of the pregnancy, he reminded himself. She was just grouchy and tired. *Let it go.* He drew a deep breath and tried to think of a way to change the subject.

The drive slipped by, and they brainstormed a list of what they'd need to buy when they returned home after the weekend: another crib, car seat, stroller. Liz jotted down the list in the small blue notebook she kept in her purse. She chewed on the end of her pen happily as she thought of more items, and her cheerfulness began to rub off on him. He imagined announcing the news of the twins to his parents, and wondered what their expressions would be, and then what his brother and sister would say. He couldn't help smiling.

—

Hilary knocked on the front door, but she was three hours early and no one answered. She looked up at the clapboard house perched on a slope overlooking the ocean. It was obvious they'd added on a side porch and a couple of rooms to the right, but the addition was tastefully done. The house had been stained a subdued gray, and tall rosebushes lined the front, the flowers electric red in contrast with the gray. She could have been looking at the pages of a magazine. Jake had done well for himself. This fact still amazed her.

She sat on the front stoop, rubbed her fingertips together, an old habit, and reached in her handbag for a piece of chewing gum. She'd had to give up smoking six months ago and, well, that'd be one thing her family would be grateful for. Not that she'd ever smoked in front of them. Only Daniel. Only he could handle such a thing, and only he knew that she was pregnant.

Leaving her suitcase, she walked around the house and down a sandy path that had been cut into dense reeds to a rocky beach where seagulls pecked at an enormous black lump. The air smelled of something dead. She turned from the birds and the water rumbling in short waves to the shore. Hilary had never liked the beach, the sand everywhere, invading shoes and bags and books and food, the men and women who were content to sit still for hours outside until their skin resembled cured meat, but in Maine the beaches were different and far less crowded. They were rockier, more dangerous, and the weather was entirely unpredictable. She respected these things. She'd only been to Maine once, in high school with a friend, but she still remembered walking barefoot on the beach at night and skinny-dipping in the frigid water with some older boys they'd met.

Yesterday, she'd taken an overnight flight from San Francisco and, from the airport in Portland, a bus to the ferry. A short old man who worked on the boat had carried her bag up the gangplank and offered to buy her a soda. Another had gingerly lifted her bag down the gangplank and led her to a cab. She wouldn't have expected such kind treatment—she'd all but written off Northeasterners as stoic and icy. The cab she took to Jake's house was a beat-up station wagon painted pink and purple, and the driver a funny elderly woman who told raunchy jokes the entire way. Hilary listened as she struggled to remember the punch lines and accidentally gave them away too early. "Christ," the woman said, "I do that sometimes."

"It's all right. No one's perfect." When they'd reached her brother's house, Hilary pressed a large tip into the old woman's hand.

Now she decided to walk the mile or so back into town to kill time. She rarely walked much of anywhere anymore and she thought the exercise would probably do her good. She'd never been to Great Salt Island. So far it appeared to be a typical New England tourist spot: quaint, candy-colored houses with picket fences, and, back near the ferry, an ice cream stand, a seafood restaurant named the Mermaid's Table. She didn't see the appeal of such a place that throttled visitors with its cuteness. She walked along the road and a stooped old man looked up from his yard at her, this tall, pregnant thirty-five-year-old woman with black hair, pasty skin, a nose ring, several tattoos. She wore large black sunglasses, a floppy straw hat, a black sundress and carried an oversized black bag. Hilary called loudly, "Well, hi there, sir. Nice day, isn't it? It sure is beautiful," and the man nodded carefully and turned back to his house.

In town, she found a bookstore, Books & Beans, where she ordered decaffeinated tea and sat on a tall stool at a metal table. The place smelled of San Francisco—of coffee and musky incense and something clean and fake, maybe room deodorizer. In the corner stood an unmanned counter where lottery and ferry tickets were sold. As far as she could see, she was the only customer in the place. The weather was warm and sunny except for a few scattered clouds, and everyone else on the island was probably at the beach—except for the boy, or man, who'd sold her the tea. Now he was wiping off the table next to hers with a stained brown rag, and he cleared his throat. Something about him was faintly familiar. Tall, somewhat attractive, with an endearingly round face and a closely trimmed beard, he could have been anywhere from eighteen to thirty, maybe older. Hilary picked up a magazine that lay on the stool next to her.

"It's nice out there today." His voice was quiet and deep.

"Nice enough," she said.

He turned and continued wiping the tables.

She rubbed her fingertips together, looked at her watch and saw that she still had over two hours before she had to be at Jake's. With the money her father had sent her, Hilary had been able to travel across the country. Five years ago she never would have come, though her father would have insisted and her mother would have told her she was being selfish. Jake would have called and lectured her about being a good daughter, and Daniel would have sent her a drawing of him alone on a beach, half smiling, half frowning.

But now, of course, everything had changed—and even more than they knew. It wasn't just her pregnancy. Her father and mother were getting older, her brother was in a wheelchair. The three Miller kids were about to become parents. Her life had seemed one long, faintly wavy gray line until a year and a half ago, when the line began to go haywire after Daniel's accident. She now tried to define what her life had become—a spastic electrocardiogram? or a circle? She wasn't quite sure yet where or in what way, exactly, her life would continue, and she constantly, desperately worried about her lack of a plan. So she regularly reinvented her future, and at first she'd considered not keeping the baby. As she stared at the plus sign on the plastic wand, she said aloud to herself, *What is it, one percent that the pill doesn't work for?* She'd worked in a clinic when she first moved to San Francisco, registering quiet, sad, newly pregnant women—and quickly nullifying the whole thing would've been easy. She'd just go to the clinic and get rid of it and continue on as before. But after a pregnant friend showed her ultrasound images of her own baby, and Hilary saw the spine like a strand of pearls in one photo, the boy or girl's upturned nose in another, she began to wonder what the tiny embryo inside her looked like, and what sort of person it would grow into. She didn't have too many more fertile years left, and why not just move forward with this? She vowed to become a great mother. She'd learn to cook and clean and dote on the child, and, well, that future quickly came to seem ludicrous—after all, what about work and money and other burdens of reality? She considered asking her father for more money (but she couldn't; once or twice a year he secretly sent her what he could, but she knew he couldn't afford any more), or just finding a higher-paying job, day care, then trying to partner up with some friend or man who had kids too and forming some patchwork family. Ideas came and went, each one eventually turning unappealing or unrealistic or just plain impossible. And in the wake of an idea gone sour, she felt a sharp panic that, when combined with thoughts of her parents and Jake learning of her pregnancy, kept her unable to sleep at night.

She was now considering staying on the East Coast, maybe finding a smaller town here and starting over. A week ago, her apartment was robbed when she was at work, and she'd lost her television and computer. Fortunately, the robbers hadn't found the ruby earrings and necklace Daniel had given her for her twenty-first birthday, or the ebony bracelet she'd bought herself last year. A few days later she'd witnessed a mugging on her way to work: a pretty, youngish woman in a suit, a long-haired man, a gun. Hilary saw him approach the woman, grab her wrist and press the nose of the gun into the small of her back, and Hilary did nothing—but what could she have done, she asked herself again and again later. He grabbed the woman's purse and a duffel bag she was carrying and tore down the street. The woman screamed. A crowd gathered and swallowed her and Hilary continued on to work, but all day the sight of the gun pressing into the woman's back stayed with her. Crime rates were up in her neighborhood, the only one in San Francisco where she could afford to live, and she felt increasingly unsafe as she lay in bed alone each night. Her contract through the temp agency with the insurance company would be up soon—thankfully, since everyone else there was meek and boring and appalled by her, she could tell, appalled just by the look of her. Her hair color constantly changing. Her clothes, her perfume, her jewelry, large and sharp and silver and menacing. And worst of all, she was pregnant with no husband at the ripe age of thirty-five. She had to assume what her coworkers were thinking because they never got close enough to her to express one thing. They just hovered near her, tentatively dropping folders on her desk, smiling tautly. But again, her contract was almost up and her rent even in her neighborhood was ridiculously high and everyone in San Francisco looked happy all the time, carefree, oblivious to the crime, and wealthy and healthy, and eventually she'd come to miss the East Coast, its moody people and weather.

She had no pets, no plants, nothing that needed tending. Her lease was month-to-month. She'd let several friends know her apartment would be available soon, packed and left.

Behind the cash register now, the boy/man read a magazine about guitars. Hilary watched his head move slightly as his eyes took in the words.

"Do you like living here?" she said.

He looked up. "I like it, but in the summer there are too many tourists."

"Ah. What's it like before we get here?" she asked.

He leaned on the counter and rested his head in his hands. "It's nice. Everyone knows everyone."

"What's it *really* like?"

He looked at her sideways. "Less crowded, as you might guess."

Hilary was disappointed. She'd wanted more, a surprising secret maybe, something only the people who lived here knew. She continued flipping through the magazine on the table, glancing at the advertisements for women's shoes, handbags, jewelry, perfume. "Maybe you could show me around the island," she finally said to him, and thought a moment. "I'd pay you to be my tour guide."

"I don't know about that."

"Come on. It'd be easy money, and an adventure."

"I guess I could."

"Just for a couple hours."

He shrugged. "I'm free after my shift is over, if you want to wait fifteen minutes."

"It's a plan."

He pulled the rag across the front counter. His arms were lined in small muscles and his shoulders stretched wide. It finally dawned on her—of course, he looked a little like one of the possible fathers, Bill David. So ridiculous, she still thought, his two first names. Bill, her neighbor, was a struggling musician by night and a secretary at a real estate firm by day. She'd pictured him in a tie, his hair pulled neatly back, bringing other men coffee and typing up their letters. Inexplicably the images touched her at first. Bill had a cat, also strangely touching, who regularly climbed out his window and onto the ledge of hers. Beatle scratched at the wooden frame and refused to stop until she let him in. The first time she heard the scratch of claws, just after she'd moved in, she thought someone was trying to break in. She grabbed an umbrella, the closest thing to her, and hid in the kitchen. The scratching continued, and then a whining, something she mistook for a door creaking. She panicked and sat on the floor of her kitchen, brought her knees to her chest and edged herself back against her cabinets. She remembered reading something yesterday about another attack in the neighborhood. She pushed her lips together, squeezed her knees tighter. An eternity passed, and the clawing continued, the whining, and then came a louder noise, a definite meow. She slowly uncurled herself, her chest still thumping, and headed back into her bedroom, where she made eye contact with a heavyset tabby. "Fuck you," she said aloud. "Fuck you and your family and your owners." She went back to what she was doing. What was it? Reading? Was she about to take a shower? The scratching continued, the meowing grew louder. Hilary walked back to her bedroom window and engaged in a staring contest with the cat, who made it clear that he was going nowhere, not now, not ever, until at least she let him inside. So she did, hoping that if the thing got inside it might realize her apartment was nothing special and finally leave her alone. Hours later, when Beatle was nestled like a hen at her feet as she read a magazine, a knock came at her door, and it was Bill David.

The boy/man motioned for Hilary to follow him. A stout older woman appeared behind the register and he handed her a set of keys, then led Hilary through a storage room, its walls lined with boxes of cups and lids.

"What's your name?" she asked.

"Alex."

"Alex, I'm Hilary. You're not going to take me somewhere and hurt me are you?"

He laughed. "That's not exactly the way we do things here. This is probably one of the safest places on earth."

"Good to know."

In the unpaved parking area, he pulled a set of keys from his pocket and unlocked the door of a small, beat-up green car. He got in and reached over to unlock her side, and she squeezed herself into this car that smelled of gasoline and animals. She was reminded of Bill David and Beatle again, and Bill's girlfriend, a short redhead he brought home a few weeks after he and Hilary had begun sleeping together. He was very open about Jackie, a name that made Hilary think of clowns, for some reason. Bill introduced them and beamed at Hilary when he brought Jackie home for dinner, as if to say, *Isn't it great? Isn't she great?* Hilary winced—she would like to have been consulted, at least, especially when Bill and Jackie decided soon after to move into another apartment together—but all the while, down in San Diego was George, Possible Father #2, whom she saw every few months, and who made the situation, if nothing else, more balanced.

They drove out of town and passed the ocean beneath a steep hill to their left. "So you're pregnant," he said.

"Indeed."

"Any father for it?"

"Actually, I'm going to have the baby on my own," she said. She'd said the words plenty of times before, but they still sounded odd. Her mother would faint. Jake would be speechless.

"I figured as much."

"You did? You figured at all?"

"Sure," he said, and slid his hands from the top to the bottom of the steering wheel. "I imagine what's going on with most of the customers. How do you think I stay awake at that place?"

"Coffee?"

"Ha."

They passed a large pond on the right where a group of kids fished and another skimmed stones. Hilary thought it an odd but happy sight. Kids here still skimmed stones over water. It seemed something that would have faded with black-and-white television and poodle skirts. She decided her child would skim stones. She would teach her, or him. He/she would climb trees and swim and they would go camping, she thought, though she'd only been once herself, and only as an adult, but as a child she'd always wanted to load up the family car and head into the woods with her brothers and parents. She remembered suggesting this and her mother balk-ing at the idea of bugs, her father saying he'd done his sleep-ing outside in the war, Jake whining about bears and coyotes. Daniel liked the idea, and promised her he'd take her one day when they were old enough, and eventually he did. Alex probably went camping with his family when he was young. He probably still camped.

"What else did you imagine about me?" she asked.

"You're the youngest."

"How did you know that?"

"You've got this rebellious way, but all you really want is to be different from your older siblings. It's a classic thing, really."

"You sound like a book."

"I can't help it. I work around them."

"What else?"

"I can't figure out the father thing. A friend, maybe? A coworker?"

Hilary held her hands together on her lap. "Could be."

"You're not going to tell me."

"No."

"Well then. Be mysterious."

She leaned the side of her face against the cool window. "What about you? Tell me something about yourself. Do you have brothers and sisters?"

"I'm an only child. I'm pretty textbook—self-absorbed, immature, all the good stuff. I live for adrenaline. Get bored easily."

"And apparently you're self-aware," she said. She couldn't help thinking he was trying to prepare her for something. "Where are you taking me?"

"It's a mystery."

"I see. That's how it works here." She didn't know who'd
started this banter, but it buoyed their conversation, and
though she wanted to hear more about what he apparently
knew about her, she couldn't think of a way to turn the conversation back without seeming self-absorbed. She decided
just not to say anything, to let him take her somewhere and to
try to enjoy this private tour. She looked out at the passing
houses perched like eager girls wearing pastel dresses close to
the side of the road, and soon the houses became more dilap-
idated, their porches sagging and paint peeling. On one
house hung a battered Soviet flag, on another an enormous
sheet spray-painted with a peace symbol.

Hilary often wondered what she'd tell her child about its
father once it was old enough. She could tell him or her something romantic: your father died for a cause, in a war, for me,
for you. But when she thought about her child she pictured a
smaller version of herself, and how could she really tell this
person such a large lie?

Daniel had asked about the father after she'd told him over
the phone that she was pregnant. When she confessed that
she didn't know who it was, that it could have been more than
one person, he said, "You're kidding." "I'm not." "How
straight out of a soap opera. I love it." She begged him not to
tell the others she was pregnant, as she wanted to herself and
in person. They wouldn't take it as well, especially Jake, who'd
been trying to get his wife pregnant for years. Hilary figured
that in person they would have to be at least slightly polite
and supportive. And she supposed that another, smaller part
of her just couldn't resist opening a door, standing there and
looking at their stunned faces.

Alex pulled off the road and onto a small dirt path and the car rumbled through sparse woods. "Almost there," he said, and suddenly she felt a flash of concern—what had she been thinking, jumping in his car so eagerly? He could be a murderer. But she told herself to calm down, this was New England, Maine, a small island. An enclosed, finite place where no criminal would be able to hide for long. He was calm and in control and seemed in no way psychotic.

He stopped the car and cut the ignition. They were at the end of a dirt road, facing a sprawling field of tall grass and brown reeds, the sky now solid gray above them. They could have been in the middle of America. The ocean, even the sound of it, was gone.

2

Dichotomies

Daniel only had a few memories of his family trip to Great Salt: his mother squeezing his hand as they walked off the ferry amid a small crowd of tourists, his father hoisting him onto his shoulders after the two had played Frisbee on the beach. They were, in fact, memories of being tended to more than specific images of the island itself. When he and Brenda went on vacation, they preferred to travel farther, or at least to more interesting places, although traveling anywhere had, of course, become more difficult now with the wheelchair. As they drove toward the coast of Maine, Daniel thought about Jake's vacation home being no more than an hour away from his house in Portland. "We should have taken my father somewhere like Paris. Or Istanbul. Somewhere with monuments and mosques. He loves his war and history."

"Has he been to Europe?"

"He and my mother went to Italy years ago but my father's wallet was stolen. I think they had a terrible time. And of course he was there in the war—but he was practically a kid then."

"Your dad seems happy with their trips to the Cape and D.C. That was the last one, right?"

"Niagara, and I think that if he were given the chance, he'd be more adventurous. After all, it is his seventy-fifth. We should've gone to Istanbul."

"Don't be silly. This is easier and cheaper. Hilary and your parents could never afford Turkey." She turned the car into the fast lane.

"Hilary would love Istanbul—all the ancient history, all those mosques and palaces. She studied anthropology in college." He traced a square on the window. It occurred to him, and not for the first time, that they wouldn't be able to travel as much with a baby. In three months Brenda wouldn't be able to jump in the car and drive to a store the way she could now; they wouldn't be able to work late or sleep in on weekends. Andrea had told them that the donor would not even know of the baby. The man probably had other children at that point, several or more. Hundreds, even, all across the country. The thought was an almost pleasant one, as it made the man seem more a distant, avuncular patron than the father of Daniel's wife's child.

When they stopped for gas, Daniel watched Brenda lift the pump from its holder and shove it into the gas tank. She yawned and leaned against the car, her head to the sky. *She thinks I've become a grouchy old bastard,* he thought. *She'll grow tired of me and leave me.* He swallowed his breath. When she finally looked at him, he formed what he considered a sympathetic smile.

Across the parking lot was an old man selling corn from the back of a pickup truck. He sat on a beach chair with his legs stretched flat, tapping his bare feet together and reading a newspaper. Beside him was a young boy kicking a bottle. The boy saw Daniel gazing at him, smiled wide and waved furiously. Daniel wondered if he thought he knew him, and wasn't sure whether to wave back. He lifted his hand and held it there for a moment.

Brenda walked inside the small building to pay, and when she returned she looked over at the truck. "I suppose you're going to comment on that man's bare feet being an affront to humanity."

"No, actually I wasn't. I was going to say that it's cute, a boy and his grandfather selling corn."

She revved the engine and headed out. "Why do I doubt that?"

"Because you think I see nothing positive in the world any-more? I do, you know, see positive things. I did think that was a sweet sight back there."

"All right."

"You don't believe me." He pressed his hands against his lap. "I did think it was nice. It seemed like some kind of pure sight, almost like an anachronism, and, and why why why am I trying to convince you that I'm not a horrible person right now?"

"I don't know."

He adjusted his glasses and inhaled a long, slow breath. He had several projects due next week: a book jacket for a novel set in Cuba, and a pamphlet for the Children's Museum, and a menu for a bar his friend owned back in Brooklyn. The projects couldn't be more different, and in his mind he tried to merge them. A palm tree; an inflatable toy palm tree; a small plastic palm tree sticking out of a margarita. He'd drifted so far from his earlier work, his abstract drawings and paintings. It'd been years since he'd made any real art.

Brenda wore her new perfume today, something she'd bought on a recent work trip to New York. It was a sweet scent of pears and cinnamon. She hadn't worn perfume in years, since they'd met, really, and Daniel appreciated her wearing it today, when they would see his family.

"You smell nice," he offered. He reached for her stomach and pressed his hand where he imagined the small head might be, but he couldn't feel any movement. The baby seemed to be able to sense when his hand was near— inevitably it stopped moving. "Anyone there?"

"Move for Dan, little one."

"Kick for your father," he said.

"It's been calm today. Maybe it's tired from dancing around so much this week," she said. "Maybe it's sleeping."

Daniel leaned over and kissed her neck and chin. He reached between her legs and she squirmed away from him. "Hey, I'm driving!" she said. She grabbed his hand, guided it toward her stomach again and said, "Here, try now," but Daniel pulled away. "Let's give it a chance to wake up," he said.

He held his hands together and looked out the window at the other cars and minivans on the two-lane highway. He'd refused to even consider buying a van equipped for a wheelchair. He'd seen them driving down the highways like tall buildings. He'd seen the newer models, loaded up with electronic ramps and levers and sleek handrails. At least when he was in their car, he was just an ordinary man sitting beside his wife.

He thought back to the rehab hospital and his physical therapist, Tammy Ann Green. He and Brenda always called her by her full name, as she'd introduced herself this way the first time they'd met. "It's one of those Southern things," she'd said, "giving everyone so many names." She'd been assigned to him while he was in the hospital, and every day at two P.M. her wide, flat face appeared in his doorway. "Danny," she'd say, "I know you're awake. I saw you shut your eyes when I walked in. Come on. We'll make this fun." She used the word "fun" promiscuously. It was a word Daniel thought defined its users, a word that for better or worse he rarely chose to say. "What is fun about learning to sit again?" he asked her once.

"Think of it as a game. If you give yourself little rewards each time you make progress, it could be fun. In case you haven't noticed, I've been rewarding you with lots of praise."

"I'm not a puppy."

"Fun is a choice we make," she said. "So is no fun."

There was one positive thing about Tammy Ann Green. A couple of days a week she worked for a doctor who was researching different types of laser surgery for spine injury patients. If there was something Daniel looked forward to about her visits, it was her updates on the research, though she was always vague and faintly confused about the more technical aspects of the study, as well as careful not to offer too much hope. "It's a little itty-bitty newborn baby, this procedure. Barely out of the womb. Give it a chance to grow up before you start banking on anything."

Brenda was able to hide her bemusement at Tammy Ann

Green, and once in a while even allied with her when Daniel was being particularly resistant, when the task before him was excruciating and Tammy Ann Green insisted cheerfully, mercilessly that he continue. When, for example, she demanded that he pull himself across the entirety of the therapy gym using only the parallel bars as support. The first time, halfway to the far wall, his arms began to pulse and his face grew hot and he finally said, "No more." He looked at these two small women next to him, their arms folded across their chests, so cavalier about being able to stand unassisted on usable legs. "No more." He looked to his wife for support. Any kind. Physical. Psychological. But she stood there quietly, her mouth pressed shut, and stared at the floor.

Tammy Ann Green said, "You're almost there."

"No I'm not. Listen, really, we'll finish this another day."

"You've almost got it. Get to that wall and we'll bring you something delicious for dinner. Anything you want."

"I don't care about dinner. I want to lie down," he said. "Brenda, come here."

Her eyes still on the floor, Brenda looked as if she were the one who had the impossible distance to walk.

He finally let go of the bars and Tammy Ann Green rushed to catch him before he fell to the floor. "See?" he said, shifting in her arms. "I was finished."

The car creaked and swerved with the wind. Brenda adjusted her hands on the steering wheel. "You know, it's funny you mentioned Istanbul. I just remembered this dream I had last night that we were there. It was so vivid. We were staying at a sultan's palace, being served dinner by a cast of eunuchs."

"Jesus. How royal." Brenda had gone to Istanbul as a teen

with her family and had her first kiss there. He wondered whether she missed herself as a teen, her old, wide-eyed self.

"You were trying to send your food back. You were saying something like . . ."—she yawned—"something like the meat was undercooked."

"You're serious."

"I am." She smiled.

"You know I wouldn't send anything back at a sultan's palace. I promise."

"I know," she said, but he wondered whether she did know this. And he wondered whether, in fact, he wouldn't.

A traffic jam appeared in the distance and soon they were surrounded by cars. "Shit," he said. "If we miss this ferry, the next one isn't for hours."

They slowed to a halt. She drew in a breath and pushed it out of her chest with force. "We'll make it," she said absently.

Daniel fanned out his hands on his lap and glanced down at his ragged fingernails—he'd chewed his thumbnails to the quick. He looked ahead at the cars beginning to edge forward, then stop.

"I miss sex," he said. "You know, the way it used to be."

She nodded once.

"I miss just jumping into bed with you and pulling off your shirt. I miss popping off your bra, that little tug of the clasp and then the release of your chest into my hands. There aren't many things as great in a guy's life."

"You can still do that."

"It's not the same—there's this closed door in my head now. Nothing can be spontaneous. Nothing feels exactly right anymore."

"That lady is on top of me," Brenda said, glancing in the rearview mirror. "She's going to hit me."

"I miss feeling the blood in my legs. Feeling horny in my feet. Did you know you could get turned on in your toes? Sometimes I actually used to feel this tingle down there when I took off your bra."

"Where do you want me to go?" she yelled at the rearview mirror. "You want me to sprout wings and fly?"

Daniel turned around.

"Don't look," she said.

He saw a tiny person, barely visible above the steering wheel of a broad sedan. She could have been a teenager, possibly not even old enough to be driving. The girl looked at him with something he couldn't quite place—anger? He shrugged at her apologetically.

"What are you doing?" Brenda said.

"Nothing."

"You're commiserating with her."

"I'm not." He turned back around.

"You were. You just shrugged."

"She's not going to hit you. For Christ's sake, love, we're stopped."

The traffic edged forward and halted again.

"She is crawling right on top of me. Right. Up. My. Butt."

"Just ignore her," he snapped.

Brenda inched forward and stopped again. Daniel kept his focus on the back of the car in front of them, a beat-up Chevy with a license plate that read 349 BIG. He forced himself not to turn around again for the duration of the drive.

His turned his thoughts to the baby, and he began to wonder whether it would resemble Brenda. Maybe it would look completely unlike her, strange and unrecognizable. And what if it didn't take to Daniel? It already seemed to be sensing he wasn't its real father. Maybe it would recognize those non-father hands when it was out of the womb.

At her insistence, they had attended a workshop for parents of artificially conceived babies. In an enormous room lit by a ceiling of fluorescent bulbs, the couple seated beside them clasped each other's hands so tightly their knuckles went yellow. Another man laughed nervously at everything the workshop leader said. Ron, a bald, middle-aged psychotherapist wearing a green turtleneck, spoke in a monotone of readying one's inner and outer houses for a new member of the family, finding oneself in one's child, informing the child of its origins when the time came.

Daniel had raised his hand and asked when, usually, did a child become aware that it had come from "artificial means"?

Ron cocked his head and said, "It varies. A child might begin questioning anytime from when she's four years old to eight or nine. And of course in different ways later on." He stopped and adjusted the pen behind his ear, clearly taking note of the wheelchair and trying to think of a tactful way to adjust his answer.

"Did you have kids through artificial means?"

"We're here to answer questions about your children, Daniel."

"I'm just curious as to whether you've got firsthand experience."

The room was still. Ron said, "If you must know, my wife and I conceived naturally."

Later, Brenda reprimanded him. "What was that about?"

"I was just curious."

"It seemed a little aggressive. He's only there to help."

"He was there because he had a job," he said, and she mumbled, "You are a real ray of sunshine lately. Even Mum noticed a nasty tone in your voice on the phone the other day."

Hilary called later that night, and when Daniel told her about the workshop, she snorted. "So how *is* your inner house handling everything?"

"I think I need a maid, maybe even an interior decorator."

"Workshops should be reserved for carpenters and wood-workers. *Ba-dum-bum.*"

"I suppose they exist for a reason, though. I suppose it's not abnormal for people who use donors or whatever to get the jitters?"

"Of course it's not, Dan. And for the record, having a baby isn't only scary for those who artificially conceive."

"Maybe you need to find yourself a workshop."

"Ha ha."

"For slutty, single, pregnant women."

"You're just hilarious. I can't stop laughing," she said flatly.

There was quiet on the line, and Daniel asked her whether she was planning to come East for their father's birthday, assuming she would say, *Absolutely not.*

—

Joe drifted in and out of the lanes. He sped up without warning and then slowed, causing other cars to tailgate them or honk and zoom past, the drivers looking exasperatedly at them and then, almost imperceptibly, their faces softening as they realized it was an older man driving. *But he's not that old,* Ellen wanted to call to them, *he's just let himself go.* He'd lost a good amount of hair, and the hair he did have was paper white. Of course, he couldn't control this, but his weight—his belly made him look at once like a baby and a one-hundred-year-old man.

"Focus," she said, "focus on those yellow lines and please try to stay within them."

Joe smiled and chirped, "Yessir." Sometimes it seemed he loved nothing more than to irritate her.

She closed her eyes and tried to think of something, anything else. Her family. It had expanded with spouses and would soon expand more. She was ready, even eager to be a grandmother and was not daunted by the idea, as some of her friends were. Perhaps because her own grandmothers had been so vital and so clearly enjoyed her and her siblings and cousins. The two women, inseparable, had both emigrated from Russia at a young age. They spoke half in botched English, half in Russian. Their husbands had died before Ellen was born and they'd virtually adopted each other as surrogate spouses. They even lived together in a small apartment in Roxbury, where they hosted poker games and dinner parties for their friends, and when she and her family visited, they were served lively meals of packaged meat, soft packaged bread and salty packaged soup accompanied by booming jazz and political debates. Ellen hoped that she would be such a woman, a fun-loving grandmother who hosted raucous events. And what sort of grandfather would Joe be? Perhaps he would quietly teach the kids about cars and turtles and wars.

She opened her eyes in time to see him turn off the highway and onto a small road. She wasn't sure this was the right turn, but no, Joe had a strong sense of direction and had to know where he was going. He could find his way anywhere, unlike her. She got lost whenever she ventured even slightly beyond familiar territory. She sighed, glad to leave the navigating to him. Babe clicked about in his cage.

A couple of months ago, MacNeil asked her, "Did you choose Joe or did he choose you?" The two had been sitting in Vera's garden drinking chardonnay. Ellen had made tortellini with snow peas for supper. Joe had been somewhere all evening—playing cards with Bill, was it?

"I don't know."

"Come on. It's always one or the other, isn't it?" he asked, worrying a blade of grass in his hand.

"We chose each other, I suppose. We simply went ahead and got married. There wasn't much decision making involved," she said. When she first met Joe, she'd just had her appendix out and her parents were driving her home from Mass General. She remembered this afternoon a little differently each time, and parts of it had vanished altogether from her mind, something that bothered her now. But that June evening with MacNeil, what she recalled vividly was her stomach still sore from the operation as she lay in the back seat of her parents' car. They'd stopped at a deli in Newton to buy corned beef sandwiches, and left her alone when they went inside. A face appeared in the window, startling at first, but it was a handsome face with round brown eyes and a cleft chin. She felt her pulse ticking. When she rolled down the window, he asked if she was all right. (And what exactly had he said? What were his words, his tone? How could she not remember this?) She explained her situation, all the while thinking only of her pasty skin and unwashed hair, and when her parents returned, he nodded at them and stepped away. Ellen turned in time to see Joe wave, his black wingtips shiny in the sunlight. Fortuitously, her father ended up buying a new car from Joe two months later, and soon after he took Ellen out for martinis in Boston. Very quickly it seemed she'd known him her whole life, and six months later they were married. They were the last of their friends to have a wedding.

"I've been thinking I chose Vera," MacNeil said, holding his gaze on the metal table in front of them.

Ellen brought her wineglass to her lips. "In what sense?"

"I pulled her away from her friends and family and seduced her," he said. The words hissed from his lips.

The garden was quiet except for the rhythmic clicking of a sprinkler turning on and off. Ellen couldn't sit in her own back yard without hearing the Wenderses argue or the traffic on Main Street. She shuffled her feet beneath her. "I guess Joe chose me," she said quietly, though she wasn't so sure. "Wasn't that usually the way? It was up to the man to do the hard work?"

"Not always," he said, and half smiled at her. "Vera would have liked this, supper outside on a June evening."

"You're right, she would've," she said. "You're missing her right now. I am too."

He looked at his lap. "We were together fifty-three years. Forever."

"I know." She tried to see whether he was crying, but he'd closed his eyes. She reached for his hand and held it in the air between them a moment.

"It's like hell some days."

"What is?" she asked tentatively.

"Continuing on."

"It won't always feel this bad," she said. "It can't. I promise you."

"Can I hold you to that?"

"You may."

"Say it again, would you?"

She sat up straighter. "It won't always feel this bad. It will sometimes, but then it won't."

He nodded and attempted a smile. "I definitely chose her, and it was a great choice. The best I ever made."

"Good," she mumbled, and didn't know what more to say. She rose and explained that she had to be going, that Joe would be home and hungry for his dinner soon, and MacNeil nodded as if he understood something fundamental about her. She took her time driving back that evening. She opted for the long route through MacNeil's town, past the cornfields on the periphery, and saw a group of cows lying down on a parched field. They knew rain was coming. She drove through other, more crowded towns and then back inside the line of her own town, where smaller houses with peeling paint sat closer together, and grass sprouted from patches of dirt on the sidewalks. Tomorrow, she thought, she would wake at six, shower, make oatmeal for Joe and leave for work at seven-fifteen. She would shelve books and read to the first- and second-graders. She would have lunch with Maura Paulsen and Abigail Welty and they would tell each other whatever news they had about their families and friends. Then she would shelve more books and box up the old ones. When the workday was done, she would drive home, cook dinner for Joe, do the laundry, watch some PBS show on their old television and fall into bed, exhausted. Nothing ever changed. Even if they stopped working, how much would really change? Not that she and Joe could afford to retire right now anyway. Well, they could, but only if they wanted to penny-pinch every day, and they didn't. A few more years, she kept telling him. We'll wait until we've got a bigger cushion in the bank. But lately, Joe'd begun saying that maybe he could live with less. He could manage, they both could. She worried he'd come home one day and announce he was done with work and had submitted his retirement papers.

"Have we gone the wrong way?" she asked Joe, now certain she'd never before seen this stretch of road.

"No, I don't think so."

"Where's the map?"

"In the glove compartment?" he offered, and she could tell he'd forgotten it. Nevertheless, she rifled through the papers in there. "It's not in here. We should stop and ask for directions."

Joe continued driving, weaving in and out of the lane. "We should stop," she said again.

"I suppose we should." He didn't have a care in the world. He slowed the car and pulled into a gas station. Across the small lot, a pudgy boy dressed in stained shorts and a T-shirt stood beside a pickup truck full of corn.

Joe walked inside the small building to pay and Ellen exchanged eye contact with the boy. Behind him a man appeared, carrying a box of something. He wore no shoes, and a cigarette hung from his lips. Ellen turned away and pressed her fingers into the middle of her forehead—a headache was coming and her legs began to cramp. Suddenly the boy stood right on the other side of her window, smiling dumbly. He might have been something—mentally retarded? "Christ," she said, and rolled down the window. "Yes?"

"You got any money?"

Was he robbing her? He had no gun, no knife that she could see.

"Ma'am, you got any money?"

She fished around for her purse in the back seat. He stood there watching her, obviously with no good sense of what he was doing. She wanted to ask him why, what did he want with her money, did he even know? But she was afraid of saying something that might agitate or confuse him. Reaching inside her wallet, she handed him three dollars, all she had, and he took it and shrugged.

Joe was now walking back toward the car. "Hey!" he yelled, and rushed forward, stumbling and almost falling over something.

The boy padded off and Joe followed him but seemed to suddenly change his mind and headed back to the car. "What was that?" he asked, leaning his head in her direction as he went to the gas tank.

"I don't know. I gave him a couple dollars."

"For what? Are you all right?"

"I'm fine. I don't know what he wanted," she said.

When Joe finished, he got back in the car, turned on the ignition and said, "We were going the right way." He shifted the car into reverse. "Did he threaten you?"

"No, no. Don't we need to be on a smaller highway?"

"This used to be one," Joe said. "Did he demand your wallet?"

"I don't know what he wanted. He just wasn't right upstairs," she said. She held her hands together on her lap. "All the different ways that people can be, that *children* can be. It's awful, if you really stop to consider it."

"Of course it is. So don't, then."

They drove past motels and hotels, convenience stores. "I don't recognize a damned thing," Ellen said.

Joe began to drift toward the lane markers and then the guardrails. Ellen's nerves were shot. *They're just shot*, she said to herself, and she imagined an enormous gust of wind blowing into her and causing something to burst from her like an explosion of water. "I'm shot," she mumbled to Joe.

"What?"

"Nothing," she said. She pressed her fingertips into her forehead again, closed her eyes and made herself think once more of her family. Daniel would be a decent father, though he was so consumed with his illustrating. (Was it art? Was it really art if it was made only to sell products or services?) He had the tendency to be a little aloof like Joe, but he too was a fundamentally good person. She couldn't even begin to imagine being a parent in a wheelchair. Every week or so Daniel and Brenda came to dinner and it killed her to see her son like this. The squeak of the chair, the sound of the wheels in the next room. When Daniel got stuck going around a corner or the wheels jammed, she had to remind herself to breathe and move on, look away, do something else. She'd tried to explain it to Joe and he'd nodded vacantly—*Of course it's difficult to see your son in pain*—and said Daniel would be fine, he'd still live a good life, the outcome could've been worse. Bland comments that left her miffed and wanting more. They were supposed to be grateful that he'd survived and could still work and live a relatively normal life. *But it's more than difficult*, she'd say now if it came up. Joe would look at her, confused, and she'd say, *Sometimes just seeing him wrings me dry, it absolutely kills me*, and he'd gaze at her through narrowed eyes as if she were being dramatic, and she would want to smack him for the dismissiveness, the ability to reside within these bland clichés. Somewhere he undoubtedly felt pain about their son, but he stifled it. As he had to, as she should have tried to and did sometimes, but the sting inevitably came raging back. She grew tired just thinking about the whole thing.

Thanks to Jake's job shuffling stocks around (she could never understand exactly what it was that he did), he had more money than the rest of them combined—more money than anyone she knew, really. His family would never want for anything. Of the three, though, he was the most sensitive and therefore the least content. He always felt a little left out—and he always was, she supposed, given his overly aggressive attempts at making people like him, as well as his strict values and expectations of others. Even when they were younger, he worried endlessly about Hilary and her bad behavior and her motley group of friends. (They smoked, Ellen now acknowledged. They drank and probably tried drugs. She'd never wanted to admit it back then.) Jake had lectured his sister, leaving nothing more for Ellen to say: *the friends you make, the choices you make now*, that sort of thing. He was a person guided by rules and morals, and felt good and bad in the depths of his bones. Running a stoplight, jaywalking: these were evils to him. And the goods were holy: family, love, work. It was surprising he wasn't religious, the way he ordered his life. But the rule of man, the rule of law—Ellen supposed these were his religions.

She'd mentioned it to MacNeil recently, and then they'd discussed what they considered to be the goods of life. "Intelligence, art, beauty. Love," he'd said.

"Food," she'd added, and handed him a plate of vine-ripened tomatoes and mozzarella. She sat down across from him and they ate quietly, and she tried to think of something clever to say.

"You had your hair done," he said.

"I did. Yesterday."

"I like it," he said. "I can see more of your eyes now."

"Is that a good thing?"

"It's definitely a good thing. One of the big goods." He kept his gaze on his plate. She wanted to ask him to keep going— did he mean her eyes specifically, or eyes in general, a woman's eyes, what? Was *she* one of life's big goods for him? But she grew nervous about where such a question might lead. What if he laughed at her and said of course he'd been talking about eyes in general, what had she been thinking? Now that she thought of it, maybe she should have just come out and set the cards on the table, asked him if he too noticed that the air between them had changed.

Joe slid his hands around the steering wheel. She looked out at the houses along the street, at two young kids playing soccer in their yard. "Do you think that poor boy back at the gas station had a home?" she asked.

"He had his grandpa with him. I'm sure they live some-where."

"Where *are* we?"

"I've got it, Ell. Don't worry."

And only a few moments later she recognized everything: the town hall, the colossal flag in front, the neon ICE CREAM sign missing the R, the small parking lot and the ferry slip. She was amazed they'd made it, and in even less time than they'd planned.

Joe pulled their car under the shade of a thick oak. He opened his door, hurried to pull the bags from the back of the car and rushed away as if completely forgetting he had a wife. He shoved past a small group of people stepping out of the next car and plowed his way out of Ellen's field of vision. She decided to stay where she was and let him realize she was not beside him.

She turned to Babe in the back seat, now asleep in his shell. Did Joe assume she'd follow him, carrying Babe's enormous cage and the remaining bag as well as her purse and jacket? The turtle's clay-colored head and arms and legs pulled beneath him, he resembled a rock. The animal was oblivious to her or anything else, for that matter. But perhaps he wasn't. What if Babe in fact understood everything? He'd been in the room when she spoke on the phone with MacNeil. Babe had watched her with his unblinking eyes, the black pits unmoving beneath thick, hooded lids. He was an ugly creature, really, an animal of no color or fur, no purring or singing. Joe liked to point out the ringed pattern on his shell—*Like a face, see? The eyes, the nose, the mouth*—and the calmness, the gentleness of a creature that moved so slowly. *What's the rush?* Joe would say when Babe inched his way across their kitchen floor. *What, when it comes down to it, is really the rush?* Babe had seen everything. He was aware of her feelings for MacNeil. The turtle was not going anywhere. He was sitting there, unmoving, unblinking, communicating that she could drift anywhere she wanted. She could fall in love at this late age, she could leave her life as she'd known it, go anywhere, but *I, Babe, am not leaving Joe. I am not running off anywhere.* Like a rock.

"Ell," Joe was saying. "Ellen." He was standing just outside her door. "We're all set. Come on now." She hoisted herself from her seat, followed him around the back and said, "Take it slowly. One thing at a time." He gently lifted Babe's cage into the air.

They had twenty minutes until the boat would leave, and they found an empty bench in the corner of the parking lot. Joe stopped for a moment, clearly considering whether to place Babe's cage on the bench or offer it to her. He paused and then carefully lowered the cage onto the ground. At once grateful and annoyed, she dropped the suitcase she was carrying. "I'm shot," she said again, *who cared if he knew what she meant*, and he nodded absently. They sat and watched a line begin to form at the ticket counter. Joe set his hand on her leg. It felt solid and sturdy, almost separate from him, as if right then it was the only thing holding her against the earth.

—

Liz had napped while Jake unpacked the groceries, made the beds, opened the windows and set up the plywood ramp over the front step. Now he looked down at her on the couch, her head against her chest, her lips slightly parted, and he draped a thin blanket over her legs, careful not to wake her. He decided to go for a walk on the beach behind the house. He grabbed his sunglasses off the coffee table and headed out.

By the water, he found a yellow pacifier and turned it over in his hands. It was encased in wet sand, and he brushed it off. Jake kept a wooden box of odd things he'd found, things that for some reason seemed wrong to throw away: an old copy of the Bible he'd found in a parking lot, a dog collar outside his office, a tiny mitten, a photograph of an elderly couple. He tried to remember to bring the box wherever he went, as he was constantly finding items that belonged in it. He imagined each had a story, a rightful owner and maybe even a reason for being left behind, and collecting them made him feel good, like the one savior of all these forgotten things. Liz

didn't know about his collection—she'd have thought it sentimental. She hated unnecessary clutter, things kept only
because a person felt guilty getting rid of them. Such things,
she'd say, kept one needlessly bound to the past. But Jake
shoved the pacifier in his pocket, glad he'd remembered to
bring the box this weekend. He often forgot it, and tended to
find the most heartbreaking things when he was without it.

He crouched before the tide, dipped his fingers in the icy
water and recoiled. Maine water was invariably frigid, but it
never failed to surprise him. He turned to walk back to the
house, noting the faint smell of fir trees. He could hardly wait
for his family's arrival and to hear what they thought of his
house, which none of them had seen. He looked forward to
handing them each a drink and guiding them to the back
porch, watching them gaze out at his little patch of ocean
under the sunset. What a change this was from the house
where he'd grown up. That small, crowded Cape with the
stained carpets, the practically antique appliances, the rotting
roof. Last year he'd offered his father some money to fix the
roof or buy some new appliances or, better yet, both, but Joe
had adamantly refused. Jake remembered back in high school
joining forces with his mother as she tried to convince Joe to
tear up the carpet in the living room and put in hardwood
floors. Joe'd received an unexpectedly large bonus at the car
lot, but he'd wanted to replace a cracked toilet with the
money. Daniel and Hilary didn't much care about the matter,
but Ellen and Jake pleaded for the new floor. Jake's classmate
Henry lived in a large house that had only hardwoods and
Jake thought it made the place seem even bigger and somehow cleaner and more elegant. In the end, though, the new
toilet won out and that matted beige carpet stayed. Jake

stopped for a second just before the path that led to his back porch. Now he had two houses of his own filled with hardwood floors. He gazed ahead at the newly patched roof, the freshly stained clapboards, and reminded himself that he'd tried to help his parents. He'd done what he could.

Liz was up now and slicing mushrooms. She'd turned on the radio and he could hear the low buzz of someone talking when he stepped into the kitchen. A shred of something—a carrot, he soon saw—hung from her hair by her ear, and for some reason it saddened him. Jake reached over to remove it, and she leaned forward and kissed him on the cheek.

"They're saying rain."

"No," he said. "It looks all right out there. Just a little overcast."

"A storm moving in later, I guess, and then rain all weekend."

"Tell me you're kidding," he said. A few days ago the forecast had been for only sun. He'd planned to take his family out in a fishing boat he'd chartered on Saturday and to go to the beach on Sunday. "I didn't hear anything about a storm."

"I'm kidding," she said flatly, and popped a slice of mushroom in his mouth. "It's okay. We'll play games or cards. Maybe it won't rain the whole weekend." She turned and set the knife on the counter.

"Mom hates games. She says they're just a substitute for conversation."

"We could watch movies. We'll figure something out." Liz was only this flexible when he was not. If he'd been the one shrugging off the weather right now, she'd be the one pacing the kitchen, trying to come up with alternate plans.

The Adirondack chairs sat stacked in the corner of the

porch, and he went to set them out beneath the overhang so no one would get wet if it rained. He placed each about a foot apart, and noted there weren't enough for the seven of them, so he went to the basement to look for the folding chairs they'd bought last year. Down here were remnants of past summers—a beach umbrella leaning against the wall, rusty cans of bug spray, a basketball he'd had since he was a kid. He used to play one-on-one with his brother, who always beat him handily and would then proceed to taunt him. Once Daniel fired the basketball at Jake's head and gave him a swollen, painful bruise that lasted weeks. (What made Daniel do such things? Jake vaguely remembered having said something desperate like, "So you're good at basketball? I get much better grades than you.") They would likely never play basketball again. Jake would never lose to him again. *Thank God*, Jake said aloud, and then blanched at his words. It was a strange concept still, Daniel in a wheelchair, and as much as the thought saddened Jake, and it did, profoundly some days, it also remained plainly incomprehensible. Jake could still remember his brother wrestling him to the ground whenever they fought over whatever it was that used to rile them. Just after the accident, Jake tried to communicate his mixed feelings about everything ("After all, you used to beat the life out of me, which isn't to say I'm glad that you're in this state, but it's just so strange to see you this way, you, of all people. You've always been such a physical person, you know? This must be devastating for you"), and Daniel, not surprisingly, told him that he wasn't exactly helping. Jake tried to clarify and expand upon what he meant—that he'd always been a little scared of his big brother, that throughout his childhood Jake had only wanted his approval and friendship, really, but

Daniel just sat there, nearly expressionless, and soon Jake gave up. This clearly wasn't the time. After all, Daniel had his own aftershock to handle—he didn't need to deal with his brother's issues too.

Jake set the basketball inside a box and looked around the basement. On top of a stack of books, he found a copy of the *Kama Sutra*. He'd bought it a few years ago as a sort of joke, when sex had become tedium, nothing more than the means to an elusive end. He'd stocked up on porn magazines, but he kept these to himself—Liz had never been particularly adventuresome or curious in the bedroom. Even before they'd begun trying to get pregnant, their sex life had been fairly sparse. He now remembered he'd hidden a few magazines here—in his underwear drawer, was it? At any rate, buying the *Kama Sutra* was his first try at expressing his desire for better, or at least more varied, sex to Liz. He'd found an old copy of the book at a used bookstore, something that made it even more perfectly ridiculous and thus somehow less overtly demanding. He'd wrapped it in leopard-skin-patterned paper and had planned to give it to her that night after work. He'd gotten home in a good mood, having devised a way to save far more than expected on the firm's quarterly taxes and then later been interviewed by *The Wall Street Journal*. Liz was sitting on their bed drinking a glass of wine and doodling furiously on a sketch pad, wrecked by the news that another of her friends had just conceived. Not once since then had the opportunity arisen for him to give Liz the book. Eventually he set it aside to be taken to the island, thinking the moment might arise here. Now he brought it upstairs and found her sitting on the porch. He sneaked up behind her. "Close your eyes," he said.

"What?" She looked back at him, her face upside down.

"Close them," he said, and she did. He placed the book in her hands, and when she glanced down, she smiled at the wrapping paper and tore it off. When she saw the title, she scowled. "The *Kama Sutra*?"

"I bought it for you a while back as a joke. When sex was becoming, you know, kind of redundant."

"Good Lord," she snorted as she peeled off the wrapping paper. "Some joke."

He looked over her shoulder at something about decorating one's lover's body with flowers. He thought of the small clinic, its hallways lined with maps of the uterus and fallopian tubes. He thought of the bottles of pills she'd kept beside the sink in their bathroom—the countless bottles, the shots he'd had to give her in her thighs with each cycle of treatment, the ovulation-predictor kits, the different types of thermometers, how she'd cut caffeine and alcohol from her diet, stopped exercise, restarted exercise. All the doctors, the five failed IUIs, two failed IVFs, the bad moods, her sore abdomen, her cramps, the endless complaints. Nothing at all joyous had gotten her pregnant, nothing remotely sexy or loving, merely a speculum, an embryo-transfer catheter and a doctor.

Jake was suddenly embarrassed that he'd given her this book. Who read this stuff anyway? Who kept porn stashed away in their underwear drawer? People who thought sex was only a form of play, nothing more, nothing less. Hormonal teenagers, maybe. People who didn't need to think about procreation and biology, that was who. He tried to remember when he'd been such a person, and it seemed like a hundred years ago.

He placed his hands on Liz's shoulders and massaged them. She leaned back and said, "That feels good."

He leaned over and kissed her forehead, then her nose, her mouth. He reached his hand over her stomach, pulled up her shirt and drew his fingers across her belly button. Like her face, her stomach was spotted with hundreds of freckles. Back in college, Jake used to look for constellations on her stomach and breasts. Even then she was squeamish and faintly reluctant about sex, but he found it old-fashioned and endearing. Most of the girls there were anything but squeamish. They wore snug jeans and cropped shirts. They covered their eyes in black paint and blue powder and slunk around the boys like predators. Liz seemed to come from a different species, this healthy, tall girl dressed in baggy drawstring pants and loose, hand-knit sweaters. The two dated and drifted apart after graduation, never guessing that they'd reunite eight years later.

"Jake," she said.

"Let's go mess around a little."

"Jake, my dear, I don't think so," she said, but he managed to pull her from her seat and guide her into their bedroom. "Right now I don't feel at all . . . I'm not feeling—" She sat on the bed before him.

"Come here," he said. He stepped in front of her and pulled her head against his stomach. How could she not miss sex? "Let's just play around a bit."

"The *Kama Sutra* did this to you?"

"It doesn't matter," he said. And what did it matter why he wanted to make love to his wife? It only mattered that he did, and that they had the opportunity and the time and the space right now. He ran his hand over her hair, which was smooth

and soft, the color of tea, he'd always said, though she thought
it had no color. "Blond, brown, red, nothing," she called it. He
placed his hands against her breasts and she squirmed and
straightened her back, then wilted. "They'll be here soon,"
she said.

"I know."

"I'm not really feeling it, sweetie."

"Because you're sick? Do you feel nauseous?" he asked as
innocently as he could. He couldn't help himself.

"I mean I'm just not feeling it on another level. I'm sorry."

"The thing is that it's been ages, and in a few months you're
really not going to be in the mood, and after the babies are
born, who knows when we'll have the chance."

"So I should feel *obligated* right now? We should do it out of
obligation?" She shook her head. "We should probably get
started on dinner."

"Yes. So."

"So. Let's go to the kitchen." She stood. "Come on, my silly,
horny husband. Let's go."

"Please don't talk to me like that."

"Like what?"

He forced himself not to yell. *Focus on the real issue.* "Don't I
turn you on at all anymore?"

"Where is this coming from?"

"I just love you, okay?" he mumbled. "And you love me,
right?"

"Of course I love you, but I'm pregnant, and with twins.
Remember? I'm tired and I have to pee, and we have a lot of
things to do before your family gets here."

"I know, but—" and a jumble of words stopped short in his
mouth. *If she really, truly loved him, and if he weren't so*—but he

was taking it too personally, as he often did. "We have time for a quickie," he said. "Come on, I insist," and reached for her left breast. She turned just as he cupped her there, grabbing her harder than he intended.

"Ouch!" she snapped. She elbowed him away and covered her chest with her hands.

"That was meant to feel good," he said.

She simply looked at him, dumbfounded.

"It wasn't meant to hurt."

"Okay, can you drop it now?" She massaged her left breast.

"I'd rather not," he said, and why should he? For so many weeks he'd tended to her every need. He'd rubbed her back each night and run to the kitchen to get her saltines whenever she felt nauseous. He'd bought her flowers countless times, cooked for her, kept the freezer stocked with her favorite oatmeal ice cream.

"Well, you're going to have to let it go," she said tersely. She shook her head and turned. "You're just going to have to," and she rushed out of the room.

"A lot of women like to have sex with their husbands," he called after her. "Even when they're pregnant. *Especially* when they're pregnant." He began to pace the room. He'd read in one of her many pregnancy books that over the nine months women's sexual organs became enlarged and more sensitive, thereby increasing their sex drive. One woman described pregnant sex as the best she'd ever had; her breasts were fuller now, and in her first few months she thought she looked better than she ever had in this one particular black teddy. She met her husband each day for lunch wearing nothing more than her raincoat and said teddy. Liz's breasts were already a little larger, a little rounder, but because she found them the most comfortable, she wore only gray jog bras or thick, broad beige contraptions with enough wires and seams to support a small car. "You know," he yelled, "you've got more blood flowing down there, and everything is bigger and more sensitive right now. You might actually like it. Maybe you'll find yourself getting into it. Just try, all right? Just give it one goddamned chance. For me."

He heard the toilet flush down the hall. She hadn't heard a word.

His face hot, he stuffed his hands in his pockets and felt the gritty pacifier he'd found on the beach. Where had he put that box? He glanced around the room and remembered it was in the middle drawer of his dresser, so close to all those magazines stacked neatly at the bottom of his underwear drawer.

—

"What's this?" Hilary asked Alex.

"A field."

"That I can see."

He stepped out of the car, but she stayed inside. A brief image passed before her: Alex pulling a gun out of his pocket and then, *blast*, all gone, no more Hilary, no more baby. But no, Alex had said it himself: the island was in no way that sort of place. People here were trustworthy. In the rearview mirror, she saw him looking at the sky. He seemed interested in something up there, and she grew curious, so she joined him. But the only things in his line of vision were low, heavy clouds.

"Where are we?" she asked. The air had grown chillier and a cool breeze pushed past them. She smelled the faint perfume of flowers.

"We're at the exact center of the island. Bellows' Field, named after Edward Bellows, the first man to live here. He was a lobsterman, I think. The island used to be named after him, but it changed seventy-five years ago when this salt magnate and his family moved here and bought out the place. They lived in a mansion at the other end of this field, but it burned to the ground in the sixties and he died in the fire. His family left, moved to New York and L.A., and none of them ever comes here anymore. Some folks on the island want to rename it Bellows' again, but it'll never fly. The heirs still own too much of it."

"Ah. The rule of money." Hilary nudged a mound of dirt with her shoe. She imagined a mansion in the middle of this field, stone columns and marble stairs, gardeners and servants rushing around. Parties of badminton and croquet on sprawling green lawns, men and women sipping iced tea and lounging in the sun. The thought was almost seductive. The clichés about money always were, and even though she knew it was silly, she sometimes thought that if she were rich, life would be richer and more full of unending possibility. She could travel, she could buy houses in faraway places, she could fly her favorite people to these houses. It was pleasing to think that happiness could be so tangible.

"It's going to rain. Later this evening," he said, his eyes still on the clouds. "Maybe tomorrow."

"I'm having this sort of reunion with my family," she said, and he nodded. "It can't rain or we'll be stuck inside with nothing to say to each other."

"Mm. I can't help you with that. It's definitely going to rain later." He glanced at her feet. "Come on. Let's go for a walk."

"You can leave your car here?"

"Sure," he said. "They know whose it is."

"They?"

"People here."

Hilary followed Alex through the grass. "Does your family live here?"

"No. They live on the other coast now. I almost never talk to them," he said.

"How come?"

"Well, for starters, they're active Republicans. My father campaigned for Reagan and Bush—both Bushes—and my mother runs the church youth group."

"Ah. Scary stuff."

"You're not kidding."

"I bet they're constantly nagging you to come home," Hilary said.

He looked at her and shrugged. "They are, but I don't really listen."

She liked him. She liked him, though she knew he was putting on airs, or anti-airs, as it were. Still, there was no denying that there was something about him. She was pregnant, not dead, and it was certainly okay to feel a little turned on by someone. She wondered if she was at all appealing to him. He probably only saw the stomach, as everyone else did, though maybe not—after all, behind the stomach was a distinct personality, arms and legs (though a bit thick at the ankles, especially now) and a decent chest, an attractive enough face. She smiled to herself as suddenly the opportunity came into focus—he was a gift, really, one more little adventure before her life changed completely.

The last time she spoke to Possible Father #2, she told him she was heading East, maybe for a while, maybe to see what it'd be like to live there again. Over the phone, George had remained quiet and removed. A carpenter, he lived in a small house on a beach in San Diego with his daughter, Camille. Hilary had met them at a wedding almost ten years ago outside Los Angeles. She'd sat at their table and the three were the only ones not to get up and dance when the Frank Sinatra impersonator started singing. George and his daughter smiled at her across the empty table. Camille was eight but had the expressions and mannerisms of a much older person. She seemed to Hilary sad and graceful. George too exuded a sadness, an appealing liquidity in the way he reached across the table for salt. He asked her about her job and told her about his, and they discussed the newly married couple. Later that evening George invited Hilary back to his house and the three ate chocolate cake on the beach and talked about the movies they'd recently gone to. The sky was overcast and the stars and moon invisible. The only lights around were the distant spots on a pier and those on a few boats. Hilary, George and Camille could barely even see each other. When Camille left them alone to go to bed, Hilary said that she should leave too, but George persuaded her to stay with the promise of meeting Boris, a homeless old man who slept on their beach and told stories of his earlier life as a movie star, an astronaut and a senator. In fact, Boris appeared shortly after with a bottle of wine and a candle—"He always shows up right around midnight. Every single night," George had explained. Boris was someone Hilary would have whisked right past on the street.

But George asked him questions about stories he'd probably heard thousands of times without a hint of condescension or bemusement. Boris apparently loved to talk, and he was oddly poetic and as such almost believable, and if nothing else, engaging. Soon it seemed they were sitting on this dark beach with an aging astronaut, now telling them of the vast red oceans of Mars as if they were as familiar to him as the Pacific in front of them.

In the end, George wouldn't move north. Camille's mother lived in Los Angeles and they shared custody. Hilary tried but couldn't convince herself to move south to the sun, the beaches, the surfers. The place just didn't suit her at all.

She and Alex walked up a gradual hill and stopped. From here Hilary could see a stripe of silver ocean to the east. To the west were only the sky and its clouds, to the north more grass and what looked like a small group of cows.

"Did you grow up here?" she asked, reaching into her bag for a deck of cards. Sometimes she found she still needed to hold something the size of a pack of cigarettes.

"Yeah," he said. "What's that?"

She looked down. "Nothing," she said, and hid the cards between her hands. "You've never lived anywhere else?"

"No. I have," he said.

She turned the cards in her hands. "Where?"

He didn't say anything more and in a moment began walking again. She waited for an answer as she followed him down the hill and up another, steeper hill, and by the time she reached the top she was winded. She leaned over and caught her breath. From here she could see more of the ocean, and the clouds looked lower and solid, as if they'd become another sky.

"Out West," he said, "Montana, this tiny town there," and it took her a moment to realize what he was referring to.

"Oh. Really?"

"Yes. But I missed it here. When you grow up surrounded by water it's hard, you know, being so far from it. It's like you lose your orientation."

"This must have been a unique place to grow up."

"It was, but it was also pretty great. It's a great thing to be a kid in a small town. It's safe and everyone knows each other for the most part," he said.

Hilary imagined looking at the two of them from above. What would a stranger have thought? Maybe that he was the father and she his wife. She tried to imagine what might have been passing through Alex's mind right then—annoyance with her constant questions, maybe—and she examined what was going through her own: sudden dread mixed with anticipation about her family's reaction to her pregnancy; the desire to press a cigarette between her lips; a heightened self-consciousness in front of Alex. And a pleasant slowing down of time. She wondered if her baby was experiencing shades of the same sensations.

"I don't know who the father is," she heard herself say.

He turned to her. "Oh."

"It could be one of several people," she said. She had the strange sense that he might be intrigued by this information. "It could be someone who's already a father. It could be another man who'd make a terrible father."

"Doesn't several mean at least three?"

"Yes," she said, and shrugged. The word had just slipped out.

"So?"

"So. What does that make you think of me?"

"I don't know. Is there something it should make me think?" He took a step toward her and glanced at her lips.

"Yes. People are supposed to be appalled. People are supposed to shake their heads and pity the child that's now inside me."

"Okay," he said. He knelt down, tore a blade of grass from the ground and slipped it between his thumbs. Pressing his lips to his hands, he blew a long, shrill sound that poured around them like a wounded goose screaming. He licked his lips and blew again, now in staccato, and when he finished he smiled up at her proudly, like a child who'd just done this for the first time.

"My family doesn't know I'm pregnant," she continued.

"Ah."

"Well, my brother does, but not my parents. And not my other brother."

He tossed the blade of grass on the ground. She wasn't getting anywhere with him. She didn't know what kept her here beside this person, this stranger, really. She looked at him. Maybe the fact that he resembled Bill David, his hands now in his pockets, his mind a million miles from anywhere she recognized. And like Bill, Alex seemed staunchly unattached to anything, not money or family, not anything. Except, maybe, the ocean. She supposed it was a little romantic. Maybe she wasn't completely finished with men like Bill, though she liked to think she was. She knew she should have been, at least.

She used to be free of all attachments. She didn't know when she'd changed, but she remembered once upon a time thinking more openly about the future and making decisions based on amorphous feelings and whims. Moving to the West Coast because it was far from home, to San Francisco because it seemed the opposite of everything she'd grown up near— hills instead of flatness, style instead of tradition, the urgency of politics instead of the conservatism of history. She'd decided to study archaeology because of the posters of the mummies in the halls of the university's anthropology department, these beautifully wrapped bodies like large babies, permanently swaddled. The promise of worlds underground, of ancient rites and religions and the eeriness of the painted mummies' faces—the expressions that had been chosen for them in their afterlife. These seemed unsolvable mysteries. But she decided to drop out of school after she'd failed too many anthropology tests. It wasn't the terminology that interested her, she reasoned, it wasn't all the reading she'd been after. It certainly wasn't the knowledge of ancient embalming practices and photographs of brains being tugged through nasal cavities. It was those exotic ideas, the art and mysticism, the unknown lives that the teachers dissected and deflated and pulled apart with their scientific identifications until all the beauty of these ancient worlds had vanished. And sometime after dropping out of college she realized so many things she'd previously thought dichotomous weren't, after all, and what she'd chosen as her new life had become tedious. The hills were impossible to bike; her style had become redundant, for she'd never stopped wearing only black; her politics had become lazy, and eventually warped once she'd begun earning a paycheck and losing a big chunk of it to taxes each

month, once she'd seen enough college students demonstrate
against this or that policy, then step into their exorbitant car
and drive back to the dorms. The mystery of archaeology
became science, which became mathematics. What was once
clear was now a big blurry mess, and a part of her missed the
romance of dichotomies, and the clarity and promise that
came with such things.

Daniel once called her starry-eyed and said if she never got
used to reality, she'd never truly grow up. She'd been
bemoaning the high rents of San Francisco and saying she
wished she were a kid again so she didn't have to worry
about things like bills or taxes. "Adulthood isn't so bad," he
claimed. "You get to make your own decisions. You get to
drive and have sex and drink and vote and rent cars." But
she couldn't help it—she thought of herself as fundamentally younger than her years. Not necessarily immature, but
youthful at her core. In the end, adulthood was such a dull
concept, dull and airless, an itchy sweater that was slightly
too small.

Alex sighed. "You're not into this place," he said.

"That's not true."

"This spot usually puts me at ease."

The reeds flattened with a wind, and she breathed in the
quiet. "It's beautiful here, really. I'm sorry, I'm just tired." She
shuffled on her feet, trying to think of more to say. "Maybe we
should get going on this tour you're supposed to be giving me
and head to the next stop or something." She thought a
moment. "Where do you live?"

"In town. Near Books & Beans."

"I'd love to see your place, you know, see where the natives
live," she said, hoping she wasn't sounding too forward.

"It's not so different from any other apartment you've seen, but we could go there if you want. Or I could take you to a beach? There's a walk most tourists like to do that goes from the northern tip almost all the way to the southernmost point of the island."

"I just need to sit somewhere for a little while, if that's all right. Being pregnant is constantly exhausting." She wasn't totally lying.

He nodded. "Fine. You're the customer."

She smiled, faintly embarrassed. She walked a pace behind him back down the hill and every now and then stopped to take in the view of the slate sky and ocean. The water on this side of the country was completely different. More confident somehow, and looking at it, she felt a deep calm that she'd missed, a sense of familiarity. She could come back to this spot again this weekend, she thought, now that she knew where it was. She could take Daniel here (if she could manage to get a moment alone with him), and someday her child and maybe have a picnic, someday when her life had become an entirely different thing.

Her breath began to quicken as she walked, and she slowed.

"You're not going to have the baby right now or something, are you? Because I'm no doctor."

Hilary laughed. "Yes, I was thinking I'd hire some guy I just met to help me do the deed in a field in the middle of nowhere. You might not have noticed, but I've got a blanket in one back pocket and stirrups in the other."

He puckered his face.

Would anything ultimately happen between them today? If

she'd met him back in California, they'd undoubtedly end up drinking in a bar, then later, in her apartment, sloppily kissing, eventually passing out and probably never talking again. But she was pregnant now, and this was not California. Everything was different. Nothing, *nothing will happen*, she told herself. Then she told herself to stop thinking about it so much. She'd never done one worthwhile or smart or fun thing after thinking too much about it.

3

Land to Land

The family treated Daniel differently after the accident, and even now, a year and a half later, he caught his mother eyeing him as if she still couldn't quite believe what had happened. Jake was still obsequious, his father even more distant than he used to be. Before the accident it seemed that they looked up to Daniel and his successful career, his busy life in New York. Hilary especially, but since the accident, even she'd been overcompensating. She'd become aggressively chummy and sarcastic. His family had come to seem fragile to him, and more separate. It used to be more of a world that included him.

Brenda pulled the car into the landing just as the ferry left its slip. "Dammit," she said, but Daniel found himself almost relieved; more time would pass before they all gathered, before his mother would reach for his hand, careful not to

touch the chair, before Jake would sprint ahead to hold every
door for him.

Brenda helped him out of the car and then stood beside
him for a moment. She bent forward and closed her eyes, saying she felt light-headed. "You all right?" he asked, but she
didn't respond. The feeling apparently passed, and soon she
headed off to find a drink. She stopped to talk to a youngish
woman with short blond hair—someone she knew? But she
didn't know anyone who lived in Maine. The woman wore
ratty cargo pants and a sleeveless black tank top, and looked to
be about Brenda's age. She held a baby dressed all in white; a
white hat, pacifier, dress, booties. Even the baby's hair and eyes
appeared to be white, and Daniel drew it in his head, a set of
overlapping white circles. The baby seemed to see Daniel staring at it. Something in the small face changed, and it spat its
pacifier into the air and let loose a horrible, curdled sound.
The mother patted the back of the baby's head and walked it
in circles. Brenda glanced over at Daniel, as if she sensed he
was responsible for the baby's misery. In an attempt to look
innocent, he shrugged and picked up a flyer on the bench
next to him. "Come Sail Away!" it advertised in ribbon letters.
A poorly drawn cartoon sailboat captained by a fat, jolly man
burst through the letters. Inside were prices for afternoon
charters, prices so high Daniel calculated that for the same
costs, he could buy two four-course meals in Portugal, ten out-
fits in Zimbabwe, a night at the theater in London. "Visit the
Maine islands! Enjoy the sounds and sights! Sip champagne
while charting a coarse on the Atlantic!" Coarse. The word
stared at him like a bratty child sticking out his tongue.

Brenda returned and said, "Here's some lemonade," handing him a paper cup. "It's quite full. Careful there."

It was a truce, really. *Don't spill on yourself.*

"I love you," he said in a bad British accent. It was the start of an exchange they used to have years ago—she'd reply the same with an American intonation. He waited for her to answer. "I *love* you," he repeated.

"I love you too," she said in her nasal New Yorkese. Her American had always been so exaggerated, yet still somehow plausible. It used to make him laugh.

"You remember," he said, still in British.

She nodded.

"It's been so long. It's been since the accident, I think?"

"Could be. You're nostalgic today." She'd returned to British. "First sex, now this."

She could have used another word for sex, and he wished she had. "Maybe it's the thought of seeing my family," he said. "We haven't all been in one place in years. Maybe it's making me miss the past or something."

"That would make sense," she granted him (because he was no longer being surly, and he would maintain this demeanor, whatever it took).

"I love you," he said again in British, and she said, "We should call Jake and tell him we're going to be late. Did you bring the cell phone?"

He reminded her there was no service up here, but offered to go find a pay phone. He saw one across the dirt parking lot, which would be hell for his wheels. But never mind. He jounced his way across the lot, trying to ignore the clinking of his teeth whenever he jolted over a pebble.

Liz answered. "Jake's not here. He's down at the beach right now." Daniel's brother never used to like the beach; the waves used to frighten him. Everything used to frighten him.

He used to worry that if the sun got too strong it would actually cook him alive. Daniel told her they'd missed the ferry. "You missed it? Well, you're not the only ones who are late. No one's here yet."

"I'm sorry," he said. "We tried. We almost made it."

"It's okay, it's okay," she grumbled, audibly trying to reformulate her afternoon. "You see any of the others there?"

Daniel glanced behind him, wondering why he hadn't thought to look yet. "No."

"We'll just eat later. You'll still be here by sundown if you take the next ferry. You'll still get to see the place in the daylight."

"How're you doing?" he asked. "Last time we talked you were nauseous a lot."

"Yes, well, that seems to have subsided. Now I'm just tired all the time. Jake is taking care of everything." Daniel liked his sister-in-law. At times he felt a sort of kinship with her, and recently they'd begun to joke about his family. She was unlike the sort of person he assumed his brother would marry—maybe someone more hypersensitive. Someone more like Jake. "I'm guessing he thinks he's lost his wife and gained a walking womb. I'm not in the mood for anything lately other than napping and planning for the baby."

"And that surprises him?"

"You know your brother. He takes everything personally. One step toward a baby is one step away from him."

"But isn't it, when you think about it? I mean literally, one step toward anything is a step away from something else."

"You too? Is this fear of abandonment some kind of male thing? Or just a Miller thing?"

Daniel swallowed. "No, Jake's always been the big baby of the family. You know that. He clings to the people he loves for dear life, and when they don't reciprocate, well, he just clings harder."

"Why do you think that is?"

"Simple," he said. "He's a wimp. Psychologically, physically, through and through. He's afraid of rejection. He's terribly insecure. He was born a baby and for some reason stayed that way. Make sure you have enough diapers for when the second comes along." The words flew from his mouth, nastier than he'd meant them.

"Yikes. Sounds like someone's got his own demons."

"I'm off-limits here."

"Well, you can certainly dole it out. Why do you think you can't take it?"

"There's not much to take, really, because I'm perfect. Do I always need to remind you of this?"

"I guess you do. To be honest, it's a little easy to forget."

"How does Jake survive this kind of harassment from you?"

"Harassment? I wasn't the one to call him a baby," she said, her tone shifting.

"I should apologize for that."

"Accepted."

"He's not a baby. He's more of an infant."

"Daniel."

"Yes?"

"You two aren't so different."

He gasped. "I object! I object!"

"Go back to your wife and wait with her until the next ferry. Ask her how she's feeling. Try to help her out when you can, and give her space when she wants it."

"Will do," Daniel said, and they said goodbye.

As he made his way back across the parking lot, he felt a

raindrop on his forehead and noticed a small patch of blue sky to his left, barely visible, becoming smaller and smaller. What if Liz repeated to Jake what he'd said? She wouldn't, she just couldn't. It'd only wound him. In the end Jake had nothing to worry about with Liz. She was someone who presented herself clearly and honestly, who never withheld anything she felt. Daniel had always known that she liked him. And despite some passing irritations, she seemed to truly, sufficiently love Jake. They were certainly a strange couple—she was so much more at ease with herself and other people than he was. At times, Daniel wondered exactly what she saw in him.

Brenda looked beatific, sitting on the bench sipping lemonade and gazing out at the water. Liz had suggested he ask her how she was feeling, but he wanted to address other matters right now.

"So," he said as he stopped beside her. He paused. He would tread lightly. "I think that this pregnancy might be it for me. I'm just not sure I want to put my body through another one. All my stretch marks, all the trips to the bathroom, the morning sickness." He rested his hands on an invisible stomach before him.

She wasn't smiling.

"Would we use the same donor, our Jonathan White, again? That is, if there has to be a next time?"

"Not this."

"I'm just not sure I can go through it all again. I'm not sure I can handle another pregnancy." He'd made a circle around what he'd meant to say.

"I'm the one that's pregnant. I'm the one that's going to give birth, for God's sake." She looked right at him. "You're feeling left out again."

"It's not just a feeling." Was this what Jake sounded like to Liz? Childlike and nagging? He wanted to continue, but the woman with the baby approached and Brenda suddenly switched into her friendly-to-people-she-barely-knew mode. The woman had messy, chin-length black hair held back from her face by a thick flowered band. Her cheeks were covered in freckles, and her eyes were steely blue. She wore no wedding ring and Daniel wondered whether the baby was even hers. She was attractive in a boyish way, hardened and muscular.

"This is Vanessa," Brenda finally said to Daniel. "She lives on the island and works for Freeman Corcoran. You know, the painter."

"And this," Vanessa said, holding up the baby's hand, "is my daughter Esther."

The baby opened her mouth and grabbed Vanessa's chin with both her hands as if she were about to nurse it. Vanessa nuzzled her with her chin, and when she pulled back, a line of drool connected their lips. Daniel tried but was unable to place Freeman Corcoran's art, though the name was familiar.

"Did you even know he lived there, Dan?" Brenda asked. "I've always loved his work. His sense of humor, his sense of fun. And he handles light so deftly," she said to Vanessa. "You know, to be honest, I didn't know he was still alive."

"He's ninety-four, but you'd never know it if you met him. He still paints every day. He's still sharp as a knife. Esther and I live in the barn behind his house—years ago he made it into a living space."

"What a job," Brenda said dreamily.

"He's always having huge dinner parties for the artists or writers who come to visit him. He invites half the island, it seems. And he cooks. For days ahead of time, he cooks. Lobster bisque, breads, cakes, you name it. Everyone on Great Salt loves him to death," Vanessa said, and kissed Esther's head. "We're never bored, that's for sure. And Freeman travels a lot, and takes us with him. Next month we're heading to Madrid for a show."

"I bet my wife would love to join you," Daniel said. Another thought had escaped. They seemed impossible to censor today.

"Just ignore this person and tell me more about Freeman," Brenda said.

The light outside had dimmed and the day had grown colder. Daniel watched several small boats buzz around the harbor like flies. He wished he'd finished his earlier conversation with Brenda and elicited some kind of definitive answer from her. And then he decided that maybe, just maybe, he did not.

—

Ellen followed Joe up the aisle of the ferry until he found an empty seat beside a young woman reading a book. Joe gazed down at her, Babe's cage swinging between them, but she didn't move. "You take it," Ellen said.

"No," Joe said. He set the cage on the floor. "You go ahead."

"I'll go find another seat somewhere else. I don't mind," she said. She continued on to the front of the boat, where a few families talked loudly. She sat beside a young boy on a bench and glanced at his family across from him, now arguing about a bed and breakfast. She tried to ignore them but their voices grew loud and insistent. The mother's was nasal, with a strong Boston accent. Ellen pushed her fingertips against her temples. What would MacNeil do in such a situ-

ation? He would allow the noise to drift away. She imagined
the voices around her fading, becoming a distant din like
faraway traffic. "Morton, I can't believe you just got one
goddamn room, and that you only remembered to tell me
now," the woman squawked, and her voice rushed right
back beside Ellen, making its way beneath her skin. They
argued on and on—they were a terrible couple. So many
couples fought in public. Even Vera and MacNeil had
sparred in front of them, and always over the silliest topics.
Often Ellen thought Vera was just being obstinate for the
sake of making a point. Ellen herself had learned to let certain things go in her marriage. Of course, certain moments
stuck to her like thorns, but she tried never to argue with
Joe in public, and insisted they not argue in front of the kids.
They funneled their irritations with each other into a
friendly sort of teasing when the kids were near, an
innocent-seeming banter that no one could have suspected
hid anything more insidious. It was never necessary to let
the world hear one's ugly grievances.

Morton sneezed explosively and Ellen's heart burst in her
chest. Two girls across from her saw her jump and giggled.
Ellen tried to smile at them as she stood, pushing against the
table, and made her way back to Joe. She wobbled with the
ferry's jumbled motion as she walked.

Asleep, Joe leaned toward the young woman sitting next to
him. Ellen wasn't sure what to do. She stood there a moment,
then reached across the girl toward one of the bags. She shuffled around inside for her migraine medicine. Not that she
was certain she had a migraine, but she needed something to
help calm her and to quiet the volume of the boat's noises.
The bottle was wedged beneath keys, a wallet, several pieces

of paper and a pack of chewing gum. She grabbed the pills
and headed off to find a bathroom.

When she returned, she went to slip the bottle back into the
bag as Joe opened his eyes. "Hi," he mumbled.

"Hi."

"You want to sit?"

"Actually, yes. Would you mind?" The bickering couple
wouldn't bother him so much.

"No, of course not," he said, and shuffled around, pushing
himself up and past her with a grunt and a sigh. She slid by
the young woman, her bony knees lifted in front of her as a
bookstand, her braided hair thin and straight like a doll's.

The ferry ground forward. Ellen took the seat and gazed
out the cloudy, stained window at the charcoal ocean. She
tried to let it soothe her, for wasn't that what the ocean was
supposed to do, soothe one's nerves? The young woman
clicked her tongue as she read. Quietly but perceptibly, click,
click, like a metronome, and Ellen closed her eyes and willed
the medicine to quiet her mind. She imagined MacNeil was
the one sitting next to her and that they were headed for a
weekend on the island, just the two of them, to have long conversations and dinner and drink wine and go for walks afterward in the dark. In just five days, she would meet him at the
Gardner. The concert was at seven-thirty, and he'd planned to
pick her up and for them to have supper in the museum café
beforehand. Joe would have poker that night, and anyway, he
knew when she went out with MacNeil—Joe just didn't know
how often they went out alone, or about the sorts of conversations they had, of course, or the recent thoughts she'd had
about him. She almost wanted to tell her husband. After all,
she was used to telling him of the thoughts and feelings that

most consumed her. She wanted to share it with *someone*, at least, but of course she could not. She absolutely could not. No matter, she thought. The concert would run until at least nine, she assumed, and by the time he got her home it'd be nine-thirty, maybe later. She ran a finger across the window next to her. She could ask him to take her for a ride, tell him she wasn't ready to end the night just yet. *I'm not quite tired enough for bed*, she'd say. And then what? Would she just come out and ask him if he felt the same electricity between them? It had been so many years since she'd worried about what a man thought of her. What did one do? She supposed she wouldn't press matters. She would merely establish a setup— she would direct him to the big parking lot by the Charles, the one near the community gardens and boat rentals. They would sit in his car at first, looking out at the glistening river, and she would tell him how much she loved this spot, how it was one of her favorites, and would he like to take a little walk, maybe? See the moon, the view of the city? Afterward, she would suggest that they drive to his house. And why not? At that point, the electricity would have inevitably risen to the surface, helped along by the sight of the Charles at night, the stars, the subtle nighttime chill. He would have taken her hand as he sometimes did. He would have stopped by the water and stood just behind her to keep her warm. By then it would have become clear that he wanted what she wanted, and they would drive back to his house in Lincoln, park the car, walk up his creaky front steps, turn on the hall light, head upstairs. In bed he would be definitive and confident, she suspected, strong and slow and responsive. She held her hands together in her lap and glanced at the girl beside her. *If she only knew what this old woman was thinking*. She wouldn't sleep at MacNeil's that night. She would stay awhile, a few hours maybe, but then she would ask him to drive her home, and she would tell Joe that the concert ran late, and that she and MacNeil and some friends he'd brought had gone out afterward for a drink and dessert, and then there was the strangest traffic jam in the city. She drew a nervous breath. It was a plan. She wouldn't let herself think her way out of it.

The girl clicked her tongue and turned the page. The ferry pressed ahead. Ellen looked out the window and could see only water. She remembered that her last ferry trip to the island felt like traveling to another world, making a sort of passage between land and land. It was almost romantic, the people up on deck, wrapped in thick wool sweaters against the cool air. Looking ahead, waiting to see a sliver of land appear on the horizon. It was what she imagined her grandmothers saw when they first came to this country from Russia. A new beginning. Promise.

Soon she would be a grandmother herself. (What kind of example would she be setting, sneaking around with her dear friend's husband? She shuddered. She put it out of her mind.) She would plan huge dinners for her grandchildren: fried chicken, mashed potatoes, baked beans. Food children would love. She would keep a drawer of paper and pens and glue and tape for them to make art projects with when they visited. She would take her grandchildren to Boston and ride the swan boats with them and take them to tea at the Ritz and to the Children's Museum.

But she was not so young anymore. It wasn't as easy to get around the city as it used to be—her legs inevitably cramped, her head always began to ache. Perhaps by the time they were old enough, she wouldn't be able to do any of these things with them. If her children had had babies earlier, though, if they'd gotten their lives together earlier, settled down, just gone ahead and made their families. In a few years it might be too late. The thought wasn't a frightening one—it just bothered her to think she might not be able to see her grandchildren become young people. It irritated her, her children's disorganization. They had waited so long to even start trying. Jake had waited until he was thirty-five, Daniel until it was too late. And Hilary—who knew if she'd ever even have a long-term relationship, let alone children?

None of Ellen's children had started their families naturally, the way people used to—a husband, a wife, a bed. The other evening, Ellen raised the subject with Joe over dinner. "Isn't it strange, the unusual ways Liz and Brenda got pregnant?"

"I suppose."

"I just hope that these new methods—the donor, the drugs—I hope they work out in the end. Do you think Jake and Liz's problems might have come from us? Our genes or something?" She pushed a thumb into her palm and squeezed her hand. She guessed he wouldn't have much to say about the matter, but her questions nagged at her tonight.

"Our genes? Don't be silly. I, at least, am genetically perfect. You must know that by now. You, on the other hand—"

"I'm being serious here. What if it was our fault?"

"Oh, just try to focus on the positive—they're having families. Families are good things. Remember how excited we were when we first started ours?"

"I suppose," she said absently. "Do you think Hilary will ever settle down? What would a man Hilary married even be like, do you think? That Jesse Varnum?" In the time she took off between high school and college, Hilary had dated someone several years older than she, something that unnerved Ellen at first—she could see the lines on his face and gray hairs throughout his black beard. Hilary had only brought him home once (in the days when she used to come home more regularly than every few years). He was the only boyfriend of hers they'd ever met. The two behaved sheepishly with each other at first, but soon Hilary began to touch Jesse quite often, to play with his fingers and his hair at the dinner table, and Ellen noticed Jesse didn't return her affection. She wanted to tell her daughter to pull back a bit, not to seem so eager, so hungry like that. *No one wants to feel that indispensable when it comes right down to it.* And despite his age, there was something about Jesse that Ellen liked. He was softspoken but pleasant, and he asked them questions and seemed genuinely interested in their lives. He was intelligent and had a kindness in his expressions that made Ellen see why her daughter was attracted to him. At one point Ellen took Hilary aside and told her she liked him. Hilary looked confused, perhaps even a little disappointed, and said, "He likes you guys too." Unfortunately that was the first and last time Ellen met Jesse Varnum. A month or so later Hilary called to say they'd broken up, and when Ellen asked why, Hilary, oddly indifferent, said, "We just did."

"I don't know," Joe said after a moment. "Maybe he'd be some rock star or something?"

"Come on," Ellen said, scowling. "Really try to picture the man Hilary would marry."

"What's the use?"

He had a point. What was the use of trying to imagine someone who might never exist? "You worry," Joe said, and set his hand on her knee.

"It's not worry so much, it's more curiosity. I just wonder what Hilary's life is like. Sometimes I wonder whether she's ever been in love—maybe she's been in love a hundred times. She certainly never talks about it. Do you think she's ever been in love?"

"Sure."

"What would it be like to be thirty-five and never have had a real relationship?" Ellen paused. The thought seemed full of loneliness. At thirty-five, she herself had had a marriage, a house, three kids, a job. She'd never known what it was like to eat dinner each night alone. But of course along with being single came a world of possibility. One could travel anywhere, work any job as long as it paid the bills. True love could always be just around the corner. Ellen's own fate had been determined, she supposed, the day she met Joe. She'd never had the sense that anything could happen—she'd always possessed a more or less clear picture of her future. Until, of course, MacNeil.

"She was in love with Jesse. I'm sure she has been with others," he said.

"Has she told you about it?"

He set his fork down. "She's mentioned different people."

"Anyone in particular?"

"I don't think so," Joe said. "You know, I want them all to be settled and happy in their lives too."

"I know you do." And he did. Their three kids had been his biggest dream, and his hope for their contentment was the continuation of this dream. He was a good person, a decent man, her husband.

The ferry grumbled. She looked out the window again, and saw that the sky was no longer blue at all but slate gray, and quickly darkening. Ellen looked at her watch. They would arrive soon.

—

Unfortunately, Jake's whole family knew of his trials with infertility. He'd meant to keep it secret, as Liz didn't want them to know. But in a weak moment, he'd told his mother over the phone, who'd gone and told his father and Daniel, who of course passed along the news to Hilary. Jake confronted his mother about it—"I was CONFIDING in you, Mom, did you not realize that?"—and asked her not to tell Liz that any of them knew, and to please pass *this* along to the rest of the family. Jake should have been smarter about it. His mother or his father or any of them, for that matter, had never been able to keep a secret, but for some reason he found himself confiding in them, especially his parents, again and again.

Liz had no such intimacy with her parents, though she was an only child. She never understood his telling his family about anything at all private. Her parents were real estate developers who lived part of the year in Hawaii and the other part in Texas. Liz grew up in Oregon, though, in a small town near Mount Hood where every other person farmed marijuana. Nothing about her mother and father indicated that they were parents. They threw enormous parties where people freely smoked pot; they cooked elaborate meals from vegetables grown in their tangled garden; they collected ancient drug paraphernalia. "The hookahs," her mother once told Jake with utter seriousness, "are thought to have been the original pleasure-givers." Liz had early on admitted to Jake that being raised by such parents had led her to adopt a rather rigid system of rules for herself. He imagined her as a child, cleaning their drawers, planning their meals, and in fact she had told him that she'd once even organized their hookah collection by their country of origin. It'd broken his heart.

He considered the fact that everyone in his family knew of their infertility as he shuffled through his underwear drawer—hopefully none of them would slip up and mention it this weekend, especially after they learned about the twins. He should never have told his mother. He wished desperately they didn't all know—Liz would be even more exasperated with him right now if she found out.

He was about to lay eyes on partially clothed twin cheerleaders, the cover of the magazine at the top of the pile, when Liz walked in. He almost closed the drawer on his hand.

"Daniel called. They're going to be late," she said, and suggested they go down to the beach and relax there for a bit.

"First the weather, now this? What else can go wrong?" he groaned, and followed her through the house.

"Easy there," she said over her shoulder.

He grabbed a folding chair on the back porch and walked behind her down the path and out to a flat patch of rocks. "Here, you should sit," he said, and reached out his arm to help her.

She eased herself onto the chair and looked up at him. "I guess I should apologize about earlier, about your book and everything. You have to understand, though—I'm just not feeling exactly sexy these days."

He took a step backward, down a decline. He moved his tongue around the inside of his mouth and said, "*I* think you're sexy." He smiled at how scripted the words sounded.

"Sometimes I wish I could physically feel what you're feeling, that I could go through some of it too, you know, actually experience some of this pregnancy for you. I wish I could take some of the burden away from you. I feel kind of useless, standing here on the sidelines. I feel like I'm just in the way." He became aware of how many times he'd just said the word "feel."

Liz smiled and nudged a mound of sand and rocks toward him. "You're not useless. You're working your tail off. You got us all packed up to come here, you cleaned up the place when we got here. You've done so much for me these past weeks. "

"Yes," he said, and though he wished that all he'd done would compel her to want to give him something in return, to *want* him more, he did appreciate what she'd said. Still, he couldn't shake a growing urge to do more for her, to make something better or simply to change *something* and get rid of the tight snarl of energy within his chest. He bent down, scooped up a handful of sand and pitched it toward the ocean, but it dispersed in the wind and some of it blew directly back into his face. He brushed his eyes. When he was a kid and his parents took them to the beach, Hilary always used to throw sand at him. She was a bratty kid and had grown into a bratty adult—he had no idea why she and Daniel were so close now. Daniel, though moody in his way, had a certain quiet dignity, a clear sense of responsibility. He was an *adult* now. Hilary, on the other hand, had gone through umpteen jobs in the last couple of years, she'd lived in umpteen apartments. He imagined she still drank too much, still smoked pot. He wondered whether she kept porn. He pictured a stack of *Playgirl*s on a coffee table beside a full, dirty ashtray and a pile of caked dishes. This was one of the many differences between them: she displayed her weaknesses for everyone to see and Jake kept them hidden inside himself, where they should stay put.

Liz stood and headed back inside to get started on dinner. He looked at the house, the one light still on in the kitchen. She was so good about electricity. She always nagged him about his laziness with lights, how he left them on when the two of them went out even though he'd told her again and again that he'd felt uncomfortable leaving a house so dark when they weren't there, as if they were abandoning it. "Why the strange empathy for something inanimate?" she'd said once, and he had no ready answer. What would she say if she found out about his box of rescued things?

After a while, Jake headed back inside too. He walked into their bedroom, collapsed on their bed and glanced up at a smallish, no, medium-sized crack by the light on the ceiling. He would have to examine all the ceilings in the house. What if he found more cracks? He'd need to have the roof redone. Again. It had been no small job redoing the original roof. The guy had charged double his estimate and the men had left muddy footprints all over the new floors. Not that it would matter, as God knows when he and Liz would be able to come to the island next, given his full roster of meetings this month. And the quarterly reports that were soon due, the revised budget, the taxes. When would he be able to spend any real time with her?

He felt his pulse ticking and told himself to slow down, *breathe, breathe*. He'd read several books about reducing stress and had adopted various breathing methods that did, he thought, help. *One, two, three*, he breathed and closed his eyes, *one, two, three*.

Liz turned on and off the faucet and the house grew quiet.
One, two, three. He slid a hand down his shorts and rested
his fingers on the warmth there. *One, two, three.* Slowly his
fingers, as if independently from his brain, began to stroke
himself, slowly, slowly, and the warmth gradually bled out,
through his middle, and he began to move faster as he tried
to recall the twin cheerleaders—their blond pigtails; their
tan, full, round breasts; their long legs wide open—and he
grew hotter and thicker, his heart beating, and soon he felt
nothing but the warmth and the speed, and he continued,
on and on, until he almost burst and opened his eyes to see
his wife, at the end of the bed, several leaves of arugula in
her hand.

"Jesus," he said.

"I think I understand." She smiled kindly.

He rolled over and buried his face in the pillow. "Can you
leave me alone?" he said through the pillow.

"Feel better?"

He made a noise like a wounded cat, repeated it louder,
and kicked his feet against the bed. In a moment he heard her
walk out of the room and her footsteps grow quieter.

It was some time before he lifted his face from the pillow
and turned over onto his back. He noticed the wooden box of
odd things on top of the dresser. He rose, retrieved it and set
it on the floor. He took the pacifier out of his pocket and
placed it on top of an earring shaped like a heart. Here inside
this box was dignity. Here was something good that he'd
done. Let her find it and wonder what the hell it was. And in
the end, let her think he was pathetic, a person made solely of
desires lately. But she was too. Her desires and needs—rest,
comfort, peace, support—overrode his by necessity of the sit-

uation, and soon there would be two other sets of needs and desires that would override both of theirs.

He was sitting on the floor like a wounded child. It occurred to him he lacked a protective skin around his emotions. They seemed to him more raw than other people's, closer to the surface and more urgent.

He stood, smoothed his shorts and placed his feet hip-width apart, grounding himself. He was a man, not a child. He was a successful man at that, and he had an incredible wife—beautiful and virtuous and smart and fun, and as for the tornado of needs they'd soon face, well, they had both wanted children from the beginning, he reminded himself. It'd been something he'd always known he'd wanted. When he first met her she was forthright about it and he appreciated this. She'd said, on one of their first dates, "How many children do you want?" and he'd said, without much thought, "Two." Maxims flooded his head now: *Beware of what you wish for; Que sera, sera.* Of course they never helped much, these words.

He looked out the window at the top of the rosebushes. The only actual, concrete problem was that Liz had just caught him going to town on himself. She was probably repulsed by him right now, despite her nonchalance (undoubtedly feigned) in the moment.

But he was human, after all, and so goddamned what if he'd indulged? She hadn't touched him in weeks, no, months. It wasn't such a terribly big deal. For that matter, he might as well finish what he started. Emboldened, he rushed to the underwear drawer, burrowed beneath his socks, grabbed the magazine with the twins on the front and went to sit on the bed. Liz coughed and he heard her footsteps approach. Losing his nerve, he quickly shoved the magazine under his pillow and walked into the hallway, where she stood, pulling towels from the linen closet. He kept his eyes on the floor, brushed past her, continued on through the living room and on out of the house again, to where, he wasn't quite sure. But he felt certain he needed to be moving. Liz hollered something to him, but he didn't slow down to listen. He needed a minute to himself, at least a minute to decide what he would say to her now, and he rushed down the back path, down to the beach, and when he finally stopped moving, he looked around at the ocean and the gray sky, and sat down on the sand.

He picked up a pebble and tossed it forward. What *was* she thinking right now? What would he have thought if he'd walked in on her doing the same? He smiled. That never would have happened—especially now. She was not and had never been a person driven by sexual desire, and again, it was one of the things that initially impressed him. She seemed above this, above temptation of all kinds. She never drank in college, never smoked. She was an excellent student and such a promising artist—her drawings had even been displayed in the library during their final year. And she had friends, so many friends who seemed to adore her. Jake had always wanted to be someone like this—someone good and admirable and talented, someone genuinely liked by a group of people, and when she came up to him and asked to borrow his notes after their psychology class, when she said she'd meet him at his dorm later to return them, that she'd buy him an ice cream to thank him, he felt he had won some sort of lottery.

Later, he'd been so proud to introduce to her his family, especially Daniel, who'd never met any of Jake's girlfriends. Liz engaged them all in easy conversation, bantered with them, even joked with them about Jake a little, something that at first made him prickle. But in the end, he was just glad that she meshed with them so well. In a sense, he became more a part of his family when she was by his side.

—

A few blocks past Books & Beans, Alex pulled his car into a dirt driveway. Tucked behind the shops was a tiny white house, its paint chipped on its clapboards. The front lawn was all dead grass and dirty toys and rusted bicycles. He turned off the ignition, and Hilary, a little surprised by the condition of the place, followed him around the back of the house. The air smelled of cigarette smoke, and she heard the buzz of a radio struggling to receive a station. He led her down cement stairs and into a dark room where she heard the sound of panting. When he switched on the light, an enormous black Lab lunged forward and lapped at her belly.

"That's Rita," Alex said.

Hilary tried to fend off the dog when Alex disappeared into the next room. Around her were piles of books, magazines, clothes strewn across sagging or torn furniture. The walls were covered in tilted posters, enormous photographs of mountains and water and trees.

Rita had fastened her teeth to Hilary's shoe and was chewing and yanking, a low rumbling rising from her throat. Hilary tried to kick her away as she went over to what looked like an easy chair beneath a pile of shirts and a hammer and a camera and a cardboard box. She set these things on the ground and eased herself into the chair.

Alex appeared in the doorway holding two glasses of water. "Drink?" he said, and handed her a glass. He sat down on the floor in front of her, evidently unaware that his dog was now mangling what looked like one of his socks with her teeth.

"She your girlfriend?" Hilary asked.

"Funny." He reached over and stroked Rita's head. "She's my baby. I've had her since I was a kid."

"She's something."

"Indeed," he said. He pulled the dog onto his lap and vigorously scratched the top of her head. She squealed and licked his lips.

Hilary looked away. She closed her eyes and tried to imagine what she would tell George about this place and this person. *Young, aloof, outdoorsy—your typical Berkeley type*, she'd say, and George would ask her why she spent so much time with him, and she'd say, *I don't know, something just kept me there*, and quickly change the subject. George didn't know she was pregnant. She hadn't been down to San Diego in months, and she hadn't been able to figure out a way to tell him, or even whether to tell him at all. Now she imagined breaking the news to her family. *You're what? And no father for it*, they'd say. *How could you let this happen? You're too old for such irresponsibility. Haven't you grown out of this stage yet?* They still treated her like the baby of the family. They still assumed she had no idea how to be responsible. Every other month Jake sent her books about investing money. Her father assumed she had no idea how to take care of her car or computer and asked her, whenever they spoke, if she'd been changing the oil, checking the tires, backing up her documents. *You can't be both a child and a mother*, they'd all think when they saw her, all of them except Daniel.

Rita looked up at Hilary with widened jaws, as if she were smiling, and began slapping Alex's nose and mouth with her pale pink tongue. He turned and gazed at Hilary with a blank expression, blissfully blank. His hair curled in boyish waves around his face. His eyes were dark, his lips full. He was handsome, objectively handsome.

"I'm beat," she said, tentatively at first. "I'm absolutely fried. Maybe I should lie down for a little bit."

He looked at her in surprise. "All right."

"Bedroom in here?" Hilary asked, pointing to the next room. "You mind?"

He shook his head but stayed where he was.

With great effort, she pulled herself from the chair and lumbered into the next room, just as squalid as the other. A mattress lay on the floor covered with clothes. The room smelled of unwashed bodies. If her mother could see her now, or Jake.

"Families make you uncomfortable," George said about a year ago over the phone.

"Not yours."

"Yes it does. You don't want to be a part of something so traditional."

"Yours isn't traditional. I'm sorry to be the one to tell you, George."

"Still. You like being on your own. You like to think you're making your own decisions, that you're not being swayed by people around you who expect certain things," she remembered him saying. "You hate having to live up to expectations."

She set her hand against the wall and lowered herself slowly onto Alex's mattress. Knots of clothes pressed into her back.

"That's why you don't want to move down here," George said.

"You know that's not true. Can you honestly see me living

in that sort of environment? With all the blondes and the sun and the surfers? I'd hate it. I'd go crazy."

"Yes, I can see it."

She pulled a pair of shorts from beneath her back and tossed them on the floor.

"No you can't."

"You would laugh at them just like you laugh at those kids demonstrating in Berkeley and the healthy couples riding mountain bikes in Marin."

It was cement, the mattress, and she tugged the clothes away as she rested her head on a stained pillow with no case. The room reminded her of college, of the boys freed from their families to neglect their laundry and diet and hygiene. She'd been in rooms like this many times before, but not in years. This could have been the last time she'd find herself in such a place.

"Okay. And what would I do for work?"

"Anything. It doesn't matter. You could work at a little gallery. You could work at a bookstore. Something laid-back, something more you than filing papers for some company."

"You know I hate all that sun. It makes bad moods impossible. It doesn't allow for sloth or irony or nastiness or anything good, really. People would hate me there, and I would hate them. It's nothing against you and Camille. How many times do I have to tell you that?"

"Right."

"George."

"You don't like expectation. You don't like families."

"I've never been too good at being a part of one. Mine can attest to that. Have I told you how many times I ran away as a kid?"

"You're thirty-five, Hil."

"Twenty-six times. Of course most of the time I just went to the woods in the back of the house, but later I took a bus into Boston. Twice I hitchhiked to New York."

"Should I pity you?"

"Maybe."

"When was the last time you ran away?"

"I suppose when I moved here thirteen years ago."

"I rest my case."

"George. I'm sorry, but I'm just not moving down there."

There was silence, a swallowing and a fizzing on the line, and then the dial tone. She looked up at Alex's ceiling speckled with mildew and closed her eyes.

Alex stood above her, Rita by his side. "Everything okay in here? You've been out for a while. You want to keep sleeping?"

"No," she said. Her head was heavy, dizzy, and she blinked several times.

He sat down on the end of the mattress. "How you feeling?" he asked. He looked at her belly.

She screwed up her face. "Oh my God, I think it's coming. I think my water broke!"

He froze, then jumped up. "What should I do? What should I do?"

She smiled. "I'm kidding. I still have three more months to go. You don't have anything to worry about."

"That's not funny."

"Sure it is," she said, and gestured for him to sit down again. "You're not used to being around pregnant women."

"This is true."

"You want to feel it, the baby? It's moving now—here, give me your hand," she said, and reached forward.

His hand was clammy, and he seemed jumpy as she tugged him toward her, lifted her shirt a little and placed his palm against the side of her stomach. The baby turned and elbowed what felt like her kidney. "Is that it?" he said.

She nodded.

"What's it doing?" he asked.

"I don't know. Feels like ballet, huh?"

He smiled. "It's pretty incredible. Does it hurt when it moves around like that?"

"No. Sometimes it's kind of uncomfortable, but I wouldn't say it hurts."

He pulled his hand away.

"What do you think of this big belly?" she asked, edging up her shirt a little more, careful not to reveal the stretch marks at her sides. "You think it's ugly?"

"No, not at all," he said, glancing at her lap.

Rita whined and nuzzled her head against Hilary's leg. She patted the dog stiffly. "You can touch it again," she said. "I don't mind."

"How much bigger will you get?" He reached over and pressed his palm against her stomach.

"Hopefully not too much. I don't think I can stretch much more. You know, I used to be fairly thin."

"I can imagine," he said. He moved his hand across the top of her stomach, down one side and up toward the middle. "This is so weird."

"Thanks."

"Not you, not your stomach. I mean this situation. Sitting

here, doing what I'm doing right now. I mean, I barely know you."

She nodded. "True. But I don't mind it."

"You don't?"

"No. I kind of like it, really."

He stopped moving his hand. "What's your middle name?" It was the sort of question a teenager asked in order to quickly establish intimacy before making a move.

"Jane," she said, smiling. "And my last name is Miller. You?"

"Walter, last name Kerwin."

"What else do you want to know about me?"

He paused. "Here's a question: what are we doing right now?" He took his hand away.

"Well, just now you were touching my pregnant stomach and we were sitting here talking."

"Very good. But I think you know what I mean."

She sighed. "I guess I do. To be honest, though, I'd just rather not have that conversation right now, if that's all right. I'd really rather not dissect this moment because I was kind of liking it just as it was. I was enjoying your sitting here next to me with your hand on my stomach, and I wasn't minding the fact that I don't know whether maybe you snore loudly or have a stash of wives somewhere or that maybe you have a secret arsenal of guns. I'm okay with not knowing these things."

"I don't snore loudly," he said.

"Thank God for that."

"It's funny. You say the sorts of things that I'd say."

"You mean in this type of situation that you've been in so many times, except never with someone who's pregnant?"

"No, I mean . . . well, maybe. Not exactly, it's just that—"

"Alex?"

"Yes?"

"I'd like it if you put your hand back on my stomach," she said, and slowly, tentatively, he did. "And now I'd like it if we could change the subject." She shuffled closer to him. "I'm glad these kinds of thoughts occur to you, I really am, but I just don't think that people always need to have this conversation."

"I guess the conversation does tend to put a damper on things."

"Exactly," she said.

"We can have a conversation later," he whispered, and she said, "If we need to."

"So you're all right with this?" he asked, and moved his hand around her stomach.

"Yes." She took one of his hands and led it around her back. He ran two fingers up her spine and across the back of her neck.

"How's this?"

"Good," she said. She smiled, and leaned forward to lift his T-shirt over his head. "And this?"

"Just fine," he whispered, and then, "You sure you're okay with this?" as he unclasped her bra. She nodded, and he moved his face toward hers, then lowered it to her neck. He breathed against her collarbone, then kissed it slowly, firmly, and made his way up to her chin, her mouth. "You still doing all right?" he said into her ear. He slid his hands around to her front, and ran his fingers over her nipples.

"Yes," she said, and closed her eyes.

"Just tell me when you want me to stop."

"I will."

He lifted her shirt over her head, then pulled off her bra and cupped his hands under her breasts. *She should pull back*, she suddenly thought, *slow things down. Maybe he was right, maybe they should at least discuss this*, but then the thought passed, and as he pushed his warm chest against her side and kissed her earlobe, her awareness seemed to empty of everything but a keen floating sensation and a tingling in her chest.

Alex guided Rita into the back seat of the car, where she lay across piles of paper and books. He left Hilary to seat herself.

"Thanks for being such a great tour guide."

"Sure thing."

"What do I owe you?" she asked, smiling.

"It's on me."

"Well, thank you. You know, I feel like I have a much better sense of this place now."

"I'm sure you do."

"And the people. I like the people here. They're awfully hospitable."

He rolled his eyes, and turned on the ignition.

She noticed that the daylight had faded and the temperature had dropped. What would her family do without the sun and the beach? Her father would hide in the corner reading. Her mother would try to engage them all in strained conversation by telling them about this friend and that, this relative, that book. Daniel would doodle or read. Brenda would talk work on the phone, maybe plan her next trip. Jake would be in constant motion, trying to please them all. More coffee, tea, a blanket? Liz would join him, straightening every household item they moved. They would all press each other flat. And this would occur, of course, after they'd each had a small heart attack upon seeing her pregnant.

They drove past the shops and Books & Beans, and she directed him to Jake's house. She peeked at the sharp lines of his profile, at his small nose and scruffy hair.

"Am I going to see you again?" he asked.

She couldn't read from his tone whether in fact he did want to see her again. And anyway, what would be the point? She'd only be here for another two days. "I don't know. I've got family stuff all weekend."

"Well, if I see you, I see you."

Did he actually want to see her again? And if he did, why? "You don't want to get mixed up with some pregnant woman."

"You're probably right."

"And I don't want to get mixed up with some guy who works in a coffee shop."

"That's nice."

"I didn't mean it that way. I only meant that, you know, let's just sit here and enjoy what just happened. Let's not have that awful conversation where we attempt to figure it out or define it by trying to decide what should come next." She remembered she'd said something similar to George after their first night together. The thought of spending the entire next day with him and Camille had been stifling at the time.

"Okay," Alex said. She directed him to Jake's road and tried to think of what she might say when she left him. Why did these moments always inspire such dread? She decided to try to soften what she'd already said. "I think I just need some time to unwind right now. Remember, I flew from California last night on the red-eye? Remember, I had to take the bus to the ferry from the airport, a two-hour drive with this woman bathed in perfume who talked to me the entire time?"

"Remember? You didn't tell me that."

"I didn't?" It did, in fact, seem to her as if they knew each other better than they actually did.

When the sky opened with rain, Alex didn't slow the car any. His windshield wipers squeaked with each motion, barely clearing the glass of the small waves that splashed it. He sped through the streets (he clearly wanted to drop her off now and be done with her) and Hilary rubbed her stomach in an exaggerated manner to remind him it wasn't just them in the car, please be careful, there was a baby too. The car seemed to float above the road. It swerved and straightened. She grew dizzy. She opened her mouth to shout, *Slow the hell down*, when they screeched to a stop.

She opened her eyes and saw, through a scrim of rain, Jake's house.

"I'll see you, maybe." Hilary gathered her bag, her heart knocking in her chest. She quickly pushed open the car door and stepped outside into the storm. She rushed through the fast rain to the house and rang the doorbell. No lights appeared to be on inside. Alex's car purred behind her as she waited, then rang the bell again, but no one answered. She pounded on the door, then tried the doorknob, but it was locked. Her family was probably trying to teach her some kind of lesson by locking the door, turning off the lights and leaving. *You have to be here on time or you'll miss everything.* Her family, especially Jake, hated when she was late.

She hurried back to Alex's car and apologized, not quite sure what to do or say next. He bounced a palm against the steering wheel, his fingers rigid. Maybe he thought this was all a ploy, that she was some lonely, desperate woman—pregnant, to boot—and that now she'd want him to take her in, feed her, be a father for her child.

"Listen, I've got to be somewhere," he said, shifting into reverse and pulling out of the driveway.

"Right."

"You want me to drop you back in town?"

He was fading from her. She'd lost whatever novelty and intrigue she'd had earlier. "Sure," she said.

Rita lay flat on the back seat, licking her paws. When Hilary turned, the dog looked up at her through heavy eyelids. "Where do you have to be?" she finally asked.

He pretended not to hear her, and she repeated her question.

"I'm meeting some people."

"Who?"

"People."

Alex slowed the car a little and they plowed through a wide puddle. "Ah. Them. Girlfriend?"

"No."

"Yes."

"No."

"What does it matter?" she said. "You can tell me. I won't care—I promise." Rita whined in the back seat and slapped her leg with her tongue. "You don't call her your girlfriend," she said. "But she thinks of herself that way."

"Okay," he said.

"You sleep with her. You go to her place late at night, you leave early in the morning. You like her. You think that someday, far, far in the future, maybe you'll want to be with her more regularly, but not now. You call her your girlfriend. But something about her kind of annoys you. She's too happy to see you sometimes. She gives you little presents. But she's sort of attractive. And she has a good body."

"Amazing. You know everything about me."

"Am I right? Come on, tell me."

"You obviously want to be right."

"I've got to be close at least. Maybe there're a couple of girl-friends?"

"You want to know?" he said.

"Yes."

"You really want to know?"

"I do."

He smiled. "I'm not going to tell you."

"That's not fair!" she said. "You're such a tease."

"I wouldn't say that," he said, looking sideways at her.

She'd gotten him back. Somehow, amazingly, he'd come back.

4

Phantom People

Rain hissed down on the pavement and the grass, the cars and the ocean. A tiny unmanned boat in the bay lifted and slapped against the water. Brenda had run ahead with Esther to their car—she'd been dancing her around the parking lot just before the rain came—and had left Daniel to fend for himself. He willed his chair to move faster. Then he willed his legs to come back to life and run him to their car. He shielded his face from the rain but was unable to move the chair with just one arm, so he clenched his eyes shut and set his hands on his wheel rims. In a moment, he felt an enormous jolt. One of his wheels had slipped from the curb and he was stuck. He leaned all his weight to one side, but to no avail. His hair dripped down his face and his shirt stuck to his chest. Through the din of the rain and wind he heard a voice say, "You need a hand?" It was Vanessa.

"Looks that way." He felt his chair drop and careen forward. He sat there, riding along through the pouring rain like a baby in a stroller.

When they finally reached the car, Vanessa went to take Esther and crawled in the back seat while Brenda struggled to help him into the front. His left foot caught on the door but she didn't notice, and just shoved him harder toward the seat. "Hold it," he yelled before she closed the door on it.

"Thank you," Brenda said to Vanessa, "for rescuing my husband." *See,* she was thinking, *witness the kindness of strangers.*

Safely inside the car, his limbs happily unsevered, he shook the rain from his hair and squeezed the water from his shirt. Vanessa and Brenda caught their breath and Daniel listened to the tapping on the car's roof. Vanessa leaned in toward them. "I heard this might last all weekend."

Brenda groaned. "I certainly hope not."

"You were saying you're a photographer. What kind of photos do you take?" Vanessa asked as Esther tugged on her hair.

"Mostly boring pictures of running shoes lately to pay the bills," Brenda said, but then went on to describe her pet project, the shots she'd been taking of other photographs found in unexpected places. An old Polaroid of an elderly couple in the middle of a field, a family portrait floating on a pond. Secretly Daniel found the project sentimental and verging on saccharine. He preferred her earlier photos of grizzled monks scrounging through garbage in India and emaciated women trying to breast-feed in Ethiopia. These pictures were unflinching, disturbing, and immediate in their impact. "Maybe I'll send you one of my real photos when I get home," she said.

slipped out of the car. She scurried across the parking lot, clutching Esther to her chest.

Daniel turned to Brenda. A strange look had come across her face—shadows ringed her eyes, her lips had dried and cracked in the corners. A red blotchiness had spread across her neck. He began to wonder whether she'd looked this way all day, if he'd only noticed it now, and if he'd in fact caused it.

She helped him out of the car once more, and he squeezed his eyes shut against the rain as he headed over the bumps of the parking lot. Because apparently he wasn't moving fast enough, she stepped behind him and took over. Before long, his feet hit something and Brenda ran to open a door. The next thing he knew he was somewhere dry again, somewhere dim that smelled of fried food.

"Leary's," Brenda said. "We're here." She was completely out of breath. He wheeled toward a table and motioned for her to follow him. "Come here, Bren, you need to sit."

"I'm fine," she coughed.

"You shouldn't run like that," he said. "And you shouldn't be pushing me. I would've made it here eventually."

"I'll be all right," she said, and held the table as she lowered herself onto the chair.

"You'll think we'll ever get there?" he asked.

"Where?"

"The island."

Her breathing began to slow. "Of course we will."

"This day feels like it's lasted a year," he said, glad they were alone now.

"Two years," she said. "Didn't we leave the house before I was pregnant?"

"I think we did," he said, running his hands through his wet hair.

"If you had to draw this day, what would it look like?" she asked. This used to be one of her favorite questions—it was an easy way to access his thoughts.

He closed his eyes and imagined a tornado tossing them through the sky. He, shooting out of his wheelchair, and she, twisting through the air, her hair straight above her. And then something small and curled, something that looked like a baby flying from her and being sucked away and up into the sky. "A tornado," he said. "A monster's arm coming out of the sky. And a bubble saying, 'You think you've had enough?'" In this past year and a half, bad luck often seemed possible at every turn.

"Ugh. There's more to come?"

"No, there can't be," he said. "It's probably just my instinctually pessimistic view of fate."

She half smiled, which was something at least.

They ordered chowder and before long the waitress brought two steaming bowls. The white chowder sat before him, thick like gruel. Daniel didn't have much of an appetite. Technically they'd been in transit for eight long hours, and in that time, they could have flown to Rome.

Brenda pushed her spoon around her bowl, barely eating anything. Her hair, now soaked, had formed a cap on her head and her mascara had blurred beneath her eyes, giving her a gloomy, shell-shocked look. He wondered whether he looked this way too.

"So," she said, stopping her spoon in the center of the bowl.

"So," he said. "You think she was lying?"

"Who?"

"Vanessa."

"About what?"

"Her father. The accident. It sounded pretty over-the-top to me."

"Daniel. That is awful. You can be a very awful person sometimes."

He swallowed and looked at the table. He wanted to tell her that he couldn't help himself. She hated him right then, and she was wondering how she'd reached this point in her life with him. Married, pregnant. But not with his child, and that was the catch, really. The baby wasn't his, and she could certainly leave him, take the baby and go off, knowing that the child was hers and this other person's, this Jonathan White, this gentle but confident man from Milwaukee. Maybe this would make the leaving a little easier. Maybe one day she'd track him down and find that the man looked exactly like the baby. He was in fact closer to Brenda's age, and maybe they had other things in common. Maybe Brenda would even fall in love with him. It was an almost satisfying exercise, Daniel found, imagining a man more patient, more sunny and sociable than he. Someone she could easily make love with. Someone who could drive a car and walk a baby around a room. Daniel didn't have such thoughts with self-pity or anger, really. He experienced a subtle sense of magnanimity in creating a better man for Brenda, and he suspected such phantom people existed in other relationships, the person that fit the other in every way. He thought back to before his accident and tried to remember whether he was at least closer to being this man then. He liked to think that he was.

The waitress reached across the table and gathered their bowls. "You done?" Daniel asked Brenda.

"I'm not hungry," she said. "I'm not feeling so great." She rested her hands on her stomach.

"Neither am I," he said, though of course she'd been referring to her pregnancy.

"It's been asleep for hours," she said. "Hours and hours."

"Lucky baby."

After Daniel had paid the bill, they waited for the rain to subside. They talked about his family, and discussed what Liz might look like pregnant. "She said she's filling out already, right, even though she's only seven weeks? She was sort of, well, big to start with," Brenda said. "She does love to cook."

"How kind."

"Please. You know you're thinking the same thing. And what about me?" she asked.

"Yes?"

"What do I look like pregnant?"

He couldn't come out and say that she looked completely different, almost unrecognizable to him some days. "You look like a mother-in-the-making."

"I look matronly?"

"No, no. You look great. You do, really. Beautiful." She didn't believe him but at least he'd said it. "I love you," he added softly in British.

The rain hadn't slowed any, but Leary's was dense with cigarette smoke and Brenda insisted they wait in their car for the ferry. She also insisted on rushing him back through the rain again, fast, too fast, and he yelled, "Slow down!" but she didn't. "I'm fine if we slow down. I'm already soaked through anyway," he called, but she didn't respond. "Christ," he said once they were inside the car. "You need to slow yourself down. Please, for me."

"Here comes Vanessa," Brenda said, and Daniel saw the woman rushing toward them, Esther still in her arms. Brenda rolled down her window.

"There's a cargo ferry heading over now, and there's room for us," Vanessa said. "You got back just in time."

"Perfect," Brenda said as she rolled back up her window, and quietly, twisting with some sort of cramp, she added, "I suppose I should have taken it easier back there."

"I'm really sorry I was slowing you down," he said, and he'd meant it, but the words sounded sarcastic, almost nasty. He wondered whether he had become incapable of saying anything calming and earnest, anything at all genuinely empathetic. "I'm sorry," he tried again carefully, "I am," and this time it sounded better, a little softer. Maybe the only way they could really communicate now was by putting on voices that came from somewhere else.

They hurried out of the car again, gathered their bags and rushed toward the boat. Brenda pushed him up a narrow gangplank, and in a small enclosed area near the front they joined Vanessa, now sipping a can of soda and bouncing Esther on her lap. He caught Brenda's eye and lifted his mouth into a smile. It was not a sneer, he was sure. It was a genuine smile, although admittedly a little forced and maybe not even his, but at least someone's genuine smile that he hoped communicated he was still there, still very much her husband.

Looking directly at him, Esther released a milky foam from her mouth. The cute-moment-to-vile-moment ratio for a baby was, what, one to eight or so? Maybe Brenda would eventually tire of their baby. And she would go through the motions—change the diapers, nurse, all the rest—like she had with Daniel a year and a half ago, when she was forced to participate in every detail of his disability, to help him stand, make himself a sandwich, figure out his catheter. But maybe a part of her would drift to a place less demanding than motherhood. She wouldn't hear the crying after a minute or two because her mind would have traveled somewhere else. Next door, or across the street, across the globe, anywhere, and Daniel would find himself alone with the baby then, two people full of needs.

He was sure he caught Esther sneering at him as Vanessa wiped her mouth with her shirt. He closed his eyes and tried to imagine a curtain lowering in front of his field of vision. Daniel's mother used to suggest that he visualize a black curtain blocking out all his bad thoughts when he couldn't sleep as a child. When he was five, a rash of kidnappings spread through the neighboring towns and he lived in constant fear of being snatched off the street or from his home or bed. Posted on telephone poles and bulletin boards throughout his town were photos of the children who'd disappeared. He could still remember their names: Megan Clapham, Sarah Vincent, Edward Coombs. Adults walking alone became suspect to him, and soon his teachers, his neighbors, even his single uncle Norman who lived in the city and was unemployed began to seem sinister. And each night before bed, Daniel pleaded with his mother not to leave him alone. "We're just down the hall, Danny, just a few feet away. Nothing is going to happen to you. The windows and doors are locked," she'd say, but she could never fully convince him of his safety. "Think happy thoughts," she said, but this never worked either, and thoughts of playing soccer in a field always turned to thoughts of a man grabbing him and dragging him into a dark forest. One night his mother suggested he picture this forest, and then a black curtain descending in front of it. "Just look at the curtain, nothing else. I'll stay here," she said, "until you fall asleep," and for the first night in weeks the curtain separated him from his fear and allowed him to sleep. It was one of the many things his mother had given him.

—

Ellen and Joe stood in a bookstore watching the rain fire down outside. Jake hadn't been at the ferry to pick them up— no one had. Ellen had sat on a bench near the ticket booth, Babe in his cage beside her, while Joe went to look for Jake, and then the horrible rain had come, and Joe ran back toward her but in slow motion, trying not to slip. Each step was a strained dance, the poor, clumsy man. He said, "I can't find him anywhere," and they rushed up the street to find somewhere drier to wait.

And now they were stuck inside this bookstore that smelled of old coffee and unclean dogs. Joe wandered toward the bookshelves. Discordant music—a cello? viola?—filled the place. Where had Jake been? Ellen closed her eyes and felt herself spin a little. The medicine hadn't done a blessed thing. The world was closing in on her and would press her flat, and in the end no medicine could help that. She thought of Mac-Neil's spacious living room, its high ceiling, its shiny wood floors. She thought of the courtyard in the Gardner, airy and broad, where she would soon go with MacNeil. When she opened her eyes, she instinctively grabbed the hand next to hers. It was large and clammy, and its owner jumped a little. A look of confusion on his face, he was a young man who didn't let go at first. Ellen finally dropped his hand and made her way to a phone booth in the corner of the store. She turned and eyed Joe, now sitting comfortably on a stool and flipping through a book. Why wasn't he looking for her?

A baby wailed, a book slammed to the floor. Ellen pressed her hands to her head and held it for a moment. Perhaps she would just collapse here and now, and that would be the end. Not only would she miss this weekend, but she'd miss the births, the grandchildren, she'd miss everything. She'd miss whatever would happen with MacNeil. She straightened her spine and breathed deeply into her stomach. She was all right, she was just fine and had endless life still in her and would go to the Gardner and walk along the Charles with MacNeil and drive back to his house afterward. Everything would be just fine. Everything would be *wonderful*.

She found Jake's phone number on a slip of paper in her wallet and dialed. She let five, six, seven rings pass, hung up, checked the number and dialed again. Five, six, seven. Perhaps both Jake and Liz had come to pick them up. Perhaps they were now driving around in the rain and looking for them. Ellen hung up and went to Joe. "They're not home."

"Oh?" He didn't know what she was talking about.

"I called Jake's house and no one answered. What do you want to do now?"

He slipped a finger between the pages of the book he'd been reading and lowered it to his lap. "I guess all we can do is wait."

"For what?"

"Maybe they'll find us here. I don't know. Just try to be patient," he said. "Let's wait until the rain stops and then I'll go back out to look for them." He flattened his mouth into a sad smile and held the book above his stomach, clearly unsure whether she'd find it acceptable for him to continue reading. "You want to go buy a book?" he asked.

"No," she said, and rested her head against the stucco wall beside her. She felt the hard little peaks poke her head and catch on her hair. "Not right now."

"All right," he said. He lifted the book an inch.

Go ahead, I'll entertain myself in this crowded, uncomfortable place, she could have said. Predictably, he reached down to check on Babe.

"He's fine," she said.

Joe looked at her as if to say, *What, now you're going to take this away from me? Without Babe and my books, what is there?*

There's me, she might say. *The person directly in front of you whom you no longer see.* She felt wounded and childish, worn so thin as to be translucent. "Go ahead, read."

He froze.

"Go on ahead," she said, and he lifted the book to his face. Just as she turned to walk away, she heard him say, "They'll show up eventually. We'll find them."

She'd been too hard on him. He was just trying to calm her.

And what if in fact Jake never came? She pictured herself and Joe curled up on the floor of this bookstore later that night, trying to sleep, Babe beside them, the thin green rug as hard as cement beneath her hip. She imagined slipping off to sleep and never waking, and this, this irrelevant little store being the last place on earth she'd lay eyes on. Her mind went to absurd places.

She left Joe and wandered past shelves of novels and poetry, memoirs and biographies and spied a tiny Isabella Gardner—the Zorn painting, it was—on the spine of a book. Ellen immediately slid it toward her. It was not a biography, rather a book of the Gardner's art, and why was such a thing necessary here, in a bookstore on an island in Maine? It was some sort of sign, she thought, some sort of lovely sign— perhaps a nod to her plan. The book heavy in her hands, she flipped to the first painting, Sargent's *El Jaleo*. The Gypsy woman danced with her head thrown back, the men on chairs behind her playing guitars as other women watched and laughed. It was the first painting to be seen on entering the museum, and it hung at the end of a hallway, shrouded in small lights, amid Egyptian wood carvings, Turkish tile and the Moorish arch supported by the Italian columns. Sargent had loved Gypsy music, dance and costumes, and the wide horizontal painting was meant to simulate their stage spaces. He'd later sketched, in hard, fast lines, a Spanish woman dancing, her arms vamping, her eyes closed. He'd done a series that he'd included in an album for Isabella.

Ellen felt refreshed, like she were returning from a better place, as she walked back to Joe. "You're still here?" she said to him. "You haven't moved an inch."

He slowly lifted his eyes to her, puzzled.

"Hello, husband."

"Hi, love. What's that?" he asked, nodding at the large book in her hands.

"Art," she said.

"Ah." He resumed his reading. He had no idea what significance was held within the pages in her hands.

Across the room a boy hollered and a door slammed. Ellen looked around the place and saw next to a table, someone, yes, her daughter it was, Hilary, whom she hadn't seen in four years, and Ellen thought at first she was mistaken, for this girl was quite thick around the middle, and had tousled, shoulder-length black hair rather than the short blond hair she'd had before. It couldn't have been her, though the resemblance in the face was uncanny and there was that blessed tattoo of ivy around her wrist and as Ellen stepped closer she saw the nose ring. "Hilary!" Ellen said, and rushed toward her daughter. "Hilary! You're here!"

The girl turned and, yes, it was definitely Hilary, and her face brightened. "Mom."

Ellen went to hug her—she was so large and soft in her arms that Ellen had to restrain herself from squeezing too hard. "Oh, is it good to see you! You look so healthy, just look at you!" And Hilary did, though when she looked closer Ellen saw that fatigue shadowed the rims of her eyes and that she had put on a good deal of weight.

"What are you doing here? Where is everyone?" Hilary asked. "I went to Jake's house and no one was there." And Ellen explained the crowded ferry, all the screaming children and irritable parents, the delay, their finally reaching the island, Joe looking for Jake everywhere, the rain, their coming here to this bookstore, and where on earth were Jake and Liz? As she spoke, Hilary rubbed her fingers together the way she had as a girl when she was growing impatient. The gesture always looked to Ellen as if her daughter were trying to start a fire with her fingers. But Hilary was not a young girl anymore. She was a woman. An incredibly large woman. Ellen suddenly couldn't take her eyes off her daughter's stomach.

"So, what do you think?" Hilary finally said.

"Is that what I'm guessing it is?" Ellen swallowed, and swallowed again.

Hilary nodded.

Ellen looked around for a man. Had Hilary gotten married? But of course she hadn't—she would have told them that, at least. Or would she have?

"I think it's probably obvious to these other people. You don't need to worry about them." She gestured behind her.

"I wasn't—I just—"

"I'm due in three months. And since I'm sure you're wondering, no, there's no father. Well, of course there is biologically, but he's not going to be a part of things. I'm going to raise the baby on my own."

Ellen seemed to lose her ability to speak or even think coherently. *Pregnant.* She had collided with a brick wall, and *no father*; now she had barreled into another. "Dad is over there," she finally managed after a moment. "Come say hello."

"Congratulations, this is wonderful news! I'm so happy for you!" Hilary said in a mock chirp as she followed Ellen. "How has your pregnancy been? Is there anything you need from us? I know you're probably nervous about doing this on your own, but everything will work out just fine. And if you need help, your dad and I will be there for you."

"Oh, Hilary, stop it, would you? I'm just digesting it all. You could have told us. You could have prepared us, for God's sake."

Hilary sulked as they approached Joe. "He brought the turtle?"

"Babe, remember? His name is Babe."

Joe looked up and his eyes lit.

"Hi there," Hilary said.

"You're pregnant?" he almost yelled.

"Joe!" Ellen said. But why not just come right out with it?

"It's all right, Mom," Hilary said, and went to hug her

father. She explained what she'd just explained to Ellen and he reacted with unmitigated pleasure (although Ellen swore she caught a flash of concern when Hilary explained the single parent part). A feeling of sickness settled over Ellen as she thought of her daughter raising a child all on her own. And with what money? Did she still have that temp job, even?

Joe and Hilary chatted casually and it seemed for a moment to Ellen as if she'd seen her daughter several times over the past four years, as if they spoke regularly, not only a few times a year. It seemed as if Hilary didn't live across the country and switch jobs every couple of months and keep the rest of her life a mystery. Ellen tried to think of a way to ask who the father of the baby was, but came up empty.

"I'm going to try Jake again," she finally said, and headed back to the phone. Once more she considered calling MacNeil (she would tell him about Hilary, and she would tell him that they were stranded in this bookstore and that her son was missing). But he was not at home, she reminded herself. He was in San Francisco visiting his daughter, residing in the large part of his life that had nothing to do with Ellen. Perhaps she should call his machine just to hear his voice. Like a schoolgirl, she was. Like a ridiculous girl, and when she reached the phone, she picked up the receiver and dialed Jake's number again. Still there was no answer. Where was he? This sort of thing was uncharacteristic of him, and Ellen wondered if she'd gotten the date wrong, but no, of course not, it was Joe's birthday on Sunday and anyway Hilary was here. The rain pounded outside, hadn't slowed down a bit, and Ellen worried (and why hadn't she thought of this before?) that something might have happened to Jake. Perhaps he'd been driving to the ferry and his car had hydroplaned and skidded off the road. Perhaps he and Liz were lying beneath a pile of metal in a ditch. She rushed to Joe and Hilary and said, "Do you think something terrible has happened to them?"

Joe said, "They probably just got the time wrong or something. They'll find us. Or we'll find them."

Hilary rubbed her fingers together.

Babe clicked about in his cage.

"Here, sit," Joe said, and stood to offer Ellen his stool. She took it and tried to quiet her mind again. She asked Hilary the innocuous questions she obviously wanted to hear: how was she feeling, did she have any morning sickness, any unusual symptoms, any trouble sleeping? Each question was an attempt to avoid the real one that itched at her more and more—*Who exactly was it that impregnated you, dear?* The closest Ellen came was, in a moment of boldness, asking Hilary why he, this mysterious man, wouldn't be involved, and Hilary just shrugged and said, "Because he wouldn't be the right person."

"Did he hurt you?"

"No, no."

There had to be a reason Hilary wouldn't reveal the identity of the father. Perhaps he was in prison. Ellen shuddered. But was this even a logistical possibility? Prison did seem extreme, even for Hilary. Maybe he was married. *Married.* As Hilary stretched her back and thrust out her belly, she began to assume a dangerous air, tough and wild and willful. It gave Ellen a shiver. Her daughter was someone's mistress.

Ellen remembered the tiny Hilary—and she was tiny as a child, rail thin with long brown braids and freckles. Her lips had always chapped, and she suffered perpetual rashes, and later eczema on her elbows and knees. Ellen tried to visualize this innocent, adorable girl standing next to the adult Hilary, who was now fanning through a guidebook to the Maine islands. A little Hilary, pouting and chewing her thumbnails, rubbing her fingertips together beside her mother, secretly too insecure to join the other children. Was it insecurity that had driven her to a married man? Was she afraid to let herself be loved by a more available candidate? Perhaps she didn't think she was worthy. Perhaps the tiny Hilary had needed to be drawn out and nurtured more, and shown that she deserved good, old-fashioned love. After all, she had a lot to offer—she could be witty and adventurous. When she cared about some-one (Daniel came to mind), she'd move the world for that per-son. She had the most beautiful hazel eyes. Whatever would have drawn her to a married man?

Ellen thought of the Gardner, where the other week she and MacNeil had made their way through each room—past the Little Salon, beneath the vaulted ceilings of the Tapestry Room, stopping at every piece of art: the Venetian mirrors, the Belgian tapestries depicting the lives of Abraham and Cyrus the Great, the candelabra, the Jacobean dresser. Every item in Isabella's house was art. Soon they found themselves alone in the Dutch Room, alone save a portly bald guard holding his hands firmly across his girth. He nodded when they came in but held his gaze just above their heads. She and MacNeil stood side by side, and for the first time she thought about what it might be like to kiss him. What if they had been alone? Would MacNeil have moved closer to her? Might something have happened between them? The room was cold and drafty and Ellen wondered if it had felt this way when Isabella had lived here. Ellen imagined she'd kept the place comfortable, for what was the point of collecting so much beauty without presenting it in a comfortable environment? A voice behind her said, "That's where the Rembrandts were," and she realized she was standing between two empty frames, a small plaque with the artist's name beneath one of them. She remembered hearing about the theft years earlier. "It was an absolute tragedy," MacNeil said, and she was glad for his words, for she was sure they would have sounded over-wrought coming from her. The guard explained why the frames were kept empty—in her will, Isabella had insisted that every item in the house, every piece of art and furniture, every rug and table and frame remain exactly as it had been before she died. The guard spoke without feeling about the dates of the theft and the few breaks in the case since then— perhaps just to keep himself awake on this slow day—and his nonchalant manner made her think of Joe. She shuffled beneath her skin and considered hurrying out of the Dutch Room and back down the flight of stairs to the courtyard, where the light was brighter and the air warmer.

She had not transgressed. She reminded herself: she had never transgressed.

"You've chosen the hospital?" she asked Hilary. "You've got a good doctor?"

"No, Mom, I'm going to squat in the woods alone and have the baby there."

"It's been done before," Ellen said, glancing around to make sure no one was listening. "When is the due date?"

"November second. A Tuesday."

"Election Day!" Ellen smiled and leaned forward to push a long strand of hair out of her daughter's eyes. "A day of deci-sion," she heard herself say, then instantly regretted it.

Hilary scoffed. "You make it sound almost biblical. I'll be

having a baby, Mom, not standing in front of the Pearly Gates. At least I hope not."

"I'm just saying it's an interesting date." Ellen wanted to ask whether the father would be there for her, for the birth. Was he at all there for her during the pregnancy? She'd said he wouldn't be a factor in the child's life, but was he at least present for Hilary now? Had he ever been? Ellen hoped he had. She hoped that he'd loved Hilary, that he'd treated her well and that her choice to have the baby on her own was in fact her own, and not his.

—

Jake and Liz had left the house late thanks to him and all of his drama, and as they'd pulled onto Main Street, they'd found themselves behind a car crawling up the street. "Come on, COME ON," he moaned.

"We'll get there," Liz said. "Calm down."

"It looks like it's about to pour. I don't want them to have to wait around for us in the rain."

"There's that shelter near the landing. They'll be fine," she said, and set her hand on her stomach, then shifted in her seat.

He looked over at her. "Is everything all right? How are you feeling?"

"Okay."

"You sure?"

"Yes, Jake, I'm fine," she snapped.

He stepped on the gas and pulled up just behind the car in front of them.

"I won't be, though, if you ram into that guy. Slow the hell down."

"ALL RIGHT," he yelled, and took his foot off the accelerator. He let the car slow, and when they reached a small hill, it nearly stopped. He eased his foot onto the gas again. He'd overreacted yet again—he supposed he was still a little on edge after this afternoon. But he'd been reading too much into what was undoubtedly nothing. She knew that people masturbated—for all he knew, she'd probably walked in on similar scenes with her parents.

When they reached the ferry, no one was waiting at the shelter. And then a moment later the rain came and it was torrential. His mind raced. Once he found his parents, what could he give as an excuse for being so late? And where the hell *were* his parents anyway? Where should he even begin to look?

"We should just go home. They have the address, don't they? They can make their way there," Liz said.

"I'm not sure I gave it to them," Jake admitted. "I told them I'd pick them up. Let's drive around a little and see if we can track them down."

His parents were probably stumbling through the rain, searching for him. Maybe they were looking in the shops, carrying their many bags (they always overpacked, ridiculously so), their shoulders bowing with the weight. *We'll meet up with him eventually, Ell,* his father would say, always the anti-worrier. *It's not the end of the world that Jake isn't here yet.* And his mother would try to calm herself by saying, *Of course we will get there, and in the meantime, let's enjoy the shops here—we haven't been here in so long. Let's look in here, at the Seafarer's Gallery.*

This isn't art, she'd say once they'd entered the small general-store-turned-gallery, *but paintings of scenes that have been painted a hundred times.* Ships, waves, lighthouses, moonscapes, sunsets. *There are far better artists living here.* She'd scoff at the silly scenes and raise her nose to them, but his father would warm to them—*for,* he'd say, *wasn't a sunset or a moon-scape always beautiful? And when we see these things in person, aren't we struck, so why can't I be struck by the same thing on a can-vas? Because,* his mother would say, *because it's fake, it's a fabri-cation of a million other fabrications, and that does not make art.* Jake agreed that this might not in fact be art but could never account for the quiet comfort within whenever he saw similar paintings in his office or at the doctor's.

They drove past a couple of shaved plots of land where new houses were being built. Enormous new summer homes had begun to sprout up across the island, and Jake watched the growth with secret pleasure. Their summer house, which they'd bought for a bargain, was worth something now. Not that he wanted to sell it necessarily, but it was now worth an awful lot more than what they'd paid for it.

"They'll sink the island with those behemoths," Liz said.

"They might. Ours isn't exactly small, you know."

"I guess not, but it's not as big as those. I never thought I'd be the sort of person to own a summer home," she said. "Did you?"

"Not really, I guess. I mean, I used to hope for certain things. My mom and I used to play this game—what would you do with a million dollars."

"And now you have so many millions."

"Mm." He paused. "It's not a *bad* thing."

"No, of course it's not. It's just sort of weird. Sometimes it hits me as really strange."

"Me too," Jake said. "But good strange, you know?"

Liz reached over and set her palm against his cheek.

"You know?" he repeated.

"Sure," she said. She suggested they park on Main Street and check to see whether his family was in one of the stores there, and he agreed. He parked beside the post office, and they pulled their hoods over their heads as they hurried along the sidewalk. At one point, Liz stopped, opened her raincoat and stood, her chest to the sky. The rain pounded her face and hair. "It feels wonderful," she said, and Jake opened his jacket too. "Doesn't it feel great?" she said. Her blue T-shirt clung to her breasts and he could see the small peaks of her nipples.

"It does," he said, licking the drops from his lips, though he was in fact growing chilly, his shirt soggy. He wanted it to feel great, though. He wanted to experience joy in being soaked to the core. "And like it or not, you look sexy, my dear." He couldn't help himself.

Liz leaned back to wring out her hair. "Onward?"

"Onward," he said. He reached his arm around her and massaged her wet shoulders as they walked toward town, stumbling through the puddles and every now and then bumping hips.

Jake led Liz into a convenience store where gray-faced men in fishing clothes stood huddled in the corner, smoking. Jake and Liz then checked the gallery and the ice cream shop, but his family was nowhere to be found, and Jake was about to suggest they run back to the car when Liz cried, "They're in here!" and tugged him inside Books & Beans.

His mother's eyes were on him, wild and happy and anxious all at the same time. "Thank God," she practically shouted.

Joe stood beside her, and Hilary behind the two of them.

Jake hugged his mother and father, and as they stepped out of the way and Hilary moved forward, Jake saw that she'd put on some weight. Even her face and her hair seemed bigger.

"Look at you," he managed. He tried to make eye contact with Liz and see if she noticed the same things, but she was busy talking to Ellen.

"Hello," his sister answered. A man tried to squeeze past her, but she blocked most of the aisle. He gave up and headed toward another aisle. Jake glanced down at her stomach, which was quite protrusive. It couldn't be. He stopped breathing for a second.

"You have a good trip here?" he mumbled.

"What do you think?" she asked, rubbing her belly. She looked at him. "I'm pregnant—that's what this is, in case you were wondering. I haven't just gotten fat."

"Pregnant?" It didn't make sense. Did she suddenly have a husband?

"Pregnant. I'm due in three months."

"Wow, I can't really—I mean, how did that happen?"

"Sex, Jake. You know, a penis, a vagina. They fit together pretty well."

He glanced around them, horrified that other people might have heard her.

"Everyone has one or the other. I don't think they'd be surprised to hear about what these things can do."

"Christ, would you keep it down?"

She shrugged. "Anyway, so, yes, I'm pregnant, and just to get it out of the way, I'll be raising the kid on my own. The father won't be involved. It was sort of a mistake but I'm happy about it for the most part now."

"Oh," he said dumbly, his throat tight. "Well, congratulations, I guess." How careless she'd been, he thought, how terrifically, ridiculously careless to allow herself to get pregnant without even being in a relationship. It was willful and irresponsible and promiscuous and it had taken him and Liz over five grueling years to conceive.

Joe was glancing over at them. He held a book against his chest as if it were armor. Beside him on the floor was a cage. He'd brought his turtle. He'd actually brought Babe. Whatever for? Was this the beginning of senility? "Let's get out of here," Jake said, and with the other hand scooped up Babe's cage.

"Don't ask," his mother whispered, gesturing toward the cage.

"I won't," Jake said, but his thoughts quickly returned to his sister. *Hilary pregnant*. The idea was incomprehensible, and as they walked closer to their car, Jake worried about Liz—was she upset about it? Could she handle seeing his little sister knocked up (and this seemed a more appropriate term for the situation than "pregnant") after all they'd had to go through? He reached the car before anyone else did, and left Babe's cage on the ground in the rain as he fished around in his pocket for his keys. His father was on him, snatching up the cage and mumbling about the rain and Jake's car—Why did he need such a big car? Why did anyone?

On the way home, he found himself stuck behind yet another slow car. He hydroplaned for a second, swerved toward a tree, then back onto the road, but no one seemed to notice. Liz chattered with his mother, Hilary was knocked up and single and spoiled, his father whispered to her eagerly in a way he never did with Jake, his mother told him to slow down before her heart stopped, which wouldn't be unheard of because she wasn't young, there was heart disease in her family, and then what would happen? He slowed his own breathing, *one, two*, and lifted his foot from the gas pedal.

Carrying everyone's bags into the house was a production. Jake rushed to get the door, and Hilary thrust her bags at him when he returned to the car to help. Joe inched his way forward, holding Babe in his cage with both hands as if it were a wedding cake. The man had terrible night vision, and once Jake had deposited Hilary's bags inside, he ran back outside and snatched the cage from his father.

"Careful there," Joe said.

"I got it, Dad."

"Just be careful, Jake."

"He's fine, Joe," Ellen barked behind them, and hurried past, carrying too many bags.

Once inside, Liz hurried around, turning on lights and taking their coats, offering them all towels and dry clothes. Hilary dropped her bags with a thud on the living room floor and looked around the house. Jake watched her register the original photographs, the coffee table they'd commissioned from a woodworker in Vermont, the sofas Liz had hired a Portland furniture maker to design. He felt both proud and self-conscious.

Joe flopped down on a sofa and kicked off his muddy shoes. Jake rushed toward him and grabbed the shoes before the mud seeped into the new rug.

"Anyone like a drink?" Liz said from behind Jake, and though he knew she was really addressing the others, he said yes, "a beer, please."

Ellen stretched her arms, looked around and said, "What a lovely place, Jake. I can't believe it was ever run-down."

"We had it gutted," he said. "And we pretty much started from scratch. Liz was the mastermind behind it all."

"I wish we could've seen it before," his father said.

"You wouldn't believe how much it's changed."

Liz appeared, handed him a beer and smiled politely. "It was a ton of work, but I think it was worth it in the end."

Ellen looked around approvingly. "Indeed." She leaned forward and ran her fingers across the wood floor. "These floors are beautiful. What is this, oak?"

"Cherry," said Jake.

"Well, that must have set you back," said Joe. "Is it tough to maintain?"

"Not at all. It's no different from any other hardwood, really."

Joe mumbled something and Ellen said, "Daniel's new house has hardwoods too, but they haven't got any rugs yet, and the place looks a little bare, to tell the truth. These are gorgeous rugs you've got." She slowly knelt to pat the Persian carpet beneath the coffee table and her expression changed. "No one's heard from him?" she asked.

"Not since earlier," Liz said.

"I do hope he's okay right now."

"I do too," Jake said, aware that her concern extended to more than just this moment. After all, his did too. At the strangest moments—at a meeting or on the tennis court—he found himself thinking about his brother. What was he doing right then? Was he able to swim anymore, to lift weights? What sort of exercise was he able to do? Daniel never talked to him much about the particulars of his new life, not that they talked that frequently anyway. But when Jake did call once a month, he didn't know what to say about the matter. Or how to say it.

He had expressed as much sympathy as he could just after the accident and tried to offer everything he had—his time (he could run errands if need be), money, recommendations of the best doctors he knew. But Daniel shrank into a stone back then, and chafed at every suggestion Jake made. Daniel wasn't used to being a person in this position—someone eliciting pity, someone so dependent on others. Each night in the weeks following the accident, Jake found himself recounting to Liz every physical thing his brother used to love to do when they were young—running track, swimming, hiking, wrestling with him in his bedroom, in the swimming pool, beating the hell out of him in their back yard—as if ridding himself of something (the old Daniel?), and then drifting off to a thick, dreamless sleep. Liz knew that Jake and Daniel had never been particularly close. Jake had annoyed his brother in myriad ways. Jake told her that Daniel loved animals and had constantly begged his parents for a dog. The bigger the better, he'd said. But Jake was allergic to dogs, cats, and the twittering of his father's birds had kept him awake at night, so after the parakeet Napoleon died, the house remained petless until they'd all left for college, when his father got Babe.

After the long months that followed the accident, Jake had been glad to hear that Brenda was pregnant and that something good had happened to them, though Jake had mixed feelings about the fact of the donor. Despite everything, at least Liz was carrying his biological children. Of course Daniel and Brenda didn't have many choices in the end, but still. What if the baby didn't look like either of them? What if the donor had a history of mental illness and hadn't informed the doctors? What if the man suddenly turned up and demanded to be a part of the baby's life?

Jake took a long sip of beer and looked around his living room and down at the cherry floor, at his pregnant wife leaning against the wall and out the window at the stormy Atlantic, and grew appreciative that he had what he had, that he'd never gotten into a horrible accident like his brother, that he and Liz hadn't had to resort to a sperm donor, that he had, in fact, a spouse he loved and a beautiful house here and another in Portland. A terrific job, good friends.

Why did it sometimes feel like a mirage? Why did it often feel as if he'd wake up one morning and find that everything—his houses, his job, Liz, especially Liz—had disappeared? He glanced over at his father, now fidgeting with the door of Babe's cage, and wondered if the man ever had the similar sensation. Was Joe secure with what he had? And was he proud of his kids and his life—had that been enough for him? Jake thought that it probably had.

—

Hilary rubbed her fingers together. She thought back to when Alex had pulled the car in front of the bookstore, when she'd leaned toward him and kissed him slowly just beside his lips. He'd turned and pressed his mouth firmly against hers. He held her face in his hands and she found she'd missed being touched this way. George was much softer. Gentler, and very innocuous.

"Well," Alex said as he backed away.

"This was a great tour."

"I'll be working this weekend," he said. "You could come by."

She gathered her bag, careful not to answer him. She wouldn't see him again. There would be no reason. Rita

pointed her wet nose near her face, and Hilary squirmed
away. "'Bye, now," she said, and shoved the door closed.

There should have been a grander ending, she decided
now as she shuffled around, the baby turning inside her.
Something more profound should have happened between
them, though she couldn't say precisely what. The moment
had seemed so freighted, like she'd been saying goodbye to
more than just one man.

Her mother was going on about how she couldn't wait to
see the petite Brenda pregnant. "How can a baby even fit
inside her?" Ellen's comments seemed to mask some kind of
worry.

Next to Hilary, her father rested his arms over the cage.
Though she was surprised to see the turtle at first, Hilary supposed she was glad Babe was here. Her father without his pet
was a sad sight, a lonely boy bored and fidgety among adults.
She'd missed Joe these past years. He was never entirely himself on the phone—he spoke quietly and a little formally, asking her predictable questions about her car and her bills, and
whenever she tried to elicit more from him, was he happy, was
he doing things that made him happy now that he was
retired, he seemed not to understand that she was trying to
gather a stronger sense of his well-being. He always replied
with one-word answers—*Yes. Sure. Fine.* He tended to fade
into the background of the family, and no one paid him
enough attention. Especially not her mother, who demanded
his constant focus, but what she didn't realize was that he was
always, in fact, paying close attention to her and to them all in
his own way. When Hilary was a child, he'd wake her each
morning and ask her to tell him about her dreams. Every single morning, he'd say, "Where have you come back from?"

and she'd tell him, if she remembered. If not, she'd make up a story about someplace she wanted to visit—California, China, the moon. He'd take it all in, listening intently, as if hidden in her dreams were clues to what she really wanted in life and maybe what he might be able to give her someday. That was how he operated—he listened. He watched. He absorbed the undercurrents that guided their conversations. Then he went into the next room to take care of his turtle and allowed people time and space alone. Her mother, though, had never been satisfied with this sort of understated attention.

Hilary squeezed his arm. "I missed you," she whispered, and he smiled and said, "Me too."

Liz showed Hilary to a small pink room at the end of a hallway. In the corner sat a single bed dressed in a frilly rose-colored coverlet and piles of lacy white pillows, like a little girl in her Sunday best. "This is you," Liz said. "Towels are over there," and Hilary noticed a stack of pink towels on the night-stand with small white fish embroidered along the seams.

"How're you feeling? Are you having any morning sickness? I left work early every day for about eight weeks straight. I considered downing a case of Pepto-Bismol at one point."

"I've been constantly exhausted, and I've had some nausea." Liz straightened a gauzy pink curtain beside her. "But I'm happy to have it all, since, you know, it took us a while."

"Of course." Hilary searched for something more to say. Was she supposed to apologize for being pregnant? They'd never spent much time together—Hilary didn't have a sense of what Liz would want to hear right now. "You must be relieved."

"In a sense. What about you? Are you nervous for the baby?"

"A little."

Liz opened her mouth, closed it, then opened it again. "Will he, the guy, help out?"

Hilary was surprised by Liz's boldness. "No, not since he doesn't know about it."

"Really?"

"Really," Hilary said, wondering whether she should've said so much. "You might not want to tell Jake. He'll disown me. Actually, why not, go ahead. It's probably only a matter of time before he does anyway."

"Come on, he's not that bad."

"Oh, but he is. Did he ever tell you about the time he caught me breaking into our parents' liquor cabinet? Yes, I was thirteen, and yes, it was the middle of the day, and yes, my boyfriend at the time was five years older and waiting for me in my bedroom, but Jake, who'd gotten home early from school, lectured me for about two hours on alcoholism and statutory rape. He scared the living hell out of me. Then he made me go to my father that night and tell him everything, and when Dad tried to hide a smile at first, Jake screamed at him that he was a terrible father and that his daughter would probably end up dead on the street one day."

"You're exaggerating."

"I'm not!"

"I know he means well."

Hilary looked at Liz, and they both smiled.

"Okay, maybe not," Liz said, "but what's he going to do,

make you call the guy who got you pregnant and tell him about it? Who cares what Jake thinks anyway? It's not his life."

"True."

"So who is he, this guy?"

Hilary walked to the bed and sat down. She looked around at the room, crowded now with her bag and one of her mother's in addition to the bed and dresser, the large hamper, an overstuffed pink chair. "He's a musician," she said. She thought of Bill David, of Beatle and Jackie. Then of George and Camille. "And a carpenter. His name is George David."

"How come you two aren't together, you know, together together? How come you don't want to tell him?"

"I guess because, I don't know, I guess because I don't really want to marry him."

"Oh," Liz said. "Well, that makes sense. I'm sorry to be so nosy. I shouldn't pry this much. I promise I won't ask anything else."

But Hilary almost admired her sister-in-law for having the courage to be so direct. "I'll think of some equally probing questions for you and ask them when you least expect it."

"Deal." There was a shuffling in the hallway, and Liz turned to leave. "Make yourself at home, Hil. If you need anything, just ask or help yourself."

In a moment, Hilary overheard her and Ellen talking in the hallway about the island (people were buying up all the land) and the rain (whenever would it stop?) and the joys and trials of pregnancy. "You'll be wonderful parents," Ellen told Liz.

"I don't know."

"It's easy to imagine this house teeming with children. And you're a great cook and Jake is the biggest worrywart in the world," she rattled on. "Really, you two will be the best parents."

Hilary wished Daniel would hurry up and arrive so she could tell him what their mother had just said. They could discuss Jake's extravagant house that looked as if the entire thing had been delivered, furnished, from a catalog. She could tell Daniel about Liz's surprising candor and ask him about their father's happiness—what did it mean that he'd needed to bring Babe this weekend? She wondered what Daniel would have to say about it all.

She hadn't seen him since a few months after his accident, when she'd flown East. She'd taken the red-eye and arrived first thing Saturday morning, and Brenda picked her up at the airport and drove her right to the hospital. Daniel lay there in bed, a little thinner than when she had seen him last at their grandmother's funeral. His legs remained, of course, perfectly still beneath the sheets, and Hilary tried to ignore the nervous flutter in her chest when she first saw him. When Brenda left her and Daniel alone to go drop off some film at the lab, Hilary closed the door to his room, pulled a bottle of vodka from her backpack, and she and Daniel took swigs until they found themselves at once laughing and crying about Hilary's then-boyfriend, an undergraduate at Berkeley who'd serenaded her the night before with his mandolin.

Hilary couldn't wait to see her brother again.

5

Pronouncements on
Motherhood

The water was choppy and the ride bumpy. Brenda and Vanessa chatted the entire way about the wonders that were Freeman Corcoran and Maine and having a baby (Daniel surmised that the baby's father had been some sort of one-night stand). Vanessa said that she actually loved raising Esther on her own, and Brenda asked all sorts of questions: "Don't you ever just want someone else to change her diapers? Do you feel closer to her, do you suppose, being her only parent?"

"You know, I do. We have our own little world and our own language. I'm the only one who understands what it means when she cries a certain way or when she sticks her thumb in her ear. Freeman tries to translate, but he always thinks she's hungry. I'm sorry, but only the mom knows the nuances. I'm sure of it. I'm the only one who can make her stop crying right away." She looked at Daniel's shoes. "You love them like nothing else. It's the most bottomless love—you'll see."

Brenda gazed at Esther as Vanessa spoke. Daniel felt the steady tumble of the water beneath them. His stomach began to lurch, and then settled. He glanced up at Vanessa—at her sharp nose, her square jaw, her muscular arms. She was both motherly and fatherly. Though he couldn't remember being as young as Esther, he did remember the sensation that his mother was the primary thing surrounding him, keeping him safe and whole, a sort of protective balloon. As he grew up and when he left for college and even during grad school, he was to some degree still contained and protected by this sensation that had become a part of his consciousness until—until when? Until the accident, he supposed.

He reached over and took his wife's small hand. He felt calmer than he had all day, and he told himself to enjoy this quiet inside. He could have, after all, gotten rankled by Vanessa's pronouncements on motherhood. He easily could have grown testy about Brenda's pointed questions.

The ferry slowed, turned, pulled backward into the slip and finally jerked to a stop. They would soon be free to move forward with the day now, just Daniel and his wife, and as the people around them gathered by the door and swayed on their feet, waiting for the gangplank to be set up, as they inched forward and he pushed himself down the gangplank, his wheels brushing the wooden rails, Brenda behind him, carrying their bags that knocked against his back, and as they headed out into the rain yet again, it was as if nothing at all had wedged between them. They were headed to see his family, and he was ready now, and she was there, his wife of almost a decade, behind him and all was well again.

Beneath a small shelter overlooking a street crowded with stores, Brenda and Vanessa exchanged phone numbers and hugged goodbye. Daniel watched Vanessa squeeze Esther to her chest, hurry across the street through the rain and disappear into a car. He reached in his pocket for Jake's phone number. "See a phone?" he asked.

"There's one." She pointed across the street to a small group of people standing beneath umbrellas in front of a phone booth. He rushed down the sidewalk, and she stepped behind him yet again to push him faster (had she already forgotten how this had tired her out before?), bouncing him over the cracked pavement, off the curb and onto the street. At one point, she slowed just before a broad puddle. People ran past them, pulling their hoods over their heads. "Bren, I've got it." He set his hands on his wheels, but she said nothing. She quit pushing him and just stood there a moment. Stopped cars hummed beside them, and after another moment she followed him. Once they'd reached the tall curb of the sidewalk, she stopped again and leaned her face toward his. "It's been too long since the baby moved," she yelled into his ear.

"How long?" Daniel curled his hands above his forehead against the rain. He should've brought his raincoat. He was sure he'd brought his umbrella, but where was it now? "Listen, do we need to be discussing this out here?"

"Something's wrong, Dan. My belly and my back are cramping," she said. The rain continued, relentless, and seemed to stretch the following minutes into hours. Vanessa reappeared, Esther still in her arms, and when Brenda told her that she thought she needed to go to a hospital, Daniel said she was overreacting—surely she only needed something to eat or drink, or maybe just to rest for a while. But she insisted, and Vanessa herded them down the street a little ways and into the back seat of a rusty car, then helped Daniel into the front. She struggled to get the wheelchair into the trunk as he held Esther on his lap. She wailed and squirmed and kicked in his arms. Daniel turned to see Brenda clutching her stomach and staring at her shoes. "I don't know what's happening," she said to the floor of the car, and then Vanessa slid into the driver's seat and drove them to a clinic, a small, squat building only a few minutes away.

In a waiting room near the emergency department, he and Vanessa and Esther watched a doctor hold Brenda's arm and rub her lower back as he led her down a hallway. He hadn't seemed to notice that she'd come here with anyone else—he'd looked right past Daniel and Vanessa at first. She should have slowed down—he'd told her twice earlier to slow down and stop rushing. So what if they got a little wet? Anyway, this was surely some kind of stress or exhaustion, and he expected the doctor to give her a glass of water, tell her to relax and send them off. Esther began to wail again and Daniel said, "I can handle it from here. You should just go home."

"I'll stay. I don't mind," she said, shifting the baby on her hip. She ran her fingers through Esther's thin hair. "I want to make sure everything is all right."

They remained beside each other, neither saying any more. The waiting room was long and narrow with several orange plastic chairs and a pile of old toys in the corner: a Raggedy Ann doll missing an eye, a jack-in-the-box with a rusty spring sticking out of it, other broken toys that looked as if they were patiently awaiting a doctor. Daniel heard a high-pitched beeping somewhere, but on the whole, it was quiet. Much quieter than a hospital or clinic should be. He tried to think of something to say to Vanessa. He drew her in his head—a thin, short woman made up of lines, holding a big, round baby. Her arms in a circle around Esther. The baby began to cry again, and Vanessa said, "She's just tired."

"You should really go home. If you'd like, I'll call you later and let you know that everything's all right. Brenda has your number."

Vanessa reluctantly agreed. "Promise you'll call me. I'll be waiting to hear from you," she said, and he agreed. She leaned down to give him a stiff pat on the back, and headed off. Daniel found himself relieved to be alone.

A short doctor with a gray mustache eventually appeared and Daniel hurried over to him. "I'm Dr. Waller, the OB on call," the man said, and one half of his mouth smiled nervously. He explained that Brenda had begun to bleed heavily, and that an ultrasound had been done, and unfortunately it appeared that intrauterine demise had occurred.

"She's still alive?" Daniel blurted, and Dr. Waller looked at him sideways. "Yes, yes, but because the bleeding hasn't stopped, and because she's medically unstable right now, though most likely she'll be fine in the end, we'll have to perform a D and C—a dilatation and curettage—to remove the tissue,"

"Tissue?"

"Yes, the tissue from the fetus."

"The baby."

"Yes, the fetus," Dr. Waller said in a deliberately soft voice, and Daniel asked, "Is the tissue, the fetus, going to be okay?"

only then acknowledging the weight forming at the bottom of his throat. "I think I see."

"I'm so sorry." Dr. Waller explained the operation, and that Brenda would soon be anesthetized, but the whole thing wouldn't take too long.

"Okay." The weight rose in Daniel's throat.

"If you need anything, just ask one of the nurses. Oh, and Mr. Miller, chances are fairly good that Brenda will be able to conceive again after this. Some people, that's their first question." Daniel looked up at the man's mustache, which poked at his lower lip. "I'll come find you after the D and C, okay? She's going to be just fine," the doctor said, and patted the back of Daniel's chair. He hurried back down the hallway.

Daniel looked over at the one-eyed Raggedy Ann and the empty orange chairs lined neatly against the wall. The morning of his accident, he'd decided to stop jogging. His knees had begun to ache when he stepped out of bed. His age had been announcing itself in places he'd never much thought about before, but mostly in his knees. He'd take up something else that'd be easier on him, he decided, maybe swimming or biking. Maybe, he now thought, maybe in the end he'd unwittingly chosen his fate. He'd given up on his knees, and his entire legs—his entire life—had been taken from him. He'd grown ambivalent about being a father and spiteful of Jonathan White, and now their baby had been taken from them. But this was a pointless, suspicious line of thinking, and no one had such control over the future. Really it had been Brenda who'd been pushing *him* too hard. If she hadn't been exerting herself, or if they hadn't been on their way to visit his family, if it hadn't been raining so hard and she hadn't had to deal with his wheelchair, his goddamned wheelchair, maybe nothing would have happened.

He headed to the corner of the room, picked up the Raggedy Ann doll and hugged it to his chest.

Brenda was groggy when Dr. Waller first brought Daniel to her. Tucked under a thin white sheet, her head lolled to one side when he entered the room. He rushed to her and nearly slammed into her bed as he reached for her hands. "Mm," she mumbled. An IV tube pierced the underside of one of her wrists, and he could see the small reddish lump like a worm beneath her skin.

"Bren?" he said, and she murmured something unintelligible.

The doctor said that although she was stable now, he wanted to keep her here for at least the night, and Daniel asked if he could stay beside her, in the empty bed there. "Of course you can. I'll just let the nurse know."

Daniel sat there, listening to the noise of running water somewhere and waiting for someone to say something else. "So what was the cause?" he finally asked the doctor.

"We won't know for some time yet. A sample of the tissue was sent to Pathology down in Portland and they'll do what they can to find something. It could have been related to the placenta, but really, for most patients, I'm sorry to say it's indeterminable."

Daniel wondered if at an actual hospital better pathologists might be able to determine more. "Could we have the tissue sent elsewhere?"

"It's sent to a very reputable lab in Portland," Dr. Waller

said. "Listen, try not to think about that right now. Your wife will wake up soon and you two will have enough to deal with."

"You know," Daniel said softly, "it wasn't mine."

"Sorry?"

"The baby. We used a donor."

"Oh, well, that makes sense."

"I just meant, you know, that maybe it was something to do with the sperm?" He realized he sounded rather desperate.

"Probably not," Dr. Waller said, nervously half smiling again. "Again, it's best not to think too much about that right now. We'll try to have answers for you soon enough, and again, you'll need to prepare for the possibility that, well, that maybe there are no answers."

Brenda murmured something and Dr. Waller said he'd check in again soon, then left.

Daniel turned to her and squeezed her shoulder lightly. The corners of her lips were gummy, and he reached for the box of tissue on the table beside her bed.

"It hurts a little down there," she whispered.

"Should I go get a nurse?"

She shook her head.

"You'll probably feel better soon," he tried.

She lay still, her eyelids sinking and rising. "Did you tell them, your family?"

"No, not yet. I wanted to see you first."

"Okay," Brenda murmured, and closed her eyes.

He leaned forward and dabbed at her mouth, but she didn't budge.

A tall nurse appeared in the doorway. "She up?"

"She was, but I'm not sure she still is."

"She'll be in and out for a while," the nurse said, and

checked the chart on a clipboard hanging from the end of the bed. Brenda's head leaned to the side and her mouth fell open. The nurse returned the chart, avoiding his eyes, and rushed out of the room.

He squeezed the tissue in his hand into a ball. Brenda's hair had bent into strange angles, and she looked like a child now as she slept, incredibly young and soft and breakable, at the mercy of everything in the world.

He soon grew fidgety and wheeled back down the hallway, where the only sound was the buzzing of a distant machine. Two nurses ran past him. An old man sat bent in a green chair outside an empty room. Daniel wandered back to the waiting area, where he sat alone for a while and listened to the long honk of a car's horn outside.

—

Ellen and Joe would sleep in a square green room with two single beds. Ellen looked down at the soft beige carpet, at the thin green and beige curtains hanging by the windows, the ornate antique clock on the wall. She wondered if they'd hired an interior designer. "More towels are in the hall closet, as well as more blankets and pillows," Liz said.

Joe set Babe's cage on one of the beds and hefted his suitcase onto the other.

"Don't worry, Babe won't need his own room. He'll stay with us," Ellen said, and Joe shot her a look.

"I'm off to make dinner," Liz said, and Ellen followed her into the kitchen, where the floors were rich auburn tiles, the countertops marbled granite. Heavy stainless steel pots hung in a circle above an enormous, shiny stove. The refrigerator and sink were sleek and metal too. The airy room and everything in it looked as if they could survive a nuclear bomb.

Jake came in and took a seat at a round wooden table in the corner that was covered in separated families of food. He had met his female counterpart in Liz. Ellen wondered what made him so deeply organized, and whether she herself had had anything to do with it. Her house had devolved into chaos when he was growing up, as there had never been enough room for the five of them. No matter how hard she tried—and she tried incredibly hard—to keep the place clean and orderly, it was a constant clutter of car manuals, toys, books, clothes, notebooks, shoes, tools, newspapers. Perhaps Jake's obsession with cleanliness was some sort of reaction to his childhood home. He was certainly in for a challenge with fatherhood.

"I'm just making a simple roast chicken for dinner," Liz said. "You want to help with the salad?"

Ellen nodded. "You know, when I was pregnant with him," and she gestured to Jake, "I had the strangest cravings for chicken all the time." Liz handed her a tomato and a knife. "Dad and the butcher became good friends over those nine months."

"I haven't had any real cravings yet," Liz said, "but I'm sure I'll get them. I seem to have every other symptom. Jake, you'll probably get cravings too. What do they call that, sympathetic pregnancy or something?" Ellen wondered if he had been trying to steal the spotlight from her lately. Pregnancy did tend to make some men feel excluded, and he'd be a prime candidate.

Jake's only response was a snappish. "So Dad brought Babe."

"He did." The knife pressed against the firm skin of the tomato, pushing it into the cutting board. Ellen set the knife aside and poked the skin with her thumbnail. It parted and a puddle of seeds bled onto her fingers.

"How's he doing these days?" he asked, a concerned tone in his voice. It was a loaded question, really, one meant to prompt her to complain.

"Oh, well enough. He always has to have his pets nearby, you know that." The tomato was a little green inside.

"And how's Daniel doing?"

"*Where* is Daniel, that's the question." And why wasn't anyone else asking this? Because no one had an answer, that was why.

"I'm sure he'll call again soon," Jake said. "You know, we haven't seen him since Brenda got pregnant."

"He's fine, I suppose. Busy with work. We've invited him to dinner the past few weekends, but he's always got a million things going on. Brenda too."

"You should invite us to dinner sometime. We haven't been down there since Thanksgiving."

"You can come anytime you like, you know that."

"Invite us sometime," he said.

She scooped up a fistful of tomato and dropped it onto the bowl of lettuce beside her. It seemed Jake had always thought she preferred Daniel to him—which, if she were to be perfectly honest, she did once in a while. Any parent who claimed to like all his or her kids equally was lying. Love, that was a different matter. She loved them all deeply and instinctively. She truly wanted the best for them all. But *like*? Jake did overreact to the smallest things. He did try too hard to impress people, especially now that he'd made his money (he'd even offered to buy them a new roof for their house a few months ago—a touching but ultimately showy gesture. They would never take money from their kids). He was her son, though, and he was a good soul, an inherently kind person who only wanted others to think well of him in the end. "I'll look at my calendar when we get home and we'll make a plan for you to come down," she said.

She finished the salad and made her way back to the green bedroom. She almost tripped over Babe, who stood in the doorway looking up at her. "One day I'll kill myself falling over him," she said. Joe glanced up from a book and frowned. His glasses had inched to the end of his nose and looked as if they would slip off at any moment. Ellen moved toward him and pushed them back.

"I need to lie down," she said. The beds were tiny, really, and her feet hung off the end of her mattress. Their bed at home was luxurious, a king-sized on which they could lie entirely separate from each other. They'd splurged after Hilary moved out. Those days, the house echoed with emptiness, and they (especially Ellen) were feeling the need to be indulgent. The new bed occupied the entire room, and they even had to move their dressers into the kids' old bedrooms. When Joe said something from his side of the bed, she often didn't hear him. But if they wanted to, they could make their way toward each other, and once in a long while, after a trying day, they did find themselves in the center of this enormous bed. Now, in the green room, she noted the wide gulf between the beds. It had, after all, been a day filled with little stresses. And bigger ones—Daniel still hadn't arrived. Hilary was pregnant with a married man's child.

"Joe?"

"Yes?"

"You there?"

"Of course."

"Good," she said, and closed her eyes. In her mind, she lifted off the bed and floated to the ceiling, out of the room, down the hallway—her arms soft, like wings—and into the living room toward the front door. Down to the water where the waves tumbled in the night, the moon watched her like an eye, the stars gathered in mythic shapes above. It was a lovely thought at first, though certainly a strange one. She looked down and saw Babe now beside her bed. She thought she detected a bit of a smile on his face. And maybe it was so, maybe he was all-knowing and could read minds and was amused by hers right then. Admittedly there were times she almost liked having the turtle nearby. When Joe was engrossed in the paper or a book, Ellen didn't mind it so much because she wasn't entirely alone. Here was this creature, this witness. Before Babe there was Napoleon, the parakeet. Joe preferred mostly quiet, unobtrusive animals—and anyway, Jake had been allergic to everything else. Before Napoleon there was Ramone, the goldfish, who darted around his tank, looking wide-eyed at them. They could have been worse. The pets could have been mangy dogs or cats that scratched the furniture and left their hair in woolly clumps on the rug.

She thought again of her conversation with MacNeil in his garden—his question about whether Joe had chosen her or she him—and she tried to more fully remember the day they'd met. She did recall a few key things: the hospital, Joe's shiny black wingtips, his trying to sell her parents a car. What had drawn him to her, this random girl? She certainly didn't look her best and he was a handsome boy, with short, dark hair and olive skin, brown eyes. Tall, lanky, broad in the shoulders. She'd been impressed by the kindness of his asking a complete stranger whether she was all right. Really it was Joe who'd chosen her, who'd sealed her fate—she was sure. It was he who'd singled her out in that coffee shop—or was it just outside the coffee shop, by her parents' car? She glanced over at him on the other bed, a world away.

The house was quiet, and Ellen listened to her breath. She wondered where Jake and Hilary were right now. In their separate bedrooms? "Joe, where do you suppose Daniel is?"

"Probably waiting for the next ferry."

"The rain's got to be driving him crazy."

"Mm, I'm sure it is."

"I hope he's got his raincoat. Do you think they're waiting in their car in the parking lot for a ferry? Or out in the rain?" She pictured her son sitting in his chair in the middle of an empty parking lot, his legs swung lifelessly to one side, rain pelting down on him. "I wish more than anything he were here with us."

He closed the book. "He'll come," he said, then set his book on the floor and stood slowly, shaking his left foot awake. He sat on the edge of her bed and nudged her toward the wall. She shuffled to make room for him as he lay down beside her, just able to fit.

Hilary trudged past their doorway. "Can you believe her?" Ellen said. "I almost collapsed when I saw her in the bookstore. Can you believe they're all pregnant?"

"Barely. We'll go from seven to ten in less than a year. What'll it be like the next time we're all together?"

"I worry about her," Ellen said. "She's going to have a hard time as a single mother. She's not exactly organized. What if she leaves the baby at some tattoo parlor? Just forgets about it one day?"

"Ell, come on."

Hilary had no idea how trying motherhood would be. "Everything she does seems motivated by some need to rebel, don't you think? Even getting pregnant—and who is this man anyway? I have to say it just feels like a sort of spiteful act. Something to do just because she could."

"I doubt it was spite. You know how impulsive she can be." He pressed his fingers through the spaces between hers.

"Do you think he's married, this man?"

Joe smiled. "No."

"Well then, why won't she tell us who he is? Do you think there's something wrong with him?" She thought a moment. "Maybe he's some kind of criminal."

He looked at her as if she had four heads, and she yanked her hand away. She wanted badly to reach some sort of answer about her daughter just once—what was wrong with that? All this weekend they would tiptoe around Hilary, asking her only the vaguest, most inconsequential questions in order to avoid eliciting any melodramatic reactions.

"Jake's on edge," Joe said.

"He always is."

"This time seems a little different to me. Something's going on with him."

Joe never noticed such things, and Ellen shuddered to think what other secrets might be hiding beneath the surface of her family. "What do you think it might be?"

"I'm not sure. He just seems off."

She considered her son. "Well, if nothing else, he is a person defined by his rules. I don't think we need to worry so much about him." She turned to Joe. "I don't think he'd go sleep with some criminal and get himself pregnant."

"No, he probably wouldn't," he said, smiling, and kissed her hand.

—

"When do you want to tell them about these two?" Liz asked, rubbing her stomach. She lay on the bed beside Jake, gazing up at the ceiling. Everyone had gone to their rooms to unpack and settle in.

"Let's wait until Dan and Brenda get here."

"He said he'd call before they took the next ferry, but I'm sure they've left by now."

"What do you want me to do about it?" He hadn't meant to sound annoyed.

"I don't know, but you don't have to snap." She moved closer to him and ran a finger down his face. "Hey, where'd you put the *Kama Sutra?*"

"You're hilarious." He turned from her and adjusted his pillow, only now remembering that the magazine lay underneath it. He considered quickly grabbing it and tossing it under the bed, but she'd see this.

She twirled a strand of hair around her thumb. "Sorry," she whispered. "I couldn't help myself."

"As I said before, it was meant to be a joke," he said.

"On some level. But maybe on another level, it wasn't."

He looked at her. "I don't know. Would that be so wrong?"

"Not exactly wrong, but maybe a little misguided, at least now?" She patted her stomach.

"A lot of women like to have sex when they're pregnant,"

he tried again. "A lot of women *like* to have sex *in the first place*."

"Shh—you want them to hear you?" she hissed.

"No." He pushed his fists into the bed as he sat up. A corner of the magazine—one of the cheerleaders' thighs—peeked out. He lunged for it and stuffed it back underneath the pillow.

"What's that?" she asked.

"Nothing." He moved backward, sat on top of the pillow, but she leaned all her weight against him and tried to push him off. "You're pregnant," he said. "You shouldn't be straining yourself like that."

"Show me what that was," she said, and continued shoving him.

"Quit it," he said, and tried to nudge her away, but as he did, she managed to reach beneath him, slip a hand under the pillow and yank out the magazine.

"*Bounce* magazine?" She laughed as she read. "'Fifty Ways to Lick Your Lover'?"

He tried to grab it from her but she twisted away and read, "'The Juicy Secrets of Twin Cheerleaders'? Twins, Jake? Jesus."

Her words took a moment to sink in.

How had this never occurred to him? Just this afternoon he'd gotten himself off just thinking of these twins. He hadn't even considered the fact that these girls were someone's daughters, and could one day be *his* daughters. Not that his kids would ever pose for such a magazine. He and Liz would surely be better parents than that, or would they? He was a sick man, stashing porn in his underwear drawer like a horny teenager, and he would make a terrible father. He was a terrible husband.

"What am I going to do with you?" she said, half smirking, and set the magazine on the floor.

He stood and paced quickly beside the bed, trying to think of something to say to redeem himself, but nothing at all occurred to him. His body hummed. And there Liz sat, calmly, evenly, virtuous as a lily. In every way a superior person, and right now as smug as could be.

"Don't you ever make mistakes?" he finally said.

"Well, I'm not exactly curling up with copies of *Playgirl* these days, if that's what you're asking."

"That's right—you're a more evolved human being than I am," he said, as he was unable to think of a more intelligent or, yes, evolved reply, and stormed off to the kitchen. He almost bumped into his mother, who stood by the table, a concerned look on her face. Had she heard them? His heart banged inside his chest. "Y-you hungry?" he stammered. He wasn't about to offer her the opportunity to opine on what she may or may not have heard.

"A little."

"How about some salad?" He considered what else they had to eat, glad for the distraction. The potatoes weren't done yet; the chicken was still cooking. But he'd brought the wheat bread Liz had baked the day before, and he found the loaf on the counter.

Ellen took a seat at the table and made a spire with her arms. She rested her lips against the tips of her fingers. Then she said, "Still no word from Dan?"

"I wish there was something we could do to track him down. I don't know why they don't have cell phone towers here yet." Jake found a small bowl for the salad (even Liz's salads were morally superior. The little mandarin oranges looked like self-satisfied smiles, the spinach and arugula a fluffy bed of bitter-tasting health). "I know you're worried, Mom. I'm starting to get concerned about him too, to be honest."

"Should we call the police?"

"Let's give him a couple more hours. Maybe he just forgot to call before he got on the ferry," he said. "Can I get you something to drink? It might help you unwind. Maybe a glass of wine? We've got some nice vintages here, some pretty rare ones, actually."

She smiled. "No, no, I'm fine. You know, you really will make a good father," she said. "You stay incredibly attuned to other people. You just want them to be happy with you, don't you?" She sounded as if she was trying to convince herself of something.

"I don't know. I'm a little terrified of fatherhood, to be honest," he said, though this wasn't exactly it. Clearly she hadn't heard his argument with Liz. "I'm just not sure I'm up to the task or that I'm a good enough person, you know?"

"Oh, you'll be fine, and Dad and I will come up and help if you need us to. You really shouldn't be *terrified*. As for good enough, well, you're one of the most good people I know." She reached for his hand. "I don't think you could be a bad person if you tried."

Jake smiled sadly at her.

"And anyway, at least there will be two of you for one baby. Think of how hard it'll be on your sister."

"Mom, can you keep something quiet for a little while?" He couldn't help himself.

Her eyes lit and she nodded.

"We wanted to wait to tell you all at once, but God knows when that opportunity will come."

"Yes?"

"We're having two."

"Two what?" she asked.

"Two babies, Mom."

She blinked several times and held her fork before her mouth. "Twins?"

That blessed magazine was all he could think of. He put it out of his mind. "Yes."

"No."

"It's exciting," he made himself say. "Isn't it?"

She nodded vigorously. "Of course it is! Two at once!" she practically shouted, then lowered her voice. "I have to say I had my doubts about those treatments Liz was on. I suppose they're what caused the twins? And this must be why you're feeling so nervous, so—"

"Jake," a voice said, and when he turned, he saw Liz standing behind them, her hands on her hips, her mouth pinched shut. She pivoted and rushed out of the room.

He stood to follow her. "She wanted us to tell you when we were all together," he said to his mother.

Ellen scowled. "Just leave her alone for a bit, let her cool down."

He took a couple of steps forward, then stopped. "Maybe I should."

There was a shuffling in the hallway and Hilary appeared in the doorway, her eyes half-closed, her hair in bent chunks beside her face. Her nose ring poked out too far from her nostril. "Hi," she said. "I'm starving." She joined them at the table and sleepily picked orange slices from the salad, looking critically at each miniature smile before she popped it in her mouth.

Jake wanted to tell his mother of the dangers that he and
Liz faced with the pregnancy—all the things their doctor had
warned them of—and a part of him wanted to tell her about
the day he'd had, this trying day he'd had with his wife, and
that she didn't want to make love with him and hadn't in so
long and what if she didn't want to ever again? But he would
wait before he said anything more about their twins. (And he
would not say a thing about his day or about Liz. It was private, and she would probably leave him if he did.) He would
let Liz have some time to herself and wait until Daniel got
there before telling anyone else anything.

Hilary was all nonchalance and fatigue as she shoveled
large forkloads of salad into her mouth, followed by enormous pieces of bread. Jake had forgotten how she chewed
sideways, like a cow. He turned away.

"Slow down or you'll choke," his mother said, and Hilary
shrugged. Jake sensed something was about to erupt between
them, so he rose and went to find Liz. The hell with waiting.

She sat under the eave on the back porch, watching the
rain drip from the roof. She didn't turn when he slid open the
door.

"Hey," he said, leaning his head outside. "You'll get soaked
out here."

"Then I'll dry myself off." She held her gaze forward.

"I'm sorry," he said. "Liz, I'm sorry I told her. It just came
out of my mouth. And I'm sorry about that goddamned
magazine."

She hugged her chest. "Maybe you should find a girlfriend," she said. "You know, maybe you should have an
affair."

"What? What are you talking about? Are you trying to be funny?" He stepped outside and slid the door closed behind him.

"No, I'm not." She finally turned and looked at him. "Apparently you have these needs that I can't take care of right now."

He took a seat beside her. "Don't say things like that. You make me sound like some kind of feral animal." Mist wetted their shoes, and Jake wiggled his toes. "I love you," he said.

"I know." She pressed her lips together. "My father used to have girlfriends. He'd see them when my mother was away on business or when she had the flu or something. There was one he was really fond of, and she became the only one after a while. Her name was Elsie. She wasn't that pretty; she was on the heavy side, and had a large, sort of bent nose. But she was really good to him. And she was good to me. She brought me presents—these miniature soaps she'd stolen from hotels and motels. I collected them."

"Jesus. You never told me this." He swallowed what tasted like a stone.

"I figured it'd bother you," she said. "And make you like my parents even less."

"I like them, you know that. They're just a little strange— you know that too. And anyway, didn't it bother you?"

"I was young. I suppose I didn't really know any better."

"But it didn't seem weird to you? I assume the other mommies and daddies didn't bring their lovers home to meet their families."

"We weren't really friends with the other normal mommies and daddies," she said. "Anyway, Elsie died in a car accident when I was thirteen. We all went to her funeral and I can't tell you how upset I was. My father couldn't even speak, neither could my mother."

"So what then?"

"Nothing, really," she said. "My father never had another girlfriend. My mother traveled less for work and spent more time with him. They made do. But since Elsie died, my father's become sadder and more withdrawn. Kind of like a smaller version of his old self."

"He seems all right to me."

"You didn't know him before."

They sat there, watching the tide swell and pound the beach. Clouds hid the moon, and the horizon was almost invisible.

"Do you think I've become a smaller version of my old self?" he asked tentatively.

"Not necessarily smaller, but since I got pregnant, or really since we started trying, you just never seem content with me. I can't seem to give you enough of myself. And you keep trying to do more and more to make me happy. You take care of me and every little thing around the house, and sometimes I think you expect something from me in return to show you that I love you and that I am, in fact, happy. But I am happy, you know? I'm *so* happy that I'm pregnant," she said, and turned in her chair. "Maybe it's healthy, really, your tending to yourself like this, in this way. It's normal to have needs." She sounded as if she was sifting through piles of thoughts that she'd been having for some time.

"I don't think I'll be hooking up with an Elsie anytime soon," he snorted.

"I figured as much. But if you find yourself wanting to, just let me know. Okay?" she said. She was serious. "Just be open with me. We can at least talk about it."

"I won't want to, I promise. I would never want to do anything remotely like that."

"I know, Jake, but I just mean—"

"I absolutely can't believe you'd say these things." He looked at her. "Do *you* want to have an affair or something?"

"No, of course not."

The wind had begun to pick up, and the air was almost chilly now. "Don't you worry that once the twins come our lives will turn upside down? That we'll have no time for each other anymore?"

"I guess I think it'll be worth it."

"Let me try again. It doesn't seem like you're attracted to me anymore." He shouldn't have said it straight out. He certainly didn't need to define for her what she may not have articulated to herself yet. "Or am I just taking something too personally again?"

"Yes, you are. Think about all that my body is going through right now." It had become her refrain. There was no arguing with her. "You have to cut me some slack."

"You keep talking about my needs, but what about yours? Don't you have any at all?"

"Lately, not those kinds." She looked at him and chewed the side of her mouth. "You fed your mother part of dinner and told her our secret."

"Yes," he mumbled. She was incapable of letting one thing go.

"You did it to piss me off."

"I did it because my mother was hungry."

"That's why you told her about our twins?"

"Jesus, Liz, I'm imperfect. Okay? How many times do I have to tell you this? I'm not fucking perfect." He said this whenever he'd reached a wall in an argument, but nothing more explanatory ever came to mind.

She squeezed one side of her neck.

"I'm going to go see if Dan called," he said, and stood.

"Stay here with me for a minute," she said. "Don't rush off."

He paused. "I'm sorry, all right? What else is there to say? I'm a bad, completely flawed, ridiculous person."

"I just want to know why you told her. I want to know the real reason."

"My family is inside. Do we have to do this now? Can't this wait?"

She dropped her chin to her chest. "Here's what I think: you're mad at me for not paying enough attention to you lately, and you're worried I never will again. You're worried we'll never have sex again."

"Yes, that's it. That's exactly it. Thank God you said it."

"You were getting back at me."

"I'm going inside."

"Seriously. There are solutions. The magazine—I don't really mind, you know? It's healthy. It's perfectly okay. I just want us to be open about these things."

"You're a lunatic," he said.

—

Jake burst inside just as Hilary was about to throttle her mother. Her pitying looks and concern, her thinly veiled remarks about everything from how Hilary ate to how she'd never be able to handle motherhood on her own. "I'm not criticizing you, honey, I'm just worried you'll choke if you don't slow down," Ellen had said. And earlier, "I want to help you once the baby comes. I want you to know that we're here, Dad and I, whenever you need us. We could fly out for a week, or you could bring the baby home sometimes. I could never have done what you're doing now, all alone. I assume this person, this man, is still out of the picture?" Endless patronizing and second-guessing, and Hilary had pointed this out but Ellen had denied it. And then Jake pushed open the sliding glass door, his face flushed and wet, just as Joe appeared in the hallway. "Anyone tell me where I might find another blanket?" he asked.

Jake flew forward, emitted a loud chirp and was suddenly flat on the floor. Joe scrambled behind him. Ellen rushed toward them and Hilary couldn't help laughing.

"GODDAMMIT!" Jake screamed.

Joe knelt and flipped Babe.

Ellen stroked Jake's head. "Are you all right?"

His face tightened. He had absolutely no balance or coordination.

"Call an ambulance," Ellen yelled to no one in particular.

"I think I broke something," Jake said. He reached toward his ankle with one hand, his neck with the other.

Joe rushed Babe back down the hallway.

"That godforsaken creature!" her mother yelled after him. "Hil, call an ambulance."

"Ouch," Jake moaned.

Hilary saw her father disappear into the bedroom.

"Hilary Jane!" Ellen called.

"Fine, Mom, just stop yelling." Hilary moved toward the

sliding glass door. She pushed it open and briefly told Liz what had happened. "You're kidding," Liz said, and rolled her eyes.

"I'm not," Hilary said, surprised by her response.

"HILARY!" Ellen screamed from inside.

"Mom wants me to call an ambulance."

"There's no hospital here, so no ambulances. Hold on, I'm coming." Liz stood and rushed inside to Jake, and Hilary followed. "Where does it hurt?" Liz asked him.

His face still pinched, he pointed to his ankle.

"Don't you think he should see a doctor?" Ellen asked, still crouched beside him.

"Can you stand?" Liz asked Jake.

"I can't move," he said, squirming on his back.

Joe reappeared. "I could take him to the hospital," he said.

"God," Liz said. "This is ridiculous."

Hilary looked at her father, standing alone in the hallway. "I'll come with you, Dad," she said.

"I'm fine, I'll be fine," Jake snapped.

"Joe, come over here and help me get him up," her mother said, and Hilary joined them. The irony. Two pregnant women and an old couple assisting the person who should have been the healthiest one there to his feet.

"I'll be all right," Jake muttered. "Just get me to the couch."

"Joe, go get your coat," her mother said, but her father froze. "JOE."

"Mom, stop it," Jake said. They guided him across the room and onto the couch, where Hilary pushed a cushion beneath his leg. The leather squeaked beneath him as he shuffled around. "I'm fine. I just need to lie down."

"What if something broke?"

Liz said, "I'll go get some ice," and Hilary followed her into the kitchen. "He can be such a klutz," Liz said to her. "And anyway, he just needs to rest and stop doting on everyone for once."

"No one's stopping him from resting. He can relax all he wants," Hilary said, and thought that it had been Liz, not Jake, who'd been doting on them since they got here. Liz wrapped several ice cubes in a wet paper towel and the two headed back into the living room.

"Honey," Ellen said. "Help me convince your husband that he should be seen by a doctor. He could have broken something."

"He'll be fine, Ellen. Just let it go," Liz said, and pushed the makeshift ice pack firmly against Jake's ankle. Hilary had never seen her sister-in-law so testy. "How's it feeling?"

"Okay," he said. He pressed his eyes closed. He held his body rigid and straight, his arms at his sides.

Hilary set off to find her father, and as she suspected, he was in their bedroom, tending to Babe, setting him on the carpet and feeding him a baby carrot. It almost seemed as if she were interrupting some private conversation between them— and did he confide in the turtle? Did he tell him things he told no one else? She hoped there was someone her father could be completely open with, even if it was a box turtle. They all made too many demands on him. Of course he was drawn to something that couldn't speak or complain or demand more attention. "Dad? You all right?"

"Sure," he said absently. "You?"

She sat on the bed beside him and looked down at Babe. "Such a hectic day," she said. The turtle turned toward the other single bed. Back at home, her parents' bed sat like an enormous raft in their small room. She doubted her parents had touched each other in years.

Joe reached forward, rubbed a finger across Babe's head and handed him another baby carrot. Jake would've lost his mind if he'd seen this creature nuzzling his fine carpet, pushing a slimy little carrot toward one of the beds, then snatching it up along with a small chunk of the carpet into his jaw.

"He okay?" Hilary asked.

"I think so. Just a little shaken up." He looked at her. "And you? You're surviving the family reunion so far?"

"Seems like it."

"You need anything from us in terms of the baby? Money?"

She reached as far forward as she could to touch the turtle's cool shell. "No, I don't think so. You know, I'm considering moving back to the East Coast," she said. "I'm about done with California. My job drives me crazy, and to be honest, the people of San Francisco have begun to seem evil to me. My neighborhood's going down the drain." She drew a long breath. "I need some sort of change and I want to start over once the baby comes. I actually packed up and got my apartment ready to sublet before I came here."

He beamed at her. "What would you do for work?"

"I don't know," she said. "I haven't thought that far. I've got a little money saved up, though. Enough to last awhile, until I figure things out. As long as I live cheaply."

"We'll help out. Where would you live?"

"I haven't decided yet," she said carefully.

"We'd love to have you at home," he said.

The thought of living with her parents hadn't occurred to her before now—it was not something she would ever do. Just the idea of telling people she'd moved back home made her cringe. "I'd be a burden," she said.

"No you wouldn't." His tone changed. "Your mother would be ecstatic. We both want to know your baby." He grinned. "Really, I promise."

She didn't want to wound her father by saying any more about the matter, so she simply nodded. Maybe she'd quietly rent an apartment in Boston, then tell her parents afterward.

She leaned back on the bed and glanced at her stomach, a huge mound before her. She thought, as she had many times before, that the look and gender of the baby would be a complete surprise. And when she saw it for the first time, would she know who the father was? Would the baby have George's round brown eyes, or Bill's full cheekbones? When she'd had the opportunity to learn the gender, she had decided not to. The ultrasound technician seemed taken aback by her, this single woman uninterested in her baby's gender. But it wasn't that Hilary was uninterested. It was more that learning the gender would further humanize the baby, and though there were times she was so eager to meet this living thing inside her, there were other times when the thought of it was almost frightening, much more significant and daunting than anything she could imagine.

She leaned her leg against her father's and stared up at the ceiling. The rain hissed down outside. She thought of Alex, and wondered where he was right then. At Books & Beans, or maybe with a girlfriend? If only her family knew where she'd been all afternoon. Yes, in the moment, everything had been worth it. But in hindsight, what pregnant woman did such a self-indulgent, impulsive thing? Alex had probably forgotten all about her by now anyway. And if he hadn't, if he was in fact developing some sort of fondness for her or thinking about seeing her again, this pregnant woman who'd lured him into bed just hours after they met, then something was truly, fundamentally wrong with him.

In the next room, Jake and Ellen burst out laughing. "I knew he wasn't really hurt," Hilary said.

Joe smiled and nodded. "I suppose I did too, but I'm sure the fall did smart a little. It was quite a tumble." Her father was a born diplomat.

"Thank you, Dad."

"For what?"

"For your offer to let me move back home. For not hating me because I'm pregnant."

"No one hates you, Hil."

"Mom might a little right now. And Jake definitely does."

"'Hate' is an awfully strong word. Maybe they were just surprised?"

"Maybe," she said, unconvinced.

"How could anyone hate you?"

"I could. Sometimes I do these dumb, spontaneous things just because I can."

Joe worried a corner of the blanket between his fingers, and Hilary could almost see his heart sink a little in his chest.

"Sometimes I'm not so bad, though," she added. "Sometimes I think I'm all right."

"You're better than all right," he said. "To me, you're wonderful. You're smart and honest, you're true to who you are."

Hilary smiled and thought that her father might be the only man to ever say such things so guilelessly, so plainly and lovingly to her.

6

Good, Happy Lives

Daniel found a pay phone at the end of the hallway and reached up to call Jake's. His mother answered, thankfully, for the thought of telling his brother or Liz what had happened before telling his parents would have seemed wrong. The words sounded wooden coming out of his mouth, "We lost the baby," as if he were reading from a script.

"What?" Ellen gasped.

"Brenda started to bleed a lot and they had to do emergency surgery," he said, and she asked him what exactly had happened and when and why, as if he might know more than he did and as if perhaps he could have stopped it.

"What happened was that we lost the baby, Mom. I don't understand much more than that right now."

"Of course not. I'm sorry, I'm so sorry, Dan." She swallowed. "I love you."

"I know," he said. "I love you too."

"Tell Brenda I love her. Is she there? Is she beside you?"

"No," he said, and explained that he was using a pay phone in the hallway.

Ellen told him again that she loved him, that she loved Brenda too—she clearly had no idea what she should be saying to him, so he finally interrupted with, "I'm going to go sit with her now. I'll call you again once I know when visiting hours are tomorrow and when she'll be released."

She said something else about Hilary and Jake and the rain as if to keep him on the phone just a little while longer. "Daniel?" she finally said after it seemed she'd run out of small talk. "We'll see you soon, honey."

He tried to imagine what her face might look like right then—intensely worried, probably, her eyebrows knit together. And then he tried to picture the room in Jake's house in which she was sitting—enormous, undoubtedly, with brand-new everything. Were the others right there beside her?

"Daniel?"

"All right. I'll call you tomorrow."

He squeezed his wheel rims and headed back through the bright hallway, past the old man who now picked at his fingers, past a couple of nurses laughing and on to Brenda's room. The fluorescent lights in the room buzzed and he reached up to switch them off. Brenda slept soundly, though she stirred as he drew near. Her hands were laced across her stomach, now notably shrunken. He straightened the sheet that had tugged free to reveal her thigh, and he pulled it back beneath the mattress.

Her eyes fluttered open, then closed. "Dan?"

He brushed her hair from her eyes and for some reason

thought of their friends Ruth and Dimitri, who'd had a baby a few years ago. Ruth still carried the boy everywhere, though he was more than able to walk. At the drop of a hat she'd unbutton her shirt and release one of her enormous, marbled breasts into his mouth. He was a boy now, no longer a baby but a full-grown boy who wore boy pants and boy shirts and could clearly say his own name, Max. "Mama boo, Mama boo," he'd say, and that would be the cue for Daniel to turn his head. Dimitri, once as prudish as a monk, was oblivious to his wife's naked breasts. Brenda thought it was lovely, how comfortable Ruth and Dimitri were. "It's nothing to hide. It's a natural thing, a beautiful thing—people should accept it." Daniel didn't want to be the uncomfortable one. He wished Ruth and her breasts and her son didn't irritate him so much. He wished, in the end, it had been a lovely sight for him too.

He imagined the dark curtain lowering over Max and Ruth and Dimitri, and soon he tilted his head to the side and fell asleep for a few minutes.

"You're on my blanket," a voice said.

Daniel blinked himself awake. Brenda was leaning out of bed, yanking a thin white blanket from beneath his left wheel. He pulled backward.

"You awake now?" he asked tentatively.

She nodded and they looked at each other. He tried to remember what she'd said to him just after his accident, when he woke to a cool rush of liquid from an IV bag and a roomful of nurses. What had happened was that she'd stood stiffly, nervously next to his doctor and barely said a thing. Daniel had hoped she would come to him, kiss him and say something, anything, really, but she'd hung back and let his doctor do the talking first.

Now he moved closer to her and bent forward to hug her legs.

"Careful! I'm a mess down there."

He recoiled. "I love you," he said in British. "Do you know that?"

She glanced around the room as if she hadn't heard him.

"I just called Jake's," he said. "And talked to my mother. I told her what happened." He looked at his lap. "It made this whole thing seem much more real."

"I should call my mum," she said, and he moved the phone on the bedside table closer to her.

Brenda whispered, "Thanks," and lifted the receiver. Her fingers danced over the many numbers and she gazed at her feet as she waited for her mother to pick up. When she did, Brenda practically burst. "Mum, good, I'm so glad you're there," she began, and her eyes welled up as she went on to explain all that had happened. "I know, I know," she sniffed, and looked at Daniel. "Yes, exactly, precisely," and he wondered what the woman had just said. "It's an island in Maine, yes, not so far from the coast here. You get here by ferry, and—" Her mother apparently interjected. "No, it's not like that at all. It's smaller, not so many people, I suppose." The two went on and on, and then Brenda spoke to her father and then her mother again, and as she did, she looked out the window.

Finally she said a tearful goodbye, hung up and rested her head on the pillow. "I just knew something was wrong." She sighed. "Didn't they say the placenta was too low at my last appointment? I *knew* something wasn't right. Remember I felt it earlier—remember when I said the baby wasn't moving?" She sounded almost irritated with him.

"You did say that."

They sat quietly and he waited for her face to soften, and for her to cry again. But she didn't—she just fiddled with the sheets for a moment and then mumbled, "I should've done something sooner. We shouldn't have gotten on that ferry."

"Bren, there's no point in that kind of thinking now."

She hoisted herself upright on the bed and turned to him. "But I knew something wasn't right. I could sense it. I know myself and my body very well."

"Oh, stop this, would you? It's over. It's done, and it can't exactly be undone."

She looked at him, then at the floor.

"I'm sorry this happened. I'm incredibly sorry." He tried to sound as earnest as he could, true to what he was feeling. "But there's no point playing the what-if game right now."

"I don't care," she hissed. She awkwardly flipped onto her side.

"I lost something here too, you know."

"I just don't want to hear your voice right now." Her shoulders rose slowly and fell.

"Bren, I'm so sorry."

She didn't flinch.

"Would you please acknowledge me, for Christ's sake?" He punched the side of the bed and she jumped. "I am your god-damned husband. I am right here beside you and I love you and you need to listen to me. You need to stop fucking ignoring me."

She turned onto her back, her eyes squeezed shut, and said, "I need to think. I just need some time and I need my mum and dad," as if he were nothing but air beside her.

A hideous, deafening roar shot out of his mouth. The terrible noise echoed in his head and his shoulders and arms, and afterward he felt completely emptied and bare. Brenda and the room and the entire world disappeared for a moment and he grew dizzy and lighter, foggier. He listened to his quick breath —it was still there after all, his pulse too, and his tongue and his teeth in his mouth. "I am here," he managed calmly. "And you are here and it's just us now. And I want you to allow me to be your husband and help you feel a little better."

She looked at him, her eyes wide. He tried to imagine what she would want to see right now: strength, fortification, comfort? He straightened his posture as best he could and steadied his breath. "This day will end soon and I'm guessing that a better day will come tomorrow, and then a better one after that. You are sitting in the darkest part of the darkest time of the darkest day right now and it will improve." He didn't know where these words came from, but he was glad he'd said them.

She pulled the sheet to her face and held it over her eyes.

He reached forward and placed a hand on her head. "Shh," he whispered, and gently stroked her hair as a mother might do. "Try to give your heart a little rest." It was something his own mother used to say.

Brenda nodded again and let go of the sheet. Her eyes had filled and she pressed her mouth into something that resembled both a smile and a frown. "I want to go back home," she said. "I want to get out of this place."

"Okay," he said. "But I don't think the doctor will let you leave just yet."

"Your family will understand, though, won't they, if we just go straight home from here without seeing them?"

He'd forgotten all about his father's birthday. "I guess," he

said, though he wasn't so sure. The idea of just heading back
to the ferry, back to the car, back to their empty house in the
suburbs, just the two of them—the idea suddenly weighed on
him. "Let's go one step at a time here. Let's wait and see what
the doctor has to say."

Brenda agreed and reached for the plastic cup of water on
the bedside table. She seemed calmer now. "It's strange, my
being the one in this bed and your sitting by my side."

"Wasn't so long ago you were on duty, huh?"

She took a long sip. "It was hard for me, you know. I never
knew quite what to say to you. Or even what to think."

"I had the same problems at the time."

"Of course."

"It was like sitting in the eye of a storm," he said. "And you
were on the other side of it all, watching the whole thing
unfold."

"I wasn't, though. I was with you in the stormy part. Everyone was, you know—your family, even little Meredith Ringley.
We all still are, in a way."

About six months ago, Meredith called their loft in Brooklyn and asked him if she could come by. They'd never met her.
She'd rushed away from the accident scene just as soon as the
ambulance came, and she communicated with them only by
phone afterward. Daniel didn't know what to think as he
hung up after impulsively agreeing to meet her. Would she
expect him to assuage her guilt? He couldn't imagine she'd
feel any better when she got a look at him in his wheelchair.
She showed up a few minutes before she'd said she would.
Daniel had been watching for her and saw the blue hatchback
pull into a parking space across the street. The car's dents had
been banged out, its windshield replaced and its hood fixed.

The small car looked like any other on the street. Meredith herself was younger than he'd expected, probably in her early twenties. Daniel pushed open his door and she stood directly before him in his doorway, tall and bony, with a mottled complexion and long, fine brown hair that fell to her chest. There she stood, chewing on her thumbnail and looking at her feet. She wore thick glasses that made her head appear narrower and her eyes bulbous. She slunk into the loft and joined them for coffee at the kitchen table. She spoke in a hushed monotone about the degree she was getting at NYU in—at this he smiled—graphic design. She answered their questions but asked none, as if she had come simply to present herself, to show them that she was merely a thin, shy, slightly awkward person, no villain. And in a way, it worked. As they watched her leave their building and walk toward her car, Daniel said, "It's amazing. She's just a kid. How is it possible for someone who seems that innocent to ruin another person's life?"

Now Brenda grew teary again, and Daniel cast around for something mundane to say. "I've been thinking of ideas for the cover of that novel I'm doing. I'm thinking of a boat sailing up a building."

"I thought that was just a small part of the plot."

"Small but important," he said. "The author wants something that shows motion and contrast. It's set in Havana, in this little office building, and the guy, the protagonist, is saving up for a boat."

She wiped her eyes. "I thought the book was about politics, Castro and whatever." Tears began streaming down her face at this point, and she covered her cheeks with her hands.

He leaned forward and hugged her legs, then tried to take her hands but she kept them pressed against her face. "I really did want that baby," Daniel said, and it was true. At least it had been true after her fateful flight back from Africa, and after that, well, he didn't need to think about it right now. He looked up at her. "I really wanted you and me to have good, happy lives together."

She nodded, sniffing fiercely. "I did too," she said.

—

At first came a wave of relief—Daniel and Brenda were fine— but then Ellen grew faint as she hung up the phone in the kitchen. She made her way into the living room, where the rest of them sat looking up at her with round eyes, and she explained in a somewhat mechanical voice what had happened.

"My God," said Hilary.

Liz, sitting on a leather easy chair in the corner, rested her head in her hands. Jake stood behind her and squeezed her shoulders. "Do they know what caused it?"

"I don't think so," Ellen said. She heard the rain continue to fall outside. "I didn't really press Daniel about it. Maybe I should have. I don't know why I didn't."

"It doesn't matter," said Liz, whose face was turning a feverish pink.

"Maybe it was the donor," Ellen said. "I worried that this sort of thing would be trouble."

"I doubt it," Hilary snapped.

Joe said, "Liz is right—what does it matter?" He stood, went to Ellen and sandwiched one of her hands between his.

"We shouldn't focus on the cause," Liz said, and went on to tell some story of her friend who'd had a later-term miscarriage, but Ellen found herself unable to hear what she was saying. Daniel, her son who would live the rest of his life in a wheelchair, had now lost his baby. She moved away from Joe. Someone said something, someone else replied and she turned and headed down the hallway and into the green bedroom. Babe had moved a step forward in his cage and looked up at her. She stood frozen above him. She had no idea what to do with herself.

"Mom?" Jake suddenly appeared behind her in the doorway.

She sat down on one of the beds and felt her spine curl.

"It's awful," he said, and she nodded and looked away. He came into the room, sat down beside her, and as he did the bed sank toward him. He breathed deeply beside her, and Ellen wondered whether he now worried for his own babies. She reached for the thin curtains and rubbed them between her fingers, trying to think of something comforting to say to him.

But he spoke first. "Remember when Dan punched me out for telling on him when he broke Dad's calculator? I think I was in fourth grade, maybe?"

Of all the things Jake could say right now. "Yes, I remember." She gazed down at the curtains in her hands. Daniel was awful to Jake as a child. She probably should have intervened more, but the two always wore her down with their constant bickering and fighting, and eventually she just started ignoring them.

"He gave me a fat lip and a black eye, remember?"

She nodded.

"That was the last straw for me. He'd beaten on me so many times I completely lost my mind. I ended up telling his friends that he'd said all these terrible things about them."

Jake looked at the floor as he spoke. "I told Rick Bernard that Dan had told me about the huge, ugly birthmark on his butt—which of course *I'd* seen before in the bathroom. And then I told Mark Sullivan that Dan said he slept with his parents because he was too scared to sleep alone." Jake smiled. "I told Jeff Myers that Dan had told me he was the worst player on their baseball team. That he only played because Dan did, and he was jealous of Dan."

"Those three were his best friends," she said.

"I know."

She thought about Daniel back then. "Those boys completely dropped him as a friend after that. He didn't have friends again until he was in junior high the next year. And he started getting bad grades, and having so much trouble sleeping."

Jake nodded.

"Well, it was a long time ago," she said, trying not to betray a rush of anger.

"It was, I guess, but still. It was a cruel thing for me to do, both to Dan and to those guys." He moved onto the floor and looked up at her. "I just remember being so completely mad at him for treating me like hell and still having all these friends and people around him who thought he was so great."

Jake sounded almost like a child again. He had only wanted friends of his own. She let go of the curtain and forced herself to reach down and run a hand through her son's hair. After a moment, the gesture came more naturally. He'd done what he had out of jealousy, and anyway, Daniel was resilient. He'd made new friends, begun sleeping better, improved his grades. It was Jake who hadn't, even now, fully recovered from not being liked enough as a child.

Babe nestled beside a pile of wood chips. Jake leaned all his weight against her legs, and they stayed like this for a moment, her hand still on his head, her eyes pressed shut.

After a while he stood, said he should get back to the others and left the room.

She heard muffled conversation in the living room and tucked her shirt beneath her lap. Babe lay perfectly still now. Outside, rain pounded the roof and the sky had finally grown black. She thought of Brenda and Daniel, alone in some cold room in some clinic on this island, surrounded by night. Ellen stood, marched into the living room and told the others she wanted to go to the clinic.

"It's late, Ell, and didn't Daniel say he was going to tell us when to come *tomorrow*? Didn't he say visiting hours are over?" Liz asked.

"I'm his mother and I want to see him," Ellen said, refusing to look at her daughter-in-law, or at the plush leather furniture and cherry floors and imported Persian carpet that suddenly appeared excessive to her, especially for a summer home. "I just want to see my son."

"What about what he wants, Mom?" Hilary said, and Ellen could have struck her.

"We'll go first thing in the morning," Joe said. "We'll wake up and go right there before doing anything else. I'll see to it that we're the first people who walk in that door."

"First thing?" She sighed, defeated, and ambled to the couch. "All right."

Joe followed and took a seat beside her.

Hours later, Ellen woke to dense darkness. The only sound she heard was Joe's faint snoring. She lay in a small, stiff bed.

Had she died in her sleep? She had no idea where she was. Her eyes open to the night, she felt weightless, only a heavy torso, and she tried to wiggle her fingers and toes and was unable to at first. Soon the feeling returned, but she still didn't know where she was. Joe slept in a small bed across from her, and when she pulled herself up out of her own bed and walked across the room, she felt a coarse carpet beneath her feet. Only when she opened the door and looked down a hallway to a living room, where a line of moonlight cut across a brown leather couch, did she remember that this was Jake's house on Great Salt Island.

She made her way down the cool wood floors of the hallway and into the living room and suddenly the meaning of the silence occurred to her: the rain had stopped. It was a relief. She looked down at the stack of blankets on the couch, remembering they had been set out for Daniel and Brenda, and the day's events came back to her. She clasped her hands together and made herself move forward, then back down the hallway. Jake's door was ajar. He lay on his back, his arms across his chest in an ominous pose. Liz lay in an identical position, and seeing them, Ellen's breath caught in her throat. Liz lifted her head. "Ellen?"

"Shh, go back to sleep. I was just checking on everyone."

"Do you need anything?"

"No. Shh," Ellen whispered again, and pulled the door closed behind her.

In the next room, Hilary slept naked on her side, several pillows stuffed between her legs and under her arms. Ellen couldn't help staring and observing how much her daughter's body had changed with pregnancy. Hilary was a small whale in the darkness. Ellen couldn't see her face, but she could see the rise and slope of the girl's—the woman's—silhouette and the pillows, like another body, shoved beneath and between her.

Ellen entered the room, wanting for a second to go lie beside her daughter and hug her close, but of course this would wake her, so Ellen just went and sat on a short wooden chair in the corner. She wondered why she hadn't looked in on her sleeping children more often when they were young. Joe was usually the one to check on them in the middle of the night. Ellen was always the one to put them down but once she herself was asleep, she was lost to the world. It used to worry her, the depth of her sleep. So much could happen and she'd have no idea about it until too late. But tonight, here she was, awake. It was a sort of gift—she was the one keeping guard, watching them breathe and dream. If only Daniel were here too. If only her children were all together here, under her eye, tucked in their beds.

She stayed in the small pink bedroom for a while longer, and watched Hilary breathe.

—

Jake woke to hot sunlight on his face. He'd forgotten to close the shades, and where was Liz? He stretched his arms, blinked several times and sat up. Flames shot through his neck, and he remembered his fall yesterday. He stood, his neck stiff, pulled on his bathrobe and made his way into the kitchen, where Liz was placing sausage links in the heavy skillet.

"We the only ones up?"

"Your father and sister are out for a walk," she said. The sausages popped in their grease.

"Dan and Brenda," he said. "God, I just remembered." His mother was a ghost when she told them.

Liz nudged the sausages around the pan with a spatula. "I called the clinic this morning. The nurse said they were sleeping, and to try back in an hour or so."

He thought of their argument on the porch last night. "Come here," he said.

"I'm cooking with hot oil, sweetie."

"I don't care. Come here," he said again, and stepped behind her. He reached his arms around her waist. Her back was broad and warm against him, and he whispered, "I missed you in bed. And I don't mean in a hubba-hubba kind of way."

She turned her head and smiled back at him.

This was a miserable, tragic way to get a second chance, but a part of him felt relieved. And then guilty for this, and then merely relieved again at how silly and irrelevant their arguing now seemed.

He looked out the window and saw the ocean blinking with daylight. It was the most beautiful thing in the world, he thought, the Atlantic just beyond his kitchen window, the morning sun hovering above the rippling mirror of water. He was glad his father and Hilary were out enjoying it. He wondered what they were talking about, and what it was that they usually talked about. Unaccountably, Joe and Hilary had soft spots for each other. She doted on the man, constantly asking if he was warm enough, cool enough, hungry, tired. Jake's relationship with his father seemed to exist more in the silences between their words, in their simply listening and trying to understand each other. He wondered what it was about his sister, of all people, that his father connected with. After all, Jake was the one who called each family member regularly. He never missed a birthday, as his brother and sister often did, and whenever he passed something in a store he thought one of them would like, whether it was a sweater or a camera or a box-set photographic history of the automobile, he bought it immediately and sent it to them.

He kissed the back of Liz's neck and headed into the living room, where Hilary was now pulling the sliding glass door shut behind her. "I hope you realize you've got an incredible back yard," she said, walking inside barefoot. Joe stood by the door, brushing sand off his shoes onto the mat. Hilary fell onto the recliner, completely ignoring the sand she'd tracked all over the rug. "Smells good in here," she said, and she wiggled up her nose like a dog.

"Sausages," Liz called from the next room. "I'm making scrambled eggs too."

"What heaven," Hilary said, and leaned her head back. Joe moved behind her and draped a sweater over her shoulders, and Hilary made a silly face up at him as if she'd forgotten all about the horrible thing that had just happened in the family.

"What are we going to do about Dan and Brenda?" Jake said.

"Mm?" Hilary murmured.

"Do you think they'll even still want to come here, you know, to the house?" He thought a moment. "It's going to be hell for her to see you two pregnant."

She looked at him. "It might be."

Joe went to sit on the couch. He pushed off his shoes and peeled off his socks, lifted one foot onto his lap and began squeezing his toes.

The bottom of Hilary's stomach poked out from her T-shirt like a beer belly. "Does it make you feel a bit strange, you know, given your situation?" he asked.

"What are you getting at?"

He searched for safe words. "I mean of the three of us, you have to admit that they most deserved a healthy baby, after all he's gone through this past year or so."

"Oh, I dunno, you and Liz sure deserve it after trying for so long. So, jeez, I guess that leaves me, who certainly doesn't deserve anything good, do I?" She looked right at him.

"They're just a little more equipped for it," Jake said. "There are two of them, after all. It was something they *tried* for."

Hilary opened her mouth.

"Stop it," Joe muttered—to whom, Jake wasn't certain. Joe pushed his thumbs into his big toe over and over. "Just stop this, both of you, before you go any further."

"Jake, can you help me?" Liz called. Suddenly she appeared before him. "I need some help with breakfast." She grabbed his hand and pulled him back to the kitchen.

"What are you doing? We were getting somewhere," he whispered. "I was about to teach Hilary that she's not the only person in the world."

In the kitchen Liz released his hand. "I'm trying to make breakfast for your family and I need some help," she said. She handed him a carton of eggs.

Jake followed her across the room. "I just want to be prepared for when they get here. I don't want Dan and Brenda to feel awkward when they see Hil."

"Honey, you're not the only one who feels terrible about what happened." She handed him a bowl and he headed to the table.

"How the hell did she let herself get pregnant at this age? It's not like she doesn't know any better. No one else in this family even seems to care," he said. Perhaps Hilary rankled him so much because she didn't seem to get to anyone else at all. Objectively, factually, she was one of the most irresponsible people he knew. How did this not bother any of them? Yes, his mother seemed mildly irritated with her, but not nearly as confounded as he was. Even Liz wasn't fazed. "Anyway, it's Dan and Brenda we should be thinking about. What do we even say when we first see them?"

"We just let them lead the way and take it from there." He imagined she spoke in this measured tone to her students.

"That just doesn't seem like enough. I don't know," Jake said, and began to rub his temples. "I just wish I could do something else for them."

"To make *yourself* feel better about what happened?"

"No. Maybe. What's wrong with that?"

Liz shook her head. The light flooded in the window behind her, and he could barely see her face. "We'll need all those eggs, so get beating," she finally said.

—

They gathered around the kitchen table for breakfast. Hilary sat as far from Jake as she could, for she worried she'd wing a sausage at him if he said one more word to her. Next to her sat her father, and across from her, her mother, who'd just woken, which was strange, for Ellen had always been the first one up in the house, and often before dawn. Hilary still remembered, with some nostalgia, the sound of her mother puttering around in the kitchen downstairs while the rest of them lay in their beds upstairs. "You all right?" Hilary asked her.

Ellen gazed at her plate, cut a sausage into thirds with the side of a fork and popped one into her mouth. She swallowed and said, "I just didn't sleep so well last night."

"Maybe because you're away from home," Hilary began, in an effort to establish some civility between them, when Jake interrupted with, "It's going to be so hard on them," apparently for the benefit of their mother now. "It's going to be so hard for Brenda to see Liz and Hil. I'm not sure it's such good idea for them to come here at all. Maybe we should get them a room at a bed and breakfast or something, or maybe they should just go home after Brenda's released. I wonder if she's in a lot of pain. How do these things work, does anyone know? Is it like a normal birth?" he asked Liz. "Did she have to push?"

Hilary held a forkful of eggs before her mouth and stared at him.

"I'm going to look up D and C, that was it, right, Mom?" he asked after no one answered him. She nodded gently, and he marched off. Hilary searched for a way to stop her brother. She glared at Liz, who shook her head and then focused on the plate before her. Jake returned a moment later with a large medical reference book (and why would a person need such a book at his summer home? Hilary didn't understand one thing about him) and scanned through it until he found the page he was looking for. "After adequate anesthesia has been administered, bla bla bla. But how does it work exactly? What's the recovery like?" he said as he flipped the page, then shook his head. "It doesn't really say anything." He set down the heavy book and his glass jumped, then he picked up the book again. "I wonder if it says how common these kinds of things are." He glanced down at Liz, who stood, her face now pink, and began to clear the plates.

"I think I'll call some B&Bs," he announced, "and see if they've got any vacancies. Then I'll go to the drug store and talk to a pharmacist, see what he suggests—maybe a heating pad? We can bring some food to them at the clinic—well, just me and Mom and Dad, not you, Hil and Liz."

As usual, Ellen was the one to step in and calm the hysterical boy. "Jake," she said, and stood. She went to him and placed her hands on his shoulders. "Don't try to fix everything at once."

Standing beside the table, Liz set her hands on her hips and said, "Well, here's a way to change the subject. You *all* might as well know that Jake and I are having twins."

"Liz." Jake coughed.

Hilary swallowed the food in her mouth. "Wow," she said, and glanced at her father. He looked just as surprised as she was.

"It's wonderful news," her mother said. "It's just wonderful."

"Indeed," Joe said.

"We'd wanted to tell you all at the same time," Liz said quickly. "We wanted to sit you all down and announce it to you so we could see your faces, but if Dan and Brenda don't come, and we don't go see them, I'm not sure when we'll get the chance."

It had to be the fertility drugs, the twins. Jake and Liz were lucky it wasn't triplets. Hilary took a bite of her buttery toast, and then another. She imagined two tiny Jakes. Two judgmental little Jakes.

He went on to say that he was nervous about Liz's pregnancy, given the dangers involved in carrying twins, but Liz interrupted him and said she wasn't thinking about that, only about having a family and having it all at once. Two was the number of children they'd always wanted anyway.

Hilary considered the strange poetry: Brenda's miscarriage, Jake's twins. A loss, a gain, and she herself—how did she fit in here? Was she the balance between them, one mother, one baby? The family had become a tipping boat, Daniel now sliding down toward the water, Jake sitting happily with all his money and houses and babies up on the other end. If only Daniel were there—Hilary wished more than anything she could see his face and know, really know, that he was still above water.

"And how about you, Hil?" Ellen said. "You don't have any more surprises for us, do you?" She wanted desperately to know who the father of the baby was. Her curiosity was devouring her.

"Actually, Mom, I was telling Dad that I'm moving back East. I've put some stuff in storage and I'm going to sublet my place."

Everyone looked at her and then down at their plates. The ceiling fan above them purred.

"Do you have a job here?" Jake asked. "And what about that job you have now, the one at the insurance firm?"

"My contract ran out. I don't have a new job, not yet," she said. "But I've saved up a little money. And anyway, Dad said he could help me out if I need it, until I get on my feet with the baby."

Jake knit his eyebrows together and said, "Where will you live?"

Her father said, "Of course she'll move back home, at least for a while. We'll figure out the details later—"

"Nothing's been decided," Hilary interjected, and this seemed to quiet everyone, at least for the time being.

They continued to eat, and Hilary heard, for the first time from inside the house, the push of the waves against the sand and rocks outside. It was comforting, a sound that had nothing to do with her or her family, the ocean churning away, oblivious.

"I'm glad someone thought to let me in on this plan," her mother said finally. She was angry. She was furious that Joe hadn't let her in on their earlier conversation and consulted with her.

Liz stood and began to gather their plates. "Don't do everything yourself," Hilary said, and rose with Ellen while the men went to the living room. It was confounding how they fell into their prehistoric roles this way—sitting and talking lightly about things like cars and politics while the women cooked and cleaned. They might as well have been wearing loincloths.

Hilary stood before the sink and turned on the tap. She felt a hand on her back. "Go, sit, I'll do this," Ellen said.

"I'm fine, Mom."

"Go, honey. You too, Liz, you go sit with the others."

Liz went to join the men but Hilary remained in the kitchen with her mother, who nudged her to the side and took her place at the sink. Hilary rubbed her fingertips together as Ellen dunked the dishes in the soapy water. "So you'll stay with us?" she asked, gazing down at the metal sink. Her eyes were shadowed, hidden beneath more wrinkles than when Hilary had last seen her.

"I don't know yet. Probably not," Hilary said. "You're angry. You're annoyed Dad didn't ask you about this first, and that he didn't even tell you about it."

"It's not that," she said, "though I would like to have known. It's more that, well, to be honest, I just can't help wondering about this man, you know, this mysterious father of your child. Is it wise to be moving so far from him?"

"I told you he doesn't matter. I'm on my own in this—I'll raise the baby by myself."

"Then I suppose you should come back and be closer to the family."

"You sound thrilled."

Ellen turned off the tap and stepped toward Hilary. "Listen to me: I'm glad you're coming home."

"You're not. You think it's pathetic that I'm doing this on my own," she said.

"Why are you saying these things? I'm certainly not thinking them. Hil, if you want to know the truth, I think you're incredibly brave. I think you always have been. Sometimes I wish I had a fraction of your courage." Her words sounded thin, like words on a greeting card. *Congratulations on your bravery! Best wishes on your independence!* Anyway, it wasn't bravery that led Hilary to this decision. It was necessity, a lack of options, a blind decision to move forward, because when else might she have a chance to have a baby? She was thirty-five, after all, and had never even been in a relationship that lasted longer than a six months.

"Honey?" her mother said, and squeezed her hand.

"It's not courage, you know that. It's something else far less admirable."

"Nonsense." Ellen turned to the sink and continued washing the dishes.

"You know, I got here early yesterday so I went into town and I met this person, this guy in that bookstore." She wondered why, since Jesse Varnum, she'd never brought anyone home to meet her parents.

"Oh?"

"We drove around for a while. He showed me some of Great Salt, and brought me to this field in the exact center, and then we went back to his apartment, this place near the stores."

Her mother nodded slowly.

What was she really trying to say anyway? "He seemed to like me," she began.

"You're worried that we think no man could ever love you? Is that it?" Ellen asked sympathetically. *Was* this Hilary's fear? "For some reason the real father just isn't suitable for the job?"

"Now you're putting words in my mouth."

"Then what is this?" Ellen moved closer to her. "Help me understand what you're going through. We can talk it out and then you'll feel better."

Hilary felt herself smile. "Mom, you should have been a shrink."

"Oh, I don't have that kind of patience. If you want to know the truth, though, I sometimes wish I had been an artist." Her mother raised a hand to the side of her mouth as if she hadn't meant to say this.

"You do?"

Ellen sighed. "I actually do. Sometimes I wish I had learned to paint like the great ones. I at least wish I could have been great in some way. Isn't that a silly thing for your old mother to say?"

"I wanted to be an archaeologist," Hilary said. "I really did, I just hated the studying and the long classes and all those tests."

"You used to love to dig at the beach, do you remember that? You used to say you were sure the greatest treasures in the world were hidden in the sand. Diamonds and rubies and gold. You used to insist on staying there long after the rest of us were sunburned and ready to leave. Maybe it's not too late. Maybe you could take a class or two?"

"I'm no good in a classroom. You know I don't have the attention span." Hilary ran her finger along the granite countertop. "And anyway, I need to think about making some money now."

"Why not think about going back to school part-time? Dad and I could help pay for some of it. See if you can find an archaeologist to assist out here, meet some people who could help you?"

"Remember, it's only me supporting this baby. I don't think this is the ideal time to be chasing my dream career."

"You'll figure it out. I know you will. You'll make something work. You always do," Ellen said, her eyes suddenly bright, and Hilary understood then that her mother did think she was capable of anything. That smoking cigarettes in the woods behind the house and moving to the West Coast and having a baby alone were, in her mother's eyes, acts of courage born of a freedom, or sense of free will, that she herself never had. This thought touched Hilary at first and then saddened her a little, for it wasn't true. Fearful, insecure, uptight people were smoking and moving across the country and giving birth alone all over the place. "You won't tell me who he is, will you?" Ellen asked softly, and Hilary shook her head, thinking, at least not now, when her mother was still absorbing Daniel and Brenda's bad news.

7

Everywhere Bits of Italy

A short, elderly woman carrying an enormous bouquet of flowers appeared in the doorway. "Lydia?" she said. She wore thick glasses, and her hair sat on her head in a white bowl. "Lydia, darling?"

"You must have the wrong room," Daniel said. He sat beside Brenda's bed.

The woman blinked furiously. "Sorry?" she mumbled.

"You have the wrong room," he repeated in a measured voice, and Brenda added, "There's no Lydia here, ma'am."

But the woman made no effort to leave. Weighed down by what once could have been a garden of white carnations and yellow daisies, she appeared not to see or hear the two of them. She opened her mouth but said nothing.

"Please, you have the wrong room," Brenda said. "You might go check with the nurses down the hall."

"Pardon me? Who's there?"

"I'll show you to the nurses' station," Daniel said, and his words finally seemed to register with her.

"Well, I must be in the wrong room," she said, blushing. "Forgive me. I'll go find the nurses myself." She turned slowly and bumped into the doorframe on the way out, knocking two daisies from her bouquet onto the floor.

Daniel wheeled across the room, edged himself forward and, with some effort, scooped up the flowers. He returned to the bed, presented them to Brenda, and she smiled quickly, then set them on the bedside table. The room grew quiet and still, and he looked at her, her eyes now closed. He had an idea—he moved closer to the bed, pressed his fists into the mattress and quickly hoisted himself onto the bed.

"Ouch!" she yelped as he landed heavily on her leg. His chair spun across the room, hit the wall and rolled back toward them. Something had skewered his palm—an earring, he saw, and he pulled the small hoop from his hand. A dot of blood appeared.

"Be careful, Dan. This isn't exactly a king-sized bed."

"Is that your earring?"

She nodded and took it from him. "Really, you almost broke my leg."

"Well, at least there'd be doctors nearby."

She wriggled away from him. "You're still practically on top of me, love."

"Fine, I'll get off the damn bed," he said, and propped himself up on his elbows, but his chair was a couple inches too far away to reach. His legs dangled from the side of the bed.

"Don't be such a bloody child."

His face filled with heat. "I'm trying here, you know. I'm

really trying, but I've got to say—" He pushed himself forward—he could probably just reach the chair—but he began to slide down, holding on to the mattress and blanket, down farther, finally smashing his left hand under his leg as he hit the cold linoleum floor. "You know, sometimes you're like a goddamned rock. Ouch, shit!" He inched himself up onto his hands, his left wrist aching from the fall, his right hand still smarting from the earring, and reached over to lock the brakes. He turned his back to the chair, awkwardly tucked his feet under himself, reached behind for the wheels, his forehead growing damp and his wrists pulsing, and began to push up onto the chair. She stared down at his arms quivering, his legs now bent against the floor, his shorts and T-shirt stiff from the rain, his hair a tangled nest, and she simply turned away. He glanced at the tiny logo on the corner of the cushion, the round stamp with the robin in the center, and how perfect, he thought, how perfectly ridiculous, a bird made to represent such utterly grounded misery.

He pressed his hands together and massaged the prick from the earring and his smarting wrist, and he tried to catch his breath. He pictured himself suddenly standing, marching out of the room, out of the clinic, walking all the way to Jake's house, where his mother and father sat eagerly waiting for him, where Hilary was probably worried about him, her older brother who was still, as she'd called him since she was a child, her best friend.

"Dan?" Brenda finally said.

He remembered the first time he'd seen the chair in the hospital room, and the way it had surprised him. The chair belonged in the window of a store that sold orthopedic shoes and adult diapers, not there in front of him, soon to be a cru cial part of his daily life. He'd felt as if he was watching himself look at it. He, Daniel Miller, couldn't be paralyzed (the real Daniel Miller was a person who was constantly moving, traveling, running, biking, going *somewhere*).

"Daniel?" Her voice was nervous.

He thought of himself and the way he'd looked as a boy. He still did have that long face. The walnut brown hair hadn't changed at all, nor had the brown of his close-set eyes, the olive tone of his skin. Even then he loathed having his picture taken, and even then, in those smiles, behind those fabricated smiles, was a resistance to faking happiness. He hoped only for his mother or father to put away the camera and come sit with him or play with him, do anything else besides asking him to pose.

He was still this person. He was still, of course, a son. And a husband. An artist. He was still essentially who he was.

"Daniel?"

He released the brakes and turned himself around. His hand screamed in pain, and his forehead grew warm again.

"Can you tell me what the hell you are doing?"

"I need to go find the doctor," he managed. "And see how long they plan to keep you here. Then I'm going to call Jake's again." He left the room without looking back at her—he just needed a few moments to himself.

His mother, father and brother arrived an hour later, after Daniel had called them, after the doctor had finally come to the room and told them he wanted to keep Brenda in the clinic one more night for observation and after Brenda had wept, saying all she wanted right then was her own bed at home and her fuzzy slippers, her own terrycloth bathrobe instead of "this crap piece of tissue that I have to wear."

He'd explicitly told his mother to meet him in the waiting area so that he could have some time alone with them first, but evidently she had forgotten. And now they appeared in the doorway like a small mob, Ellen dressed in a swinging navy blue skirt and light blue short-sleeved blouse; Joe, hovering close behind her, pushing his large, round glasses up his nose; Jake, dark rings under his eyes, and thinner than the last time Daniel saw him. On the phone, Ellen had insisted they come, and Daniel told her all right, but *please leave Liz and Hilary at home*—Brenda probably wasn't ready to see them yet. His mother had said that Liz was having twins, so, yes, it was probably best she stay home, and best that they not tell Brenda this yet, and Daniel had said, *What makes you think I'm ready to hear this?*

Now they stood before him in Brenda's room, tentative, a little unsure of what to do with themselves. Daniel wheeled closer to Brenda and took her hand, maybe to show that she wasn't contagious.

"Well, you found us," he said dumbly.

Ellen was the first to step forward. She went to him and held his head to her chest. She smelled of musky perfume and felt soft, plush, and Daniel's eyes began to water. Joe followed with a tight squeeze of Daniel's shoulder and a long hug for Brenda. Daniel worried he might unintentionally hurt her, and that she'd snap at him about her soreness. Jake hung back in the doorway, his hands shoved in his pockets, his eyes fixed on the floor as if he were trying desperately to think of the perfect thing to say.

"Are you comfortable here, Brenda?" Ellen asked. "Is this

bed all right? We brought you muffins from a bakery, blue-
berry muffins. Do they feed you here? Listen, you'll come
back to the house and rest some more." She grew teary. "We
were so worried about both of you before we heard, before
you called, and, well—"

"We have to stay here one more night," Daniel interjected.

"Then we'll bring dinner to you tonight," she said. "We'll
all come here and keep you company. We can celebrate Dad's
birthday here tomorrow morning. Right?" She reached for
Daniel's hand.

He tried to think of a gentle way to tell them that Brenda
wanted to head home as soon as she was released from the
clinic, and that they'd have to forgo Joe's birthday this year.
He sensed Brenda staring at him, and he muttered, "We'll
see. Let's go talk in the waiting room and have some muffins."

"We already ate. We only brought these for you," said Jake,
but Ellen whispered, "Come on," and herded them into the
hallway. Just before he closed the door behind him, Daniel
glanced back at Brenda, but she'd already closed her eyes
again and gone somewhere else.

—

They filled half of the tiny waiting room, the men in her
family. And sitting in the plastic orange chairs, hunched
toward each other, they appeared exhausted and pale and
forlorn, except, strangely, Joe. He stirred the cup of coffee
he'd bought at a gas station on the way to the clinic, an
expression of calm on his face, and she wondered what he
was thinking. Jake asked Daniel about his work, and he
responded that he was drawing something for a book, a
pamphlet and something else—she could barely hear his

soft, terse answers. Ellen looked at her husband and it seemed his mind was somewhere safe and warm and quite far away.

The only other person in the waiting room was a man sitting across from them, holding a sandwich. As her sons talked, Ellen watched the way his mouth opened and engulfed a large part of the sandwich—and so early! It wasn't even eleven. He sniffed and swallowed in one motion, the morsel sinking visibly down his throat. She began to wish he were not there. She felt too conscious of their conversation, too aware that he could hear every strained question Jake was asking.

Joe stopped his spoon in the middle of the coffee. "You'll be all right, Dan," he said, and she looked at him. "We're all going to be happy and healthy in the end." It sounded like a passing wish that had leaked out.

"I hope so," Jake replied.

Turning to Daniel, Ellen said, "Do you think Brenda would like something to preoccupy her? Maybe some magazines?" She glanced around the room and saw a pile of ratty toys in the corner, a one-eyed Raggedy Ann holding court on top. Ellen looked away. "Or a book? Would you like us to pick up some things in town?" She searched for gentle ways to ask whether he now knew exactly what had happened to the baby and why and what would happen next.

Daniel pushed himself up several inches in his wheelchair and sank back down. "I think she just needs to rest."

"Can we come stay with you at home? Help take care of Brenda?" she pressed on.

"She'll be feeling better in a few days, the doctor said. And he said she'd still be able to have children." He peeled a muffin from its wrapping and peered down at it with a strange look of dread.

"Oh." The syllable practically popped out of her mouth. "Good," she managed, but what if the same thing were to happen again? What if the problem was something related to Brenda's physiology? Ellen reached over and took Daniel's hands. She wished she could sit him on her lap and encircle him with her arms the way she could when he was a small child. She closed her eyes and felt him breathe deeply and then she tried to rise away from her body and her family. Mac-Neil said that just after Vera died, he tended to float above himself and to watch this hapless, leaden body plod through the long days. Ellen tried to do this now but a weight inside her chest would not let her go. So she stayed within herself, kept her eyes on her son and for some reason remembered Daniel as a boy, swimming, kicking water onto everyone else in the indoor swimming pool. (And where was this? Was this in Boston?) She thought of Jake and Hilary dog-paddling around the perimeter of the pool and remembered being a little nervous about the deep water. So she thought back further, to their family visit to Great Salt before Hilary was born. (It was here, she suddenly knew with exquisite certainty.) The four stayed in one room, and Ellen remembered being the last to fall asleep each night, and appreciating that her children and husband were so close to her and therefore safe in that enclosed space.

Daniel tugged his hand away. "I should go back to Brenda," he said, and she nodded. There was nothing more she could offer him right now.

On the way back from the clinic, the subject of Hilary's moving East arose, which led to Jake ranting about how he hoped Ellen and Joe wouldn't "enable Hilary," how she would learn nothing if people took care of her all the time. Joe finally cut him off. "We're going to help take care of you too. Whatever you need from us, you let us know," which seemed to quiet him for the time being.

At the house, Hilary and Liz were sitting on the back porch. Ellen had a brief urge to tell them of Jake's sour comments (he would learn when he became a parent: rarely was it a *choice* whether or not to help your kids), but of course decided against it. She merely set her hand on Hilary's head and said nothing. It was warm and her hair surprisingly soft, and Ellen kept her hand there for a moment. She looked out at the sea for the first time since she'd been here. She'd always wanted to live next to the ocean, and was glad that at least her son was able to now. That at least someone she loved could experience such a thing. The sky was cloudy and textured, like a thousand gray sheets piled messily on top of each other, and she could barely make out the horizon line, for the water was just as gray and choppy.

She turned and walked inside, past Joe and Jake, who were now reading the paper in the living room, and on into Jake's bedroom, where she'd seen a phone on the bedside table. She picked up the receiver and without thinking dialed MacNeil's number. He was supposed to return much later today, but she wanted to hear his voice on the answering machine. As she listened to the rings, she began to worry about what she would say if for some reason he'd gotten home early. But of course—

she would tell him of the weekend's tragedies. And she would use this word. She would tell him all about what had happened to Daniel and Brenda, and then she would tell him what had happened earlier—about Jake's fall and Joe's almost getting them lost on their way there and the strange boy at the gas station. She would tell MacNeil everything, and he would understand and sympathize and utter something wise and explanatory about bad things happening to innocent people. Or would he? It was he who typically spoke of his own tragedy and she who consoled him. Would he even want to hear of her weekend? Or would he rather talk about his own? Most likely he would change the subject back to him and Vera and his grief, that darkness that always hung in the air between them. The phone rang three times, four, five, and finally his machine picked up and his voice said, "Can't come to the phone so leave a message," as if he couldn't quite bring himself to use the word "I." She quickly hung up, stood and headed into the next room, where she took a seat next to Jake on the couch. She was afraid to say anything to him lest she unleash another of his tirades.

"Mom," he said after a moment. "Have you ever collected anything?"

"No. Well, when I was a child I kept hair ribbons. But no, nothing really since then. Why?"

"What do you think of collecting? Do you think it's silly?"

She had no idea what he was getting at. "It depends, I suppose, on what's being collected. Are you thinking of starting some sort of collection?" She glanced around the room. "Art?" she asked, intrigued.

"No, no, nothing that civilized. It's just sometimes I find these things—junk, really."

"Oh?" she prodded, hoping he'd continue, but he said no more. "You know, sometimes I wish we could afford to collect art. Can you imagine original paintings on the walls of our shabby little house?"

"It's not so bad. And you could probably afford one or two. I could help out."

"No, no," she said, and smiled. "I wouldn't want you to."

"You always wanted more."

"I suppose I did. But I didn't *need* more."

"You sound like Dad, you know. Can I ask you something?" She nodded.

"I don't mean this to be rude or anything, but how come you and he never thought of getting different jobs that earned more money?"

But it was, in fact, rude. It was an ugly, distasteful question. She pushed her hand into the leather sofa cushion and looked out the window at the clouds hovering above the water. "We did well enough," she said. "And anyway, we got on our paths and then what could we do? Your dad loves his job, you know that. And I'm happy at the school. That library is what I know."

"You don't regret anything?"

She shook her head. Her acceptance and longing had lived beside each other for so many years, she supposed they'd become almost indistinguishable. She looked at him. "This collecting. You've got a room full of junk somewhere?"

He appeared stung. "*Mom.*" He took himself too seriously. She had the urge to muss his hair. "Why *do* you suppose people collect things?"

"Maybe to fill some kind of a void?"

"Huh." He suddenly looked terribly sad.

"I'm sure there are other reasons," she said. "You've secretly begun collecting dead bodies in the basement? You've become a serial killer."

"Not funny," he huffed.

"A little funny." She sounded like Joe, trying to lighten the mood, but it wasn't working. She changed tack and told him about Isabella Stewart Gardner's collection. Ellen told him that she'd been reading a book about the woman, and as she spoke she began to worry that she was saying too much. But no, she wasn't—the museum and MacNeil were two separate things. There was nothing wrong with her love of the place or her interest in the woman's life. Yes, Vera and MacNeil had been the ones to take her there first. Yes, MacNeil had taught her quite a lot about Isabella and given Ellen his book, but so what? She loved the place as a separate entity from MacNeil. She absolutely did. "After her only child died and her marriage began to fall apart, she traveled the world—Scandinavia, Russia, Vienna, Paris, later the Middle East. She went to all sorts of lectures on Italian studies, and began collecting art." Jake's eyes began to wander the room, but she continued, determined to be heard. "At first she bought Parisian gowns and jewels, and she developed this idea of her house outside Boston as a sort of Venetian palazzo. She supervised the expansion and rebuilding of the place, and decided where each pillar and arch and doorway would be. Eventually she collected 290 paintings, 280 pieces of sculpture, 60 drawings and 130 prints, 460 pieces of furniture, 250 textiles, 240 objects of ceramic and glass, as well as lots of rare books and manuscripts." Jake looked at her sideways and nodded. She had memorized these numbers just a few weeks ago. They seemed grand, encyclopedic, like the shopping list of a god, and she loved rattling them off to people. MacNeil, in a glum moment, said these numbers only proved Isabella's obsessive need to acquire everything she could, but Ellen was convinced they were a product of more than just money.

She thought of Daniel's new house and how the tall windows still had no curtains and the cold wood floors no rugs. She could sew thick, warm curtains and find them some colorful, plush rugs at a discount store. She could bring them prints, perhaps, some calming scenes of places far away to help them forget all that had happened, even if only for a second or two. Of course, they had the strangest aesthetics. Daniel, for all his somberness, enjoyed mostly humorous art. He collected original R. Crumbs and had plastered the walls of his studio with these horrid pictures of women—their breasts as large as watermelons—chasing wilted, hideous little men. Brenda had equally dark taste but preferred photographs of unhappiness and poverty, war and desperation. Ellen would bring them some La Tour or Vermeer prints, something with light and hope. She would visit the Gardner Museum shop when she returned and see what inspired her. And she would stop by the local nursery and pick up some plants with bright, lively flowers, plants that were easy to manage. Orchids, or maybe African violets, which had been Vera's favorites.

Later, Liz set out ingredients for people to make sandwiches, but no one had much of an appetite. Ellen looked around the kitchen at each person in his or her own world—at Jake, staring out the window, thinking about his mysterious collection of junk; at Joe, reading, oddly, the arts section of the paper;

at Hilary, rubbing her fingertips together; and at Liz, both
hands bracing her knees, a look of grave consternation on her
face as if she were about to give birth. And what if she were?
What if the two unformed babies came toppling out too early?

Ellen sat up straight and focused on the tiled floor, the
small squares the color of rich earth. Isabella had chosen
bright tiles for her floors, Mediterranean blues and greens.
She'd found novel ways to soften the fierce New England light
and make it resemble the coyer Italian sunlight. She spread
gray curtains of lace over her enormous windows. Around the
panes she hung paintings of the Madonna, or mythical gods,
or the baby Jesus. Paintings warm and sacred but also muted
and gentle. In a letter to her great friend Bernard Berenson,
she wrote, "I look out as I write and see the rain puddling the
snow and man and beast wallowing! Inside in this my boudoir,
where I am writing, it is charming. Everywhere bits of Italy."
Ellen had jotted down this last sentence on the back of a
receipt and now kept it in her wallet. It sounded to her like
the start of a poem.

—

It'd grown humid, the worst sort of air that caused the mos-
quitoes to descend in swarms and people on the island to walk
in slow motion, glistening with sweat. Jake stretched out on an
Adirondack chair and patted his forehead with a tissue. He
watched Liz and Hilary wander down the small path to the
water, kick off their sandals and dip their toes in the tide.
They turned to each other, talking and nodding. Strangely,
unaccountably, it seemed they'd taken to each other this
weekend. They looked almost similar from this distance: both
tall, though Liz was slightly taller; both fairly big, though of

course Hilary had grown much larger. Even from here Jake could see the shallow dimples on the back of her legs, the long creases where her arms met her torso. Liz's body was firmer, slightly muscular in the shoulders and calves, wide through the hips. She had far better posture.

While he watched them talk casually, while he lounged on his back porch, Brenda lay in that bed in the clinic and Jake now wished more than anything that he was there, not here, there beside her in her room to tell her and Daniel that he was sorry for what they had gone through. He had not said anything to her. He'd merely hovered behind his parents, mute as he searched for the best words. He should have said that there must be nothing worse than what they'd just been through, and for this to happen when they were away from home. But he'd been intimidated by the enormity of the situation—the only sentences that occurred to him were stiff condolences or unfounded assurances that he knew would only upset them more.

Low waves splashed Liz's feet and she took a step backwards. Hilary swept her hands in wide gestures. She was telling a story, maybe, and Liz nodded every few moments. She was a born listener—she managed to make everyone feel fascinating. After a while, the two turned and made their way back to the house. Playful smiles on their faces, they looked as if they'd been talking about him and he suddenly wanted to yell, *Do you know how lucky you are? How can you look so happy at a time like this?*

"Hey," Hilary called. "You should check out the water. It'll wake you up for the rest of your life."

Liz said, "She's right, you know."

He stood, lifted his hand in a wave and walked inside. His

father was sitting on the floor right next to the coffee table, his back facing Jake. Joe leaned forward and said, "That's it, honey," and when he looked closer, Jake saw Babe lolling around in one of their casserole dishes that Joe had filled with water. "There's a good boy. Your dad loves you, yes he does." Joe had never been this demonstrative with any of them. He stroked Babe's shell and continued on. "We've had a hard weekend, honey. Some bad things have happened to Dan."

Certain that he wanted to hear no more, Jake cleared his throat to announce his presence, and Joe turned around. "Didn't see you there," he mumbled.

"I just came in a second ago," Jake said. He sat on the couch next to him and looked down at Babe. "You do love that thing," he said, and his father nodded. "You can go ahead and take that casserole dish home with you."

"He's clean, don't worry. I'll wash it out afterward."

"Fine, fine," Jake said. "Hey, can I ask you something? What do you and Hilary talk about?"

Joe looked up. "She tells me about her life, I guess. And I listen."

"What does she tell you?" There was no point tiptoeing around the real questions. "Did she tell you about the father of her baby? Who he is? Did she say that she feels bad about having a baby on her own?"

"No." His father looked briefly at him and then at the floor. "Of course not."

"Well, I for one worry about what's going to happen to her."

"I worry about all of you."

"Even me?"

"Of course. You'll see, once your babies come along. You never stop worrying, even after they grow up." Babe lifted his head.

"You don't much show it."

"No," he said. "I guess I don't really see the point."

Outside, Liz and Hilary took seats on the porch. Liz stretched her arms above her head and then burst out laughing.

"What exactly do you worry about?" Jake asked, drawing his hand across his forehead. He'd grown warm again.

"Well," Joe mumbled, and pushed his hands together. "For starters, the fact that you've got two babies on the way. It'll be a lot of work. You two have someone to help, right?"

"Liz is asking around about nannies, and her friends at the school have offered to help out too if we need it. She's taken care of every possible thing, I think."

"You're lucky to have her." He paused, as if trying to anticipate what Jake might want to hear. "How could you not like her? And of course I like you too, Jake. I like each one of my kids very much."

Jake crinkled a tissue in his pocket.

"Your mom and I could've done much worse, when you think about it. I've got friends whose kids refused to grow up. Bill Dooley's son never left home. Mom's friend Maureen's daughter is in and out of the mental hospital."

Jake thought to say, *So your standards are high*, but stopped himself.

Babe's head suddenly shot to the side and the turtle appeared to be looking at Jake. "Christ," he said, and looked away. "Hey, remember that fishing trip you took me on a thousand years ago? Just the two of us? That morning we both tried to learn fishing but didn't catch a thing?" It had been Ellen's idea. Jake had been throwing tantrums over the smallest things at school, and Ellen had thought some father-son time might help.

His father sucked his lips into his mouth for a moment. Clearly he didn't remember a thing. "I'll tell you what I remember," he finally said. "This was maybe when you were ten or so. You and Hilary were riding your bikes with a bunch of kids, and she fell off hers. She broke her toe, remember? It started raining, and she couldn't walk, so you gave her a pig-gyback ride all the way home—it had to be three miles you walked with her like that in the pouring rain, and when you got home, you said you'd tried to ride her on your bike but you worried she'd fall and hurt herself again. So you carried her on your back instead." Joe smiled. "You're going to be a good father."

"I hope so." Jake said, only vaguely remembering that day. "Though sometimes I'm not so sure." He tried to think of a way to broach yesterday's embarrassments without revealing the actual details, but it seemed that their sting had faded, and soon the women came inside, and Hilary went to Joe, and Liz gave Jake a squeeze on the shoulder, then headed to the bedroom. He stood and followed her, and suggested calling Daniel to check in on him and ask him whether they planned to join them the next day for Joe's birthday dinner. Jake went to sit on the bed, picked up the receiver, and Liz stood before him, his head in her hands. As he listened to the phone ring-ing in the clinic, she pressed his forehead against the slight curve of her belly.

"Our whole family is in there," she whispered as someone at the clinic answered the phone.

"Hey there," he said happily, and tried to calm his voice to an appropriate sobriety as he asked for Brenda's room.

"Yes?" Brenda answered.

"It's Jake. You feeling any better?"

"Sort of. You want Dan?"

Jake couldn't take his eyes off his wife, who stood above him, smiling down. "All right, but first, how are *you* doing?" he asked Brenda. "We've been thinking about you all day."

"Oh. I'm fine, like I said."

He could barely hear her, she spoke so softly. Though Jake could certainly see why his brother married Brenda—she was attractive and talented, and seemed intelligent enough—he found her a little aloof. Part of him suspected she didn't like him that much, didn't like his money or his corporate job with money (not that she understood precisely what he did, not that anyone in the family really did or ever once thought to ask about it) and didn't really like their big new house or the fact that Liz was a talented cook and an organized housekeeper, such predictable wifely traits. Part of him felt extraordinarily American around her—clumsy and gaudy, materialistic.

When Daniel took the phone, Jake asked gently whether they planned to come for Joe's birthday. "Listen, Brenda doesn't need to come if it'll be too hard for her to see Hil and Liz pregnant. You could come for a little while on your own," Jake said. "And if you want, I could try to get you a room at a B&B, you know, if you want some space."

"We'll have to play it by ear and see what she's up for. Definitely not tonight, but maybe tomorrow. Tell Dad we'll try." There was a brief silence, and the two said goodbye.

Outside the bedroom, Ellen paced. "You need something, Mom?" Jake asked

"Just to use the phone."

"To call the clinic? I just called Dan, and they said they're going to try to come when they can, but no promises."

"Oh," she said, a flustered look on her face. "I actually wanted to call the neighbors."

"For what?"

"To check on things at home," she said, looking at her hands.

Jake nodded and they continued past her. He whispered to Liz, "What do you think that's about?"

"Maybe she's having an illicit affair," she muttered, raising her eyebrows.

"Ha," he said. "My parents don't do that sort of thing." He couldn't help himself.

Liz rolled her eyes and went to join Hilary, who was now snapping green beans over the sink in the kitchen. Jake returned to his seat on the couch, where he lifted his legs onto the pile of blankets and closed his eyes.

"Seventy-five." Joe's voice was a surprise in the quiet room. He was still on the floor beside Babe.

"Yes?"

"Can you believe your dad is this old?"

Perhaps with age, Joe was turning maudlin and self-pitying. "It's not that old," Jake said.

"Bull. It's old. Your dad is an old man." Joe reached for the casserole dish with both hands and began to stand. He groaned and leaned forward.

"You got it?"

His knees cracked, but he finally made it upright. "What will you do when I can't stand by myself?"

"Stop it."

"You never think about what'll it be like to get to this point. I don't mean to be complaining, but still. It's incomprehensible, sometimes." Joe sighed and started toward their bedroom.

Maybe he needed to know that he wasn't the only one worried about his future. Jake called after him, "I'm afraid of the future too, Dad."

"Hmm?" Joe stopped and turned.

"I worry too, you know, about getting older."

Joe leaned against the wall and frowned. "My parents were a burden to me, you know," he said. He rarely spoke about his past or his family. Joe's father had died before Jake was born, and his mother had lived with him until he was twenty-five, also before Jake was born. Joe had taken care of her and tended to her when she had cancer. But he never spoke of it, and Jake knew only the bare facts. "I suppose I'm better at taking care of people than being taken care of," Joe finally said.

"Dad, you're not sick or something, are you?"

"No, I'm fine. Just a little preoccupied on my birthday, I suppose."

Jake nodded slowly.

Joe shrugged and shook his head. He was done talking about himself. "And what about you? You holding up this weekend?"

"Sure," Jake said.

"Everything okay with Liz? At work?" He sat down on the edge of the easy chair and set Babe, in his dish, on the end table.

Jake edged closer to his father and told him that in fact he'd had a few arguments with Liz because he'd done some stupid things this weekend. That work would get busier soon,

that his nerves had been frayed, that he'd wanted this weekend to be perfect, for everyone to enjoy the house and the
beach and to love this place as much as he did. He'd just
wanted to make everyone happy, he finally said, and now so
much had gone wrong.

Joe looked at him. "It was a good thing, getting us all
together. "

Jake nodded.

"And the rest of it. Well, I think that's pretty normal, you
know."

"What do you mean?"

"All those nerves and everything. They've got to be normal
for what's going on in your life." He seemed as if he wanted
to say more.

"You think so?"

Joe gathered the dish and stood again. "Sure."

Jake set a hand on the dish to steady it. "Thanks, Dad."

"For what?"

"For saying that."

Joe adjusted the dish in his hands. "It wasn't anything."

"Sure it was."

"Time for Babe's nap," Joe said quietly, and headed back to
the bedroom.

—

Hilary had told Liz about meeting Alex, about Bellows' Field
and the salt magnate and his heirs, about Alex's apartment
and about what had ultimately happened between the two of
them. Hilary had only met her sister-in-law a few times, and
in the end didn't dislike her as much as she thought she
might, though there was something in Liz's healthy complex-

ion and her wholesome manner—she'd said "fudge" when she dropped a plate earlier; she'd alphabetized the bottles of herbs in her spice rack—that Hilary didn't entirely trust. But here they were for the first time alone and Hilary found herself strangely eager to tell someone the details of her first few hours on the island (as if to verify that Alex actually had existed), and Liz eager to hear them when they walked down to the water. "You went back to his place?" Liz had asked, more impressed than horrified. "And then he said what?" Hilary had repeated the facts excitedly and set her hands on her hips. "Let's go to Books & Beans tonight." "Not a chance," Hilary had said, "I don't want him to think that I expect anything from him, or that I'm suddenly smitten with him after one day," and Liz'd argued, "Oh, come on, let's go, if for no other reason than so I can get a look at him." Hilary was surprised at Liz's interest, as well as her easy acceptance of the whole thing. Hilary had been hesitant to mention it at first, as it felt a bit like admitting promiscuity to a virgin. Not that Liz herself exuded prudishness, but her life with Jake did seem clean and white and pure as new soap. "What would be the point in going back there? I think we both knew that this was a onetime thing," Hilary finally said. "Is this just some desperate attempt for you to find someone to father my child?" Liz groaned and laughed. "You give me too much credit. I'd never try to scale that mountain." Hilary swallowed hard, faked a smile and suggested they head back inside.

Now they stood in the kitchen preparing dinner. Hilary found herself wondering about Alex again, trying to guess where he might be and with whom—but what was the point? And why did he keep reappearing in her thoughts? "Liz,"

Hilary said as she snapped off the end of a bean and tossed it into a bowl. "Can I ask you a weird question? You might hate me for it."

"Sure, those are the best kind," Liz said.

"What was it about Jake? What made you first want to be with him?" she asked. "And please don't tell me it was the sex."

Liz smiled. "It wasn't the sex," she said. "I don't know. He was the opposite of everyone I'd ever gone out with, I guess. Sometimes I think that the preconditions of love determine everything. Everyone I'd been with before, I'd had to chase. I'd always been drawn to these distant types who inevitably broke my heart. And then came Jake, this person who displayed his fears and weaknesses on a tray and wanted more than anything just to be with me."

Alex was yet another in a line of similar men. Another Bill David, another Jesse Varnum—and why was she, Hilary, still drawn to them? Maybe her heart hadn't been broken badly enough yet. Maybe she hadn't allowed it to be completely broken—but why should she? "Were you attracted to him?" she couldn't help herself.

"I was attracted to someone wanting to be with me, and yeah, that was him. So yeah, I was."

"Are you still?"

"Sure," Liz said, and leaned in front of Hilary to grab a bean. She popped it in her mouth and her eyes fell to the floor.

"He's crazy about you," Hilary said, and reached for a bean. She felt a flash of sympathy for her brother, but tried to ignore it. "You want me to set the table?"

Dinner was filled with long silences punctuated only by Ellen commenting on the food or Jake on the weather. Hilary glanced around the table at each person quietly eating dinner. Maybe her family had used up all of their conversation. She had always thought that they had a limited number of things to say to each other. After all, here were five very different people. How did any family have anything to talk about after this many years? Such silence was to be expected, she supposed, though she was never comfortable with too much quiet, no matter what the situation was. With men, it seemed to indicate some sort of failure on her part or his. With coworkers, it indicated boredom. She worried she'd have to endure great silences with her child. Before he/she could speak, of course, but later, when it could, when she'd run out of things to say because she and the child were now a family too and by definition had a limited number of things to say to each other.

Liz pulled Hilary aside when she and her mother were washing the dishes and whispered, "Tonight? Books & Beans?"

"I thought we'd scrapped that idea."

"Not officially."

"You didn't tell Jake about it all, did you?" Hilary pressed her fingertips together.

"No, I didn't. Though he'd probably welcome the distraction at this point."

The idea of leaving this increasingly quiet house and seeing Alex once more did, despite herself, appeal to Hilary. It was growing dark outside. She heard a heavy gust of wind whistle past. "I guess we could drop by," she said. "Just for a minute."

"There you go."

Hilary went to the bathroom to look herself over in the mirror. Her face had become a bloated moon with the pregnancy, her lips were chapped. She was a lost cause, and considered calling it off and telling Liz that she didn't feel well. But of course Liz wouldn't buy it.

Liz knocked on the door. "Ready?"

Hilary opened it and nodded reluctantly.

Her father approached them in the hallway and asked where they were headed, and before Hilary could stop him, he was saying he'd like to join them and Liz was leading him toward the front door.

Hilary and Liz chatted all the way to town, Joe in the seat behind them. "What are you going to say when you first see him?" Liz asked, and Hilary shushed her, gesturing to her father. "He doesn't care, do you, Joe?"

"No, I'm no one. I don't hear anything," he said, and Hilary turned to him. "Liz wants me to go say hi to this person I met at the bookstore earlier yesterday, when I was waiting for everyone."

"Oh?"

"This *guy*," Liz added.

"It was nothing," Hilary said. "She is just unhealthily curious."

"I see," he said, and smiled sympathetically. "We can browse the books while Liz talks to him, then."

"Hilary's just playing coy," Liz said. "She likes him. She just won't admit it."

"I don't!" They sounded like teenagers.

Joe smiled at her and shrugged. "It's okay if you do."

"I don't, Dad," Hilary said. "Honestly." They were calling

too much attention to the whole matter, and she was protesting too much.

They parked on Main Street and walked quietly past the general store and the small gallery. The air was still thick and warm, the sky almost dark. No one else was on the sidewalk. "How about we just check out that gallery instead?" Hilary mumbled at one point, and Liz said, "Not a chance."

Inside Books & Beans, Alex leaned against the wall behind the register. Next to him stood a tan girl, a rope of black hair resting on one of her shoulders. The two whispered about something and Alex brushed his hand against her waist. Joe and Liz and Hilary, who quickly ducked behind the tall shelves of books, stood there for a second, watching. Hilary's chest squeezed at the sight of them. "Let's go somewhere else. This is idiotic. I don't want to make him uncomfortable," Hilary said, but Liz took her arm. Her father headed off to the biography section. "Go talk to him," Liz hissed. "She probably just works here too."

"I don't want to," Hilary said. She stepped back behind the shelves, which when she looked closer she saw held self-help books, and pulled out one about fatherhood. Liz hovered at the end of the aisle, peeking out at Alex and the girl. "It does seem like they're just coworkers or friends," Liz said unconvincingly. "He *is* good-looking. I see what you mean."

"Liz."

Liz went over to her and took the book from her hands. "*On Becoming a Father*?"

"Maybe I should buy it."

"We're here so you could forget about that for a night."

"I can't forget about it," Hilary said. She grabbed the book. "And anyway, I don't want to." She drew a long breath and looked at her sister-in-law's expectant face. "God, this is just ridiculous," Hilary finally said. She pushed past Liz, marched to the counter and handed the book to Alex.

"Hilary!" he said, as if he hadn't seen her approach.

"Hello. I'm buying this for my brother," she thought to say. "And my sister-in-law. The one back there, hiding."

Alex looked behind her and smiled. The girl beside him tugged on her braid and licked her lips. Her eyeteeth protruded just slightly from her other teeth. She had pale blue eyes, heavy lids, a spray of freckles across her face. She was both beautiful and homely.

"How's it going with your family?" he asked as he rang up the book. The girl watched them closely.

"Not so well, really." She hesitated, but then the words just came. "My brother and his wife lost their baby yesterday."

"Oh. God, I'm sorry," he said dumbly.

Hilary handed him the cash, and he paused at the money between them. He pushed her hand back. "Go ahead. It's yours," he said.

She felt like a ridiculous spinster, now beset by tragedy. "Take the money. If you want, keep it," she said.

"I'm sorry," he said again.

The girl looked at Hilary's stomach.

"I'm pregnant," Hilary said to her, lest the girl think she was just fat. This probably communicated that there was nothing to worry about, that Hilary was just some friend of Alex's, someone completely nonthreatening to whatever agenda the girl might have. She turned her eyes to the floor, inched closer to Alex and said, "Congratulations," with either irony or sincerity, Hilary couldn't quite tell.

"We're going now. Goodbye." Hilary turned, her chest

pounding. She headed toward the door and slipped her arm through Liz's.

"Nothing? You want to invite him back to the house?"

She tugged her forward. "Let's go find Dad."

He was thumbing through something with a pale woman's face on the cover, and though he didn't seem ready to leave yet, he quickly slid the book back onto its shelf and followed them out.

On the way home, Hilary stared out the window at what she knew was the water but was now only darkness. How embarrassing this all had been. How utterly stupid of her to let Liz talk her into it. She felt her baby shift inside her and poke her . . . her what, her liver? To her left, Liz squirmed in her seat, complaining of pain in her legs as she wriggled around, trying to find a more comfortable position. The car jerked forward each time she moved and leaned on the gas. Hilary flipped open the book on her lap but couldn't read a thing in the dark. She would read it when she got home. She would try to teach herself all about what it meant to be a father, and maybe, then maybe, she could show everyone that she was fully capable of handling this other life on her own, this little person who would be so dependent on her. She rubbed her fingers together. None of them thought she'd be able to handle it. Well, maybe Daniel. But Jake, and probably her mother—they thought her child was doomed.

"He didn't seem so great," her father said from the back seat.

"Thank you, Dad."

"You've got enough to focus on anyway."

"Exactly," she said.

"You're past all that," he said so quietly it was barely audible.

"Past what?" Liz asked. "Men?"

"Men, boys, whatever," Hilary said with as much conviction as she could muster. She turned to her father, who looked at her proudly and smiled.

8

The Sound of Forgiveness

Brenda asked Daniel how long Vanessa had stayed at the clinic and whether she knew what had happened, and he told her that he'd promised Vanessa they'd call her. He found her phone number in his wallet, and Brenda picked up the receiver beside the bed and dialed. Someone else answered, and Brenda spoke quietly, Britishly, as she asked whether Vanessa happened to be available. She covered the receiver and mouthed, "Freeman," and Daniel nodded once. When Vanessa came on the line and Brenda described what had happened, she turned away from him and her shoulders dropped. "No, they had to operate," she said, and then, "I know, I knew something was wrong. I hadn't felt anything for a while." She reassured Vanessa that she was fine now, that the clinic seemed good enough and that no, there was no real need for Vanessa to come back, Brenda had just wanted to let her know what had happened and thank her for the ride to the clinic. "Yes, all right, and I'll call you when we get back home. Maybe we can arrange another trip up here, maybe next summer or something, or maybe you could come visit us," she said, and Daniel pictured all of Brenda's strange, situational friends—Vanessa and Esther, Morris Arnold and his girlfriend, as well as his foul dog Rex, Freeman Corcoran, even—crowded in their living room, having a drink.

After Brenda set down the receiver, she tried to stand beside her bed but began to sway whenever she took her arms away from the rail. After a few failed attempts, she sat back down.

"What is it about us that seems to invite such bad luck?" Daniel asked.

"Don't be glib." The fluorescent lights above them flickered and buzzed.

"I'm not. I'm being serious. Look at us."

"I'd rather not," she said, and draped the sheet over her legs. "I'd rather not just sit here and think about misery, to be honest."

He adjusted his glasses. She was never one to want to dissect unhappiness. He was the analytical one, the stereotypically female one in that respect, he supposed. It was strange that his own wife didn't share this tendency. "Can I ask you a question?" he pressed on. He began to have the sense that if he didn't ask these questions, they would devour him. "Do you still like me?"

"Yeah, sure," she said, her eyes on the bed. "But I dunno, sometimes you can be tough, Dan. You know that. Sometimes I think about when we first met, and what I liked about you then. I liked your grouchiness, I suppose, because you weren't grouchy to me, only to everyone else. It made me feel as if I'd been admitted to some sort of club. And I liked your deep voice. I liked your nose."

"My nose?"

She licked her lips twice. "I thought you had a good, strong nose, just the right length, no bumps or jags. It gave you a strong and decisive look. I didn't know very many decisive men back then."

"And now?" He drummed his fingers against the arm of his chair. He knew he should be asking her how she was feeling and whether she needed anything from him—a back rub, a glass of water? "Do you still like my nose?" he asked.

She shrugged. "Mum says you know what you need and want and at least you can articulate that, which is more than most people can."

"How come you never told me any of this? I never knew you liked my voice. Or my nose, for that matter."

"I suppose I just forgot to. Anyway, you've always known most everything else that I think of you."

"That I complain too much, and that I've become a depressing person to be around."

She nibbled her lip. "You've been through so much hell."

"So have you now," he said. "We aren't such different people, you know." He remembered when they'd lie in bed and he'd sketch her knee or her chin using only words. This seemed like decades ago.

"We both hate anchovies," she offered.

He nodded. "We both love Barcelona and Lagos and our little island in Greece." They'd spent their honeymoon on one of the smallest islands in the Aegean.

"Though you hate Nice, and I would be happy living

there." She often spoke of happiness in a stingy way, as if it were only available to her, as if it were something he'd never attain because he wasn't emotionally or perhaps biologically capable. At times, it seemed she did connect it with gender: only other women—her mother, her friends, even Vanessa—could understand her search for happiness, and could truly experience happiness themselves.

"Nice is expensive and overrun with snotty Europeans," he admitted.

"We both sleep on our left sides, even now," she offered.

"Some things haven't changed."

"A few, I suppose."

"I'm still the same person for the most part, just living inside a slightly less functional body." He wasn't certain he fully believed this downplaying of the accident, but maybe just speaking the words was some sort of progress.

She made no expression, as if she too wasn't convinced.

"We both lost something in the middle of a street," he said, and swallowed. It hadn't come out the right way at all. Brenda's eyes filled, and he moved closer to her bed and sandwiched her small hands in his. "I'm sorry. I shouldn't have said that."

She shrugged and took her hands back. Quietly, almost inaudibly, she said, "You're forgiven."

He wanted to ask her if he'd heard her correctly, and if he had, to please say it again, again and again, but he worried she'd take it back or say he was pulling too much from two little words. Still, he began to let himself think that she forgave him more than just this one insensitive comment—his loathing of Tammy Ann Green and Morris Arnold, his sharpness with Vanessa, all of his bitterness and despair both before and after the accident. Indeed, he hadn't changed all that much. She'd just gotten to know him better over the years.

He looked at her, then out the window at the leafy ash trees, their branches bobbing in the wind. He thought of their friends' newborn baby who was born breech and of the Korean baby that Evan and John were going to adopt. He thought of Lily and Maria, or was it Marie?—twins Brenda's cousin recently had in London, and the photograph of the two dressed in tiny hot pink jumpers and holding on to two enormous teddy bears wearing matching jumpers. He thought of James Roger McDonald, who was born to Daniel's agent Richard the year before. He was a handsome baby, with soft blond hair and round, liquid blue eyes and Daniel squirmed when Richard handed him the baby for the first time, as he had no idea how exactly to hold him. The boy weighed nothing in his hands, and his head rested in Daniel's palm like a baseball. He looked up at Daniel, right into his eyes, and Daniel leaned over to kiss his forehead. He smelled of bananas, and Daniel reached down to kiss him again. It was amazing to him that this was a whole life in his hands, and that a life could weigh so little. Daniel was surprised he remembered the boy's full name now. He was usually terrible with names.

Brenda soon dropped off to sleep again, and Daniel dozed off too and was woken a while later by a nurse, who helped him onto the other bed, where the pillow was flat and the sheets smelled of mildew. He tried to make himself drift off again despite the too soft pillow and the smell. Brenda was now sleeping soundly. Or maybe she was just pretending. He'd done the same recently, when he heard her stirring in their bedroom, unable to find a comfortable position for her stomach. Now it seemed the worst sort of betrayal.

He considered what it might be like to return home and to step inside their house for the first time without the baby and without a plan for what would come next. First he would call their counselor at the sperm bank and let her know. Then Brenda would phone her doctor and her family again. And then what? What to do when there was no one left to notify?

Suddenly he remembered Freeman Corcoran's work—his childlike paintings in electric primary colors of houses, happy little houses flying through the air or floating on the ocean, drifting past beneath the sun or the moon. Fish, boats, whales drawn in bloated, silly shapes. It was a crime, the acclaim Corcoran got for these blocky, simplistic scenes that any five-year-old could have painted. People paid a fortune for his work. Brenda had to be lying when she said to Vanessa that she loved it. She had to be—it was the sort of art they loved to hate. Obvious, pretty, infantile art created for the widest possible consumption. "Fun" art.

He thought of Tammy Ann Green. And then it dawned on him. He would call the doctor she worked for when they got home, and Daniel would ask to meet him and hear more about his research on spinal cord injuries. Why hadn't he thought to do this yet? He wouldn't tell Tammy Ann, as she'd discourage him, so he'd do some research of his own and track down the doctor himself. Hell, he already knew the man's name because Tammy Ann had mentioned it so often. It was a plan, and Daniel smiled to himself. Maybe he *would* walk again.

262 The Birthdays

—

"Did you buy any books?" Ellen asked Hilary when the three returned from Books & Beans.

"She bought something about parenting," Liz announced, and smirked at Hilary. The two were in cahoots over something, Ellen thought disdainfully, and rose from the couch. If they wanted to have fun during this sad time, let them. "It's late and it's been such a long day. I'm going to bed," she declared, and Joe followed her into the green bedroom.

"What are they up to?" she asked. The curtains swayed.

"Boys."

"What?" Ellen went to open the window a little more, and breathed in the scent of the ocean, briny and pungent.

"Liz wanted Hilary to see some guy she met earlier."

It was some sort of breakthrough; Joe never paid attention to incidents such as these, and certainly never reported back about them. "She mentioned someone to me earlier, I think."

"I couldn't tell his age. But he looked younger than Hil. Anyway, it was unsuccessful. She decided against it at the last minute."

"It? What 'it'?"

"I'm not sure, frankly," he said, lifting his shirt above his head. "I wasn't about to ask."

"I suppose not," she said. She pulled her nightgown from beneath her pillow and slid off her skirt, and realized that for the first time in hours she was not thinking about Daniel or Brenda or, for that matter, MacNeil. "Did she tell you who the father of the baby is?"

"No."

"You'd tell me if she did, right?"

"Ellen."

"Well?"

"Of course I would, but she won't, and you should stop letting it nag at you."

She tried to pull back a little. "It'll be good for Hilary move back home."

"It will. We can help her with the baby when she needs it."

"Just don't leave all the hard work to me," she said, apropos of nothing, for when the children were small, Joe actually did help more than the other young fathers they knew. He was an expert at changing diapers and bathing babies. His greatest contentment was seeing the kids in their pajamas first thing in the morning, rubbing sleep from their eyes, gathering around the table for breakfast and filling the room with noise.

Ellen lifted the sheet and blanket on her bed and slid beneath. Joe switched off the lamp between them and took a deep breath. He would be fast asleep in seconds, but she wasn't tired yet. Her mind spun. Hilary and a baby alone—it was still hard to fathom. She replayed the conversation she'd had with her daughter earlier. Why not research archaeology, learn about the best people in the field living in Boston and bring Hilary to them? Once the baby was a little older, she'd have time. She'd need a job. Why not try to find one she liked? Joe could help. He loved research, the hunt for attainable answers.

But Daniel and Brenda needed her and Joe more right now, at least more urgently. Her primary focus over the next several weeks would be filling their house with art and color and life. Improving their immediate surroundings—beautifying their world. Once Isabella's young son and later her husband died, she threw herself into the building of the museum, the collecting, the details. It was only then, after so much tragedy, that she became a true curator. Two great sorrows, in the end, had prompted her toward such happiness.

The next morning she stretched her arms, sore from her sleeping in the same position all night, and tiptoed out of the room. Apparently she was the first one up. The living room had flooded with the early morning sun, the strongest sun since they'd arrived, she thought as she stepped out onto the back porch. Her cotton nightgown billowed in a cool breeze, and she felt almost naked, standing outside like this. She hurried to one of the Adirondack chairs and sat, tucking her gown beneath her legs.

Mornings were always her clearest time, and once in a while, just to think, she stayed in bed well past the time that Joe had woken and fixed himself coffee. Whether spent in bed or puttering around the kitchen, mornings gave her a sense of freshness, of newness and perspective. And after the rain and then the thick humidity, this particular morning was a relief with its dry, warm air, the quiet of the house and the rhythmic wash of the ocean before her, pushing and pulling its tide from the shore. Not one person could be seen on the beach, and she felt it was all hers for the moment, the great, wide Atlantic, all its fish and plants, its tides. And how perfect, how kind that the sun had chosen to shine like this today, on Joe's birthday. Was it the sunlight, not the time of day, that gave her this rush of contentment in the face of everything? Either way, she felt more optimistic than she had in a while, and she began to plan what she would buy at the grocery store for Joe's birthday. She'd convinced Liz and Jake to allow her to buy this, at least. She decided she would cook flank steak, baked stuffed potatoes, Caesar salad, biscuits. It would be an unhealthy meal, full of fat and grease, but she would not let herself think about it, as these were Joe's favorite foods.

Another breeze pushed against her legs. She tried to imagine what a weekend here with just Joe and MacNeil and Vera might have been like. Joe and MacNeil weren't great friends but they seemed to respect each other. When Vera had been alive and the four had dinner, the men discussed sports and politics, predictably, but mostly they shadowed the women's conversation, adding only incidental comments here and there. While the women chatted about Vera's travels and growing art collection, Ellen's children at school and the movies they'd seen recently, the men nodded and inserted words of support—"It was the coldest, the absolute worst weather to be in Venice," MacNeil would add to his wife's description of their Italian vacation; "He really is a little hellion," would be Joe's confirmation of Ellen's story. Undeniably Vera had been the force that brought them together, the one who arranged the dinners in Lincoln, the trips to the museums, the one who got the conversations about love or sex or politics or art up and running and the one who kept them going, really, through the wee hours of the night. Vera had been the most charismatic of them all. Ellen considered the past few weeks. Whatever the deeper motivation to be with MacNeil was—a longing for a different life? envy of his financial and spiritual ease?—now seemed laced by a simple sort of pity, a draw to take care of this man in the aftermath of death. He needed her comforting words and her endless listening. Even now, so many months later.

Liz appeared behind her, her face puffy and her eyes pink. "The sun," she said. "I'd almost forgotten it existed."

"You're up early," Ellen said, and looked back at her. "What's it like to have two? What does it feel like? Maybe it's a little too soon to really feel them?"

Liz's face brightened. "I'm constantly hungry, but as soon as I eat anything, I feel full and bloated. I'm tired a lot," she said, and looked at Ellen. "But excited. It's still so amazing to me that I'm carrying two babies right now. Sometimes I feel afraid that something will go wrong," she said, and worried her fingers before her mouth as if she hadn't meant to allow herself these words, at least not in Ellen's presence. Liz smoothed her sweatpants against her legs and looked out at the ocean. "How was Daniel yesterday?"

"All right," Ellen said. "Well, not really. I expect he's not fully equipped for this, though who would be? You keep thinking the worst has already happened—and then comes something else and you just wish it could've been you instead. You'll see, when the babies come, that you'd be willing to experience their tragedies for them. You honestly would be." Ellen stopped. "I'm sorry. I shouldn't go on like this."

"No," Liz said. "Don't apologize."

"You two will be natural parents. Jake will work himself to the bone taking care of the babies. He was born to be a father."

Liz smiled. "It's true. He too would experience everything bad for the people he loves if he could. He works himself into a frenzy over other people's problems. He gets so worried when things don't go just as planned, or when he can't fix something. He loses his mind."

"He can't help it," Ellen said.

"I know. I guess not." Liz ran her hands through her hair, smiled sweetly and headed inside.

A large cloud swam in front of the sun and Ellen watched the shadow of her hand fade from the arm of the chair. She remembered leaving MacNeil's house after their first tea. She'd gone home and struggled with a piercing headache, and every thought she'd had for the remainder of the day had been of MacNeil, now alone. He had cataloged to her all that needed to be done—box Vera's clothes, cancel her subscriptions—and she'd offered to take care of the clothes, the subscriptions and whatever else needed to be done. And now, when she thought of it, when she remembered the continual headaches and lethargy, the hollowness as if she'd lost a significant part of her interior, she resented MacNeil's so easily giving away what he should have kept for himself. The next time she saw him he was a little brighter, a little less preoccupied, and even talked of subscribing to an experimental theater Vera had always mocked. Ellen had felt glad initially—she was successfully helping him through this difficult time, though later that afternoon came a creeping melancholy as she thought about Vera's traditional taste in theater. Ellen realized now that it'd stung her, even insulted her—yes, that was the sensation—when MacNeil said flatly the other day that he wasn't sure he'd be able to revive the garden, and that he'd probably just let it go. Unless, of course, she wanted to take care of it.

She'd never much had to comfort Joe about anything, even through the worst of times—what had happened this weekend, even, or Daniel's accident, or earlier, Joe's car lot going bankrupt, his bypass four years back. He withdrew, he grew a little testy, but he kept it to himself for the most part. He'd always been the one to comfort others, even in the face of his own struggles. He'd never expected her to absorb any of his sadness.

While the others woke and took showers and read the paper, Ellen and Hilary walked down the street to a small market. A couple of cars blew past them and startled Ellen. "It's easy to imagine what this place might have looked like a hundred years ago," she said, "before the cars and people took over."

"Sure, just a little piece of land in the middle of the ocean."

"It must have been beautiful."

"It still is, if you look between these huge houses." Hilary gestured to the massive wooden skeleton and backhoe on their left. Just past it, the land carpeted in tall grass sloped down to the water.

"Mm, true," Ellen murmured.

They reached the market and Ellen found a plastic basket at the front. As they strolled past bins of soft tomatoes and hairy onions, she asked Hilary about the details of her move— had she hired a mover yet? (No.) Had she telephoned doctors in Boston yet? (No.) Hilary grew quieter and quieter until she mumbled, "I'll go get the meat," and hurried toward the butcher's section.

Ellen let her go, not wanting to force her way into whatever it was that was irritating her daughter, and resumed gathering groceries.

They reunited at the checkout line. Hilary rubbed her fingers together vigorously and looked up at the ceiling. "Something bothering you, honey?" Ellen asked.

"No, Mom."

Ellen thought of last night's mysterious trip to the book-store. "Is it a man? Is it this man, you know, the father, that's on your mind?"

"God, would you drop it?" Hilary's nose ring shifted as she spoke.

"It's fine, you know, if you don't want to start a new rela-tionship right now," Ellen said, only then realizing that she probably wasn't supposed to know about last night.

"What are you talking about?"

She swallowed. "Dad told me about that person at the store."

"Oh. Well, it was nothing. I hope he told you that part."

"You'll meet the right one someday," she said.

Hilary shrugged, a sour expression on her face. The cashier waved them forward, and Hilary began placing items in front of him. If only she stood straighter, wore a touch of makeup now and then and got rid of the hideous nose ring and tattoos. She had the loveliest face, really, the most beauti-ful hazel eyes.

The cashier pulled a sack of potatoes toward him. He was an attractive young man with shaggy brown hair, heavy eye-brows and dark eyes, and Hilary seemed to be avoiding eye contact with him. Ellen wondered if he resembled the one they'd gone looking for the night before. Did she find this young man attractive? Sometimes Hilary seemed fundamen-tally lost, floating through life aimlessly, trying, in vain, to find love just like so many other people, while at the same time resenting the world for expecting her to.

—

Jake stepped away from the tide as it approached his sandals. He had been walking on the beach with his father for a while now and chatting about his hometown, where Joe and Ellen still lived in the same small house on the same small street they always had. Real estate prices there had soared, and a new community had suddenly sprouted up a few streets over. Its houses were enormous, ridiculous hotel-like structures for small families, sometimes even childless couples, his father said. "They have wrought-iron gates and bushes shaved into globes," Joe lamented. "Their cars are all fat and blocky. Everything they own seems to be huge. Their dogs, their cars, even the doors and windows of their houses. Your mother and I sometimes go for walks there and try to imagine what's going on inside."

"I hope you're not bothering anyone. Everyone likes their privacy, Dad."

"We're just going for walks. We're not committing any crimes."

"Still." Jake used to see random people roaming his own neighborhood in Portland, craning their necks as they passed each house. He'd finally decided to have a wall of bushes planted near the end of his driveway so passersby couldn't glimpse him and Liz having breakfast or going about their daily business.

The water glittered with sun. It was, after all, a picture-perfect day, and a good number of other people strolled the beach. A family who'd just moved in a few houses down sat by the tide, and the children buried a young boy in sand. The boy didn't appear to be enjoying it at all. In fact, he was complaining loudly.

"I hated that when I was little," Jake said. "Daniel and Hilary used to bury me and then leave me there for hours. Remember?"

"It wasn't for that long. And you know we wouldn't have let anything happen to you." A small girl danced around the boy's head, sprinkling sand on his hair and singing a song about a bluebird. "Children do that sort of thing. You let them," his father said, and Jake didn't know whether this was a command or just a statement.

The two continued on. Jake realized with a pang that he could now see the top of his father's head, the shiny scalp barely covered by stray threads of hair. He looked away, and then he had an idea: he would give his father the box of things he'd collected over the years. He'd explain how he'd rescued these items that would otherwise have been thrown away or destroyed, and how he'd found each one somehow poignant. The unpainted, sturdy oak box in which Jake kept the items reminded him, in its plainness and utilitarianism, of his father. Jake would tell him that he taught him how to be a good person, how to work hard and steadily and how to love one's family.

When they returned to the house, Jake went to find the box. Hilary and Ellen sat in the living room sipping glasses of lemonade, and Joe joined them. Jake would present his gift later, when they were alone, for he didn't want his family to know about it. They would think it strange and sentimental, and they wouldn't see the point. He and Liz had bought his father a sweater and shirt for his birthday, as they did every year, but Liz reveled in predictable presents, having grown up receiving miniature statues of Buddha and crocheted prayer shawls as gifts. He brought the box down to the basement, where he found a roll of wrapping paper and ribbon.

When he came back upstairs, Hilary was reminding Joe of earlier days. She was talking about the times he brought her to work at the lot and let her sit in the driver's seats of the most expensive cars. "I still remember that popcorn the guys there used to make. I think I still associate Chevies with the smell of butter."

Jake made his way around the edge of the room and dragged in a chair from the kitchen. The room grew silent and he said, "This is nice."

"Mm," his mother said. "My family in the same place."

"Almost," Hilary said. "Has anyone talked to Dan?"

"When I called earlier, he said they'd try to come later today," Ellen said.

"Well, if they don't come, it'd be okay," Joe said firmly. "It's enough that you all are here with me."

"I don't know. I sort of hope that they do come," Hilary said, and Jake agreed.

Liz, Hilary and Ellen shuffled around the kitchen and Jake stood behind them, asking what he could do to help—cut the biscuits? slice the steak? "You just relax," his mother said, and then suddenly, "You know, with your interest in collecting, you really should think about art."

Hilary nudged past him, a bowl of salad in her hands.

"Nah," he said, worried she'd press him on the subject. Why had he brought it up earlier? He supposed he'd been feeling a little pensive all day. More reflective, even, than usual.

"You ought to. I could help you."

"I'm not a big art buff, you know that, Mom." Liz elbowed him aside as she made her way to the stove. "I like my pictures of sunsets and forests. I don't have an eye for the really expensive stuff. Or the interest, really." He glanced at his wife. Did she see that despite his success, he was still the same down-to-earth person he always was?

Ellen shrugged and went to the refrigerator, and soon he began to feel that he was in the way, so he turned and left the room. His father sat on the back porch reading a newsmagazine, and Jake hurried off to get the box. When he returned, Joe made no gesture of acknowledgment. The beach had emptied, probably because it was lunchtime. Only a group of seagulls circled the messy mound that had earlier buried the young boy. Jake wondered if the family had left food there, or their beach toys, and considered walking down to check. Perhaps he would start a new box now, and maybe someday he could give it to his children. He could start two new boxes, one for each.

"I can feel myself sitting still," his father said.

"Hm?"

"I can feel my bones even when I'm not doing a damned thing. That's when you know you're old."

"Dad, you're not all that old." Jake quickly handed him the present. "Here. Something from me alone. It's a little different." He waited quietly while his father tore open the wrap, his hands a little shaky, and held the wooden box before his face. "A good box," his father said, and shook it.

"Yes, that's how I think of it," Jake said.

Joe removed each item—the dirty dog collar, the heart-shaped earring, the stained Bible, the pacifier, the photograph of the elderly strangers—and held it to the light, turning it slowly.

Jake grew embarrassed by these things that now looked so old and worn. "They're things I've saved," he said. "Things I've found over the years."

"Trash?"

"Sort of, I guess. But not really. They're things people left or forgot somewhere, things I didn't feel right throwing away. I've been collecting them since I was a kid."

"You have?" His father lowered the box to his lap.

"I wanted to thank you for being good, and I wanted to show you how I can be good, I mean how I can be considerate—"

"I know that already," Joe said.

"I guess I like to think that behind each of these things is a person, you know, a whole life." His words sounded silly. They'd made more sense in his mind. "Each time I find one and bring it home, it sort of feels like I'm saving something important."

Joe nodded. "It's a nice thought, isn't it?"

Jake watched the lines of the tide as they pushed toward the shore and bled across the sand. He wondered if it looked the same to his father, the water pooling into fingers, piles of wet, shiny seaweed like neglected, soggy clothes. "You understand why I gave you this?"

His father nodded again and stood, his legs creaking. "I do."

Jake looked at him. "No one else knows I've been keeping these. Not even Liz."

"I won't tell them." Joe stretched his arms.

This hadn't happened the way Jake had hoped. "Do you think I'm crazy for keeping these things?" he said.

"No, I don't," Joe said. He looked down at the box in his

hands. "I was just thinking that you're a little like me. When I found Babe on the side of the road and when I wrapped him up in that shirt and brought him home, it was the best feeling."

"I thought you got Babe at a store."

Joe smiled at him with a sparkle. "Don't tell your mother."

"I won't," Jake said.

Joe squeezed Jake on the shoulder and headed back inside, the box in the crook of his arm.

—

Hilary slipped off to the pink bedroom to lie down for a while. The mattress, yesterday too soft and short for her, now felt only a relief, and she closed her eyes.

Outside the room she could hear Liz ordering Jake to clean off the table, get her two eggs, find the mixing bowl, and Jake snipping that he was only capable of doing one thing at a time. Hilary could also hear her mother in the next room, picking up the phone receiver and setting it down every few seconds. Each time she did, the phone beside Hilary's bed clicked. Finally Hilary picked up the receiver to hear ringing on the line and then a man answer, a voice that was faintly familiar. Ellen and this man asked each other about their weekends, and then she told him about Daniel and Brenda, about Hilary's surprise pregnancy ("and she won't tell us a *thing* about the father"), Jake's beautiful house, the bad weather, and then returned to Daniel and Brenda, and the heartbreak of it, all of the unbearable heartbreak Daniel had weathered.

Hilary froze, her hand curled tightly around the receiver. When her mother finally stopped talking, there was an awkward pause in the conversation and the man said, "I'm sorry," and then nothing. Ellen continued on, repeating her sadness about Daniel's fate as if she were trying to elicit something, anything more from this man. "I just don't know what to say to him. I mean, what do you say to your son after he's been through this?" she finally asked, and the man said, "I wish I knew. Wasn't it Oscar Wilde who said, 'Where there is sorrow there is holy ground'?" "Oh, I don't know, but I'm not sure that would be adequate anyway," Ellen said, and the man gently changed the subject to his daughter in San Francisco, and her kids, and what they'd all done together while he was there. Hilary tried in vain to remember which of her mother's friends had kids in San Francisco—wouldn't Ellen have given her their names and told her to look them up? He went on about MoMA, the Matisses and the Diebenkorns, all the exquisite daguerreotypes, and Hilary could practically hear her mother's mind wandering back to Daniel and Brenda. Hilary considered hanging up but didn't want them to hear her, so she stayed on the line. The man mentioned some plans they'd made for next week, some concert at the Gardner and maybe supper, and finally they began their goodbyes. "I miss you," her mother said in a hushed voice, to which the man responded, "À bientôt, E."

"Do you miss *me*?"

"Of course I do."

"I mean, do you miss me as a person? I don't mean the time we spend together, or the things we do. Do you really miss me?"

He paused. "Yes?" he replied tentatively. "Is everything all right?"

"Sure," Ellen said. "Oh, I don't know. Nothing here is

really all right at this point, is it? Haven't you heard what I've been telling you?"

"What can I do?"

"You could say more. You could tell me that everything will be fine, even if it won't. You could *comfort* me a little." She paused. "You could come here."

"I can't do that. You have your whole family there. I've just gotten back and—"

"I know, I know."

"I'm not sure what you want from me right now."

"I suppose I want you not to say things like that. I want you to do something, *anything*, M. Let me ask you this: what is it that *you* want from *me*? What is it that you even feel for me?"

He swallowed. "Gratitude. The deepest, warmest, loveliest, most loving gratitude."

Hilary held the phone away from her ear, then brought it back, just in time to hear her mother say, ". . . more?"

"Of course. I couldn't have survived these last months without you. You've been my lifeline, you know that, my rope to sanity. I miss you and I do want you to come back here. I want us to go to the Gardner this week and I want to give you something I bought when I was away. It sounds corny, I know, but I do need you. I absolutely need you and I do love you and—"

"I have to go."

"E?"

A man who was not her father had a nickname for her mother. He loved her and had given her a nickname and this vaguely familiar but ultimately unrecognizable voice, this complete stranger had now learned all about the weekend. Ellen said again, "I have to go now. I'll call you when we get back," and quickly hung up. Hilary slammed down the receiver and looked around the room. She grew light-headed—had she imagined this? Maybe through her growing fatigue and surging hormones she'd conjured this phone conversation. Maybe, in fact, this whole weekend was some sort of mirage, and she'd wake to find herself back in her apartment in San Francisco, Beatle scratching at the window, the sirens screaming past on their way to the hospital down the street.

"What the hell is she doing? What is going on here?" she said into the air. She ran her fingers in circles around her belly and tried to imagine a baby curled inside her, its head to her side. She could feel it there, positioned in such a way that it could have been looking up at her face. "Married people are nothing but miserable. You might never have a father, little one," Hilary whispered. "I might be both of your parents. What do you think about that? Would that be all right?" The baby stayed still beneath her hands.

She sighed. She would try to find a place where neighbors watched out for each other, a real community. She would move somewhere less crowded than San Francisco, somewhere more contained, where everyone knew everyone and she'd get help raising her child merely because she lived here. She closed her eyes again and laced her fingers across her stomach. Despite everything that had gone wrong this weekend, there was something about this island, its unpredictable weather and small streets, its history, its people—the men who worked on the ferry, the cabdriver. They exuded a sort of innocence and earthiness and history—they seemed to have lived here for thousands of years. She thought of Alex. Maybe, she thought, maybe she could rent Jake and Liz's house until she found one of her own. But there was the girl in the bookstore, Alex's messy apartment, his intrusive dog. More worrying and potentially more troublesome in the end, there was the way he drifted from Hilary when she was mid-sentence as if he were plotting an escape. There was no reason he should be a cause for her to move here. There was no good reason at all. What kind of person would move here for someone she'd spent one day with?

But he didn't own the island. He shouldn't have any purchase on her future one way or the other. If this was the right place for her, then so be it. She could find a job at one of the stores in town, or at a restaurant. She'd waitressed plenty of times before. She smiled to herself, relieved to have a new plan finally. And only then did she remember the phone call, and her mother, and the fact that soon she and the rest of them would all be seated around the dinner table, celebrating her father's seventy-fifth birthday.

Hilary stood in the corner of the kitchen and watched Liz pull a steaming chocolate cake out of the oven. Ellen sat at the kitchen table.

"Have you been to the Gardner recently?" Hilary asked. She couldn't help herself. Her mother looked up, surprised.

"Yes. I'll take you when you move back home, if you'd like."

"Actually—" Hilary said, but then stopped herself. She would wait until after dinner to announce her revised future. She didn't want to upset anyone now, before the birthday celebration—and her mother, not to mention Jake, might well disapprove of her new plan to move here. *What sort of opportunity is there in a place like this?* they'd say. *What sort of men? Why must you change your mind every five minutes? Pick something, any-thing, just make a plan and stick with it.*

"Actually what?" Liz turned.

"Nothing," Hilary said. "Forget it."

She helped Liz prepare the icing for the cake, and as they worked, as her father dozed in the living room and her brother puttered around somewhere else, maybe on the back porch, Hilary noted a pleasant silence in the house. So much could be said right now—so many concerns could be expressed, so many accusations made—but no one was saying a thing, and this made her grateful. Hilary heard her father shift on the couch. Nothing was changing. Nothing was happening. Even Jake had let them be.

For her father she had brought a framed photograph of herself holding his hand on her seventh birthday (the two stood next to each other in front of an ice cream stand on the Cape), and another photograph of them a few years ago, when she'd come East for her grandmother's funeral. (Hilary had just told him she'd gotten a new job in insurance, and he'd seemed skeptical even then of this career choice for her.) She'd also brought a third frame that was currently empty. In a few months, she would give him a picture of the baby, herself and Joe. The past, present and future, all neatly framed for him. She'd considered giving him photos of the entire family but her mother had filled their house with these. He had none of just her and him, and none of her recently. She'd wrapped each frame separately. They now sat on the bed in the pink room, and she went to gather them and asked Liz where she could start a pile of presents.

The cake was frosted, the steak nearly ready. No one knew whether Daniel would join them, but everyone seemed content to let the subject rest for now.

"You're almost there," Hilary said, taking a seat beside Joe on the couch. Ellen was having an affair, but Hilary put it out of her mind. "Wasn't it three-thirty P.M. you were born?" She remembered finding her parents' birth certificates years ago on her father's desk.

"I'd like to just stop forever at seventy-four."

"Hear, hear," she said. She grabbed a pen from the side table and held it in front of her mouth like a microphone. "Any last words of advice? Thoughts, impressions, hopes, wishes?"

"Nah," he said. "Well, there is something you told me when you were about eight, it had to be. You'd run away into the woods and your mother sent me to find you, and when I did, you'd climbed way up high into an oak tree and I stood there down below you, wondering what on earth to do. I tried to talk you down. I started climbing up, even, but you yelled down to me, 'Stop trying so hard. Just let me stay here, because eventually I'll have to come down. You can't always fix everything.' You remember that?'"

Hilary tried but didn't remember this particular scene. She'd escaped to the woods so many times they'd blurred together in her mind. "I said that?"

"You did," he said. "It was good advice. You might want to remember it with your child."

Hilary nodded. It seemed to her that her father had in fact

fixed quite a lot in her life; he'd listened to her litany of complaints about school and her mother and Jake over the years. Joe had decoded some of the mysteries of her brother; her father had secretly sent her what money he could when she'd needed it. She considered the ten or twenty birthdays that lay before him, the awful days to come that marked only the passing of time. She took his hand and squeezed it tightly.

"I'm not going anywhere," he said, as if he sensed what she was thinking.

Liz had bought silver ribbon to wrap around blue silk napkins, and went to the deck to get two bouquets of daisies—and where and when had she gotten these? Hilary wondered as she stood to help. Liz stepped back into the living room and handed Hilary a handful of tiny plastic silver stars to sprinkle around the table. "Yes, I know, I go overboard," Liz said, but Hilary replied, "Nah, it's nice." And it was, and Hilary was glad someone was guiding the day back to the reason they were all here—her father. She held the stars in one palm and they felt like sand in her fingers as she sprinkled them across the white tablecloth. They glinted in the day's sunlight. Liz wrapped the napkins in the ribbons and carefully set them equidistant from each other—Hilary thought she noticed Liz's eyes move in even paces between seats—and then went to the freezer for the chilled glasses.

With the three babies on the way, they would celebrate so many birthdays in the coming years. Hilary thought of Daniel and Brenda in some clinic on this island, then of the first time she saw Daniel in the hospital after his accident, his legs absolutely still beneath the thin blanket. She focused on the table before her and the hundreds of tiny silver stars and thought of her own baby, how she would celebrate its first birthday here on the island with a roomful of new friends and neighbors, maybe even Alex, though maybe not. Probably not.

Liz turned on Hank Williams, one of Joe's favorites, and asked her if she wanted anything to drink. Leaning against the kitchen counter, the two sipped glasses of lemonade, and Hilary asked Liz what she thought of the island as a place to live year-round, how many families lived here and what were the schools like. Liz looked at her sideways and asked what she was getting at, and when Hilary told her confidentially of her new plan, Liz clapped her hands and said it was the best idea she'd heard in years. "You can live here and be our caretaker," Liz said happily. "And maybe when things get serious with that guy at the bookstore, he can move in."

"Liz."

"Yes?"

"He has nothing to do with my idea to move here."

"Okay," Liz said.

"I've only known him for two days."

"Okay, okay," Liz said. "I promise not to bother you about him anymore."

"Thank God."

"But promise *me* something. That when something more does happen with him, you'll tell me about it."

"Why are you so fascinated by this subject?" Hilary asked.

"What's more fascinating than sex? What's more interesting than pure physical attraction?"

Her words were laced with an uneasy combination of judgment and titillation and maybe something more that Hilary didn't particularly want to consider. She shouldn't have told her about any of this. "I can think of plenty of things," she finally said.

Hilary watched her mother touch her father's arm (acting, she must have been, completely and utterly lying to them all) as he took his seat at the head of the table. And here they were, most of a family gathered to usher in their father's seventy-fifth year. It was four o'clock, too early to be eating dinner, and Hilary felt suddenly alone amid the two couples, this group that despite everything continued to expand.

9

Gregory Peacock in Flight

Daniel and Brenda waited for Dr. Waller to come to their room, hand them their discharge forms and say goodbye. Earlier she had decided she wanted go to Jake's house for Joe's birthday after all. She'd have to see them eventually, and she and Daniel already made the trip here, and had Joe's present. They'd go for a couple of hours and then head home, she'd said defeatedly. Now she sat on the end of the bed, flipping through pamphlets about pregnancy loss and stillbirths, and Daniel looked out the window at the cloudless sky. He tried to listen for the sound of the ocean, which couldn't have been far, as the island was so small, but he was unable to hear it.

He began to want to stay here in this clinic on this island. Not that he particularly liked the clinic, of course, or even Great Salt, which he'd seen virtually nothing of since he was a child. But he found himself wanting to keep Brenda and his family close to him, and in a place separate from the rest of the world. He and Brenda used to dream of living on an island someday. For their honeymoon, they'd flown to Athens, then sailed to Rhodes and then Lipsos, a tiny Dodecanese island closer to Turkey than to Greece, where Brenda's friend had recommended they go if they wanted privacy. To the dismay of their parents, they'd gotten married at City Hall in New York. They had neither the money nor the desire for all the trappings of a wedding, and were far more interested in spending what they did have on the honeymoon. Lipsos rose from the ocean, hilly and electric green, brightened by the azure of the sky, and the colors there later inspired entirely new palettes in his work. They stayed on the top floor of the only inn on the island, and in the afternoons lounged in bed, trying to find markings they'd never seen before on each other's body—Daniel found a tiny fan-shaped birthmark beneath Brenda's left breast, and she found a faded old scar to the left of one of his ankles. They made love in the bed and on the floor and in the shower, where Daniel now remembered lifting Brenda against the cool blue tiles and feeling the plush inside of her body, the exact center of her, he'd thought. Then they fell into the deepest sleeps, woke, and made love again. They were the only guests of the innkeeper, a squat old woman with soft white fur around her mouth. She spent her days by the water, screaming at the fishermen as they pulled in their nets. By Daniel and Brenda's third day there, everyone on the island recognized them as the newlyweds. One man knocked on their bedroom door and, bowing, presented them with a bouquet of orchids and a bottle of ouzo. Another sat with them as they ate breakfast at the inn and told them, in broken English, of his title and record as best diver on the island. Brenda was charmed. Daniel was too at first, but soon grew irritated by the lack of privacy (he would later tell Brenda's friend about this), and all the strangers who approached them and pointed, smiling, toward their hearts. By the blowsy old man with feathering eyebrows who fell at their feet and crooned a song about—Daniel gathered—love.

She set the pamphlets on the bed now.

"Should I go look for Dr. Waller?"

"No, let's give him a few more minutes."

Eventually this weekend would become a part of her past, a distant turning point—though toward what, Daniel wondered. It was in her nature to fully recuperate after setbacks, large or small. For him, though, such events had unfolded differently, of course. Calamity had stuck to him—he found himself unable to ever completely shed it. It warped his moods, it soured his outlook. It stayed imprinted on his memory. He knew that years later he would still vividly recall the details of their stay in this clinic: the sight of the two daisies on the shiny floor, Dr. Waller's mustache, the one-eyed Raggedy Ann doll in the waiting area. He would always remember the sting of the earring in his palm as he lay in a small bed beside his wife who'd just lost her baby.

He could try not to dwell on just the hard times. He could remember the Sundays they'd lie in bed into the evenings, the dinner parties in Brooklyn with their friends, the many trips they used to take. *What was your favorite thing about Lipsos?* he could ask her now to help distract her. *What do you remember most clearly?* He wanted to tell her that he would be a better husband from now on because he finally understood that he was fundamentally the same person he'd always been. The accident hadn't changed who he was, just how he functioned.

But he looked at her in her blue linen maternity dress sitting at the edge of the bed, her hands cupped together, her eyes on her feet, and he thought these words would sound too tidy to be believed and come much too late to even be relevant to her. What would he say, *I'm better now?* This wouldn't resurrect anything. In fact, it would undoubtedly make matters worse.

Dr. Waller finally appeared in the doorway, a pen in his mouth. "You'll need to take it easy on yourself. No exercise or heavy lifting for a couple of weeks," he said to her. He told her which pain relievers to take and how much rest she'd need. She should wait three months before starting to try again. She might consider wearing a firm bra, he said, to help suppress the milk that would come. Pads instead of tampons for the vaginal bleeding. Daniel imagined him scanning down a checklist in his mind. "Anything else?" he finally said, and when Brenda asked, he told them they could pick up the ashes outside the nursery. The crematorium had done a rush job, given the fact that Daniel and Brenda were only here a short while. A nurse would be waiting in the nursery to assist them.

They sat in the back of a cab, the heavy plastic cylinder with the ashes now inside the suitcase. Retrieving them outside the nursery had been a conspicuously unceremonial event, and Brenda had tucked them away between her clothes before he could come up with a better idea.

He had not definitively told his family that he and Brenda would attend his father's birthday dinner, for he wanted to maintain the option of backing out if she wanted to. Then, as they were leaving the clinic, he'd decided that this would be his real present to his father: their attendance. *Her* attendance. They'd brought him several armchair travel books about Europe, but this, their coming when Brenda had such mixed feelings about it, would be their real gift. They'd surprise everyone by just showing up in a cab. One of the nurses had looked up Jake's address in the phone book.

The cab's brakes squealed as they rounded a corner. "You sure you're still game? This might be our last chance to turn back," Daniel said, and she answered, "We'll go for a while and then it'll be done and we can head home."

She had never completely taken to his family. Her closeness with her own family would always make them somewhat unnecessary to her, little more than a duty.

Daniel stared out the window. The sun beat down through tall oaks and maples that lined the road, and moments later they passed several shops. The island drifted past him and he took in sights he hadn't seen two days ago: a café where several women in loose, brightly colored dresses milled and chatted with each other; a store called Books & Beans, small tables lining the sidewalk outside it; a restaurant called the Mermaid's Table; a small ice cream stand—typical touristy sights. The road dipped down close to the shore, and the ocean appeared to their left in countless shades of blue. Gulls bobbed near the water, and no one lay in the sun on the rocky beach that separated the ocean from the road.

Jake's house was big for a summer home, but also understated, its shingles weathered gray and the front door a muted blue. Rosebushes bloomed in front, and the lawn was striped diagonally from being recently mowed. Daniel still couldn't believe his younger brother—who used to cry at the drop of a hat as a child and seemed to fail at everything he tried, every sport, every friendship, every girl he had a crush on—was now able to afford two houses and had married someone as likable as Liz. Daniel wondered how Liz felt about their new money, whether she was comfortable with it or whether, at times, she found it strange suddenly being able to afford so much after a lifetime of less. Her eccentric parents had raised her in some shack in Oregon, he recalled. Or was it a commune?

They paid the driver, who helped them with the chair and their bags. Their small suitcase on his lap, Daniel wheeled himself over the sharp gravel and watched Brenda walk in front of him to the door. Jake had laid out several long pieces of plywood as a ramp. He was nothing if not considerate of Daniel's needs now. Brenda, on the other hand, didn't look back once to see whether he was still behind her, whether he was having a difficult time with their bag and pushing the chair over the gravel.

Once he caught up to her, she shuffled on her feet after she rang the doorbell. He tried to imagine what was going through her mind right then—reluctance at having to face two pregnant women? Maybe she was cramping, her breasts swelling against her shirt with milk. He was about to ask her if everything was all right, when Liz threw open the door. Daniel was glad, even a little relieved, to see her freckles and overlapping teeth, her broad grin. She gathered them into a flurry of hugs and smiles and concern and chatter. Ellen squeezed his shoulder and ran her hand through his hair.

"Do you want something to drink or eat?" Jake rushed over to them. "Or do you want to relax for a bit before dinner? Do you want a tour of the house—but no, of course, you must be exhausted—" and Daniel finally said, "Easy there."

"We just sat down for supper," Ellen said, pushing her way back to Joe, who stood a few feet behind the others with Hilary. Pregnant, she was twice as big as Brenda had ever been. His sister was tall and healthy, and he hadn't realized how much he'd missed her and her expansive presence, even more expansive now. She exuded herself—she was the sort of person who hid nothing. She was flipping through a magazine as if she didn't want to appear eager to see them or to participate in the flurry that was this family, and most likely she had no idea what to say to him or Brenda right now anyway. So Daniel said, "Hey there, Larry, you look like a different person."

"Danielle." She nodded. They'd never used these names in front of the family—they'd made a pact ages ago to keep them secret, but right now Daniel didn't care. He couldn't help himself. She went to him and planted a firm kiss on his cheek, and did the same to Brenda, who smiled politely as she offered the side of her face. She was becoming well-behaved Brenda, the steely person no one could upset.

Liz moved behind Daniel and helped him forward into the aggressively matching and overly designed house and he found himself at a table covered in tiny plastic silver stars, a napkin and utensils set in front of him, a plate of food before him. He glanced at Brenda, young and silent and tiny between Hilary and Liz, so tiny she looked as if she might suddenly shrink away to nothing. She kept her focus on the plate before her. "Do you want some lemonade?" he asked her, and her "no" was quick and muffled.

No one spoke for a moment and Daniel heard the push of the ocean outside. There it was, all that water around them and beneath them. He wondered if Brenda heard it too, and he was about to say something about it when Jake insisted on getting her *something* to drink.

—

Ellen could relax now that everyone was here. She sliced her meat and savored the rare center. It was pink and would clog her heart but who cared? This was no time for discipline.

MacNeil did not love her. He loved her care and sympathy, he loved her attention and the things she did for him, and this was, at least to him, a sort of love, but as for loving *her* and wanting her as a person. Well. She had for once offered him her sadness and he had done nothing but ramble on about Oscar Wilde and MoMA and all he and his daughter's family had done together, how big his granddaughters had gotten, what a scenic neighborhood they lived in ("on the Pacific, I mean right on the Pacific"), as if he were chatting with their mother. No one in the world cared as deeply about your kids as you did—this was a fact Ellen had learned early on in parenthood. Clearly he didn't know this, or more likely just didn't care. She took a long sip of lemonade. He'd been talking about them more and more recently. "I think about living closer to them," he said the other day, and she worried he was actually considering moving across the country, but he then said, "I just want them back here. Do you ever wonder why Hilary went so far away?"

"No," she'd said. They sat in his dining room over backgammon and Pinot Noir. "It made perfect sense to us that she chose to go to school out there, given the way she operates," aware of the intrusion of the word "us."

"I find myself taking it personally. They grew up here in the East. We loved it, Vera *loved* it. We never wanted to live anywhere else."

"Everyone moves these days. It's nothing to take personally." She shook the dice in her fist.

"We sound so old."

"We are," she said, and smiled at him. She rolled the dice. "It's all right that they're gone."

"It is?"

"It is," she said, though she knew it wasn't for him, especially without Vera. Still, today Ellen didn't want to mourn with him. Today she wanted it to be just her in the room with him, just Ellen and MacNeil. "Do they like where they live?"

"Yes," he said.

"Well then." She glanced down at the board—she'd just won the game.

"Selfish or not, I still wish they were closer," he said, and rose from the couch to go to the bathroom. It seemed an hour of silence—of worrying she had pushed him too far, that perhaps she was the one being selfish here—before he came back, turned on some Bach and showed Ellen a book he'd just bought of Klee, painting after painting of what looked to her like scratches from a cat's claws against brash colors and bright shapes pressed together. She hadn't known he liked Klee, whose name, MacNeil now said, meant "clover" in German—and what reaction should this have elicited? She simply said, "Oh," and continued to glance down at the book, faintly dismayed. She felt these paintings excluded her. They knew something or lived somewhere that she did not. "Daniel loves Klee," she said. "He could have been a real artist."

"He is a real artist," MacNeil said.

"In a way."

"I'm sure he'd say he is."

"You're right, he would." She nodded. "He is incredibly talented. He could draw so well even when he was small. He was a terror on the playground and not such a good student in school, but with crayons or paints he was an angel." And now he lived his life in a wheelchair.

MacNeil seemed lost in a painting of curved lines against a pale blue background and Ellen wondered what the significance was, whether this was a painting that had meant something to him and Vera. The book was enormous in his hands, and a luxury, really, a book like this. It should have been enough for a person to look at art in a museum. Why was it necessary to own such a book, a book that cost, Ellen had noticed with some alarm, seventy-five dollars?

He did not love her outside of his grief. And perhaps she did not love him.

"A toast." Joe lifted his glass of water, and everyone turned to look at him. "To me," he said, "and to all of you making it here this weekend."

"To our growing family," said Jake, and Liz dropped her fork. The clink startled everyone, and Jake's face flushed. He took a long sip of wine.

"It's all right," said Brenda, her eyes fixed on her plate.

Ellen couldn't think of a thing to say that would make the moment pass more quickly.

"I didn't mean that," Jake said. He swallowed the rest of his wine and refilled his glass.

Brenda pushed her hands against the sides of her face and squeezed her mouth forward.

"Do you want to go lie down, sweetheart?" Ellen asked her, but she mumbled, "Everyone please just ignore me. Really, I'm fine." Her accent sounded more pronounced.

"Of course," Ellen said, and looked down. The food on her plate became terribly unappetizing.

"Tell us what would be best for you, Bren," Jake said. "Do you need some time alone? It's a nice walk down on the beach." Hilary shot him an annoyed glance. Brenda kept her eyes on her plate, and Jake plowed ahead. "It must have been devastating. It must be incredibly painful for you to be here right now." He believed he was so sensitive to other people's needs, and that he, more than anyone, knew what was best for everyone in the family because he paid so much attention to his own army of needs. What had she and Joe done, Ellen wondered, to foster this in him?

"Perhaps I'll talk about it later, but I'm not quite ready now. I'm sorry."

Thankfully, Joe began to ramble about some book he was reading, and Liz eagerly joined him. The two chattered on while the rest of the family ate quietly. And when they'd exhausted this conversation, a silence swelled.

"I'm staying here on the island," Hilary suddenly announced. "I'm not going back home with you and Dad." Six pairs of eyes looked at her. "Liz agreed to let me stay here in this house until I find a place of my own."

"She did?" Jake's lips were lined in blue from the wine.

"I did," Liz said, calmly slicing her meat.

Ellen stared at her daughter, now vigorously rubbing her fingers together. Perhaps she would finally start a fire. Perhaps she would light the house on fire and they would all rise up in smoke.

"Oh, well then," Joe said.

"That's all you can say?" Jake snorted. "Oh? Well?" He turned to Hilary. "Have you thought about how you are going to support yourself? How you are going to take care of a child alone here? Who's going to help you? How you'll afford to live? And what winters are like here? Have you considered *any* of this?"

"I knew you'd say these things," Hilary responded, a spot of potato on her chin. "I shouldn't have told you. I shouldn't have said a fucking thing until I got settled here."

Ellen had to restrain herself from leaning forward and wiping her daughter's face. "Shh, please," she hissed. Her temples throbbed. "Hil, does the man even know you've decided this? Does his wife?"

Brenda glanced around and traded a look with Daniel. Joe stared at his plate.

"Who are you talking about?" Hilary barked.

The beast was out of the cage now—what was the point in whispering around it anymore? "The father of your child, for God's sake."

"He doesn't have a wife, Mom."

"Then why won't you tell us who he is? I assumed . . . I mean I guessed—"

"Because I don't know *who he is*, all right? And *he* doesn't know who *he* is because there were *two different men* and it could be either, and this only happened because I'm an irresponsible slut."

Ellen shuddered. Did the others know this? Had Joe known and kept it from her because he figured she wouldn't be able to handle it? And the answer—was it better or worse than she'd thought it would be?

"It's okay, Hil," Daniel said. "You're not a bad person."

Liz reached forward and squeezed Hilary's shoulder.

Two men. Ellen looked at her daughter. Her face and neck flushed as she drank a half glass of lemonade in one gulp, then slammed the glass on the table.

Others were suddenly talking about the food and the wine.

Ellen finally made herself say, "So you'll live here for a while."

"She won't be that far away from you, and she'll be closer to us," Liz said hopefully, to which Ellen automatically replied, "But she'll be all alone here."

"And that's the real problem, isn't it, Mom, that you can't picture a person, worse yet a parent, really living alone? You can't stand loneliness and you're lonely with Dad because you think he doesn't pay enough attention to you, which, by the way, he does, but that's why you're going to the Gardner Museum next week with some other man." Her face bloomed red again.

Ellen planted her hands on either side of her plate. Joe looked at Hilary. Liz glared at her plate. Daniel puffed out his cheeks as if he were about to blow into a trumpet.

"I'm sorry, Dad," Hilary said in a loud voice, a voice complicit and selfish and full of uninformed anger. The spot of potato finally fell from her face. "I'm really sorry."

As she stood, a flood rising within her, Ellen regarded her family around her. "I have plans with MacNeil Burgess to go to the Gardner Museum next week," she said as if in time to a metronome. "He has been our friend, and Vera was my good friend for many years and she recently passed away."

Hilary glared at her, waiting for her to continue. Joe looked at her blankly. He did not know her as a whole person. None of her family did and it angered her, how little they knew of her soul—that thing she'd ignored for so long—and the larger things it craved, and how little they cared. For she knew each of them inside and out. She had known them since they were born, and how they cried, and what it took to comfort them, what they loved to eat, to see, to smell, to hear, and later, what made them laugh and shudder and sleep. And as for Joe, Ellen knew him all too well. She knew how he took his tea, that he woke at six-fifteen every morning, alarm clock or not, and let himself doze for fifteen minutes. That he loved certain animals because of their quiet, and loved children because of their innate energy and curiosity. He loved her because she was his wife, because she was there beside him and had been for most of their days, every single morning and evening. Because in life, one was supposed to love, and one was supposed to love one's wife, and that was enough for him. She knew him as an old man and had known him as a younger one, a new husband and new father, a manager of a car lot. Though there was, of course, another person that she barely remembered anymore, her first Joe, the boy she first met on her way home from the hospital. She desperately missed the clearer memories of the day they met. She missed the strength of her attraction to him, and the enormous promise of it—she couldn't even recall what that felt like. Bits of the day had faded with time and no longer seemed to exist. She missed the exciting uncertainty of that day and of so many after, the sense that time was a vast, uncrossable galaxy that had no other side.

"I'm well aware that your mother and MacNeil are friendly,"

Joe said calmly. Ellen felt herself wobble a little, a fork in one hand, a napkin in the other. The faces around the table softened. "Vera was her good friend, after all. And I'm well aware how much she loves the Gardner."

"Your father knows that MacNeil has been grieving and has turned to his friends for comfort," she finally said, but how much *did* Joe know? What *was* there to know about the matter in the first place? The facts were these: She was helping a friend weather the passing of his wife. She herself had been mourning the passing of this dear friend. There was nothing else she could name about the matter right now that seemed at all consequential.

Brenda hung her head like a young girl. Everything seemed to be spinning and Ellen felt weightless, and steadied herself on the back of the chair. Vera was gone. Ellen's unborn grandchild had died. Her son sat broken in a wheelchair. Her daughter would live her life alone. Ellen's forehead had grown warm. She felt Jake's hand on her arm and Hilary's on her leg, gently pulling her to the side and then down. Ellen let herself sink slowly back into her seat, and landed with a small *whump*.

—

Jake exhaled. It seemed that he'd been holding his breath for hours, and, his face damp, he reached for his glass of wine. Something had popped in the family. Where had Hilary gotten this nonsense? Their mother, another man—it was ridiculous. She was an old woman about to become a grandmother. And she loved his father. Of course she had male friends. Of course she and Joe argued and ignored each other, but what married couple didn't? Hilary simply didn't understand the nature of long-term relationships. She ran from conflict, as she was too stubborn to work through it or wait it out—and look at her. Emotionally, she hadn't grown a day over the years. And now she would be a mother and Liz had promised her their house without even asking him. Hilary managed to coast over life's speed bumps, always rallying someone else to take care of her.

"You know, Hil, I don't much like the Gardner," Joe suddenly said. "It's a little dusty for me, and a little too quiet. Your mother knows I can't walk all those stairs anymore."

Ellen nodded and smiled, and Jake sensed his parents were tacitly agreeing to something. He finished the wine in his glass and poured himself more. "You took us to the Museum of Fine Arts once on a snow day, Mom," he said. "Remember? We dug out the car and slid our way to the city. That drive scared the hell out of me—we kept spinning out, and nicked the guardrail at one point. When we got to the museum, we were the only people there except the security guards, and you told us to pretend this was our house and that we were princes, I think it was, and that you were the queen. Daniel's bedroom was the one with the Van Gogh sketches, right? And mine was the one with all these ancient sculptures."

"I did?" Ellen said. "How inspired of me."

"I don't remember that," Hilary said, and Jake said, "It might have been before you were born. Dan, do you remember?"

Daniel didn't respond, and Jake wasn't certain he'd even heard his question. Daniel had barely said a thing since they arrived. His hair was a mess, and he looked as if hadn't slept for days, which he probably hadn't. Jake grew a little weak in the stomach just looking at him.

"I remember that snow day," Joe said. "I stayed home and worked, but I remember you three coming back all abuzz like you'd just visited some other country."

Liz stood and walked the tray of meat around the table, offering each person more. She smiled flatly at him and Jake felt a rush of gratitude for her. She would not have fallen in love with him, he thought, if they had met earlier, say in high school. He remembered her old sketchbooks that he'd found about a year ago in their attic when he was looking for a hose. The first book he'd opened contained childlike drawings of adults above her parents' names, and other names he didn't recognize. The lines were messy, the colors ridiculous. Eyes were crossed and ears were drawn to look like wings. He recognized her trademark humor and the comic way she really saw people. And she was just as methodical as a child as she was now—she'd even dated each page. Her self-portraits back then were adorable: an enormous head, eyes practically on top of each other (still a hang-up for her), an absurdly long nose, puffy lips, tiny hands, an egg-shaped body. He flipped through her drawings as a six-, seven-, eight-year-old. He looked at her friends, then her parents lifting those idiotic hookahs to their mouths. He flipped through her adolescence, past boys drawn with less exaggeration and more details. Standing in the dim light of the attic, Jake stopped at a drawing of a blue-eyed, yellow-haired, angelic-looking boy named Gregory Peacock. The boy was rendered much more realistically than the others, and the skill she had as an eleven-year-old was remarkable. When Jake looked closer, he noticed faint pencil marks beneath the marker lines so straight they must have been drawn with a ruler. Gregory Peacock appeared on several more pages with her parents, next to animals, beside a tree, caped and flying through the air—this was Jake's favorite. He'd undoubtedly been her first love, her earliest, purest desire, and after looking closely at all the drawings of the boy, Jake found himself flipping through blank pages until he reached a piece of mole-colored cardboard at the end of the book. She'd stopped with *Gregory Peacock in Flight, December 14, 1977.* She'd been eleven years old. Jake set down the diary and picked up the next, which resumed on April 21, 1988, when she was twenty-two. He tried but was unable to find the journal that covered the missing ten years. She'd most likely skipped them. And from April 21, 1988, onward the drawings were completely different. They were harder and less playful, and infused with a more critical eye. Lines were more angular, expressions more serious. She no longer drew her parents, and the boys became larger, leaner. None smiled or even looked to be moving. Certainly none flew. Jake flipped through pictures of a pudgier Liz hidden beneath long, straight hair, her hands always clasped together. He saw pictures of her next to young men with facial hair— and why, at that age, did everyone hide behind their hair? These young men wore dark clothing and unhappy expressions—their pouts and brows and sneers became the exaggerated aspects of her drawing. Jake wished he could have seen pictures of the missing years, for he thought he might have learned something important about Liz from them. Eventually the pages led to him, a tall, skinny young man wearing a broad smile. He'd never seen these pictures of himself. Liz had shown him later sketches, but never these, and he examined the freer lines, the pliability of his fingers and toes and lips and eyes, and thought he did offer something, after all the hard lines of those dour boys. Something lighter. But not as light as Gregory Peacock. Not as pretty or as studied as that young, yellow-haired, flawless boy. She'd drawn Jake's glasses, his enormous brown eyes behind them, and his wide mouth, his smile as big as a slice of watermelon across his face. He looked cartoonish, he thought. Silly almost. Soon enough there she was beside him, her hair shorter and fuller, a watermelonlike smile on her face too, and they looked like cartoons of two children, brother and sister almost, smiling up at him with no idea what was in front of them. There was none of the care, none of the erased lines or detail that her earlier drawings had. Jake never told her he'd found these journals—he wasn't entirely certain that he'd want to hear what she might say about them.

Fuck Gregory Peacock, he murmured to himself. He sighed. He was tipsy and well on his way to drunk. "I'm getting drunk," he said, though it seemed no one heard him.

Hilary's fork scraped her plate. He supposed it wouldn't be the end of the world if she stayed at his house—he just hoped she wouldn't do something careless and burn down the place. Perhaps he could introduce her to the shop owners and the other summer homeowners they knew here. Perhaps someone could hire her to do something. She'd appreciate that— and she'd appreciate him for doing it. She'd have to. He could help her get her feet on the ground, and after all, she would be on the East Coast now. Not across the country. Not in their parents' house, as Liz had told him was her earlier plan, reliving her youth. It was a start, at least.

Ellen had a faraway look on her face—she was probably still thinking about the MFA.

"I loved loved loved pretending that museum was our house," Jake said, aware that his words had slurred from his mouth. "It felt kind of sad, pulling into our little driveway after a snow day there."

"Well, be happy you had a driveway," his father said. This was a version of his clichéd refrain, especially when they were younger and Jake and his mother played their game of imagining the great things they would buy if they had a million dollars.

"Of course, Dad," Jake said. "I'm sorry, I'm just a little drunk."

"If I could have bought you all the Gardner, I would have." It sounded almost as if he were mocking them.

Jake wondered what his father thought the first time he saw their wrought-iron gates and the long driveway lined in dogwoods and the groomed lawns at their house in Portland. On that morning they first visited, Jake had been so busy chatting with his mother he hadn't paid much attention to Joe. Now, when Jake thought of it, he remembered the man fidgeting with his sweater sleeve, looking around and above himself as if he had just landed on the moon. Jake refilled his wineglass and took a long sip. Wasn't his father at all proud?

—

Evidently Hilary knew nothing about her mother or father as people separate from the family. She knew nothing about anyone in the end, only what she thought she knew. Her accusation seemed only to draw her parents closer. And her mother's reaction to her admission about her baby's father. A married man! Well, Ellen certainly could've thought worse—was she now thinking that the two possible fathers were brothers, or criminals, that Hilary conceived the baby during conjugal visits at San Quentin? Ellen sat wilted in her chair, overwhelmed.

She seemed to have grown grayer, and her eyes droopier just over dinner. Hilary glanced at the clock on the wall. It was only six-thirty. Was it possible to age visibly in just two hours? She now regretted saying anything at all. Later, she would take her mother aside and apologize for doubting her and tell her that she would visit her and her father often, and to keep that guest room ready for her.

But she would also say that she still didn't understand the tone of her mother's voice in those moments over the phone, and what all that secrecy between her and MacNeil was about, and why the mention of love? Why did her mother need to call him and tell him about this weekend? Was he really just a friend, and if he was, did that make things any better? Hilary guessed that certain friendships lasted longer and plunged deeper than many marriages.

Everyone had planned to leave the island Sunday evening, after Joe's birthday dinner. Ellen had a dentist appointment the next morning and Jake a meeting with the partners back in Portland. But given all that had happened, they decided to stay on another night. The appointment and meeting could certainly be postponed. The only person who was hesitant about staying on was Brenda, but in the end she'd agreed.

They would save the cake until a little later, they'd decided, until they weren't so full from dinner. As they cleared the dishes and tidied the kitchen, Hilary stepped into the living room to see whether anyone had left glasses or dishes on the coffee table. Jake followed close behind, and bumped into her when she stopped short in the middle of the room. "Oops!"

"Careful," she mumbled, and flashed a look at Daniel, who

sat near the couch in one corner of the room. Brenda was in an easy chair in the opposite corner. Hilary went to the couch. "Hi Danielle."

"Hi Larry."

Was there room for so much sadness in one marriage? She kept her eyes on the floor. "What kinds of projects are you doing for work lately?" she asked him.

Jake came over to the couch and sat at the end of it, practically on top the wheelchair, but Daniel seemed barely to notice.

"It's okay," he said to Hilary. "You can ask about *it*. I mean—" and he glanced at Brenda, who nodded. Hilary guessed that Brenda liked her, at least sort of. Brenda liked that she was self-deprecating and utterly nonthreatening, that she adored Daniel in what she saw as an innocent, younger sister way.

"You sure, Bren?"

"It's your family, after all. Of course you want to tell them about it." She spoke as if Hilary weren't there.

Joe came in and sat on the arm of Brenda's chair, and they listened to Daniel's story of that Friday evening, of Brenda's creeping fears and her abdominal and back pains. Of Vanessa (Hilary would look her up—she sounded interesting) and Freeman Corcoran and the rain, of the doctor and the operation and the old woman carrying daisies. As they spoke Hilary conjured several possible scenarios: She could move in with them and her baby would, by its sheer proximity, become like theirs. Or she could just give them her baby or find an apartment close to their house and spend most of her time with them. But these options seemed more like fantasies than anything else, and not necessarily realistic or even welcome remedies to anyone's problem.

"Dan became obsessed with the donor," Brenda said quietly. "He made up a whole personality for him."

"Really?" Jake said.

"It's amazing to me that he won't find out what happened to us," Daniel said.

"Maybe he will," Hilary suggested. "Will the sperm bank tell him?"

"Not unless the autopsy shows that it had something to do with his sperm. But the doctor said it's unlikely they'll find anything," Daniel said. He paused. "Maybe it's better for him not to know. I guess there's no point in upsetting the guy."

"Did I just hear you say that?" Brenda asked.

"It probably is better," Jake said. "I mean, do you really want to involve him now?"

Hilary looked at Daniel. "What was he all about in your head, Dan? What sort of person was he?"

"We called him Jonathan White," Daniel began, then looked at Brenda and shook his head. "It's silly, I don't want to get into it. I'm sure he's a nice person."

"What about his job? His personality?" Hilary asked. "I bet you thought of that."

"You know what?" he said slowly. "I just don't think I should talk about it."

Joe said, "There are always other people who come and go from your marriage—your kids and friends and family. But it doesn't change the thing that connects the two of you." He wasn't normally the sort of person to bestow truths or sage advice, but he stretched his arms and went on. "It doesn't change that thing that brought you together in the beginning and all the years you've gone through together."

No one moved. Hilary looked at Brenda, who was gazing

out the window. Jake stared at Daniel, as if waiting for him to agree.

"Dad, you've become sentimental in your old age," Daniel finally said.

"I suppose I have." Joe smiled.

"I don't like it," Hilary said. "I don't want to be the only cynic left in the family."

"What about me?" Daniel said. "I taught you everything you know."

Jake groaned. "Oh, please. Hil, you were born cynical. Dan had nothing to do with it."

"I don't know. I like to think I had an influence," Daniel said.

Hilary rolled her eyes at him.

Jake mumbled something under his breath.

"What was that?" Daniel asked.

"I just said that you two can be insufferable. You act like you're the only two people in the world."

"What does that mean?" Hilary asked.

"Maybe you could remember that there are other people in the room?" He gestured toward Brenda. She glanced back and forth between them, probably thinking about her own family and missing them right then. Hilary knew she was particularly close with her mother—Daniel had mentioned their outrageous phone bills at the end of each month.

"You okay?" Daniel asked his wife, and she nodded. He looked at Jake. "I'm not seeing the problem here."

Jake curled his lips into his mouth.

Ellen stepped into the room. She went to the couch and took a seat right next to Jake. It seemed none of them could be close enough to Daniel.

"Forget it," Jake finally snapped.

"Forget what?" Ellen asked.

"Jake thinks we're excluding him again," Hilary said. Too many times, they'd had some version of this asinine conversation. Too many times when they were younger, Jake had tried to sabotage her relationship with Daniel by telling him the "bad" things she'd done (stolen Jake's toy, used Daniel's skates without asking him, and later, drank, smoked dope, had too much sex) or by telling Hilary that she should stop being such a puppy to him and tailing him everywhere, that she'd eventually drive him crazy. And it wasn't just *their* friendship that Jake couldn't stand. It was Daniel's many friends, it was Hilary's many boyfriends. It was all the friendships and intimacies in his life that Jake had never been invited inside.

"Oh, give me a break," he laughed. "I was just thinking that it would be considerate to include Brenda in this conversation, or Dad, since it is his birthday."

"I'm all right," Brenda said.

"Well, good," Jake said. "I wasn't sure."

"You were just trying to be thoughtful," Joe added. He was maddeningly diplomatic.

"I wouldn't call it thoughtful," Hilary said. "I'd call it insecure."

"Hilary," Ellen hissed.

"You know what, Hil?" Jake said. "I don't think I want you staying in our house after we leave. I don't even want you living on this island, to be honest."

"Fine. That's fine with me," Hilary said.

"Jake, come on," Liz interjected.

"You don't appreciate one goddamned thing anyone does for you," he said. "You expect everyone to take care of you and support you in every idiotic choice that you make. And the thing is, they do! This whole family thinks it's great that you're pregnant, that it's just so great that there's some man out there who doesn't even know he's got a baby. I guess I just don't understand this, and I don't understand how you take it for granted that everyone else does."

Hilary blanched. "You know what? I actually do. I appreciate it enormously when people treat me with respect, and like I'm an adult, which, I hate to tell you this, I am."

"Really? Because you've never seemed like one to me."

"Jake, stop it," Daniel said.

"You shit," Hilary said to Jake.

"Hilary," Joe said.

"You insecure, judgmental piece of shit," she said to Jake.

"HILARY," Joe boomed.

She stood, rushed down the hallway and into her bedroom and slammed the door shut as hard as she could. She grabbed her clothes on the floor and began stuffing them into her bag. A moment later she heard a tentative knock on the door, then a slightly louder knock. "It's me," her father said, and reluctantly she let him in.

"What are you doing?" he said, eyeing her bag. "You can't leave yet."

"I think I should."

"Hil. Put down that shirt and stop moving for a second."

She squeezed the shirt in her hands but stood still for a moment. Her whole body seemed to be palpitating.

"Jake doesn't think you're a bad person. He doesn't think you're a child or a slut or anything else, for that matter."

"Would you like to place a bet?" she said, and sat down on the bed.

"He just wants to be more a part of things, he always has. You know that. And he knows just what to say to get under your skin." He paused. "He knows the things that you think about yourself."

She put down the shirt and sat on the bed. "What do you mean?"

He looked at her, then sat down beside her. "You don't exactly hide them."

But earlier Jake had chastised her about her not having informed the father of the baby about her situation. He had chastised them all, in a sense, for allowing her to do this and, by extension, for allowing her to get pregnant in the first place. This was pure Jake. This wasn't him sensing her deepest worries and exploiting them in some warped attempt to draw closer to her. This was simply him proclaiming his verdict on her. She pulled the blanket over her face as her eyes began to fill. She considered her father's words again, and wondered if there wasn't a hint of truth to them. "He's such a very enormous dickhead," she said into the blanket, and Joe said, "He can be sometimes. But I don't think he means to be."

"Dan and Brenda shouldn't have to deal with this sort of crap tonight."

"I'm guessing Jake's thinking the same thing."

He was probably right. She let go of the blanket. What would come of Daniel? And Brenda? What would come of Hilary for that matter? "Dad? Do you think I'm going to be a terrible mother?"

"No."

She lifted her head. "I have no idea what I'm doing. I don't even know how to change a diaper. I've never changed one in my life. Not even one," she said, and he leaned toward her, set his hand on her arm and said, "That's what we're here for."

She looked up at the ceiling. "I hate Jake."

"I know. But sometimes you don't."

"Most times I do."

He squeezed her arm and sat quietly beside her, probably more distressed than she was right then.

"I know, 'hate' is an awfully strong word," she said, after a while.

"It really is," Joe said.

10

The Presence of the Past

Hilary and Joe gently interrupted Jake's reading of the ferry schedule (even inebriated, Jake loved to organize and plan). "How about you open your presents now?" she said to Joe, her eyes red and raw. Jake looked at her, then at Joe, and agreed this was a good idea, and just like that, the air in the room seemed to loosen.

Brenda trudged to the corner of the room where their suitcase sat in a small pile. Daniel watched her rifle through her clothes and noted the container of ashes next to her toiletry case. He tried to give her a sympathetic glance when she turned around, but she avoided his gaze. He shouldn't have agreed to stay on another night—she obviously didn't want to. She was somewhere else in her mind again—where? Back at their house, chatting with Morris Arnold on his porch? More likely she was across the ocean, on that dusty blue couch beside her mother, the two of them talking nonstop. And most likely, in her mind, Daniel wasn't in the room with them. She placed their present on the table and returned to the easy chair.

"You didn't have to get me presents," Joe said as Hilary and Liz set more boxes on the coffee table before him. "You know I don't need anything."

"Oh, just go ahead and open one," Ellen said. She sat in the other easy chair, her legs crossed at the ankles. "No need for the disclaimer." Daniel thought of Hilary's strange accusation during dinner, and then he thought of the Gardner Museum, that enormous dark house near Boston. He'd gone by himself one rainy Saturday when they first moved back to Massachusetts. Brenda had dropped him off and then gone to run errands downtown for a few hours. He remembered sitting beneath Sargent's painting of Isabella Stewart Gardner in a black short-sleeved dress with strands of pearls and rubies around her small waist, a ruby around her neck. She stood before burgundy and ochre wallpaper. The design on the paper made it look as if an autumn tree grew from her head, the focal point of the painting. Her skin and face and hair did not match the richness and luxuriousness of the rest of the picture, the fall color of the wallpaper and the warmth of her rubies. Her skin was the color of winter and her hair light rust, a neatly piled wreath. But most striking was her expression. Daniel remembered staring up at this woman's pursed face that seemed to have been caught mid-sentence. The pink corners of her eyes, the lines that held her mouth—she appeared afraid, or angry, as if what stood before her were not these priceless paintings and sculptures and furniture but something much more disappointing. The way her mouth looked, she could have been saying, *Stop* or *Hold on a moment.* He remembered wondering what made Sargent want to capture this particular look.

Jake and Liz gave his father a version of their annual gift: a short-sleeved blue-checked shirt and a beige cotton old-man cardigan. He held them in the air before him and thanked Jake and Liz politely.

Hilary handed him three small boxes wrapped in black paper. She was so predictable in her aversion to color, even down to her choice of wrapping paper, and it was one of the things Daniel adored about her, her absolute, unwavering consistency. In each was a small framed photo. "Past, present and . . ." Hilary said, pointing to the empty frame, "future. To come: a photo of me and my baby."

"Ah! What a sweet idea," he said. "You'll come home sometime and help me find the right place for them." He set them in a small pile on the table.

"Who's next?" his mother asked. "Daniel?"

Brenda handed the silver box to Joe, who held his head down as he tore off the paper and carefully lifted each book. He was never comfortable receiving gifts. He much preferred giving them, and avoiding the spotlight at all costs, or at least shining it on someone else. Daniel could sympathize with him.

"France, Germany," Joe recited. "How wonderful." He fanned through the photographs of each country, then placed the books on the table and looked around the room. "This has all been too much. And just because I'm getting older. It's a funny tradition, isn't it? Celebrating this day that brings you closer to the end?" He spoke lightly, as if the gravity of his words hadn't occurred to him.

"Wait, wait! We're not done yet," Ellen announced, hoisting

herself out of the easy chair and shuffling into the kitchen. She returned with a few small boxes wrapped in pale blue paper. The first contained an ornate silver tin of jasmine tea that Daniel suspected was more something his mother liked than his father. The second was a Red Sox cap. "His old one is about to fall apart," she explained, and his father unwrapped the final present slowly, carefully peeling off each piece of tape, folding it neatly and setting it aside.

"Go on," Ellen said. "There's no need to save the paper."

Inside a small rectangular plastic box was a deck of playing cards, each with the same photograph of their family on one side. "I found this shop in the mall that makes your photos into decks of cards," she said. "Now when we play hearts or gin we can think about you all. They also made coasters and place mats, but I couldn't imagine setting a drink or my dinner on your faces." She smiled and folded her hands on her lap as he examined the cards.

"What a great idea, Ell," he said. "Maybe these cards will bring you good luck. Maybe you'll finally win a game."

Daniel's parents loved to be the bantering couple, but he knew the banter turned darker once the two were alone. He'd grown up listening to them argue about money or Joe's job or Ellen's friends in the bedroom next door as he was trying to fall asleep. The arguments were consistent, if nothing else: Ellen had always wanted more of something—for Joe to be home more, for him to be more social with her friends, more interested in her latest interests, and Joe had always maintained that he was only capable of so much, that he had limits, that the world had limits and that this fact was not such a terrible thing—one had to just accept it at some point in one's life. Daniel remembered slipping farther beneath his sheets and trying to block out the noise of their sharp words by bunching his sheet and blanket next to his ears. And the next day, as if they'd now purged themselves of something poisonous, they'd joke with each other and sneak a kiss or two when they thought the kids weren't looking. They'd laugh and flirt, and all would be well for a few weeks or longer, until Ellen's moods would start to turn. In the end, Daniel couldn't imagine being married to someone for as long as his parents had and still feeling playful together. Perhaps in moments of nostalgia, but newfound playfulness? It seemed impossible.

Daniel saw that on the cards was a photo taken at least ten years earlier, when Hilary had come home for Thanksgiving. The five Millers stood on their front stoop, and Daniel remembered it had been their neighbor who'd taken the picture, Mr. Simons, or Mr. Simonson, was it?—a widower who listened to talk radio so loud they could hear it from their living room. None of the spouses were in the photo, and Daniel wondered whether his mother had purposefully excluded them (would Brenda be offended?), and why she'd chosen such an old photo, one taken, he realized, before he was in his wheelchair.

"Look at us," Hilary laughed, grabbing one of the cards. "Look at me! My hair is so blond it's green!"

"God," Jake mumbled, burping into his fist, "I must have been ten pounds fatter there."

Daniel took a card and saw that indeed his brother was rounder then, before he'd met Liz, before he'd grown more disciplined about himself and his life. And his mother's hair was a little less gray. His father stood on the far right, his shoulder touching hers. He wore a faint smirk, an expression hard to read, and one of his eyes was just slightly closed.

Daniel himself appeared in the middle of the group wearing an old sweatshirt, still faintly tan from the summer. His hair was longer then, and fell just over his eyes. He stood with his legs apart, his hands on his hips. He'd just met Brenda and would soon bring her home to meet them, once he'd finally told her he loved her, he remembered thinking now.

Brenda ran her hands through her hair. She was so pretty, he thought as he looked at her, an objectively beautiful woman. But so much about her had changed and continued to change, or *was* it even she who was different now? Maybe it was more the way the air circulated when they were in a room together—maybe it was only this that had changed. Whatever it was, she was gradually stepping away from him in order to save herself. This much was obvious. His heart seemed to grow thick in his chest.

—

Persistent thoughts about Brenda's miscarriage (was it a stillborn? At six months it seemed closer to that than a miscarriage), and the conversation with MacNeil, and Hilary and Jake's argument suddenly vanished, and Ellen found herself merely buoyed by feelings of kindness and gratitude toward the improved weather and the smell of the ocean, toward her children and Joe. "Oh, it's good to have my five kids here with me tonight," she said. She now sensed that choosing a photo of just the blood family for the cards might have been a little exclusionary, but at the time it seemed more a fond nod to the past than any statement about the present.

She leaned back in the soft chair and thought of Vera. Maybe in fact she was here right now, a part of the air. Maybe she and Ellen's parents and grandmothers were in the room with her and her family, watching them. It was a comforting thought, that the dead never truly left.

Daniel, Joe and Jake chatted about taxes. Liz muttered to Hilary, "You'll stay here. Jake will be fine, just leave it to me," and although Hilary seemed reluctant, the two did begin to discuss the logistics of living here. Brenda looked on, listening to their conversations. None of them were alone here. In this moment, no one Ellen loved was truly alone.

MacNeil had recently stumbled across a new biography of Isabella, one considerably less laudatory than the other he'd given her. In the end, he'd told Ellen, after her young son and later her husband had died, Isabella became the sole proprietor of her house. It was her one motivating force, building the museum and gathering art and filling its walls (this part was common knowledge), but before long she became quite a dictator in this quest. Though she had one of the first phones in Boston, she used it only to summon others, and refused to take any incoming calls. She ordered the architects and landscapers around mercilessly, and after the museum was up and running, she was known to bark at visitors if they overstepped their bounds. "Jesus Christ, madam," she said to a woman touching everything she saw. "This is no menagerie." Those paying attention developed a panorama of views about her, and not all were positive. Bostonians thought her greedy and showy. Henry James, across the ocean, had written in his journal, "The negation of work, of literature, the swelling, roaring crowds, the 'where are you going,' the age of Mrs. Jack, the figure of Mrs. Jack, the American, the nightmare—the individual consciousness—the mad, ghastly climax . . . The Americans looming up—dim, vast, portentous—in their millions —like gathering waves—the barbarians of the Roman

Empire." Ellen had almost laughed when MacNeil first read her these words. They sat in his living room, dissonant jazz clamoring from the stereo. MacNeil called it free-form.

"Such drama," she said. "How can you fault someone for wanting to surround themselves with beauty?"

"It's the trying so hard, the need to outdo everyone else," MacNeil said. "It's such an American thing, really, wanting to be the best, no, to *have* the best and the most beautiful."

"But you yourself love the finest art. You love superlatives—and you love the Gardner Museum as much as I do."

"I do, is the funny thing. Even Henry James, once he came to visit, fell in love with the place."

"So how do you reconcile this, your scorn and your admiration? How do you reconcile your being an American with your European heritage?" Ellen had only been to Europe once, and that was many years ago. She and Joe had gone to Italy to tour Tuscany and then the museums of Florence. On their second day Joe's wallet had been stolen, and on their last day Ellen was struck by a stomach flu. In the end they saw far less than they'd planned. Joe liked his domestic vacations: the Grand Canyon, Niagara. He always said what's the point of traveling so far when you haven't seen everything in your own country yet?

"I don't know if you ever can," MacNeil admitted. "Maybe Isabella made do by cramming so much of Europe into her Boston house. Outside was the gray weather, the naysayers, all the jealous people. Inside was her real life."

"I am American and happy to be," Ellen said, and straightened her posture. "My grandmothers struggled in order to get here and build a life for their families."

MacNeil nodded and smiled, bemused. "My parents did too, you know."

"I think the only difference between Americans and Europeans is that Americans are more open about their longings. I don't see anything wrong with that."

"I suppose it's the lack of subtlety, the inherent gaudiness of it."

"Everyone experiences desire," she said.

"I don't disagree."

"What does it matter, then, how we show it?"

He shrugged, and before she realized it, he'd changed the subject.

This was the last time she saw him before he left for San Francisco, and she drove away from his house thinking that perhaps he had a point in the end. Everyone in her family was so clumsy in their desires, fumbling aimlessly and openly toward that which they could never fully achieve. Joe groped about for knowledge, bargains, the most efficient, the best this, the fastest that. Brenda and Daniel wanted a child so blindly they'd bought a stranger's sperm. And now, remembering this conversation, she reluctantly added another to the list: in her ill-informed search for companionship, Hilary had fallen into motherhood.

But no, Ellen decided, MacNeil just could not see the sheer liberation that came from admitting one's true desire. Without the confession of this desire to another and without attempting to act upon these longings, one was truly alone in the end. A widower in a sparkling, sanitized house. A shrinking old woman in a cavernous museum, who let her stockings split with holes and her dresses grow thinner as she desperately conserved her money for the endowment of the museum. One night close to the end of her life, a servant found Isabella wandering the second floor in her nightgown, approaching a window. The servant gingerly led her back to her bedroom. No one ever discovered whether she had been sleepwalking or what her true motivation had been this night, if there had been one. Ellen liked to think that Isabella had just been having a sleepless night and gotten up for a stroll to admire her paintings, that the woman, despite everything, had found her favorite things in life and merely wanted to be beside them. The alternative thought was too much, that so much could come to nothing in the end.

Joe was listening to Daniel talk about his work. Her husband was a man who could hear what a person was really saying and really meaning better than anyone she knew. It was, she thought, a rare talent.

She closed her eyes and listened to the voices of those she loved pool around her.

—

"I'm just warning you that the weather here is terrible in the winter. All those nor'easters, and snow like you've never seen it. And if you're thinking about buying here one day, the property taxes are outrageous," Jake said to Hilary, not that she'd ever be organized enough to buy a house here or anywhere else, for that matter. He couldn't believe that he'd let Liz talk him back into this just now. ("She needs this from you," she had said, and in the moment, it seemed like the noble thing to do.) Hilary's eyes drifted around the room as he spoke. Facts and practical advice merely bored her. He wanted to tell her that over a hundred people heeded his advice every day at work. "You're really going to do this, move here?" he finally asked.

"Yes."

"Our kids will be able to see their cousin a lot," Liz said quietly.

"I know, I thought of that too," Hilary said. She had responded more to Liz than to him this whole weekend. "And since I doubt they'll have brothers or sisters, I think that'll be important."

He craved another glass of wine but there was no more, and anyway, he supposed he'd had enough. "Maybe you'll meet some great man and get a great job and have some great life here. You never know what kind of things could pop up along the road, the path or whatever of life when it comes to our futures." He'd meant to sound positive and inspirational, not drunk.

Hilary shrugged.

Liz set her hand on Hilary's knee and said, "There's always Alex," and Hilary shook her head and said, "How about the cake?"

The two rushed off to the kitchen. Would they become good friends, his wife and sister? Would they share their secrets or even talk about him to each other? He shuddered. And who was this Alex? He supposed it wouldn't be so completely terrible if Liz and his sister became friends. If nothing else, it might make Hilary like him a little more.

Jake turned his attention to Daniel and his father's discussion of tax laws and was happy to correct them when they bemoaned the new deductions. "No, they haven't disappeared," Jake said, and explained the restructuring of the laws, the rationale for the government to withhold a slightly higher percentage on income taxes, but offer breaks on other deductions. "It's actually pretty progressive," he explained. As he continued, he sensed they weren't quite following what he was saying.

Liz returned to the living room and handed him a glass of water. "Drink this," she whispered. "No more wine, okay?" His mother sat across from him with a faint grin on her face, her eyes closed. And in the other easy chair, Brenda looked through him, an almost ghostly expression on her face. Jake rose to find a blanket or a magazine, something, anything, to give her.

"I'm thinking of hiring an accountant this year," Daniel explained, mentioning someone their friends had used who'd saved them thousands the year before. Just as Jake opened his mouth to suggest his own accountant, the lights in the room dimmed and Liz and Hilary drifted in from the kitchen carrying a large white cake ablaze with a ring of candles. Everyone sang "Happy Birthday" and his mother added the harmony as always. Brenda didn't open her mouth, and Daniel barely made a sound, and at the end of the song, the women stood in a cluster before his father. Everyone watched Joe gather air into his lungs and blow the breath from his body, flattening the tiny flames and turning them to dark strings of smoke.

Jake reached forward and plucked the candles from the cake. He walked into the kitchen and stood against the counter for a moment, willing away a sudden rise of melancholy. He counted to three and thought of happy sights—his bright green lawn, Liz's sleeping face on the pillow next to his each morning. He closed his eyes and grew a little dizzy, so he opened them, and after the dizziness had abated, after the sadness had ebbed, he walked back into the living room to rejoin his family.

Liz was cutting the cake and Hilary handed each person a slice. Jake imagined this room full of them and their twins and Hilary's child, three generations of Millers all together. It was a welcome image, a room brimming with energy and chatter, the excitement and bustle of children.

The light outside gradually began to dim, and after they brought their plates into the kitchen and Liz made coffee, Jake led everyone out to the back porch. The seven barely fit here—he would have it extended farther out so it could accommodate them, as well as the twins and Hilary's child and whoever else might join the family someday. Daniel's chair occupied at least half of the porch. Liz awkwardly perched on one arm of his chair (*For God's sake, be careful!* Jake almost said. *We don't need any more accidents in this family!*) and Hilary sat on the floor on the other side of him. They began a game of fish, the only game everyone knew how to play. Joe dealt the cards and Ellen reminded them of the simple rules.

As they played, Jake kept his eyes on the low waves rolling onto the beach, the rocks tossing in the water and spilling onto the sand. The sun had dipped into the horizon, but some measure of light remained, a muted shade of apricot that seemed almost to rise from the ground. For a short while longer, they could stay out here and still see each other's expressions—for a short while longer, it would be neither day nor night.

The cards sat in a messy pile on the small wooden table and at one point a few of them lifted into a breeze. Jake stood to grab them before they flew too far. "Ha, got you," he said. "Now my family's going nowhere. I've got you in my hand."

He slammed the cards down on the table too hard, and the glass top of the table shook a little.

"At least for now," his father said, and Ellen grinned at Jake with a strange mix of pride and bewilderment.

Brenda, seated in an Adirondack chair, lifted her knees to her chin. She carefully plucked a card from her hand and set it on the discard pile. Jake watched her face and was struck by the sudden sensation that he might not see her again. He wanted desperately to say something that would endear him to her, as well as to the rest of them. He thought of mentioning the way Daniel first described her after they'd met as "young but only in looks, and funny, and incredibly smart," or how his own parents had met, how his father had sold his mother's parents a car just to get to know her, or how he and Liz often talked about wanting to fly the whole family to Disney World one day. But he didn't know Brenda well enough to sense what would win her over. She'd always remained quietly by Daniel's side, a little unsure of where or even whether she fit into this family. Perhaps it was her age or her nationality that made her always seem almost like a stranger among them. Or perhaps it was just her desire to remain at a distance from the center of things. Whatever it was, it was a desire Jake didn't understand at all.

The evening grew darker and it became difficult to see the cards in the waning light. After Daniel had won (Jake had secretly slipped him the strongest hand when it was his turn to deal), everyone headed back inside. But Liz stayed to gather the cards and straighten the chairs, and Jake helped her.

"How're you feeling?" he asked. He reached out his hand.

Liz took it, moved closer to him and pressed her cheek against his.

Her face felt cool and plush, and he smelled the frosting on her breath. "I love it here," he said. Without thinking, he reached his hand around her back and pulled her even closer, then slipped his fingers up her shirt and touched the side of her breast. She didn't wince or swat him away. "This is okay?" he whispered, and she nodded. He wanted no more than this right now. He didn't want anything more from her at all, and for this he was grateful.

The two stood silently until they could no longer see the ocean and the sky had gone black. Then they turned and went inside.

—

They'd all said good night to each other and gone off to bed, and now Hilary found herself staring up at the ceiling of her room. Her pillow was too soft. She'd grown sweaty beneath the sheets, but once she tossed them on the floor, she became chilly. After a while she stood and wandered down the hallway and through the living room, where Daniel and Brenda lay on the fold-out sofa. Jake and Liz had insisted they take their bed, but Daniel had said the bigger room would be easier for him to navigate. Hilary looked down at them and wondered whether either was really asleep right now.

She crept past them, carefully pushed open the front door and closed it as quietly as she could behind her. The night was cool but not cold, and she could hear the distant buzz of an airplane as she stood on the front steps in her pajama pants and old T-shirt. After the buzz faded, the only sound she could hear was the waves pushing again and again onto the sand. She made her way down the driveway, cursing to herself as the sharp gravel dug into her feet. Across the street, she found a tree stump shaped like a chair. She eased herself onto it, shifting over a forked ridge near the side, and remembered the many times she ran away as a kid, when she sat high above her house in those trees. What was it that sent her away in the first place? She looked back at Jake's dark house, everyone in their beds inside. It had always been the smallest things: her mother's insistence that she clean her room before going to a friend's house, Jake's refusal to let her borrow his calculator. Each no seemed an infringement. She supposed she hadn't changed all that much. Nothing riled her more than a boss asking her to complete a project differently than she had, or a boyfriend wanting her to drive slower. Such minor requests made her feel sewed inside a tight sheet, and now she wondered why.

A bird squawked down by the shore, and she looked around. The road was a rich auburn, the sky the darkest maroon— everything had taken on warm colors. If a night here could be so hospitable, she thought, if people could leave their cars unlocked, if this Vanessa person was so interesting and welcoming, then this island would indeed make a good home.

She saw a car's headlights in the distance, and as it approached, she wondered if for some reason it was Alex. But why did she keep thinking of this person who undoubtedly had a girlfriend, or maybe a few? Soon enough he would become just another part of her past. Her future was the baby, herself and an entirely new life.

As the car drew closer and then stopped, she saw to her surprise that it was him. He pulled over to the side of the road, turned off the ignition and stepped out. She was suddenly embarrassed to be sitting outside alone in her pajama pants late at night.

"I had this strange sense that I should check in on you. I just finished up at work," he said.

"What if I hadn't been sitting out here? Would you have rung the bell?" She gestured toward the dark house.

"I don't know. Probably not."

"Lucky I'm out here, then," she said. He came closer and sat down on the ground next to her. "Were you on your way to see that girl?"

"What? Who?"

"The girl you work with?" She didn't want him to have to cover something up.

"No," he said. "You know what? I've been a little worried about you since you came into the store last night."

"You have?'

He nodded. "How's your brother?"

"He's managing, I think."

"Does it make you scared that, well, something might happen to your baby?"

She smiled. "Not really. Maybe it should. But I guess I'm just not letting myself think that way."

He wrapped his fingers around her ankle and held on as she swung it in the air. "What happened between us," he said, "you know, at my place—I'm sorry about that. I really am. I'm not sure what I was thinking."

"You weren't alone. It wasn't only your decision."

"I guess you're right. But still, I mean, you're pregnant. You're, what, six months' pregnant? And we'd just met? It's not exactly Boy Scout behavior."

"Do you do this all the time? Sleep with people you've just met?"

"No. Do you?" he asked.

"Every day." She glanced down at him and smiled. "I enjoyed it, to be honest." What was the point in lying now?

"You did?"

"I really did." She rested her hands on her belly.

"Okay," he said, and let go of her ankle.

"You didn't? You thought it was too weird."

"No, I liked it too. I promise. But Hilary, you know, I can be an asshole. I'm completely unreliable. I'm selfish, I tend to leave people in the lurch, and you deserve better than that."

"Alex?"

"Yeah?"

"Shut up."

"Okay," he said.

"I get the sense that you've said this so many times, it barely means anything to you anymore. You don't need to break up with me," she said, and set her hand on his shoulder. "And you don't need to apologize for sleeping with me. You certainly shouldn't apologize for that."

He kicked a pebble onto the road.

"And one more thing, just for good measure. I don't do this sort of thing all the time either."

"I didn't think you did."

"Really?"

He looked up at her, and though she could barely make out his face in the darkness, she thought she detected a smirk. He stood, turned to her and said, "Hi, I'm Alex."

"Hi, Alex, I'm Hilary."

"Do you need a ride somewhere? Is that why you're sitting out here on a tree stump in the middle of the night, Hilary?"

She considered suggesting that they go for a drive and then maybe, just maybe, they'd end up at his place again, but then she thought of her family just feet away from them, of Daniel and Brenda, of her father, her now-seventy-five-year-old father, and said, "No thanks. I just came out here to clear my mind, and I think I should head back inside now."

"All right," he said, and shoved his hands inside his pockets.

"Oh, and I have a bit of news for you," she said. "I'm going to stay here on Great Salt for a while. I kind of like this place, and my brother offered me his house—well, my sister-in-law did really, but that's another story."

"Good. I'm glad you're staying."

"You're glad, but you're a little worried that I'll want too much from you."

"I'm sorry, what did you say your name was?"

She laughed. "I don't want anything from you. I promise."

"Hilary, right, that was it."

She moved closer to him and rested her head against his arm. He stepped behind her, slipping his hands around her stomach. "I'm not worried," he whispered, his lips against her ear.

They stayed like this for a few moments, until Hilary said, "I should go."

"How long do you think you'll stay on the island?"

"I'm not sure. I'll see how it goes, and whether I can find any work."

"You want me to ask if they need anyone else at the store?"

"Sure," she said. "But I've got a little saved, and my folks are going to help out. I'll be all right for a while."

"Hil?" he said.

"Yeah?"

"Sleep well."

"Good night," she said, and reached forward to take his hand. She kissed the top of it, probably longer than she should have, and headed back to the house. Maybe they would sleep together again—a part of her hoped they would—or maybe something more would happen between them. Most likely, though, they would become some version of friends in the end. The thought wasn't entirely unpleasant. They could see each other every once in a while for dinner or a drink and talk about the others on the island, the latest gossip, and their own gossip, whom they were currently seeing or wished they were seeing. They could give each other advice about these women and men, they could discuss where they hoped to travel, what they hoped to do with their lives, as Hilary suspected this was a subject she would never tire of, even after the baby was born. In the end, it was the imagining alternate futures more than living them that seemed so necessary. The reminding herself of the many options for a person in this world. And she thought that Alex would agree.

She tripped over a pair of shoes by the front door, and Daniel shuffled in his bed. "Larry?"

"Sorry, go back to sleep," she whispered.

"I can't. I wasn't sleeping anyway."

"Is she up?" Hilary asked, motioning to Brenda.

"No. Hear the breathing? Sit with me awhile. I can't fall asleep." He gestured to an easy chair.

Hilary crept to the chair. "You sure we won't wake her?"

"Nah. What were you doing outside?"

"Just had a moment of claustrophobia in here. I needed some air," she said. "One thing they don't tell you about being pregnant is that your body temperature goes haywire. I'm always either hot or freezing."

"I'm not sure she ever got to that point."

She moved a few pieces of clothing from the chair and sat down. "I'm sorry."

"It's all right," Daniel said. He pulled himself up in bed and adjusted the pillows behind his back. Hilary couldn't quite see his face in the darkness of the room. "She did have other things, a lot nausea and headaches, mostly in the beginning."

"I know what that's like."

"I used to think that her being pregnant would put us on a more similar footing, you know, physically. That we'd both be at odds with ourselves. To be honest, it drove me crazy that although she had all these aches and pains and morning sickness, she remained basically happy."

"You were a miserable wreck before your accident, Danielle. I'm sorry to tell you this, but you've never been 'basically happy.' Or maybe you were, I don't know—were you? Maybe that's me I'm talking about, never fundamentally content about anything."

"I don't really know. But I must have assumed that the discomfort and all the changes that come with pregnancy would in fact bring us closer. We needed that after the accident and after I'd begun to hate everyone and everything. Here's something: I think that deep down I wanted her to suffer like I had."

"That's probably normal."

Daniel whispered, "No one should want another person to suffer, especially his wife." Brenda let out a short sigh. "Let's try to keep it down."

"You've been through a lot," Hilary said as quietly as she

could. "Nothing can operate by *shoulds* after that." She tried to think of something more comforting and specific to say about the matter.

"I suppose. But now, I don't know. I don't think I'm making her feel any better after what just happened to her. I've tried, but I don't think it's worked."

"Maybe she just needs to feel like hell for a while."

"Maybe. But I wish there was something I could just say or do or give her that would help just a bit." He twisted a corner of the sheet in his fingers. "She's so far from home over here."

"What do you mean?" Hilary looked at Brenda, her small thumb beside her open mouth.

"She's so far from London, from her mother and her family."

"But she's lived here for ages."

"I know. Still, at a time like this. You should've heard her talking to her mother and how relieved she was just to hear her voice. I know that I needed you all around after my accident."

"You just needed the distractions of liquor and stories of my pathetic love life," she said. "You know you're lost without me."

"Oh, I think it's the opposite, Larry."

Brenda turned again and Hilary stood. "I'm going to let you two sleep."

"Don't leave me," he half joked.

"Oh, Danielle, dahling, what do you want me to do? Should I crawl into bed between you two?"

"Okay," he said sadly.

Hilary touched his shoulder and turned to leave. She stood a moment, unsure whether she should actually leave, and if she stayed, then what? Could she sleep in the easy chair? She considered it, but then glanced at Brenda, a tiny heap next to him. She would wake the next morning and wonder when Hilary had joined them, and why.

She crept down the hallway and into her small room, where she lay down on the bed. She closed her eyes and shuffled beneath the sheets, but remained unable to drift off to sleep. How did her brother's marriage continue day after day? How did anyone's, for that matter? In general, it seemed a strange institution to have lasted so long. In this time when babies could be created by joining chemicals in a glass tube, when divorce was at an all-time high, ye olde institution of marriage was alive and well, and not just for dogged traditionalists: gays and lesbians sought the right to marry, artists married, musicians and loners and sociopaths and geniuses— virtually everyone. Smart, funny, creative people like Daniel fell in love and believed that this heightened, blissful state of attraction and adoration would last forever (for if they didn't believe this, what was the point?). And then slowly, surely, the bliss began to fade—the adoration became affection, then comfort, then stasis, then irritation, and these people clung to each other long after anything good between them had slipped away, and why, what for? Hilary turned over and faced the ceiling. Surely there had to be a reason all these people stayed together.

11
A Completely New Experience

After Hilary left, Brenda began to twist and turn in her sleep. She kicked Daniel and flopped onto her back, then shot her arm into the air. "You okay?" he whispered, but she just sighed restlessly. What a sight they were right now, Brenda thrashing about in her sleep, Daniel sitting upright and scrunching the sheet into a ball. And what if she had heard the conversation he'd just had with Hilary? What if Brenda was incorporating it into some nightmare? But they'd spoken quietly. She couldn't have heard them—and anyway, it might not have been such a terrible thing if she had. After all, he hadn't said anything that wasn't true. He'd merely spoken of his growing concern for her. He let go of the sheet and lay back down.

They would wake tomorrow, say their goodbyes to everyone and head off to the ferry. When they arrived on the mainland,

Brenda would help him into the car, and later into their house (his hands always got stuck between his wheels and that blessed doorjamb—he'd been meaning to have the door widened for months). She would check in on Morris Arnold, do their laundry, tidy up the place since they'd had no time to clean it before they left, make dinner, and later she would help him out of his chair, into his pajamas and eventually into their bed. Daniel adjusted the pillow beneath his head and tried to get comfortable, but the pillow was too soft, the mattress too hard. The waves pressed against the beach again and again. Before they dropped off to sleep, he would tell her that he'd been thinking about starting to lift weights again and build the strength to manage better on his own. He wanted to at least be able to get in and out of the car by himself. He'd tell her that tomorrow, he planned to call the doctor Tammy Ann was working for and ask about his research, then volunteer to help him. Maybe the man was close to finding a cure—maybe he could tell Daniel about some of his discoveries, if nothing else. Daniel pictured himself and Brenda beside each other in their bed at home, beneath those heavy cotton sheets she'd bought at that British housewares store, and he tried to imagine what her reaction to these things might be. Would she be relieved? Would she even care? After all, minimizing his burden on her was not the same as tending to her. He tried to imagine what tending to her might actually entail—trying to clean the house himself? Cooking her favorite foods? Chatting up the neighbors in her stead? The overall task seemed much larger than these superficial things, more nebulous and permanent and, he began to fear, next to impossible.

She sighed again. The waves seemed to whisper, *shh, shh,* and he fell into a fitful sleep. A while later, he woke to a fully formed thought: on the other side of this ocean was her mother, starting her morning, undoubtedly worried sick about her daughter. She, more than anyone, would know how best to tend to Brenda.

She folded the crisp white sheets and set them in a small stack on the coffee table. Her back to Daniel, she began tidying the room, adjusting every pillow and frame and book. He kept finding himself directly in her path.

"I'm thinking . . ." he finally said, and drew the deepest breath he could. "I'm thinking that you should go home to visit your family for a while. It might be the best thing for you right now." He'd rehearsed the words in his head the night before. He thought of gentle, convoluted ways to suggest the trip, then sharp, aggressive sentences; bloated, melancholy pleas. In the end, he'd decided just to be direct and honest.

"Oh?"

"Maybe for a week or two. Play it by ear, see when you've had enough. I think it'd be good for you to be back home. Don't you?" A heavy sense of doubt crept through him, but no, he was doing the right thing for her.

"I don't know if the doctor will let me go just yet," she said tentatively.

"Well, whenever he gives you the green light."

She held her eyes on the floor. "You could come too?"

He shook his head.

"You're trying to get rid of me?" She forced a smile. "Anyway, I can't leave you alone, you know that. You'd do nothing but let yourself lie in bed all day. You'd grow bedsores and go completely mad."

"Thanks for the vote of confidence, love," he said.

"I'm just saying what's true. And don't be sarcastic with that word."

"You've gone away before, Bren."

"But not since your accident," she said.

"What word? What word are you talking about?"

"Love," she said. "All right? Love. I hate that you only use it these days when we're arguing. We both do. Like it's some sort of ammunition."

"I hadn't noticed that. You're right, though," he said, and then, more quietly, "What a terrible thing."

"It is a terrible thing." She stood and pressed her hands over her face.

"I'm so sorry, Bren." His eyes began to sting.

She sank into the couch. "Are you just saying that, or do you really believe it?"

"I'm sorry for all the sarcasm. I'm so sorry." He brought his fists to his eyes. "Please believe me."

She leaned her head back and looked up at the ceiling, and Daniel felt a tightening at the bottom of his stomach. He wanted to take back his suggestion that she go home.

"I guess I would like to be with my family for a while," she finally said. "I do miss them right now."

"I know," he said, trying to sound strong and empathetic. Decent. "I can imagine."

"You sure you wouldn't mind?"

He managed to shake his head. He thought of her struggling to help him out of his chair and into their bed. Then he thought of their house without her, of lying in their bed alone, his empty wheelchair next to him. He pictured Morris Arnold next door, waving hello and looking around for her. And then

Daniel had an idea. "Maybe I'll just stay here and let you have our place to yourself for a while if the doctors don't want you to fly home right away. Maybe I'll just stay here with Hilary, at least until you get back."

"But what about your work? Don't you have that book jacket due this week?"

He said that it could wait. Once everyone learned what had happened this weekend, they would extend his deadlines.

"Of course," she said.

Hilary appeared in the doorway, rubbing her eyes and yawning. "Danielle. Brenda. Morning."

"Larry, what do you think of me staying here with you? Just for a little while?" He briefly explained that Brenda might head home alone.

Hilary nodded slowly, clearly trying to decipher what this news might actually represent. "Sure. The company would be nice," she said. She stood with them for a few awkward moments, then shuffled off to the kitchen.

Daniel glanced back at Brenda. He wheeled toward her, reached over and linked his fingers with hers.

"I should probably just slip out before everyone else gets up," she said, slowly pulling away.

"No, don't go yet," he said. "Say goodbye to them before you head out. There's no need to make everyone worried about why you left so quickly."

Thankfully, she agreed.

"What's going on?" Jake said, when Daniel explained the change in plans. Jake stood above him in the kitchen, a mug of coffee in his hands. "Shouldn't you two be together right now?"

"It's what she needs," Daniel said. He knew he sounded curt, but he couldn't help it.

Jake opened his mouth, then closed it. Maybe he was finally learning that he couldn't always have a say in everyone else's business. He meant well, Daniel knew he did, but sometimes it seemed as if Jake had been born without any innate sense of when to keep his mouth shut.

Daniel headed back to Brenda. He would see her again in a couple weeks, of course he would. He helped her separate their clothes and set hers back in their suitcase. "I'll just throw mine in a plastic bag or something when I leave," he said.

"All right." She glanced down at their things. "I'll put this somewhere safe for now," she said, gesturing toward the container of ashes.

He nodded. "Put it where you think it won't hurt too much to look at."

"I will," she said, and he began placing his clothes in a stack on the easy chair, wishing she'd said a little more just now, though what precisely, he wasn't sure.

Evidently Jake explained the situation to his parents, for about ten minutes later, when Brenda's cab pulled into the driveway (she'd insisted on avoiding any awkward goodbyes near the ferry), everyone seemed to know that she was leaving by herself. She gathered her bag and jacket and said goodbye to the loose group that stood before her in the living room. She thanked Jake and Liz politely for their hospitality, and Daniel followed her outside and pulled the door closed behind him so he could see her off alone. The plywood slipped beneath him, and his left wheel dropped onto the gravel before the right one did. She walked silently beside him as they crossed the rough gravel toward the cab. He reminded himself again that this was the best thing he could do for her. "Call me when you get home today," he said when they finally stopped on a grassy patch. "And after London, we'll see." He sat as straight as he could despite a sudden pull of gravity. "We'll just see how you're doing at that point, all right?"

"Thank you," she said.

He hoped she did see at least a small change in him. After all, he could have said, *Can't you see how hard this is for me? Look at what I'm doing here: I'm giving you a gift. I'm trying to do what's best for you, even though it's making me want to burst right now.*

She stood there, looking down at his feet, maybe trying to think of exactly what to say. The taxi driver drummed his fingers against the steering wheel.

"Goodbye for now," he finally said, and she said, "Thank you again for this," and her words made him realize that, yes, she appreciated him right now. He was indeed doing the right thing, and later today and tomorrow and the next day, she could think of him with some degree of gratitude.

As she slid her bag into the back seat and climbed into the taxi, Daniel held his breath. She pulled the door shut, and he slowly lifted his hand and waved goodbye.

The air was cooler today, the sky covered by a scrim of clouds. He squeezed his knees. Even now, the nothingness beneath the skin there amazed him. Not a single pinch or chill. Sometimes it was infuriating, other times just strange. How could he lose so much and continue onward even for a minute? How could he continue on as an artist and husband and almost become a father in the face of this nothingness? It

seemed impossible to comprehend, and in a way, it was unbe-
lievable that he had.

—

Ellen could no longer stand to see Daniel sitting in the driveway by himself, so she went outside. "Come back in," she
insisted. "Come and be with us before we head out," and kept
a hand on the back of his chair as he turned himself around.

The others sat in a circle in the living room, eating their
breakfast. "Here, have something," she said, and rushed to
the kitchen, where Liz had set out fruit salad and bagels. Ellen
fixed him a plate and returned to the living room. "You'll stay
here until Brenda comes back from London?"

Daniel nodded. And would he and Hilary be able to take
care of themselves here, let alone each other? Would Hilary
be able to handle getting Daniel in and out of bed, helping
him in the bathroom if he needed it, all of this by herself?
Ellen sat on the sofa, took her plate in her lap and moved a
square of cantaloupe around a grape.

Joe soon appeared in the hallway carrying several bags in
one hand and the cage in the other, his glasses perilously resting on the tip of his nose.

"Oh, I'm not ready. I hate to leave," Ellen said, and went to
fix his glasses.

"We'll see you again before too long, Mom," Jake said. His
eyes were pink—he was undoubtedly hungover and now
regretful of having polished off a bottle (was it more?) of wine
last night. This weekend had crushed them all. "Maybe the
next time we see you will be when Hil has her baby?"

Ellen glanced at poor Daniel. Of course he knew the others

would still have their babies, but she wondered whether he'd have the strength for it.

"Ell," Joe said in his let's-get-things-moving voice. "We don't want to miss the ferry."

"I know, I know, but hold on a moment. We need to say proper goodbyes. Daniel," she said, and leaned down to him, "you'll let us know if you need us. You'll let us know when Brenda comes back and if you need us to help out or do anything, do anything at all, you know, grocery shopping or cooking for you, whatever you need, cleaning or decorating. Because I'm thinking that what we need is to get you some beautiful new . . ." There was no stopping the words that trailed from her mouth, though what she really wanted was to ask him when Brenda planned to return—would she even come back? *She would, of course she would, how could she not?*

"Mom, I'll be okay," Daniel finally said.

Joe squeezed Jake's arm. "I loved all that you did for me this weekend, and the gifts. Your gift. I won't forget it."

Ellen was glad that Joe thought to say these things. Sometimes such niceties escaped him and she was left to compensate for his frugality with tact.

Liz helped them carry their bags outside and Joe toted Babe's cage behind her, and before Ellen could stop to enjoy one last moment with her family, they surrounded her and Joe and said their farewells. They all stood beside the cab that Liz had called. Ellen had suggested it, since Liz and Jake would take the next ferry and were in the middle of packing up their car. Soon, too soon, Ellen found herself sitting beside Joe inside the moving cab, Babe to his right, the island rushing past them on all sides.

"I can't stand leaving them," Ellen said. "I never can."

"I know."

"Can you?"

"Ell," he said quietly, and rested his hand on top of hers. She waited for him to say more, but it occurred to her that of course he would not. He never did. But he did keep his large, soft hand on hers for the duration of the ride, until the cab had finally stopped and they could see a few people moving up a gangplank, onto the small ferry that rose and sank on the dark gray water.

They found two empty seats next to the engine room, though the blare here was deafening. The boat lifted anchor, and Joe fiddled with Babe's cage on the floor in front of him. The turtle snuggled into his wood chips. He had become like another child to Joe, and Ellen was suddenly grateful for it.

She closed her eyes and tried to ignore the roar of the engine. Soon she would see MacNeil again at the Gardner. She pictured the Tapestry Room lit with candles and lanterns, throngs of people piling in and walking toward their seats. "You know," she said loudly, and nudged Joe, "the opening night of the Gardner was on New Year's Eve. Fifty members of the Boston Symphony played Bach and Mozart, Chausson, Schumann. Can you imagine it?" It felt like a cruelty at first, speaking so admiringly of this world to Joe. But it was not, she reminded herself. There was nothing wrong with adoring a place.

"It must have been something," he said into her ear. The engine droned behind them.

"Back then there was a two-story concert hall. Now the Tapestry Room is what the upper floor used to be. Isabella hung lanterns from the balconies and candles from the arches and windows. She filled the hall with flowers, every sort available. Think of the scent! And there were fountains everywhere. It makes me happy to think about. I know it's silly, being so enamored of a museum and a woman, but it does."

"It all seems otherworldly, doesn't it?"

"Mm," Ellen said, unsure what he was referring to.

"Like a dream, really," he said, his lips now against her ear. His warm breath gave her a rush.

He'd startled her, his face in the window of her parents' car that day so many years ago. She didn't know what made her roll down the window for him. Now no one would so easily talk to a stranger, but back then, she supposed, it was a different planet. Joe had leaned his face almost inside the car, asked, "You all right in there?" and looked down at her, and she'd been at once taken aback and exhilarated and ashamed of her unkempt state. "Sort of," she managed. "You look good to me. What's your name?" "Why do you need to know?" she said in her deepest voice, and she felt the warm rush of his breath on her cheek as he said, "It's just a feeling I have, that it's something I ought to know. I'm Joe Miller," he said, and he smiled, and right then her parents approached from behind him and he pulled back, taking away his breath and his eyes that had looked her up and down so audaciously. "Goodbye for now, Joe Miller," she said, and waved two fingers as she rolled up the window.

She would cancel her plans with MacNeil and bring Joe to the Gardner; after all, the tickets to the concert were hers. So what if Joe didn't like it there? She'd plead with him and find some way to convince him to go with her.

Or she would go alone. She would call MacNeil and tell him that she'd caught a nasty cold. She would drive herself into the city, park beside the skinny river nearby and walk toward the great house by herself. She'd never been there alone, and it would be a completely new experience. She felt something inside her loosen, as if from a tether.

—

Jake drew a map of the circuit breaker box on a scrap of paper while Liz showed Hilary how to use the washer and dryer. His head throbbed from all the wine he'd drunk the night before. It was the oddest thought, leaving his house to his brother and sister, and Jake began to wish he could stay on with them, show them around the island, charter them a boat and have long chats with them in the evenings over dinner. But he had an annual meeting with the partners the next day and Liz had a doctor's appointment the following day.

He found Daniel sitting by a window in the living room, sketching something on a pad. Jake handed him the map of the circuit breakers. Daniel briefly glanced at it and set it aside. "This is just in case one of the breakers blows. We blow them more than we should. I need to get the electrician back in here." He looked down at Daniel's pad. "What are you drawing?"

"I have this book jacket due soon. I'm just doodling some ideas. It's for a novel set in Cuba."

"Ah," Jake said. How different their jobs were. The next day, Jake would sit in a room with ten other men and discuss stock portfolios and bonds, the revenues of smaller financial firms, current trends in fiber optics and computers and entertainment conglomerates. The last time he sat down to draw anything had to have been at least twenty years ago, and it struck him as infinitely strange that his brother actually made a living this way. "You think that you and Brenda really will try to get pregnant again?"

Daniel thought a moment. "Probably not. This might have been it for me." He looked down at his hands. "This whole thing wasn't easy. But I guess ask me again in a year or so." He glanced up at Jake. "Who knows?"

"You're right. Who knows?" Jake said, and set his hand on the side of his brother's chair. He didn't know what more to say about the matter without smothering him in sympathy. "This weekend was nothing like I thought it would be."

"You're telling me."

Jake moved his tongue around his mouth. "What was all that stuff Hilary was saying about MacNeil Burgess? It was ridiculous. Sometimes I think she would learn a lot from just being in a relationship for a while. And a job too, for that matter."

"She seems pretty happy to me."

Jake reluctantly agreed that his sister did seem more content than she had in a while. Pregnancy actually suited her. "Still, I think it'll be tough for her to be a single mother."

"You're in for something yourself with those twins," Daniel said, and Jake wondered why no one in his family ever really agreed with him about anything. Except for his father, in his quiet, passive way. And as for Daniel—he was just protecting Hilary, who had no one to really protect her in the end. Though of course she'd brought this on herself, she always did. She'd made her choices.

"I guess we are in for something."

"Hey, thank you."

"For what?"

"For letting us stay here," Daniel said.

"I'm happy to. Can I do anything else for you?"

Daniel shook his head. "This is plenty. You've been so generous," he said, as if forcing himself.

"No I haven't."

"You have. All weekend. I know Dad was touched."

Jake looked at him. "Well, thank you," he said. "You know, you can stay here as long as you want. I like knowing that someone's here." He wanted to discuss what had happened to Brenda and to tell him how very sorry he was, how unfair it was to the two of them, who'd already been through so much. And he wanted to apologize for fighting with Hilary and ask his brother if he and Jake could start over and try to talk more frequently, visit each other more often and be more a part of each other's lives, but Liz and Hilary walked into the room.

"Jake, our ferry is waiting," Liz said, and moved beside him.

Hilary went to sit beside Daniel. "There's a map of the island in the kitchen drawer. And a tide schedule there too," Liz said. Jake looked at his sister and brother, a pregnant single-mother-to-be beside a paraplegic man—how had his family come to this?

"We won't have any parties," Hilary said. "We won't tear the place down."

"Ha," Jake said.

"Thanks again," Daniel said.

"Really," Hilary added, looking at her feet. "Thanks for this."

For the first time in too long, Jake swore he noted a brief but definite fondness on their faces.

In the rearview mirror, he watched his house grow smaller and he tried to imagine what his brother and sister were talking about. Him? Liz? Their parents? He tried to estimate where Joe and Ellen might have been at this moment. He looked at his watch and figured they had to be in their car, driving home, sitting side by side quietly as they had thousands of times over the years, as he had so many times with Liz. There was nothing like sitting in silence next to his wife after a weekend on Great Salt, he decided. There was nothing to compare to that kind of solace.

Liz ambled up the gangplank, as did Jake behind her, wobbly with all of their bags. He could hear her heavy breath, or was it his? Liz collapsed on a bench on deck and Jake took the seat beside her. He lifted her hand and set it on his lap. She'd leaned over and laid her head down and Jake watched her breathing slow. Her hand sat like a heavy sponge on his legs and he lifted it, but it dropped with the weight of a brick.

"Hello? You there?" he said.

"Mm. I'm tired. I'm spent. I'm not sure I've ever been so spent," she said, and he wanted to pour gratitude upon her for all her work this weekend. And for more—for her being willing to endure all the infertility treatments, the long bouts of sadness, the constant anxiety in order for them to have a family, and then he wanted to apologize again for the *Kama Sutra* and the magazine (which in the end she'd thrown away with the rest of the weekend's garbage). But if he thanked her profusely and apologized as urgently as he felt he should have, she would prickle with irritation. She would cut him off and he would apologize again and none of it would ever really stop. This rhythm would continue to pulse beneath them even when they went about their business separately or held each other affectionately. Beneath the surface of everything, beneath the balance of his entire life was an unstoppable pendulum that constantly threatened to knock him off-kilter.

He counted to three in his mind before he said anything. Liz began to lift herself and sit upright. "Got it?" he said.

"Got it." The ferry pushed away from the dock and the foghorn blew.

"Do you worry about the babies? You know, after what happened to Brenda?" he asked her.

"I did even before that," she said.

"This morning I was reading that medical book, and it said that this kind of thing is really rare, and that it almost never happens. I'm glad we have that book up here, you know?" They'd bought it at Books & Beans a year ago, along with several others about fertility and pregnancy.

She nodded vacantly.

"Our babies will be fine," he said. "I really think everything will work for us. I have this gut feeling."

"You do?"

"Don't you?" he asked.

"I suppose so. But to be honest, I'm trying not to think about all that right now. Right now I'm trying to think about sitting here on this ferry and then just making it home. I'm trying to ignore the pain in my back and the fact that I can barely keep my head up. I'm sorry, honey, I'm just a little out of it."

"That's all right," he said. "That's perfectly fine. Liz?"

"Yeah?"

"I was pretty drunk last night, wasn't I?"

"You really were," she said, smiling.

"It's been years since I was that drunk," he said, and returned her smile.

—

Hilary struggled to help Daniel across the sand and rocks. He hadn't been down to the water since he'd arrived, and though getting him there proved next to impossible due to the weight of the chair, the rocks on the beach, the sand, the mud, the seaweed, the wind, she was determined to do it. Together they managed to move him close enough so that he could just reach a finger to the tide.

"I never liked the beaches in Maine. What's the appeal, all the rocks and the freezing water?" he said as a skirt of seaweed tumbled onto the ground before them.

"Yeah, I know, but it's like a difficult child, this place. You can't help admiring a beach that refuses to be sunny and soft, and water that makes your bones ache just looking at it."

"I guess you're right," he said.

She steadied her arms against the top of his chair and gradually lowered herself to sit on the rocky sand. She kicked off her sandals and mashed her toes against a pile of wet pebbles.

"It's funny. I never really knew what Brenda was thinking this whole weekend," Daniel said. "I could guess, of course. But she never admitted much. I did all the talking. I told her how I felt and I asked her a million questions." He paused. "Maybe it's her being British or so much younger than me or something, but she's always stayed about a half pace away from me."

Hilary nodded and said, "You can never really know what anyone else is thinking."

"But it's different when it's your wife. I'm sorry, but it is."

"Of course it is. It's probably more frustrating then." She leaned forward, picked up a pebble and tossed it into the water.

"There have to be plenty of people who understand what's going on in their spouse's head," he said.

"I'm sure you can always sense it on some level. But maybe you just don't always like it, so you convince yourself everything is their fault, that they're too distant or aloof."

"Maybe."

Hilary had listened to countless friends complain about their relationships and marriages over the past few years. "Can I ask you a question? Why do people stay together for so long?"

Daniel held his hands together in his lap.

"I'm sorry. That was a horrible thing to ask."

"No, no, I'm just thinking about us," he said. "I don't know exactly why we have. It's worked pretty well, for the most part. I like having someone around to watch out for me, someone else to be a witness to my life." He swallowed. "For me, so much of it is predictability and knowing that every morning, there'll be a warm body beside mine and I'll know exactly what size she'll be, what she'll say and where I'll fit next to her and where she likes me to touch. When that predictability started to fade away because she was out of bed early or didn't respond to me like she used to, when there was this big part of my body that could no longer feel a thing next to her, that's when everything started to go haywire."

Hilary looked up at him. "That makes sense."

"It does?"

She turned her eyes to the ocean and the horizon line far away. "Sometimes my favorite part of sex is the stillness afterward, just lying next to someone and feeling them right there beside me."

"You're such a girl."

"And you're not?" she said. "What were you just saying to me?"

"True."

Hilary smiled up at him. "If I wasn't pregnant and tired right now, I'd strip down and run into that water."

"No you wouldn't."

"I would."

"If I had legs that worked, I'd join you," he said.

"Excuses, excuses."

They sat for a while longer, and once the wind grew stronger and the air chillier, they made the journey back to the house. They were like an old, broken-down couple, Hilary thought as she used every ounce of strength she had to help her brother back up the beach and onto the gravel path that led around to the front door.

"You weigh at least a thousand pounds," she huffed.

"So do you."

"Always the charmer, you." She went to push open the front door.

"Someone has to be." He moved onto the plywood ramp and inside.

That evening, they sat over plates of food leftover from the birthday dinner. Hilary told Daniel about what had happened with Alex, about Bill David and George and Camille, and about how she sometimes thought about calling George but she wasn't sure she should; after all, what would be the point? Daniel said she was probably doing the right thing, moving here and starting over on her own. "Starting over is usually the best thing for you," he said. "But this Alex guy? I'm not so sure."

"Well, neither am I." She stood to clear the dishes. "But I'm telling you, he knows his way around a bed."

"Sex—I think I remember what that is."

"I'm sorry," she said.

"Don't be."

"I can't help it."

She left their dishes in a stack in the sink, vowing she'd wash them soon, or later that night, or maybe tomorrow, and she went to the living room to join Daniel, now flipping through a newspaper. As she glanced out the window at the fading gray sky, she decided that this must have been what a good marriage was like: sitting in a room together, unremarkably reading a newspaper and not worrying what the other person was thinking or trying to come up with something to say. She knew Daniel's humor and temper and fears like she imagined an old wife would know her husband's. She loved him despite the things she didn't love about him, that he could be moody and a little bossy, a little too parental with her sometimes. She loved him ten times more than she didn't love these things.

Hilary rested her arms on her stomach and felt a stillness inside. The baby had been turning all day, and must have finally fallen asleep. It was the strangest sensation, something inside of her drifting off to sleep while she sat there, awake and alert. Something so very separate from her at the very core of her body, someone she'd never seen or heard, but felt distinctly every day.

Outside the cold water continued to spill onto the rocky beach. The moon became sharper in the blackening sky, and she could just see the sliver from where she sat. Daniel breathed a sigh and turned a page of the newspaper.

In loving memory of my mother,
Joan Ruth Pitlor (1941–1984)

Acknowledgments

For various colors of wisdom, support, friendship and generosity, my deepest appreciation to Jill Bialosky, Evan Carver, Chris Castellani, Bill Clegg, Jessica Craig, Emily DeGroat, Henry Dunow, Hannah Griffiths, Nicole Lamy, Don Lee, Winfrida Mbewe, Amy Robbins, Deborah Weisgall and Susie Wright. Also to my sister, Margot Geffen, for her insights and enthusiasm; my family, my first experience of love; and mostly, to my husband, Neil Giordano, the first to believe, and without whom I could never have written this book. Thank you.

THE BIRTHDAYS

Heidi Pitlor

THE BIRTHDAYS

Heidi Pitlor

READING GROUP GUIDE

DISCUSSION QUESTIONS

1. Compare the ways in which the women who have married into the family interact with Ellen and Joe. Why do you think Liz connects with her in-laws, while Brenda doesn't seem to?

2. At one point there is an exchange between MacNeil and Ellen where Ellen says of Daniel, "He could have been a real artist." MacNeil replies, "He is a real artist." Is MacNeil, a relative outsider, able to make a better assessment of Daniel? Does this relate to Ellen's inability to understand what it is exactly that Jake does for a living?

3. What role do age and age differences play in each of the relationships? For example, Brenda is much younger than Daniel—how does this affect the way they relate to each other? How is Ellen's affection for MacNeil, and for Joe, different from the affection expressed between the younger couples?

4. In addition to this, discuss the role of generational differences in the book. How do the parents' expectations for their children affect the children's own wants and goals? To what degree have Ellen's and Joe's philosophies on life rubbed off on their children?

5. Discuss which characters you most identify with and why. Is it easier to feel sympathetic to those whose difficulties are externally caused or accidental (like Daniel) than to those whose situation is largely due to their own choices (like Hilary)?

6. Do you agree with Brenda and Daniel's decision to use an anony-

mous sperm donor (and artificial insemination)? If you found yourself in a similar situation, would you choose this solution?

7. Likewise, Jake and Liz have gotten pregnant with the help of modern science. Do they seem to have grappled with much of a moral crisis in making this decision? What do you make of our society's embrace of reproductive technology?

8. Discuss Pitlor's narrative approach. What is the effect of her telling the story told from all the different points of view?

9. Pitlor uses metaphor frequently. Discuss some of the most significant metaphors in *The Birthdays*. For example, does Joe's turtle signify anything? What is the role of the art of Corcoran?

10. Why do you think Pitlor chose to set the book on an island? What role does the setting play? How can setting add to a story?

*Available only on the Norton Web site:
www.wwnorton.com/guides